LOST IN THE FOG

A Novel By
Michael Ostrowski

Published by Inkshares, Inc., Oakland, California
www.inkshares.com

Edited by Caroline Tolley
Cover design by CoverKitchen
Interior design by Kevin G. Summers

ISBN: 9781950301119
e-ISBN: 9781950301126
LCCN: 2020932778

First edition

Printed in the United States of America

For J'Nell, my family,
and for everyone who pre-ordered my book
and supported the publication campaign, especially
the Grand Patrons. I appreciate you
more than you'll ever know.

ACT ONE

PROLOGUE

San Carlos, California
October 30, 2008

WITH A CRACK of an elm branch a squirrel did its best imitation of a monkey. The creature leapt expertly from tree to tree over a creek, finally landing on the side of Camden Swanson's apartment building and defying gravity by scampering up to the roof. More squirrels followed in its path, and none of them fell into the shallow stream of water or tumbled to the ground.

Camden watched intently and raised his bottle of beer in appreciation.

It was dusk, and his posterior was firmly entrenched in his frayed camping chair on his back porch. He finished his last sip of beer and reached into his cooler to find nothing but water and ice. He heard a knock inside his apartment, but before he could stand up, the door creaked open and then shut.

From his vantage point on the back porch, through the large screen door that looked into the living room, Camden watched a strange woman wearing a short skirt walk toward him. She stopped about three feet from the wire mesh and stood next to a shelf that was packed with his collection of vinyl records. At first glance he couldn't tell if she was the tallest lady he had ever seen or the prettiest. When she lit a cigarette with a Zippo and put it up to her full lips, he was sure she was the sexiest.

"Your door was open," the woman said.

If he wasn't so buzzed, Camden likely would have been startled by the intruder. The alcohol instead dulled his senses, and emboldened him where he might have been more alert to potential danger. Also, like many men, his good judgement dissolved in the presence of an attractive woman, and there was an almost atavistic need to be agreeable with her.

"Come on in," he said, quickly realizing it was a stupid thing to utter since she'd already had.

Camden thought he might have seen her before but couldn't be sure because his girlfriend, Georgia, often had all kinds of people show up unannounced at their doorstep. Georgia was a well-respected artist and had both welcome and unwanted visitors. Usually the latter were male fans, groupies who loved her work and found her alluring. The uninvited women were almost always art dealers desperate to get her to showcase at their galleries, though Camden had to shoo away a few horny female Georgia admirers. This woman, however, seemed too put together and too confident to be a groupie, and he figured her for someone who wanted to buy or sell his girlfriend's work.

"I'm guessing you're here for Georgia," he said. "She's out. And I'm not authorized to do anything with her pieces."

"Georgia Léveque is a very talented artist, but I want to talk to you, Mr. Swanson."

Camden stayed seated and peered at his towering visitor. Her slightly tousled ink-black hair fell to her shoulders. A fringe of bangs covered most of her forehead. If she wasn't an art dealer, who was she?

He could only think of one other thing. The previous year, one of his mistakes, or actually a series of them, led to bankrupting the newspaper he used to work for in Los Angeles. She could be a reporter looking to do a where-are-they-now article.

"I'm long over talking about what happened in LA. And it's hardly news anymore."

"I know all about how you were fired for 'egregious disregard for facts,' as I believe it was officially stated," the stranger responded, and then took a long drag of her cigarette. "But I'm not a reporter, and that's not why I'm here. However, there's quite a bit I do know about you. Thirty-five years old, from the Boston area, and you've lived in California for about seven years. You've won awards for your reporting, used to be a mini-celebrity in LA because of your TV news appearances. That all went away about a year ago, and your more-than-generous girlfriend has been trying her best to help you turn your life around. Without much success."

Camden stood up, which he hadn't done in over an hour, and with all the beer he had consumed, wobbled just slightly. His intuition had been blunted from months of apathy, but something was wrong here. She could be a thief, a person he had unknowingly wronged from his past, or possibly there was a guy in a white coat right now running after her with a giant butterfly net.

"Okay, you've Googled me. Can I ask why?"

"My research has gone far beyond the internet. I've been watching you. Pretty sure you've been wearing the same pair of jeans all week. The only variant is your Red Sox shirts. How many do you own? I'm also curious if you have written any poems today?" she asked.

"I haven't catalogued all my shirts, so can't answer the first question. I have, in fact, written some poems, but not even Georgia knows I do that. There're only three other people on the planet who know my little hobby. Did Dickie, Sal, or Rubbish send you here as a joke?"

"I've seen you with your friends, but I've yet to have a conversation with them. While I'm sure deep down they're all nice people, I hope it doesn't have to happen. But I'm curious as to why you write poems."

"Because it keeps me sane standing in a museum gallery all day doing fuck-all nothing. All right, Twenty Questions is over. Who the hell are you, and why have you been watching me?"

Camden had been on the back porch for the last two hours, unprepared for his encounter with the mysterious, tall woman. With the squirrels his only companions, he had eaten seven pieces of string cheese, drank five beers, and had written three haiku. He had recently gotten into the Japanese poetic form after watching *Winter Days,* a short anime film based on the poetry of Bashō.

Camden wrote better when he was working at the museum, but there was one with promise he had scribbled earlier in his tiny notebook:

Cracking branches!
San Carlos dusk.
Vanishing squirrel.

"We have important business to discuss," the woman said. "Should I join you on the porch, or would you like to sit in the living room?"

"Don't take another step until you tell me who you are," he said and pulled out his phone. "I'm on my way to being sloshed, but I can still dial 9-1-1."

"There's no need for that. I'm here because I have a serious offer for you. One that could change your life."

"Can you get me my career as a journalist back? That's the only thing I want."

"Unfortunately, I don't have the ability to pull off such a miracle, but you will want to hear what I have to say nonetheless."

Camden opened the screen door and entered the apartment, instinctively sucking in his belly and attempting his best to appear cool in front of her. He ruined it when he belched.

"Excuse me," he said. "Must have been that soda water with cranberry juice."

"Or possibly all the Lagunitas you've had," she said. "You usually get a six-pack of that brand, but then go back to the supermarket for more. You switch to a less expensive option, I imagine, due to the size of your bank account."

"Are you going to guess my weight next?"

"You don't want that," she said with a smile. "I'll take a glass of wine, if you have it."

"While I'm at it, I could cook you dinner. I think there might be some filet mignon and lobster in the fridge."

"My apologies. Since you're drinking, I'm being polite by asking to join in."

"My mom raised me right, so I'll get you a glass. But let's cut to the chase."

Camden went to the cupboard in the kitchen and selected a bottle, set behind several choices from top Napa wineries, of Trader Joe's Two-Buck Chuck. It's what Georgia used to make sangria. He then poured it into a plastic San Francisco Giants cup and handed it to her.

The woman sipped her wine and did her best not to grimace. She left a trace of lipstick on the cup when she set it down on the end table. She then eyed an Impressionist-influenced watercolor on the wall of Parisians crossing the Pont Neuf, painted by Georgia when she was nineteen.

"Is your girlfriend named after Georgia O'Keeffe?" she asked, wandering around the living room. "Or something more prosaic like the state?"

"If I'm ever asked to write her biography, I'll be sure to find that out. Her dad owns a few O'Keeffes, but I've never heard him talk about them."

"I'm familiar with your girlfriend's father as well," she said and picked up a framed photo of Georgia wearing a graduation gown standing with her dad. "Mr. Léveque is an impressive collector and from all accounts a true gentleman. Nice picture of them. Are they why you took your current job as a museum security guard? A way of getting into the family business?"

"More prosaic reasons, to borrow your phrase. Money, a J-O-B, the means to pay the bills since nobody will hire me as a reporter. And before we go any further, you have five seconds to tell me why I shouldn't call the condo security. The fact you know all these things is creepy. Or as the kids say these days, creepy A-F."

"Mr. Swanson, money is the reason why I'm here. I'm going to present you with an offer where you can make lots of it."

"Swanson makes me think of frozen dinners. Call me Camden."

He didn't take his eyes off the woman while she continued to poke around the apartment. She scrutinized more photos, the stack of Camden's vinyl albums next to the Bose speakers, and then picked up a tiki mug shaped like a coconut. While she didn't touch it, the woman bent down for a closer inspection of a foot-high abstract sculpture Georgia had done when they first met. She had given it to him as a birthday gift.

Camden was 94 percent certain the lady was a con artist, but he owned next to nothing and had no access to any of Georgia's work or valuables. He could have called the building's security and had her thrown out, but she had stirred an emotion inside he hadn't felt in a long time—curiosity. So he decided to give her five minutes to explain her "offer," and then he'd get back to the squirrels and his haiku.

"Camden, I'm here because you used to have a career as a journalist. But now you're a guy approaching middle age who punches a clock at a museum for minimum wage."

"It's fifty cents higher," he said. "Got a raise."

"I can't imagine you find any satisfaction with your current job," the woman said.

"Are you kidding me? There's tons of job satisfaction as a museum gallery attendant. I get paid to stand. I stand with my arms behind my back for eight hours a day and tell kids not to touch the art and old folks not to lean against walls. Occasionally a teenager gets a backpack through, and I ask them to check it. That happens infrequently, but when it does, it goes right in my diary. But let's get back to your fantastic offer that's supposed to change my life."

He went to the fridge, reaching past Georgia's vanilla soy milk, for another beer. He popped it, returned to the living room, and plopped down on the couch. The woman sat right next to him and he got just a hint of perfume, or possibly it was just lavender body cream.

Camden watched her swirl the purple liquid in her plastic cup, smell it, and then put it back down without taking a sip. She crossed her long, tanned legs and studied him. Her look was a mixture of curiosity and disgust, akin to a seventh grader's gaze at a formaldehyde-imbued frog.

"Camden, I'm here because I think you can help me."

"How?"

"You work at a museum. I want to rob it."

1

Camden Swanson and the Odalisque Sculptures
Three Days Earlier

CAMDEN STOOD ON the elevated commuter train plat-
form in San Carlos, gazing north up the tracks toward the city.
The train was late, which in and of itself hadn't bothered him,
except he had hustled down the street so he wouldn't miss it.
Sweat now ran down his ears and neck, beading in his hair. He
wanted to be back in his bed or else on a Hawaiian island.

With a whoosh of air and the screech of metal, the train
disrupted the stillness of dawn. The doors clanked open and
Camden took his usual top seat in the second to the last car.
He recognized most of the faces, as the commuters from the
Peninsula all seemed to enjoy the same spots to place their
asses. Tired and hungover from a night of drinking beer on his
back porch and communing with the squirrels, he could only
stare slack-jawed at the lavender and pink clouds crashing like
waves over the East Bay sky.

At San Francisco's Caltrain Depot, Camden exited with the
mass of people and began his usual walk up 4th Avenue. After
crossing over to Ellis and passing under the unlit neon sign of

John's Grill, he was around the corner from the Matisse Hotel, his place of employment. But instead of a direct approach, he circled around the block over the hill to the loading dock, what he referred to as his "sneaky back way." While he did have to pass a sex shop and had been asked to purchase heroin on a couple occasions, it became his preferred route because he could bypass the commotion every morning.

The employees of the hotel were all on strike, and they were in their usual places, holding signs and banging trash can lids. It was a city-wide labor action at most of the large hotels due to the union and the hotels' months-long stalemate on signing a new contract. Back when he was a reporter in Los Angeles, Camden had done pieces on the transit and janitor strikes there, and those scenes were contentious. But the hotel strikers had only perpetrated violence against San Franciscans' eardrums with their chants, megaphones, and trash can drumming.

"Jingle Bells" was the melody, but the lyrics remained a mystery. A megaphone helped deliver the message, but the tiny Asian woman held it too close to her mouth to be decipherable. However, even if she had been more adept with the contraption, Camden wouldn't have understood because the words were in Mandarin. But the next scream out of her mouth did not need a translation.

"Scab!"

The comment had been directed at an elderly woman entering the six-month-old Matisse Hotel. While it was true the woman in question had crossed the picket line of union workers, if the octogenarian wearing a Chanel suit and carrying a Tiffany bag was a replacement worker serving food or cleaning rooms, Camden was prepared to strip down to his underwear and board a cable car singing Randy Newman's "I Love L.A."

The Matisse Hotel, housed in a restored early-twentieth-century bank, drew visitors not just because it was the newest luxury property in San Francisco; the hotel had also become a destination for its prestigious Museum of the Twentieth Century, located on the top floor of the historic building. Included in the collection were works by Pollock, Hopper, O'Keeffe, Rothko, and Picasso. But the jewels of it all were the three eponymous Henri Matisse odalisque wax sculptures, reputedly worth one hundred million dollars.

As a museum gallery attendant, his position was nonunion, and Camden was not directly involved in the labor dispute. Except he had to cross the picket line every day or choose to work elsewhere. With the competitive San Francisco job market and his inability to work in his chosen profession of journalism, he wasn't quitting despite the hassle and the shitty pay.

He accessed the hotel's side entrance from the loading dock, which couldn't legally be blocked by the strikers, and entered through the revolving glass doors without being bothered. He went through the lobby, with its wrought iron and painted glass dome and black-and-white-tiled floor designed for the guests to think they were in Belle Époque Paris. After getting downstairs to the employee area, he grabbed his uniform from the community closet. Recently dry-cleaned, it reeked of chemicals.

Harry Hipple stood next to Camden's locker dressed in the gallery attendant attire of blue blazer, striped tie, and black slacks. Hard-Case Harry, as the twenty-five-year-old was known to his coworkers, piqued his interest only because the guy could somehow remove his pants without taking off his shoes.

"Fucking assholes," Harry said. "And it ain't the democrats this time. The fucking assholes I'm talking about are the fucking assholes who're holding the picket signs and calling a good, God-fearing American like myself a scab. We're not in the goddamned union. If we don't cross the picket line, which liberal smart-ass group is gonna support us?"

"They don't know who you are," a young guard named Timmy responded. "They're human beings who have rent to pay and kids to support. Overnight, a group of strangers took their jobs. They're angry and have a right to be."

"Then why in the holy hell did they vote to go on strike?"

"If you're going to criticize unions, Harry, lest you forget that the concept of not working Saturday and Sunday and the forty-hour work week was also established by them."

Camden's head was beginning to hurt, and he wanted to move as far away from Timmy and Harry as possible. There were pieces of art that needed guarding, but he kept fumbling with his tie. Over and over he made it either too long or too short.

"Why don't you go into the hotel via the loading dock from the top of the hill?" Camden finally asked, hoping to shut his colleagues up.

"And walk next to a filthy sex shop?" Hipple replied.

Camden finally got his tie right, resisted the urge to give Hipple the finger, and went to the auditorium for the gallery attendant pre-shift meeting. From the back row, he watched Larry Aberlour, the director of security for the Matisse Hotel, cough, scratch his ass, and then begin speaking. His boss recycled the same information over and over, and in his six months of employment, Camden only knew of four pre-shift meeting topics: terrorism, vandalism, falling asleep in the galleries, and being vigilant for thieves.

"We could be a target," Larry said loudly to the fifteen people assembled in the auditorium. "You might think it won't, but it could happen to you. If a security guard leaves his post for one minute, people could die or art could be stolen or destroyed."

Larry began pacing, appearing almost like a penguin as he walked back and forth.

"Should you wander over to your gallery neighbor and begin talking, you're inviting chaos." He then lowered his voice a few octaves to mimic a dunce. "Hey, look at me. I don't care if that guy leaves a backpack full of explosives next to the Picasso. I'll just go talk to Sally Sue over here."

Larry walked back to the podium and spoke into the microphone. "Well, you will care when boom, you're all dead! C'mon, people, I can't stress this enough. While you're off gabbing or gawking at the art, that gives the bad guys the opportunity they're waiting for. Whether it's ripping a painting off the wall or leaving behind a swath of carnage and destruction. You have to stay alert, team."

Camden looked around the room to take in Larry's "team," who were mostly frail art students and seventy-something-year-old men. Maybe three of them were listening. Cell phones were used to surf the web and send text messages, and hearing aids were switched off. However, Larry likely believed he had a captive audience.

"Yes, there is a full-time security force that works inside the hotel. And yes, there are cameras in every nook and cranny inside our museum. But you are the first line of defense. You're not just for show."

Camden inadvertently laughed with a loud "ha." The thought of him, or anyone else in attendance, as being any kind of defense, was that ludicrous.

The laugh and the "ha" caused a wave of giggling. Larry glared at Camden.

"I'm glad you all find protecting priceless artwork and people's lives funny."

"There's nothing funny about it, sir," Hipple responded.

"Thank God we have you."

Another burst of laughter welled inside Camden. He slouched into his chair, gritting his teeth to avoid releasing it. There was a chance his kidneys might rupture.

"And remember what I've pre-shifted the entire week. The hotel's owner, Mr. David Bouchon, is supposed to visit the museum. I don't want you to embarrass me. Now get your keys and radios and be at your posts five minutes before we open."

Camden tried his best to blend into the crowd and sneak out of the room, but Larry walked right up to him and blocked his path.

"I expect that kind of bullshit from the college kids, but not from the adults," he said.

"My sincere apologies. I didn't laugh because of you," he lied. "I was thinking of something funny my girlfriend said last night."

"Bullshit, Swanson. I'm writing you up for today, and if you do anything stupid while Mr. Bouchon is here, expect another one. I don't have any problems coaching you the hell out."

Camden had rehearsed at least a dozen eloquent ways to tell his boss to fuck off, but he was in no position to use any of them. He needed to be responsible, apologize, and accept his punishment. He managed to do that without vomiting in his mouth, but it would be an epic challenge to keep quiet for the rest of the day and not get fired. He hoped Larry Aberlour would stay in his office.

* * *

More than halfway through his shift, Camden, who had a degree from NYU and twelve years' experience as a professional journalist, had to tell a woman not to touch the chest of a statue. It was a Pop Art marble slab of a woman with enormous breasts and a tiny waist. He had lost count of how many times patrons of the museum had fondled it.

He was standing in the 1960s gallery, which featured works by the usual suspects of Warhol, Johns, and Lichtenstein. Before taking the position as museum security guard, Camden had never given pop artists a second thought. But six months of staring at their work had forced him into an opinion: much of their revolutionary art from the hippie days had not aged well. He enjoyed Jasper Johns, Lichtenstein, and several others, but to him many of the pieces seemed gimmicky.

However, there were scores of twentieth-century artists, such as Hopper, Braque, Modigliani, Klee, and Pollock, who interested Camden. And so did Henri Matisse, the deceased man who lent his name to the hotel. He especially liked the early paintings, such as the woman in the multicolored hat displayed at a rival museum.

Except the Matisse odalisque sculptures didn't do it for Camden, and it didn't matter people had ventured across the world to gawk at those objects costing an unfathomable amount of money. With plenty of time to study the pieces when the gallery was empty, he could only see the three-foot-tall bulky black wax pieces as billowy shapes that barely resembled women.

Before dating Georgia, he had only known the names of four artists: Picasso, Rembrandt, Michelangelo, and Raphael. And the latter two were due to animated, crime-fighting turtles. Up to that point he had been inside two museums; the Cordovan in Boston because of a story he had reported on, and the Guggenheim in New York on a date. However, from his romantic relationship with an accomplished artist and his job as a gallery attendant, he had absorbed a modicum of art appreciation through osmosis.

But right then all he truly cared about were the wallet-friendly Irish coffees at the Gold Dust Lounge. Camden retreated to an innocuous corner and stood and guarded and tried not to think about the concept of time. Glancing at your watch was an occupational hazard for security guards everywhere and made the shift drag on and on. Which is why he had sold his at a pawn shop a few days after he took the job.

* * *

Camden's shift rotation, after his stint with Pop Art, went next to Art of the Freedom Movement and ended with Beat Culture. He had become fond of the Beat room, which featured framed handwritten poems by Kerouac, Ginsberg, Snyder, and Gregory Corso, because he could read them when pedestrian traffic slowed down. Although at first he took in the free verse to battle time, he now looked forward to it. These works inspired him to write his own poems. In his tiny notebook he had scribbled:

Charbroiled soul on a wing-tip bun / Monkey-faced Monets sleeping on the run / Give me two dollars for some nickels / Extra plutonium but hold the pickles / X-ray murals now on the moon / With ruby slippers, minus the cartoon / A harem of raindrops frozen into glue / Climate-controlled whiskey, at a theater near you.

Camden had been engrossed with his poem and failed to notice his boss walking into the gallery with Mr. David Bouchon. In a charcoal suit that likely cost more than Camden made in several months, and walking with an ivory cane, Bouchon was in his late fifties with short brown hair flecked with gray. He was fit and seemed ten years younger than his age, despite the cane. The hotel's owner approached Camden with furrowed brows and spoke in a slight French accent.

"May I ask what you're writing, young man?" he asked.

The universe was tempting him. Camden wanted to say he was cataloguing all the reasons why Larry Aberlour should be featured on a new reality show, *World's Most Douchiest Bosses*. Instead, without a word, Camden handed over his poetry notebook.

Larry looked as if his face were going to melt and burst into flames. The Frenchman read the poem with a roguish grin and gave it back to Camden.

"Influenced by Bob Dylan, no?"

"I'm not sure where that one came from," Camden responded. "When the muse hits, you gotta listen to her."

"Please do not write when patrons are in the galleries. But if you're alone, I'm happy to see you indulge in some artistic expression. Standing here must get tedious at times, no? *Au revoir.*"

* * *

When his shift ended, Camden changed into his usual civilian outfit of jeans, Red Sox T-shirt, and black windbreaker, when the weather called for it. He did it so quickly he left no time for either Harry Hipple or his boss to speak to him. His job was his to keep for at least one more day. When Camden reached Powell Street, he almost started to skip into the Gold Dust Lounge. Dickie, Sal, and Rubbish, the three other members of what Camden had dubbed the Unsuccessful Men's Club, were already in a booth.

"The protector of antiquities," Dickie said after Camden had ordered a drink.

"Good to see you were able to pry your thumb outta your butt to make it," Sal added.

Camden's three friends had all gone to San Francisco State together and were co-owners of a sports memorabilia shop in South City. He had met them walking out of the Balboa Theatre after a screening of *Blade Runner* when Camden complimented Dickie's "Replicants Rule" T-shirt. They ended up talking about the film, Philip K. Dick, and dystopian sci-fi over several beers at the Hockey Haven. He thought his new friends to be strange and interesting, and they were the only ones he had.

The trio were each five feet, seven inches tall and dressed in the same manner of cargo shorts and hooded sweatshirts or T-shirts (though they never wore the same colors). They eschewed any clothing with logos because, as they would tell anyone who would listen, they refused to be walking advertisements for fashion designers, sports teams, or products. But they each had a wardrobe full of ironic T-shirts and sweatshirts.

Though the three were of the same height and body type, they were never confused as being triplets. Dickie had long greasy hair, wore spectacles with enormous rims, and his fleshy skin was barely a few hues past a corpse. Sal's pockmarked face was mostly covered with his bushy beard and muttonchops, and a tweed scally cap shielded his bald head.

Rubbish was the quietest of the three and had a bald, misshapen head. He hadn't said one word or even noticed Camden's entrance, but instead stared at a tall, gorgeous woman in a tan skirt and black blouse. The lady did not pay any attention to Rubbish, a reoccurring phenomenon in his thirty-seven-year-old life.

"Hey, Rubbish, the peep shows are in the Tenderloin," Dickie said.

"She's gotta be six feet five. And super fucking hot," Rubbish responded. "The peep show girls are all skanks."

"Fine, but if her boyfriend wants to kick your ass, I'm holding you down."

"If she's got one, he ain't here," Rubbish said. "She's been at that table all by herself since we walked in. Three guys approached her, all shot down."

Camden glanced furtively in the tall woman's direction, and then his attention focused on the waitress putting a warm beverage laced with whiskey in front of him. He put it to his lips and savored it and let the other members of the Unsuccessful Men's Club continue their banter. After ordering another drink, he studied the cherubs on the ceiling mural and then his eyes drifted to the painting of a reclining nude. He'd eaten nothing all day but half a bag of barbecue chips, and the Irish part of the coffee was beginning to create a fine haze in his mind.

"Written any new poems?" Sal asked Camden.

"Several," he answered, pulling out his notebook. "Here's a crowd pleaser:

I'm a free-range chicken, with FDA approval and honey mustard dressing

Standing all day with tie and blazer I keep nobody guessing

So I look at a Matisse portrait with no oil, or canvas, or even genius

Too bored with words and ideas I don't even want to rhyme this with penis

I'm a hundred years too old, or a hundred and one years too young

Just a dishrag mopping up the mung

So pelt my organs, my molecules, with heavily salted nuts of corn

I'll just keep on babbling and babbling and babbling, wishing I was never born."

"Let's get on to business," Dickie said with head-shaking disapproval. "Who wants to start the discussion?"

Although Camden had deemed it the Unsuccessful Men's Club, the four guys met under the auspices of a movie group. Like some do with books, once a week Sal, Dickie, Rubbish, and Camden met to discuss a film. Sometimes a new release, but often the movie was at least a decade old. They prided themselves on choosing obscure titles. Tonight's topic was to be an experimental Korean film made in 1974.

Nobody had been able to find it, so Camden's three friends began passionately discussing the work of Lee Chang-dong, Bong Joon-ho, and So Yong Kim. He was not at all familiar with their films, so instead he retreated to his mind and the booze he kept ordering. A haiku started to form in his head, but he could only get the first line: *Rock bottom dweller.*

2

Veronica Zarcarsky and the Matisse Hotel

EARLIER THAT DAY, Veronica watched Ryan Crimsone, the director of human resources for the Matisse Hotel, step one of his size-fourteen shoes out of his office, while the other held his fleshy body behind the doorframe. Her boss's preferred mode of communication was to yell from his desk, so whatever had him standing now had to be important. His perpetually reddened and puffy face had a quizzical look on it.

"Veronica, can you pull the file on Harry Hipple?"

A staffing agency had sent her to work three days at the hotel. That was a month ago. Due to the labor dispute and the quality of her work, she kept being asked to return. Five days a week she descended into the basement of the hotel to the HR office wearing her outlet-mall-purchased business suit to fax, file, collate, and run errands. While it wasn't what she wanted for her career, she took pride in doing a good job, even if mostly everyone referred to her as "the temp."

Veronica moved quickly to a metal cabinet, thumbed through the Hs, and extracted the Hipple file. Ryan lumbered over, snatched the folder, and squinted as he read through the pages. She counted the number of hairs (fourteen) sticking out of her boss's veiny, bald skull.

"I knew that name rang a bad bell. Why do they want to nominate that guy for Employee of the Month? He's had at least three complaints against him."

Carmine, the HR coordinator, plucked a piece of lint off his designer sweater vest and said, "When I took his ID picture, he asked if I was a Jew."

Bonnie, the assistant director who always wore stylish business-appropriate dresses with a blazer, stepped out of her office and said, "I interviewed him."

As Ryan rifled through the papers in the file he asked, "How did it go?"

"When I asked the 'Explain a situation where you had to make a critical decision when your supervisor was not present,' Harry Hipple went on a five-minute diatribe about how he tried to make a citizen's arrest at the jewelry store he once worked at. Some guy came in to buy an engagement ring. Mr. Hipple swore he had seen him on *America's Most Wanted* the night before. Turns out the gentleman was an investment banker."

"How the hell did he get hired?" Ryan barked.

"Three guards had quit during orientation before we opened, and our director of security was desperate," Carmine answered. "At that point we were all so crazy busy, and he kind of slipped through the cracks. Hipple had a lot of security experience. Larry Aberlour said he would keep him in line."

"Hipple wins Employee of the Month when I win Miss Teen USA," Bonnie said and then winked at Veronica.

Even if it was nowhere near the path she wanted to take in her career, she enjoyed working in the Matisse Hotel. Sure, there were too many mundane administrative tasks, but Veronica took satisfaction that her role in the office expanded each day. Her duties now included taking photo IDs for the scores of replacement workers being hired every day, giving out and keeping track of locker assignments, and maintaining an updated list of all the new temporary employees who were continually being "termed," which stood for terminated. She had even been given her own office.

Which is where she went after getting the Hipple file for the director of HR. The office was a laptop computer on a metal table inside the dank storage room that housed the additional employment records and anything else that wouldn't fit in the office. The HR team referred to it as the "Scary Room" because it was constantly in disarray. Chock full of detritus, nobody liked going inside. While the place needed better lighting and maybe a couple of air fresheners, Veronica was proud to have her own office.

She had been working steadily for a couple of hours and wiped a bead of sweat off her forehead when Carmine entered and tossed two file folders on her desk.

"Two more terms," he said. "One temp they caught naked as a jaybird taking a shower in one of the guest rooms. Claimed he was cleaning it and got too wet with his clothes on. Term number two is another theft case. Man, is stealing a couple of beers really worth losing your job over? While our security team might not be the best and brightest, and they're woefully underpaid despite our protests, they're likely gonna catch you walking out with bottles of Heineken in your pants."

Without waiting for a reply, Carmine exited the Scary Room, his musky cologne lingering as Veronica placed the files into her in-box. She returned to her spreadsheet and her fingers danced across the keyboard at seventy words per minute.

Even though she displayed a Zen attitude to the rest of her human resources team, she did keep a few secrets from her coworkers. She had a master's degree in journalism from Berkeley and her goal in life was to be an award-winning investigative reporter. While she had done plenty of articles for her college paper, since graduation Veronica had only managed to sell some freelance pieces to dog magazines (her French bulldog, Sabrina, provided a lot of material). She planned to put herself on the map by writing an insider's expose on the labor dispute and had been covertly gathering material over the last few weeks.

She finished processing her last termination file and powered down the laptop. After being stuck all day in the basement, she eagerly awaited getting outside for a walk. That's when Bonnie called.

"We need to clear out more women's lockers for our new-hire temps," she said. "Think you can stay an extra hour and help me tag and bag?"

Dim fluorescent lighting, concrete floors and walls, and the odor of dirty clothes mixed with perfume, it was not a place to spend five minutes. But Bonnie was her favorite person at the Matisse Hotel, and Veronica didn't hesitate in agreeing to the task. She secured the door to the Scary Room and met her manager at Ladies Locker Room C.

Bonnie was in the process of holding a pair of shoes by the laces and dropping them into a plastic bag. She turned her head away in disgust as a female security officer stood there expressionless with a clipboard. Veronica was already familiar with the process. Because the workers were not allowed to enter the hotel after they went on strike, and their replacements needed lockers, the hotel had a space issue.

The personal belongings of the union employees on strike needed to be extracted from their lockers and placed into plastic bags. All bags were numbered so they could be returned into the appropriate lockers once the labor dispute ended. Illegal items, such as pornography and weapons, were destroyed. Uniforms were sent for cleaning and equipment put back to its proper place. Security was always there as a witness.

"Kind of makes you feel like a—I don't want to say Nazi 'cause that's too hyperbolic, but doesn't feel right," Bonnie said once Veronica began to help. "I know we're not confiscating any of their stuff, unless it's illegal, and they'll get it back, but it feels weird."

"It does," Veronica agreed. "But the workers here now need lockers."

"You're always so positive, Veronica. And you're really good with people. You'd make a good front desk agent, or even concierge if you know the city well. Are you from San Francisco?"

"Santa Rosa, but I went to Berkeley."

"You may have bigger ambitions, but a full-time job at our hotel would look good on your resume."

"Agreed, and I appreciate that," Veronica said.

She worked along with her manager and a taciturn security guard to clear out fourteen lockers over the next hour. The bagged items were dumped into a bin and Veronica wheeled it into the Scary Room. She would need to use the events of the night for her article on the strike, capturing the sights and smells to bring the story alive.

She clocked out and while leaving the hotel was screamed at by several of the striking workers, mistakenly identified by them as a scab. She held no ill will toward the group, and instead kept her head down with a blank expression and moved quickly through the placard-wielding mob.

The frosty, fog-swept air cooled her face as she headed down O'Farrell Street and then up Grant. After the gloominess of the locker room and the overtime she had earned, she planned to treat herself to a book. Usually she'd go to Green Apple Books in her neighborhood, but she decided on City Lights in North Beach as a change to her routine.

She wanted a spark to help her write her article on the strike and went in search of tomes on unions and the labor movement. But after browsing several that made her eyes heavy, she ascended the creaky wooden steps to the top floor and selected a Gary Snyder off the shelf. The City Lights Poetry Room was one of her favorite nooks in the city.

Her next stop was only a few feet away to Vesuvio's, a bar that Jack Kerouac used to frequent. At a wooden table on the second floor she sipped wine and read several poems. Later in the evening, she made her way to Sacramento Street and boarded a #1 bus to the Richmond District. Less than half an hour later she walked toward the recently restored white, bow-fronted Edwardian on 20th Avenue where her basement apartment was located.

Veronica noticed a very tall and beautiful woman leaving from the front door of the house, someone who did not seem to fit in with her roommate's stoner crowd. She was on the opposite side of the street, and while she wasn't sure why, she walked past her apartment entrance. Veronica then circled back toward the house and watched the tall lady walk up 20th and take a right on Lake. She followed her.

Before reaching Lake, Veronica ducked behind shrubbery and saw the stranger enter a gray Mercedes. She mentally noted the license plate. Her heart raced, and she calmed herself down by acknowledging it was just a silly thing she was doing, an act brought along by reading too many mystery books. The car drove about twenty yards and then turned around.

Under the streetlight on the corner of Lake and 20th, no more than fifteen feet from where Veronica stood, the Mercedes stopped, and the window rolled down. Veronica was paralyzed with fear. She could not see clearly inside the car but could easily discern the finger that pointed out the window and wagged back and forth at her. The glass then went back up, and the Mercedes peeled off and zoomed down the street.

3

Georgia, Mr. Léveque, and the Cordovan Museum Robbery

THREE TIMES DURING the night, Camden almost walked to the fridge for a glass of water. On each occasion, he couldn't muster the energy to hydrate himself, and upon waking at 10:00 a.m. his throat was scabrous. It hurt to cough, which he had been doing all night because of the cigar he had smoked. He would have paid the contents in his wallet for anybody to bring him water.

The only person who could have carried out the task had left the apartment a few hours before. Nor did she have any use for three dollars. Camden imagined that Georgia had stood over him for a few seconds before leaving, disgusted that he was phlegmy and smelled like alcohol; she never would have considered getting him a glass of water.

But Georgia had left a typed note.

After a shower, four frozen waffles, two pints of water, one string cheese, and a Gatorade, Camden picked up the note. Being so hungover, it had taken all his energy not to topple in the shower. But he was finally able to get his—as Jim Morrison once said—fragile, eggshell of a mind to read:

Dear Drunky,
We're not talking about a matter of "philosophical differences," as you're fond of saying. Right now there are only facts, not abstract mind concepts. And here they are, blunt to the bone:
- *You're a child when it comes to our problems. You think that not talking about them will make them go away. It makes them worse.*
- *You're doing nothing to improve your career situation. The security job was supposed to be temporary, something to get you on your feet. Six months later you're still doing it and not even applying to other jobs, ones that suit your education and experience.*
- *You drink way too much. You might have the cute smile and good looks, but lying next to you at night when you're wasted has utterly turned me off to you sexually. If you think I'm being too harsh, or a bitch, then it's because of problem number one.*
- *You refuse to talk about anything important, and then I build up all these complaints and I explode.*
Call me when you get up.
—Georgia

She of course was right about every bullet point, but Camden had felt paralyzed to take any action to change the person he had become. They had met a little over a year ago in Los Angeles, when he was a successful journalist and she was being interviewed at a TV station where he made regular appearances as a special contributor. She had stuck with him during his whole fiasco of getting fired and the public embarrassment that followed. She deserved better, and that made him feel even worse. He wanted to call her and to make a pledge to be a better boyfriend and partner, but at that moment he had to battle the hangover engulfing his head.

The only physical activity he could do was put on a DVD, and it seemed like a *Big Lebowski* sort of day. It was on Camden's top-ten list, to the dismay of the rest of the Unsuccessful Men's Club, who preferred the Coen Brothers' other work like *Miller's Crossing, Barton Fink,* and *Fargo.* But the Dude and his quest for his rug that really tied the room together always made Camden feel better.

Yesterday he'd promised to make the 10:00 p.m. Caltrain to be home by eleven. But he'd stayed out carousing with the Unsuccessful Men's Club until last call and got a ride home from Sal. His girlfriend had every right to be pissed.

He paused the DVD, freezing the image of the Dude's face being covered with Donnie's ashes, and picked up his cell phone to call Georgia. But instead of pushing the button in his address book, he put it down and made a turkey and avocado sandwich with oil and vinegar. When the film was over and only crumbs remained on his plate, he finally called.

"Just getting up?" she said.

Saying he had eaten a sandwich and watched Steve Buscemi portray Donnie before calling was not an option. Neither was claiming that he'd slept until 1:00 p.m. But there was another lie that might work.

"I just saw your note, Georgia."

"Bullshit. I put it on the fridge, and there's no way you didn't at least get yourself a glass of water. You must be hungover as fuck."

"That's why I didn't notice it," he said.

"I honestly don't have time for you now. I'm at the studio, and I'll be here late."

Georgia's workshop was an old log cabin in the Santa Cruz Mountains just off Skyline Boulevard in Woodside. The small plot of land skirted the State Game and Fish Refuge and boasted spectacular views of the bay. Her father had purchased the cabin in 1977 and for two decades spent several weekends a year in it. He gave it to his daughter as a place to paint and sculpt.

"Do you want me to make dinner?" Camden asked.

"Don't bother. I have a lot of work to do and I might even spend the night."

"I thought you get creeped out when you spend the night there alone."

"I do, Camden, but I have that exhibit in two weeks. I'll be fine."

"Do you hate me?"

"You said you'd be home by eleven and you didn't even call. Then you're all liquored up and wake me."

"It wasn't that I wasn't thinking of you, it was that I was drunk."

"We really need to talk. We're both very good at avoiding confrontation, but we're in dire need. And it must be said in person, not over the phone. The note is the preamble to the conversation we need to have."

"Are you breaking up with me?"

"Let's talk in person, Camden."

"Do you want me to drive up? I could bring Chinese food and a bottle of port for dessert. Just an hour and I'd leave you alone."

"I have to get my work done," Georgia said. "Tomorrow might not be good, either, but let's count on meeting the next day."

"Should I send you a calendar invite?"

"I wish you weren't such a smartass and that you'd actually take that kind of initiative. But no, don't bother. I'll call you tomorrow when I know I have some free time to meet."

"So you can break up with me."

"Hey, I think my dad is going to stop by today. I know you guys have gotten close, and I'd rather you not talk about our troubles, okay?"

"Good luck getting everything ready for your show, Georgia."

Between his fluctuating work schedule and her preparing for her show, he hadn't seen much of his girlfriend over the past few months. And here was yet another day for Camden to spend alone. He should start searching for his own apartment since their breakup was imminent, but that seemed too exhausting. There was little doubt he would begin drinking, but there was no beer in the fridge.

While Camden was thinking about going to purchase the new Lagunitas seasonal release, Georgia's father entered the apartment. The door was unlocked per usual and the trim, six-foot Frenchman with matching bushy gray hair and mustache did not knock nor announce himself. Mr. Léveque carried a case of wine and showed no surprise in seeing his daughter's boyfriend lying on the couch watching TV with a hand down his pants.

"*Bonjour*, Mr. L," Camden said as he removed his hand from his crotch and sat up.

"*Salut*, Camden."

Over the last six months, from when he and Georgia had moved from LA to San Francisco, Camden and Mr. Léveque had spent many a night drinking wine and discussing books, films, and whatever topic each found interesting. Sometimes Georgia joined them, but often they had spent time alone while she had been working. He had come to relish the hours he spent with Mr. L.

"Sorry to intrude on your demanding afternoon," Mr. Léveque said.

"Can I help you with that box? An old man like yourself shouldn't risk a hernia."

Mr. Léveque, who wore a corduroy sports jacket over a black T-shirt and jeans, smiled and placed the box he had been holding on the floor. "The day I can't pick up a case of wine is the day I am checking out of our world."

After shaking hands, Mr. Léveque grabbed a bottle from the case. He showed the label and smiled. Camden couldn't make out a word on the bottle except "Product of France."

"It's an '03 Gérard Raphet Charmes-Chambertin."

"What does that go for, about ten bucks a bottle?" he asked.

Mr. Léveque laughed deep in his belly and answered, "Slightly more."

"If it's more than fifty, I'm going to have to ask you to leave it outside. It would offend my sense of American democracy."

"That's because you couldn't tell the difference between a piece-of-shit American wine and a work of art from one of the most prestigious plots in Burgundy."

"Why don't you try me?" Camden asked.

"I knew I was goading you for a reason. Let's get it opened."

Camden leapt from the couch, high-fived his girlfriend's dad with his right hand and with the other grabbed the bottle of wine. He studied the label as he carefully removed the cork, figuring it and its eleven partners of the case were worth more than what he had paid for his first car. He smelled the wine, taking in the earthy fruit notes.

"Where is Georgia?"

"Mademoiselle is at her studio. Her show opens soon."

"It is a fine thing she does not indulge in your slacker ways."

"When you say *slacker* it almost sounds respectable."

"I just don't get you, Camden. I remember your appearances on the TV shows in LA; you had so much charisma and confidence. I've read your articles. You're a smart guy and could be doing something better than working as a gallery attendant. That's for students or retirees my age."

"Hard to explain. It's almost like I've been a spectator in my own life. I'm embarrassed about who I've become, and I want to change, but ever since being fired, I've been in a fog. Like I'm walking around with a concussion. Have you ever had one?"

"Thankfully, no."

"I played football and got a few, and it's the only comparison. But before we get into the sad saga that is my life, let's have some wine."

Camden used Georgia's Riedel glasses and slowly poured the wine. The two men enjoyed drinking on the patio and watching the squirrels prance over the creek. The Frenchman was out there leaning against the porch railing, and Camden joined him with the wine. They swirled, smelled, clinked glasses, and tasted.

Camden asked, "Has anybody at a wine tasting ever stood up and yelled, 'Holy fucking shit'? Because that's what I want to do right now."

"It is a fine Burgundy."

Before dating Georgia, he hadn't ever tasted a bottle of wine that retailed for over twelve dollars. But through his girlfriend and her father, he had been given the opportunity to sample some of the best in the world. Beer was still his first choice of alcoholic beverage, but more glasses like this and he would only want fine wine.

"It's light but complex and it's almost sweet," he said, "but then you have that intense plum and black cherry taste."

"Monsieur Camden has become a sommelier."

"It's also menacing," he continued, "with a hint of clowns on a bright summer day."

"Clowns, yes. I'll suggest to Gérard to put that description on the next vintage he bottles, you fucking smartass."

"I thought the French created sarcasm. Don't blame me for your country's influence."

"Okay, I enjoy joking with you immensely. But it's time to get serious. I'm glad Georgia is working. I've been wanting to speak with you for some time."

"Uh-oh."

"I'm fond of you. I understand what my daughter sees in you. She sees you for what you truly are, not what you are currently doing."

"Okay, Papa."

"How old are you?"

"Thirty-five."

"*Quoi?* Only thirty-five and you've quit? When I was thirty-five, I was making decent money, not rich but getting there. Then I lost it all on a business venture. Every cent. Georgia was was not even a teenager and her mother divorced me. So what did I do? I fought my way back. At forty, I was a multimillionaire. If I sat around all day crying, I would have ended up a wino on the streets."

Camden raised his glass and said, "I'll be there soon enough."

"You joke, and it is always good to joke. But sometimes you need a strong kick in the pants. I would never interfere in my daughter's personal life. But I know her. She's loving, she's caring, but she has never tolerated mediocrity."

"Getting back to my concussion analogy. I want to shape up, get my act together, embrace the power of positive thinking, and any other self-help platitude you can come up with, but I just can't seem to do it. Something keeps getting in my way."

"Life gets in your way, Camden. But I hope you can overcome your troubles. I've seen Georgia work months on a painting only to rip the canvas into pieces. She's smart enough to know when to give up on a lost cause."

"She pretty much told me she was going to break up with me today. Honestly, the only reason she hasn't done it sooner is she's been too busy getting her new show ready."

"So you cannot get hired as a reporter. At first I thought it was an exaggeration, but then I made a few calls myself. So why not start your own magazine? I will be your investor."

"You'd be throwing your money away," Camden said. "I'd love to be a reporter again. I think it's the only thing that can save me now. But starting a magazine requires a lot of energy and enthusiasm. And those are two things I don't have anymore."

"And those are qualities you cannot fake. But maybe someday you will rise from your funk. But it sounds like my daughter will have moved on by then."

"I have a friend that owns a little rental villa on the North Shore of Oahu. He keeps asking if I want to run it for him, and maybe the time has come to say yes. A complete do-over of my life might be in order. But truly, Mr. L, that seems too exhausting as well. I wouldn't even know how to start."

"Lao Tzu once said the journey of a thousand miles starts with one step. Nobody can do it for you. But after step one, things should fall into place. And I am offering my sincere help once you make the first move. Now that we've gotten that out of the way, let us enjoy our fine Burgundy and watch these squirrels."

* * *

After Georgia's dad left, Camden decided he would be down-right foolish not to open a second bottle. There would still be ten left, and his days of drinking fine wine in San Carlos were surely coming to an end. But while he savored the taste of the burgundy, the alcohol had begun to stimulate his memory, bringing back all the poor choices he had made in his life.

His mind wandered back to his first big-city newspaper job in Boston. He thought of the redbrick building and the beers he had after work at the Sevens, the look of the city as he crossed over the Mass Ave. Bridge after covering a story in Cambridge, and the drool-inducing meatball sandwiches he used to have at Mangia Mangia in the North End.

He covered school committee meetings and peppy man-on-the-street pieces, but he quickly proved he was worthy of more. He graduated to the police beat and it was everything he had dreamed about. He'd been thrilled to report on the crimes that took place in the city, be they petty theft or murder. While he wasn't seeking it, a sensational story found him.

The Cordovan Museum art heist was the second biggest in Boston's history, falling quite short dollar-wise of the Gardner theft, but no less an atrocity. The thief took Ingres. He pilfered Degas. He even snatched up three Monets. It was a veritable French artist bonanza, denting the private museum's collection. The alarms had been disabled, and the security guards were taken out with precision by tranquilizer darts at four in the morning.

Nobody saw anything.

Except for Camden.

He had been working on another story, the source for a cocaine dealer, which had brought him to a South End location. Acting on a tip, a bogus one, unbeknownst to Camden, he concealed himself in some sickly hedges with a thermos full of chicory coffee and rum. For five hours he had his binoculars on the window of a dilapidated three-decker house where a massive drug deal was supposed to occur.

With boredom, his binoculars wandered. First to a couple having sex, then to various constellations he couldn't name, and finally to a man dressed in black, hang gliding and holding duffle bags. He watched the stranger sail toward the direction of Commercial Street and Atlantic Avenue, where his trajectory would take him to the pier.

The hang glider was a hell of a lot more entertaining than a phantom dope deal. And with his coffee gone and the rum boosting both his confidence and stupidity levels, Camden got into his car and followed. He watched the person land with expertise on a patch of grass off Atlantic, leaving the contraption behind to sprint up the bridge of Seaport Avenue.

Camden parked on Atlantic Avenue, cutting the motor one hundred yards before he stopped, and followed the man dressed in black. Almost to the end of Seaport, the mysterious person climbed up over the railing with his bags and disappeared off the bridge. Crouching low, Camden moved in tiny steps down the bridge. He reached the place where the man jumped over and got on his knees to look through the railing fence. He watched the guy haul up the anchor that was keeping a boat in place.

He never knew if it was the booze in his blood or the Good Samaritan instinct to stop a crime. But just as the thief started the engine and diesel fuel filled the air, he jumped over the metal railing of the bridge and landed chin first into the boat. Camden wrestled with the man and was able to push him overboard. The cops arrived soon afterward with sirens, spotlights, and guns.

He not only had uncovered the story, he had saved an invaluable amount of art. His story ran with photos of him at the pier holding up a Degas painting. He got the key to the city and a promotion to the investigative staff.

The Cordovan robbery became an even more compelling story when the art thief turned out to be a local junior college art professor. Bo McClennan had a PhD, a face that resembled Matt Damon's, and he had written two well-received books on art. Camden not only covered the trial but also had to give testimony. McClennan went to jail and Camden became a star reporter.

After a few more years in Boston, Camden felt he deserved bigger and better. Los Angeles called with an offer to be a columnist. Like most bad ideas, it seemed like a terrific one at the time.

Before accepting the *Los Angeles Item* job offer, Camden's managing editor in Boston, Naushad Badini, pulled him aside. His dark eyes were bleary, which was to be expected after working sixteen straight hours, and his tie had three different colors of food stains on it, not surprising after eating breakfast, lunch, and dinner at his desk.

"What the fuck are you doing?" he asked.

"They're going to give me a column, and it's more money than I'll ever see here."

"You're right, we can't top the cash," Naushad said. "And you're too goddamn young in this city for a column. But what we can do is make you the lead of our investigative team."

"It's tempting, Naushad."

"Hey, I get it. LA and the money and the big fake boobies and the sun and all that jazz. But I know you. Some people can sell out, cash their checks with a big grin, and sleep like fucking babies. You are not one of them."

He thanked Naushad and then gave his two weeks' notice.

Once taking the new job and driving all the way across the country and eventually reaching the 101 freeway in Hollywood, his life would never be the same. His column became popular, he became a frequent contributor to the local news and radio stations, and many believed he would soon take his talents to the national level. Long-term-career journalistic success seemed inevitable right up until the day he was fired.

Being terminated for making factual errors was nothing new for a reporter. Even with such a blemish, a respected columnist had a legitimate chance of landing another job. Under the pressures of deadlines, even the most seasoned newspaperman can falter. Mistakes do happen, but what Camden did went beyond the scope of a typical journalistic blunder.

The official reason listed for his termination was "misconduct by egregious disregard for facts." His superiors claimed he maliciously fabricated a story to create an Orson Welles–type *War of the Worlds* hoax. But at the time of the incident, Camden believed the city was being attacked by half-monkey, half-snakelike creatures. Dropping acid can do that to you.

* * *

Whenever he thought back on his time in LA, he was certain his demise began the day he arrived in the city. Despite making considerable money, living in a spacious apartment in the Silver Lake neighborhood, and writing a column read by thousands of people in one of the most glamorous cities in the world, he was miserable. He complained to anybody who would listen about a David Lynch–type cloud of dread, complete with a nondescript industrial droning he heard whenever the sun shined too brightly.

He had a column every Tuesday, Thursday, and Sunday. It was called "The Outsider's View" and featured the recent transplant's views on his adopted city. The owner of the paper, a man from Kansas, believed the too-numerous-to-count expatriates living in Los Angeles would love Camden's caustic opinions on the city. The Boss was right.

"I'm fucking miserable," he told Bradleigh Chen, his one-time friend and editor.

"That's why everybody loves your column. You're miserable and you're funny."

"I'm bored. I got into journalism so I could make a difference. But now I spend eight hundred words describing a guy picking his nose on the 405."

"Just barely being involved in a six-car crash and then being stuck in traffic next to a guy who won't keep his finger out of his nose is amusing," Bradleigh said.

"I don't want to be amusing. When I was in Boston—"

"I did important stories," Bradleigh droned in a mocking tone. "I'm going to put it as delicately as possible. Get fucking over it. This is your life, and you can either sulk and pout or enjoy your success."

Camden chose to sulk and pout, usually while downing various alcoholic spirits.

4

When Harry and Larry Met Candy and Mandy

DURING THE SAME time when Camden was drinking wine with Mr. Leveque, Harry Hipple stood erect, hands clasped behind his back in the center of the gallery. His eyes swept the entire room to the limits of his peripheral vision. After repeating his lighthouse approach a few times, he turned around and did the same thing.

Whenever he happened to notice an attractive woman, like the college student in tight jeans and a belly-baring shirt, he'd imagine dead dogs covered with flies. Thinking of sex, or God forbid, getting a hard-on, was the surest way to lose focus of his important duties. Hipple was so concerned with keeping his mind pure, he even bought saltpeter because of what he'd heard about it. But whether it would have kept his private parts at ease, he would never find out. What he purchased turned out to be nothing more than a filed-down Flintstones Chewable. Hipple had punched his cousin in the nose several times for selling it to him.

"Lighten up, dude," a twelve-year-old kid with a potbelly said to him.

"I don't get paid to 'lighten up.' Enjoy the artwork while keeping a safe distance from it, young man, and don't worry about me."

The kid laughed, put his headphones back on, and flipped him off as he walked away. Harry spotted an elderly woman leaning on the wall and moved toward her. But before he could chastise the white-haired lady, the silence of the gallery was broken by the high-powered hum of indecipherable chatter. And then the room filled with twelve-year-old kids. It was now his time to shine.

Lower your voices. You're too close. If you touch that sculpture again, you'll be sitting on the bus for the rest of the day. He moved about the gallery and kept order, informing nine children that they were in direct violation of museum policy. When the last kid left, Harry sighed in contentment, as if he had eaten a satisfying meal.

It was time for his break, and he watched Timmy stroll over to relieve him of his post. Hipple had recognized him as the tall hippie prick defending unions the day before. He had never been in the same rotation as the guy and wanted to leave his presence as soon as possible.

"Man, don't you hate school busses?" Timmy said once he reached Hipple. "I mean, I think it's terrific they're getting kids interested in art, but a museum isn't Disneyworld. In such large groups, they're gonna socialize. And besides, it makes us work twice as hard."

His blank expression had not changed from the second Timmy had approached him. He thrust his radio at the college student and left without saying a word.

On the way to the break room, a woman bumped into him. She was of average height and looks and wore a gray dress. The woman slipped an object into Hipple's pocket and whispered, "That's from you know who."

She then looked indignant and said loudly, "Watch it, asshole."

The Tall Woman had told him she had hired someone to give him the key, but he was not expecting to receive it in such a hostile manner. He also figured it would happen outside of the museum and the cameras. To make it worse, the woman had hit him flush on his bum shoulder. But after his irritation subsided, Hipple could only grin. Good things were on the way. Very good things.

* * *

The day before he had received the key, a very tall and pretty lady had approached him at his bus stop on California Street. She had asked him to do four things for her in exchange for seventy-seven thousand dollars. Hipple had made minimum wage his entire life, and while he initially turned the offer down because he wasn't sure he had the nerves to do it, he capitulated after she whispered in his ear: "I know you can do it, Harry."

He had gotten goose bumps and an erection. The former would stay and the latter would dissipate after the next thing she told him: "I need to be very blunt with you. These four things should be very easy for you to do, but they must be done on two conditions. You can never, ever, tell anyone that we've met or talked. Can you do that?"

"Yes," Hipple croaked.

"And when you get the backpack, you must never look in it. Do you understand? You cannot, under any circumstances, look inside the backpack. My clients wish to keep the contents a secret and will not appreciate any breach of trust."

"If I'm doing something illegal, I should know just how illegal it is."

"We are paying you an awful lot of money to complete simple tasks," she said. "Somebody will give you a key, you use it to get a backpack out of a safety deposit box. You take a backpack and put it in a locker where you work. The night before the robbery, you take that backpack out of the locker and put it in the stairway outside the museum doors. Mr. Hipple, a chimpanzee could do it. If you don't like the instructions, then we'll find somebody else."

"All right, all right, I won't open the stupid bag. But for the sake of argument, let's say I do. Let's say the bag rips and the contents fall out. What would they do?"

"I don't issue threats, Mr. Hipple. But my clients value tact and secrecy above all else. Violate it, they'll weigh their options. And sometimes violence is one of them. Now, do you still want that seventy-seven thousand dollars?"

His hands were trembling and it took a few seconds, but he was able to get out a hoarse "yes."

After receiving the key when his shift was over, he proceeded to do the second of four errands to get paid more money than he'd ever seen in his life. The key would open a safety deposit box located in a building on an alley off Third Street, a few blocks away from the ballpark. He began sweating and his stomach felt sour just thinking of the task.

Hipple didn't spend much time south of Market and had difficulty finding the location. He lived with his mother on Clement Street in the Inner Richmond and thought it too expensive to see a Giants game or dine in a SoMa restaurant. The sign on the faded redbrick building was small, and the one window next to the dented metal door had been painted black and was covered with bird droppings. He never would have imagined that such an establishment would rent anything with the word "safety" in it.

"Do you speak English?" he asked the caucasian man behind the plexiglass window.

If the slender person with the hairy arms was insulted by Hipple's question, he didn't show it. "Are you a cop?" he asked.

"I wish I was."

"The fuck kind of answer is that? Are you, or aren't you?"

"I'm not," Hipple said.

"Do you have a box, or would you like to rent one?"

Hipple reached into the pocket of his tan corduroy pants for the key the stranger had given him in the museum. He had to fish around coins, a pocket knife, and a can of mace to extract it. He thumped the blue key on the chipped linoleum counter and slid it under the glass.

The skinny man disappeared behind a tattered velvet curtain, leaving Hipple alone with adrenaline whipping through his veins. Sure, he needed the money, but he didn't have the stomach to associate with seedy characters in sleazy situations. The place smelled like cat urine.

There was a loud buzz, and somebody yelled, "Open the fucking door."

Hipple did as he was told and jumped when the solid metal door slammed behind him. He now stood in a concrete hall lit with a bare light bulb. A door in front of him opened and the hairy gentleman stood there with a metal box the size of a briefcase. He suddenly thrust it at Hipple, nearly knocking him over.

"You're allowed five minutes in a private room if you wish to take anything from the box. If you're gonna take the whole enchilada, here's what happens. I turn around, you take it and fuck off."

His third task was to take the backpack from the security box and put it inside locker number 333 in Ladies Locker Room A at the Matisse Hotel. Despite the woman's warnings, he had to know what he would be carrying inside the place he worked. Yes, the security officers did not search each other when they entered the building, and he could get the bag inside without issue, but it could have been drugs, weapons, or human organs.

This is it, he thought. It's the only chance he'd have to find out how evil his deeds would be. Maybe whatever was in the bag was so bad it would cause him to tender his resignation.

"Ahh, I'm not sure if I want the whole inchilloada. I'd like a private room, please."

"It's enchilada, you fucking idiot, and are you sure that's what you want? I have instructions, and you peeking inside weren't part of them. It was a test, Mr. Harry Fucking Hipple, and you failed."

The sound of his name from such a man's lips unnerved him. He felt bile coming up from his stomach. His hand began shaking.

Hipple lifted the top of the metal security box, grabbed the heavy backpack from inside, and was out the door so fast he almost tripped over his legs. Once on the street he inhaled deeply, anticipating fresh air to soothe his nerves. Except a bus had just passed and the exhaust made Hipple cough and then gag. After wiping the drool from his mouth he hailed a taxi.

"The Matisse Hotel."

* * *

A couple days after successfully putting the bag inside the locker and managing to not dissolve into a panic attack at any point during his shift, Hipple sat on a beanbag in front of a bulky nineteen-inch television in the house he shared with his mother on Clement Street. His boss at the museum, Larry Aberlour, was seated in an aluminum folding chair next to him.

Hipple had stopped him from using the plush recliner because it was his mother's, and she would know if somebody's behind had messed up her groove.

They watched a show on tank warfare while drinking sparkling wine and taking drags from cigars. Hipple had purchased a case of ersatz champagne at Walgreens after returning from the hotel, and he had poured it into the finest glasses he owned, collectable *Return of the Jedi* cups from Burger King. The cigars he bought at Cigarettes R Cheaper! on Geary and were the least expensive items they sold.

"What kind of shit champagne did you buy?" Larry asked as he stared at the tiny bubbles floating just below the rendering of Jabba the Hutt.

Hipple was insulted and his face showed it, but since Larry was his boss he didn't respond. He instead got up for the bottle, poured more sparkling wine into his glass, and collapsed into the beanbag chair, the air hissing out of the foamy leather-lined seat in an elongated sigh.

"Nothing like watching a good tank fight," Hipple said. "Me and Ma love this show."

"For creeping sake, Hipple. Your mom isn't coming home tonight, is she? What about the entertainment I arranged?"

"She's in Palm Springs. And Mr. Aberlour, we could have gone to your place."

"Just busting your balls a bit, Harry. So you getting excited about the girls?"

"They're escorts, right? Not whores."

"Are we going to the opera? The only place they'll be escorting us is to the bedroom."

He was conflicted. The thought of paying for sex had always repulsed him, yet he had never possessed enough money to do so. When his manager mentioned he could hire escorts for their celebration, Hipple agreed. But now he wanted to leave the apartment and get far, far away. His hand was shaking, and it was hard to drink the champagne.

"Drink up, my good man," Larry said. "We're going to do it up right tonight. Because after the, ah, job, we keep a low profile. Our tall friend was very clear about that."

"What's her problem?" Hipple asked with a jittery voice, recalling the seedy safety deposit man. "I don't like to be threatened."

"It's not her. It's her—"

"Clients. I'm sick of hearing about her clients. Who the hell are they?"

"What do you care if they're fucking leprechauns?" Larry said. "We're both getting paid a lot of money to do an easy job and keep our mouths shut. And we're both going to do just that. We're talking serious shit here, Harry. I'm not risking anything."

"I know. I don't like to be threatened, is all."

"We shouldn't even be talking! Remember what she said. Neither of us should know the other is involved. But since we both let the cat out of that bag during your performance review today, I need a goddamned drink."

Hipple could barely hear the plastic cork popping when his boss opened two more bottles of sparkling wine. Larry gave him one and then raised the other for a toast. After clinking the bottles and chugging straight from them, they waited for their escorts to arrive. For the money they were paying, Hipple thought, they better be pretty as hell.

Candy and Mandy, each wearing a hip-hugging dress the color of their hair, arrived twenty minutes later. Hipple was relieved to see they were attractive in the way good clothes, good makeup, and good surgeons could provide. Candy was a redhead and Mandy a brunette; both were in their mid-thirties and voluptuous.

It took three more bottles of sparkling wine, two strip-teases, and a hand job for both men to break the promise of confidentiality they made to the Tall Woman.

Having just returned from the bathroom, Hipple was now drunk, relaxed, and full of misplaced machismo. His eyes were glazed over, and when he tried to sit on the beanbag with Mandy, he misjudged by a few inches and thumped onto the floor. He laughed it off, but then he was worried over noises Larry was making after taking a puff on his newly lit cigar. But Hipple was relieved to see, after the coughing jag subsided, that his boss was able to pour wine for the whole group.

"Money to burn, ladies," Larry said and collapsed on the couch next to Candy. "We have money to burn."

"Yeah," Candy deadpanned as she noticed Princess Leia on the side of her glass. "I can see you're a couple of high rollers. Secret agents or mafia?"

Larry laughed and said, "This place is just to keep our cover. But I bet you get that a lot. Guys bragging about them-selves, making their lives seem more interesting."

"Nah, they're usually happy to spend hours yapping about their wife, dog, and desk job."

"You're a spunky one," Larry said. "I like that."

"It's the wine. My sense of humor gets heightened when I drink bubbly piss."

Mandy whispered to Candy, "Are you cray-cray, these guys might be a couple of jokers, but they have some money. They're good for more if you keep your mouth shut. The less said the better. Guys aren't interested in listening, only talking."

"Candy is just playing," Mandy said. "The champagne is delicious."

"Besides, I've done enough E to get a fat-assed baboon high," Candy said.

"She's a spunky one, like you said. Especially when she's having a good time. We feel really comfortable here. Can I have some more champagne?"

When Hipple was able to get off the floor and onto the beanbag with Mandy, his escort ran her fingers over his crotch.

"Tell us what you do," Mandy continued. "You're both mysterious and that turns us on."

"Well," Larry said, "we do have interesting occupations."

"I'd love to hear about it," Candy said, finally getting on board. "But you only asked for a two-hour escort."

"Two hours and a hand job for a thousand," Hipple muttered.

"That's our standard escort, boys," Mandy said in a breathy voice.

"Ladies, he's kidding." Larry took out a wad of cash and fanned the bills. "A thousand to us is Monopoly money."

"We figured that," she said. "And you know, a couple of players like yourselves, you're probably into some dangerous shit. Hearing about danger gets us all wet."

"Speak for yourself. I'm drier than all those towns you drive by on the way to Vegas on a hot summer afternoon."

"Excuse us," Mandy said and led her partner to the kitchen.

"Neither of us is getting sexually aroused from anything these two losers are saying. But we have them hooked for more money, so let's keep them talking and drinking. Two hours are gonna pass before either will think of unzipping their pants. I know this is your first night on the job, but if you would have listened to me on the ride here instead of dropping E, you wouldn't be trying to fuck it up. Now get back in there and keep your mouth shut."

Larry counted out two thousand and shoved the money down Candy's lacy underwear when she returned to the room. "We're thieves," he said, "but I can't say what we steal."

"Because it's dangerous," Mandy purred.

"I want to get hot," Candy said. "Tell us all about it."

"We're international thieves," Larry said, hoping that would be enough.

"So you're international thieves who steal . . . ?"

"Sculptures," Hipple blurted out. "The odalisque Matisse sculptures."

Larry looked like he was going to have a seizure. "That's another one of our covers. The truth is we're gold thieves. International gold thieves. We specialize in coins and bars."

"I've heard of those sculptures," Candy said. "I was with a client so I didn't get to the museum, but the suites were the bomb." She ran her hand down Larry's back. "So, you're going to steal them. They have to be worth a fortune."

"They sure are," Hipple said.

"If that was, in fact, what we were in town to steal," Larry said. "But we're gold thieves. And a shipment of, ahh, Krugerrands, has just came in from Antwerp."

"There's been months of planning and we're part of a team," he said.

Larry grabbed him by the arm and whispered in his ear. "What the fuck are you doing? Do you want to get us killed?"

"C'mon, who's gonna know? Mr. Aberlour, I've never done anything interesting in my life, and there are two hot chicks who want to hear about it."

"Tell us more, you sexy beasts," Candy said in her best Marilyn Monroe impersonation.

And they did. The liquor flowed and the story of how the Matisse sculptures would be robbed came out of both mouths. The warnings of the Tall Woman were distant echoes in the drunken men's minds.

5

An Offer You Can't Refuse

ON THE MORNING of October 29th, Veronica walked fifteen minutes from her basement apartment to a bluff overlooking Baker Beach. She sipped coffee from a thermos and watched two elderly ladies practice Tai Chi against the backdrop of the Golden Gate Bridge. She liked how the clouds drifted over the Marin Headlands and cast enormous spaceship-like shadows on the ocean. She inhaled the scents of dirt, grass, and ocean air with a meditative smile.

Being in the moment was much better than worrying about the mysterious woman in the Mercedes, wondering why she had wagged her finger at her. If Veronica had to think of anything, best it be the article she was writing on the hotel strike. It was her day off from her temp job, and she needed to make progress with her free time. She had her notebook and laptop and while drinking green tea and eating a banana, she reread all the information she had gathered. Afterward she switched on her computer and double-clicked the icon on her desktop titled "The Article." The first page read: "Untitled Hotel Labor Dispute Article."

Those were the only words.

She typed an opening paragraph to the article and then, like the dozen or so before them, deleted it. She made several more attempts, and two hours later gave up. She was frustrated at not being able to write, so instead she listened to waves crash against the shore with her eyes closed. When the image of the woman in the Mercedes popped into her head, Veronica shuddered, opened her eyes, and then hurried the ten or so minutes back to her apartment.

Sabrina, her French bulldog, greeted her with a bunch of snorts and a wagging tongue. While she was setting out a bowl of dog food and some water, her room had begun to fill with secondhand smoke. Sarah, Kutra, and Le Ned, her roommates on 20th Avenue, had begun their daily abuse of marijuana inside the house.

Veronica, living in the basement, smelled traces of the cannabis just about every day. She didn't partake, but such a minor nuisance wasn't worth complaining about. However, the smoke now seemed to be seeping through her ceiling and she needed fresh air. She could have gone outside to the backyard, but with no food in her fridge and the banana the only thing she had consumed all morning, she decided to get an early lunch. She had a separate entrance through the basement, but her roommates, who were also the owners of the house, always had their cellar door open. Many times, while attempting to leave, they would shout down to her, asking if she wanted to "burn one." Veronica believed they were all likable people, but she didn't smoke marijuana and their stoned musings bored her.

Hoping her roommates were too engrossed in their conversation about *The Lord of the Rings* to notice her, she made her way to the door. She found the right moment to leave when they began talking simultaneously about their perfect synergy with the hobbits. Veronica was almost outside when Kutra yelled, "V-Ron!"

Kutra was nineteen years old with a long-distance runner's build and wore her hair in a beehive. Despite the fact she was stoned every moment of her life, the young woman was focused and alert. That was probably because she had a penchant for snorting her ADD medication. Like her cohorts, Sarah and Le Ned, Kutra had never worked a day in her life. All three subsided off trust funds.

Veronica wanted to sprint away from her roommates and their masticated brains, but she didn't believe in rudeness, and also didn't want to jeopardize her living situation. Regardless of her room's basement setting, peeling wallpaper, and capricious plumbing, the house was minutes away from the ocean. And since the owners of the house were all rich and clueless, her rent was far below market value.

"Where ya going, V-Ron?" Kutra yelled down.

"Just for some coffee," she fibbed.

If she had divulged her actual destination, Tommy's Mexican Restaurant on Geary, she would have been obligated to bring them takeout, which she could not afford. Combining their being born rich with their cannabis intake, Kutra, Sarah, and Le Ned did not comprehend such variables as disposable income.

"C'mon up. We'd like to hear how you'd feel about living in Middle Earth. We're totally interested in somebody else's opinion. We're smoking some serious shit, too."

None of them ever remembered that Veronica did not smoke pot.

She politely declined and rode her bike to Tommy's for a burrito and a margarita. While absently staring at the cartoon image of a sombrero on the place mat, she wondered why she had to resort to freelance articles when she should have been hired by one of the Bay Area newspapers. Her favorite professor at Berkeley had gotten her a few interviews, but none had resulted in a job offer, even though she felt she had aced them. But Veronica decided to stop her line of thinking, as she knew her aunt, who was a staff reporter at the *New York Times*, would have chided her for.

"No excuses and no complaints," Aunt Becky often said after one too many martinis at the rare family gatherings she made it to. "Very few people are handed anything, and the rest of us have to work our asses off for whatever it is we want."

Aunt Becky was a big role model and influence, but so was Nellie Bly, the pioneering investigative journalist from the late 1800s, early 1900s. She was put to sleep with stories of Ms. Bly going undercover and writing about injustices at sweatshops and mental asylums. Her aunt hooked her on journalism at an early age, and Veronica was determined to be successful in it.

Temp work gave her access to various businesses, some of which she hoped would be corrupt. Her first assignment was passing out 401(k) information to a bunch of accountants in a downtown skyscraper. Going floor to floor and handing out booklets to balding men with bellies who ate greasy lunches at their desks offered no chance to uncover fraud. The most intriguing thing she learned was that the company gave their meeting rooms names that she found depressing. It made her feel sorry for the people who had to sit for hours in a place called "Morning Tranquility" when it was anything but.

The next assignment was the Matisse Hotel, and the strike was her opportunity for a compelling story. After work, Veronica took copious notes of the day's activities, every detail she had seen and heard regardless of how trivial they might have been. She had almost filled an entire notebook.

But when she tried to write the article, she never got further than the first paragraph. The goal was to give an insider's glimpse of the strike, but that wasn't enough. The daily newspapers had only culled quotes from either the union's or hotel's spokespersons. The main issues of rising healthcare costs and wage increases had been given some ink, but coverage had shifted to the strike's effect on the San Francisco economy. But even that angle had waned, and Veronica was no longer sure if anybody who wasn't involved cared.

But a talented reporter can make the public care. That's what she believed, and after she finished lunch, she boarded a 38 Limited and made her way downtown. A hotel worker rally was happening in Union Square, an event that could open her story up visually since all her notes were derived from inside the basement office. Veronica knew she needed to give the piece a real voice instead of prepackaged public-relations prattle.

By the time she made it there, the rally was more than halfway over, but she did get to hear a few impassioned speeches and was able to interview several of the employees who had been watching. It felt good to be doing real reporting, and hopefully this would spur her to finally work on the article that evening. But the labor rally would not be the most interesting thing that happened to her that day.

* * *

After Veronica finished gathering quotes for her story, she needed a coffee. Since the sun was shining and the late October temperature allowed San Franciscans to shed jackets, she decided to find a place with sidewalk seating. Wearing a sun dress and sneakers, she ascended the steep slope of Powell with short, choppy steps as a cable car rumbled past her. When she reached Sutter, she paused for a few seconds to catch her breath.

"Ms. Zarcarsky, I was wondering if I could have a few minutes of your time."

She turned around and looked at a lady who was taller than the starting center on the women's basketball team when she was at Berkeley. The stranger's long tan skirt billowed in the wind. Veronica recognized her as the woman in the Mercedes, and she instinctively took a few steps backward.

"I didn't mean to scare you last night. I should have just kept driving and not let you know I had spotted you, but it was the end of a long day and I was annoyed at my carelessness. Letting emotions get the best of me, I made a second mistake by wagging my finger. A good lesson to always stay in control of your emotions."

"Why are you following me?"

"I have a business proposition for you."

"That takes you to my house at night, and then following me here?"

"I wasn't ready to speak to you last night, but yes, I followed you here today. Please, let me buy you dinner and I'll explain why. Any place, my treat."

"You got me a bit freaked out, to be honest with you. And I have no interest in sales or pyramid schemes or religious cults," Veronica said.

"It's none of those things, Ms. Zarcarsky. And I'm sorry to have scared you last night. But if you let me buy you dinner, I can give you all the details. You can of course say no, but then you'll never know why I've been following you."

Veronica wanted to believe in karma and that everything happened for a reason. On some days she did, but mostly she saw life as random. And she cherished bizarre encounters and situations that varied from her everyday routines, even if there wasn't a greater purpose behind them. She also figured if the woman really wanted to do her harm, there was no reason she'd offer her a free meal.

"I'm still full from lunch, but was on my way to get a coffee."

They walked to Jasmine's Café on Bush Street in silence. The strange woman ordered for them both inside, and they now sat at a sidewalk table in the shade. They sipped cups of coffee and tried to size each other up.

"Do you work for the hotel?" Veronica asked.

"No," the Tall Woman answered. "But the reason we're talking is because you do."

"Well, technically I work for a temp agency. They have a contract with the hotel."

"Even better."

"I appreciate the coffee, but are you going to keep being cryptic?" Veronica asked.

"I apologize, let's get down to business. What I'm going to ask you is confidential. I would have rather met in private, but your roommates seem to never leave the house."

"You've been stalking me."

"Watching, per request of my clients," she answered. "We weren't even sure if we would need your services, and I actually began watching you for insurance reasons. Given an unforeseen event, it has paid off for my clients and me."

"And who are your clients?"

"The less you know the better, but they are people who need a valuable bag that they own recovered. You are in a perfect position to get this item for us."

"Legally?"

"Somebody who reads poetry and writes at the beach doesn't see the world in black and white. So I think you can understand when I say there's nothing immoral or illegal we're asking you to do if you don't ask any questions or seek a greater purpose than your task. Stay in the dark; you'll like it there."

Veronica watched as two businessmen passing by on Bush Street turned around to stare at the person sitting across from her. The lady's long legs were a detriment to the small iron chair.

"What do your clients need?" Veronica asked after she took a sip.

"Just a backpack."

"Does it belong to your clients?"

"It certainly does," the Tall Woman said. "And the contents inside the backpack are important to them."

"Why do they need me?"

"The backpack was put inside a locker at the hotel by an associate of ours. It was secured by a private lock, but it's come to our attention that the lock was cut and a new one placed on it."

"Employees aren't allowed to put personal locks on hotel lockers," Veronica said. "It's against policy and we've cut dozens of them."

"And that's why we need your help."

"You want me to break into a locker?"

"Not break," the Tall Woman said. "You have the combination."

"It's on a master list inside the HR office."

"And you work inside the HR office."

"That doesn't make it okay for me to give out combinations," Veronica said.

"But what's inside the locker belongs to my clients. The backpack is theirs."

"What's in the backpack? And why is your client's backpack in a hotel locker?"

"It is to your advantage that you do not know," the Tall Woman said.

"So when I get caught with a pound of marijuana, I can plead ignorance?"

"I promise you there are no drugs inside the backpack. In fact, there is nothing illegal about the contents."

"Then why can't I know what's inside?"

While Veronica welcomed the bizarre, the reporter in her wouldn't allow her to simply nod and listen. Who? What? Where? When? And how? Questions had to be asked.

"Who are your clients?"

"They wish to remain anonymous," the Tall Woman said.

"Are they terrorists?"

"Ms. Zarcarsky, my clients, if anything, are capitalists. And they're willing to offer you an ample sum of money to carry out a simple task."

"How ample?"

With fluid movements, the Tall Woman took a pen out of her designer handbag. She wrote a figure on her cocktail napkin and slid it across the table. Veronica quickly surmised she could pay off her college loans and have plenty of money left over.

"All I ask is a simple task, and complete discretion."

6

Miles Krakow and His New Creative Medium

LATER THAT DAY, Georgia, wearing a loose, paint-splotched cotton dress, moved around her sculpture titled *Buddha on Broadway*. She used all five feet, nine inches of her body, along with a wooden step stool, to reach the top portion of the object. She inspected her sculpture first in totality, and then took off her black-framed glasses to scrutinize it up close.

When chicken wire snagged her index finger and blood streaked down her hand, she was more annoyed at the interruption than in actual pain. She continued curling the wire around the base of the sculpture, and it felt good to have been working for two hours straight. But when she noticed the circles of blood on her dress, Georgia dropped her pliers and went to the bathroom for a Band-Aid.

"It's goddamn brilliant," Miles Krakow yelled from the other room.

Upon returning from dressing her wound, she found Miles sitting on the floor with his legs crossed. After lighting a cigarette, he continued in his praise. "Fucking brilliant."

"It's not finished."

"If I were you, I wouldn't put another finger on it," Miles said.

"You're not me, and there're some finishing touches to be done. And that doesn't even include casting the bronze."

"So what do we have here?" Miles leapt up and began circling the six-foot-tall sculpture. "Chicken wire, wax that will become bronze."

"Some of the wax will stay wax," Georgia said.

"And there's some sandstone, and I guess that's a plastic trash bag? Can make out a hint of a Buddha as it abstracts into a wonderfully bizarre frenzy of images. A religious piece?"

"Do you think it is?" she asked.

"I'm not sure. Since your mom is from India, shouldn't you have used Ganesh or Shiva?"

"Fuck you. I'm half French as well, Miles. And even so, the Buddha was born in India."

"Well, whatever your intentions are, it blows me away."

"Thanks," Georgia said. "But I'd rather be painting."

"Please, darling, don't give me that shit again. You're more known for your sculptures, and you need to embrace that. Anyone can get famous for painting. I mean, look at me."

Georgia stared at Miles, dressed in the hipster fashion of skinny jeans, irreverent T-shirt, and aviator glasses. She didn't need anyone to tell her how famous he had become for his paintings. After his first exhibit, one esteemed critic claimed that Miles combined all the best of Van Gough, Dalí, and Pollock on his epic canvases to create original masterpieces. Heavy praise for an artist, especially a fourteen-year-old. After his first show he became a sensation, a child prodigy who was loved by critics and the masses. Georgia naturally had some jealousy issues over this.

His success lasted a decade until Miles woke up one day and decided he never wanted to paint again. At least that was the way he described it in interviews. Georgia had known the truth: he had been growing bored with the medium for years. But when he announced his retirement, nobody believed him. Miles Krakow and painting were synonymous.

Eight years after declaring he was finished, he had stayed true to his word; however, the man had not given up on art. And his new creative medium had kept him in the public eye.

Georgia snatched the cigarette from the artist's hand and took a long drag. At thirty-four, she was older and less success-ful than Miles. She had even studied him in college, a bizarre fact she couldn't expel from her head. She took one more drag and tossed the cigarette into a cold cup of coffee.

"No smoking in here."

Miles smiled and instantly took another cigarette from the pack.

"My dad shows up without warning, and you know how much he despises cigarettes."

"It's your cabin," Miles said.

"Don't give him another reason to hate you."

"Georgia, your dad loves me."

"He used to."

"C'mon, he can't still be upset."

Her father had progressed far past the emotional realm of being upset. He was upset when she and Miles ended their five-year relationship. He was disappointed when he retired from painting. But Miles had done something to cause her dad to percolate with an anger that would never subside.

"You set fire to one of his Picassos."

"One of *my* Picassos," Miles said. "I bought it from him."

"And when you told him what you planned to do with it, your so-called 'new artistic expression,' he demanded it back," Georgia said.

"Your father has such an astute eye for art, in time he'll come to understand my vision. Not only that, I guarantee he'll eventually want to buy my piece. He'll see the genius in it."

Georgia was disgusted that Miles's new medium was the desecration of established artists' work. So far he had set ablaze the Picasso lithograph; took a chainsaw to a Henry Moore; ripped into tiny pieces a Winslow Homer; and urinated on one of his first oil paintings, which he then melted with acid. Miles performed these acts of vandalism in front of a cheap video cassette camera from the eighties.

He claimed to be inventing a new form of art, one that reflected the violence and barren culture of the twenty-first century. The world did not agree. He was assailed with eggs and rocks at his first exhibit. Numerous death threats were issued. And just last week, several countries passed laws prohibiting the sale of any artwork to Miles Krakow or anybody acting on his behalf.

"My dad lives for the preservation of art," Georgia said. "He loathes you."

"Frenchie will come around."

"You're a fucking lunatic. I'm afraid to be seen in public with you."

"History will judge me differently."

"First I thought you were being eccentric in a sort of Andy Kaufman manner," Georgia said. "Now you've launched into full-blown Howard Hughes craziness. Seriously, you need to stop taking so many pills."

"I indulge in the occasional red or blue or green pills. Sometimes yellow and orange."

"How long are you going to keep this up? I mean, nobody will even sell you a painting anymore. And you sold every piece of art you ever made or acquired when you retired."

"Poor planning on my part, an impetuous act that I deeply regret."

"You regret all that money you made?" Georgia asked. "How much was it? One hundred million?"

"Loads more than that. Which is why I'll find somebody to sell me an artistic treasure. And if not, maybe I'll pay somebody to steal one."

"Don't even joke about that."

"Because it's in your family history?"

"Fuck off, Miles."

"I'm sorry, I don't believe the stories about your dad stealing those Rembrandts in the seventies. And I'm sure he had nothing to do with the Gardner and Cordovan heists. But you gotta admit, it sure is fun to think about. Your papa a real-life *Thomas Crown Affair*."

"Screw you. You can continue to slander my father and I'm going to throw you out, or you can cut the shit and we can take a drive over to Half Moon Bay. I need some fresh air, and a burger and a beer sounds really good."

"Consider the shit sliced and I'll drive."

* * *

Several hours later, Georgia was eating lukewarm Chinese food on the hardwood floor of her cabin with Miles. Although there was a fire crackling, candles lit, and both were wet from taking showers, the mood was several notches below romantic. In fact, she wasn't speaking to him.

Georgia had accompanied Miles out of the city and intended to have a burger and a beer at Half Moon Bay Brewing Company. After heading over the Santa Cruz Mountains, they parked by the restaurant and took a stroll by the water. It was windy, but she said the salt air would do them good.

And it had, right up to the point when they were pelted with clams.

The art society of a local Christian high school had returned from a whale watch. Eager to try something new, many of the teenagers bought fried clams. Despite being doused with tartar sauce, the mollusks did not agree with most of the students' palettes. Upon sighting Miles Krakow, who had been the subject of a recent "Art of the Devil" lecture, they found use for the unwanted food.

From the students faces, it was clear they took great joy raining greasy clam strips, dripping with tartar sauce, onto both Georgia and Miles. Their teacher looked to be encouraging them, and the kids turned to french fries when the shellfish ran out. When there was no food, they threw rocks.

Georgia's pleas of mercy did not deter the students.

"Monster!"

"You'll burn in hell!"

Miles said he wanted to whip his penis out and yell blasphemous obscenities, but she grabbed his arm and yanked him toward the car. When he refused to get inside the Jaguar, she threatened with absolute conviction to abandon him. He eventually climbed inside the vehicle, not before extending both middle fingers to the students. As penance, she made him buy dinner at a Chinese restaurant.

Now sitting on the cabin floor with the takeout containers scattered about, Georgia said, "That's the last fucking time I'll ever be seen with you in public."

Those were the first words she had spoken in an hour. But Miles had not been daunted by the silence. He sang. He lectured on the importance of art in a free society. He even put on a puppet show with a clam and a fry that had stuck to his jacket.

"I have enough problems without factoring you into my life," Georgia said.

"Other than that waste-of-space boyfriend of yours, you seem to be doing well."

"You were at my last exhibit," Georgia said.

"You sold some pieces. The *Chronicle* gave it a decent review."

"Decent is death. God, I'd almost prefer being despised like you than to be decent."

"Who cares if some newspaper reporter said it wasn't your best work?" Miles said.

"Far from my best work."

"It was a stupid newspaper. Your boyfriend used to write for them. How's he doing now?"

"I don't feel like talking about Camden."

"Why? It's such fun," Miles said.

Georgia sighed and grabbed the bottle of wine that was between them on the floor. It was a Cliff Lede Poetry Cabernet, which they had purchased several years ago when they were a couple on a trip to the Stags Leap District in Napa. They had already consumed a bottle of Chimney Rock Reserve Cab bought on the same excursion.

"You better go easy with the vino, there. After that bottle and the one on the table, I only have one case of Opus in my trunk."

"And you better haul it out and leave it as a fucking peace offering. Fried clams! And you wonder why I dumped you."

"We parted ways mutually," Miles said. "Long before I found my new artistic genius. Fill me up."

She poured one splash into Miles's glass and put the bottle down.

"God, I would love to get in your pants again," Miles said.

"Gross. And even if I mostly can't stand looking at his stupid face and I plan on breaking up with him, I have a boyfriend."

"If you tell me you haven't cheated on him, I will laugh in your face," Miles said. "There are rumors about you and Bouchon. Cheating on your boyfriend with the owner of the place where he works. Brilliant."

"I'm not going to have this conversation, especially with someone who cheated on me."

"I had a few moments of weakness, which is pretty commendable for a young, successful, and filthy-rich artist. And I'm sure you did, too, when we were a couple."

"Never," Georgia said.

"I might be apt to believe you. But it's only because you were a nobody back then. Now that you're successful, you've earned the right to have any cock you want."

"That's horrible. I feel awful I've cheated on Camden. And what do you know about my relationship with David?"

"The art community treats me as an outcast, but I have my spies. But back to my original argument. I'm sure Camden was Mr. Faithful. It's only 'cause he's a drunk working for minimum wage."

"He was a successful writer once. Who—"

"Won awards for his column," Miles continued for her. "I'm familiar with the Camden Swanson dossier. He might have had things going for him, but he pissed them all away."

"Just like you."

"The difference is that one of my scribbles used to sell for a million dollars."

"If you could have only seen Camden the night I met him. He was so funny, so smart. I met him at the TV station where I was being interviewed for that show I did in Westwood."

"I think it's hilarious he basically published a science fiction story on page one of a major newspaper."

"I thought if I got him up to San Francisco, he could start working on a novel or do some freelance. I thought he could reinvent himself and I wanted to help. I really did."

Miles got to his knees, kissed Georgia on the cheek, and said, "He shouldn't be your problem anymore. And I have more pressing things on my agenda than Camden Swanson."

7

Nightmare on Elm Street

AS THE SKY turned a bluish gray and the trees became silhouetted on October 30, the Tall Woman drove south down the 101 Freeway and exited at Holly Street in the small Peninsula town of San Carlos. She always gave fake names while working and had the necessary documents to become any of these people. But for the Matisse job, she made the decision to use no name at all.

She thought of herself as an independent movie producer, a job she'd done well for several years in her early twenties. Her duties back then were preproduction, all the planning and pulling the necessary strings for the director to make a successful film. She was an expert in logistics and had built a reputation in Hollywood for never overlooking a single detail. Her work ethic carried over into her current, more lucrative profession.

She was very careful in choosing her partners whenever a job came her way. Her clients, as she referred to them, were a group of men that she had worked with a few times in the past. They were very careful, which she respected, and they could be trusted. Every team she partnered with had their plusses and minuses, and with these clients the only bad thing was their reliance on superstition. They all seemed to believe in tarot cards and numerology. She didn't believe in bad luck, only bad preparation.

Stealing the Matisse sculptures from the Museum of the Twentieth Century would not be easy, but it could be done. It was what happened afterward, the moving of the stolen art, that was always the hardest part of the theft. But there was no issue there, as she had been propositioned to commit the crime by a buyer who coveted the pieces.

With a team of proven professionals ready to liberate the sculptures, there was only the matter of hiring people from the inside to help. With museums, the employees were almost always low paid and living paycheck to paycheck, and with careful observation she could choose the right ones. With this particular job, there were the striking workers and their replacements, which offered a great distraction and a bounty of people to choose from.

Veronica was perfect because she was employed by a temp agency. Hipple was the dumbest of the gallery attendants she had met and would make an excellent patsy. After the robbery, as a matter of course, the police would watch all available security camera footage and they'd surely see the woman she'd hired slip the key in Hipple's pocket.

She thought the toughest person to hire would be the director of security, but Larry Aberlour was downright gung ho about ripping the place off. He felt he was grossly underpaid and wanted a career change. He was primed as the second patsy.

For the last insider, there was one person who clearly stood out. He didn't fit with the rest of the gallery attendants in the museum who were mostly college kids or retirees, and after learning that he was fired for making up a crazy story and printing it in a major metropolitan newspaper, Camden Swanson would be the third patsy. He'd think he was being hired to be a hostage, but they'd plant evidence to make it look like he was responsible for the crime.

With her objective in sight, the Tall Woman parked her gray Mercedes on Elm Street, brushed the creases out of her pleated tan skirt, and strode toward Camden Swanson's apartment. She didn't bother to wipe the perspiration off her forehead. It would make her more attractive to him if he wasn't too intoxicated to notice.

At the complex's entrance, she held the door for a young couple who was leaving with multiple pieces of luggage. She entered the building and walked down the hallway to Swanson's door and knocked twice. She was ready to pick the lock, but figured to try the handle first. It was open and she went into the apartment.

* * *

While Camden was annoyed that his day of squirrel watching and guzzling beer had been interrupted, the amazon woman now had his full attention. The fact that someone so attractive had been watching him and apparently needed his help was too bizarre to compute after all the beers he had consumed. He couldn't have guessed what her proposition would be, but he hadn't expected her to say: "You work at a museum; my clients wish to rob it."

"I'm on some sort of reality TV show now," he said, "or else someone is fucking with me. Either way, you got the wrong man, and I got some drinking to do. You found your way in and I'm sure you can find your way out."

Camden went to his turntable and pressed the button that spun the record and dropped the needle on it. As the warm crackle came from the speakers and Robert Earl Keen began to sing, he crossed back to the patio with his beer just as a squirrel scampered across the porch. When he sat in his camping chair, the music stopped with a scratch and the balcony door slid open. The woman, who towered over him, wiped a wisp of hair from her forehead.

"Nobody is fucking with you," she said.

"Humor me. How much we talking here?"

"Seventy-seven thousand. My clients are very superstitious."

"I would think aiding and abetting a felony was worth more."

"High standards for a guy making minimum wage," she said.

"The fifty-cent raise boosted my self-esteem. Or else, if I'm risking a lengthy prison term, I'd be wanting a little more security."

"Nobody will even know you're involved. All team members have a specific, independent task that is clandestine. I assure you there is no risk on your part."

"What all crooks think until they get caught," Camden said. "Ask Bo McClennan."

"We all know Bo McClennan very well, and your involvement in his arrest when you were a reporter. There's quite a bit of irony here, and I'm glad you brought him up. But I need to know. Have you had any contact with him recently?"

"Not since I interviewed him in prison nearly a decade ago. There's no way in hell I'd ever allow myself to get behind bars. I wouldn't want that nightmare."

"We have assembled the right crew and have a perfect plan. Nobody will get caught."

Camden looked into his bottle, hoping to find more than the two or three sips. He knew most heists were inside jobs, and he would naturally be a suspect if he agreed to help them. He wanted to tell her to go to hell, but the words would not come out of his mouth.

"We need a hostage," she said.

"Never seen that in the want ads."

"Normally the standard operating procedure is to take a hostage by force. But there's an element of risk involved, especially when you're dealing with security personnel."

"I work with college kids and old men."

"That's another reason," she said. "My clients do not want to deal with the irrationality of youth or the frailty of old age. We do not like to take chances."

There was still time to get back to his life of being a nobody, to return to his beer, Robert Earl Keen, and the squirrels. But the haze he had been in, the concussion-like feeling that had engulfed him for so long, was starting to lift. It was exciting, it was dangerous, and with the way his life had been going, he really had nothing to lose.

"Why me?" he asked.

"To be blunt, your life is far removed from the American dream. You're a failure and you'll never, ever, otherwise see the kind of money we're offering in one lump sum."

"And I wouldn't tell anybody because it would require too much effort," Camden said. "I'd have to have a closed-door meeting with my manager and fill out paperwork and get the police involved. And of course, they would all think I'm crazy."

The Tall Woman rose, moved languidly into the kitchen, and returned to the patio with a fresh bottle of beer. Camden figured he should watch her, but he never once turned in her direction after getting distracted by a squirrel bounding straight up the side of the building.

"When you finish your shift tomorrow," she said, "I will meet you at the corner of Fourth and Bluxome. We will go to an undisclosed location to meet my clients."

"I haven't said yes," he said.

"You will be paid very well."

"Just to be a hostage?"

"They did a job a couple years back, one I wasn't involved with, where their hostage was a martial arts expert," she said. "They killed the guy, but not before millions were lost. So my clients are paying you for peace of mind and efficiency. Their plan will run at its optimal potential if you do absolutely nothing. Something you are clearly good at."

"What was that cross street again?"

8

Friends of the Devil

THE NEXT MORNING, Halloween Day, with the Richmond District veiled in heavy fog, Veronica rode an early morning 1A Express bus to downtown. She brought her new poetry book to read, but her conscience was too busy justifying her decision to help the mysterious tall woman. It was more money than she had ever seen at one time, all for simply giving a combination. But whatever was in the bag, even if not necessarily illegal, would surely be part of some larger crime. As the bus turned left on Bush Street and the skyline of downtown gleamed through the clearing fog, she decided she would use the money as capital to start a freelance career.

But the little cartoon angel on Veronica's shoulder kept reminding her that helping the Tall Woman was wrong, and waves of nausea undulated through her belly. When she got to work and grabbed the file folder containing the new locker combinations, she began hyperventilating and slumped onto the floor against the metal filing cabinets. Luckily the office was empty, Carmine having gone to lunch and the two managers in meetings. Veronica's hand shook as she scribbled down the combination to locker 333 on a piece of scrap paper. She thought back to her conversation with the Tall Woman the day before.

"The bag must be inside the locker," the Tall Woman had said and then provided instructions: "It's imperative. The combination means nothing if the bag isn't there."

"A lot of temps threw their stuff in lockers and used their own padlocks. We'd just cut theirs, put a hotel lock around it, and make them come to HR."

"How could you tell if it was a temp or a regular employee on strike?"

"Well, first we have the master list," Veronica said, "which tells us who should be in the locker and whether or not it should be empty. If there was no assignment and the locker had stuff inside, it was pretty easy to differentiate."

"I only care about number 333 in Ladies Locker Room A," the Tall Woman said. "To repeat, the combination is worthless to my clients if the bag is gone. You would then need to locate it."

"If for some reason it wasn't in there, it would be in the Scary Room."

"Scary room?"

"It's the auxiliary storage room where they keep the old records. It's kind of my office."

"Are you going to help my clients, Veronica?" she asked.

The answer "yes" came a lot faster than she'd expected.

Now the time had come. She was to meet the Tall Woman tonight at Lefty O'Doul's and give her the locker combination. With the number to locker 333 in Ladies A in her hand, her throat went dry. A sharp pain welled in the back of her head. Bonnie walked into the office just as Veronica was about to go to the locker room.

"Sorry to startle you," Bonnie said. "God, you look awful."

"It just came on strong. I hope it's not the flu."

"Like everybody since the strike, you've been working crazy hours. You're worn down."

"I'll be okay," Veronica said.

"There are couches in the locker rooms. Why don't you lie down a bit? If you don't feel better, go home and get some rest. 'Cause we'll need you tomorrow for the job fair."

Veronica thanked Bonnie, took a deep breath, and rushed toward the locker room. Rounding the corner at an increased speed, she walked straight into one of the gallery attendants, easily identified because of his blazer and striped-tie uniform. They both fell to the floor with a loud thud.

"Oh my God," Veronica said. "I'm so sorry. Are you okay?"

"I'm fine," the guy answered. "Not a scratch."

Veronica looked down at his arm and saw a five-inch scratch made from a pen sticking out of her notebook.

"Well, I guess one scratch isn't so bad," he said.

She laughed and said, "I'm Veronica."

"Camden Swanson at your service."

Veronica got to her feet first and extended two hands out to help Camden up off the floor. He accepted the assistance but did his best to push himself upward.

"I'm so sorry. Do you need a Band-Aid?"

"I'm fine, thanks. You must be on your way to an important meeting to be moving so fast," he said.

"Just the bathroom," she said, not wanting to arouse suspicion in the man wearing a security guard uniform. "I, ah, have to pee."

"Well, that's important, too."

"Sorry again," Veronica said as she hurried away.

The locker room was empty, the dim florescent bulbs casting shadows off the benches. It took a few minutes to find number 333, for they weren't in true sequential order. Every creak, every clank of a pipe or distant noise in the hotel made her nervous.

Veronica looked at the piece of paper and turned the lock to the proper numbers. She misread her handwriting, mistaking a seven for a one. The lock didn't open. She tried again.

The round piece of metal clicked, and the latch sprung open.

The locker was empty.

* * *

Camden couldn't stop thinking about the woman who had to pee. He liked the way her beauty wasn't ostentatious; he needed to think about her for a few moments before it became clear. And not only had she laughed at the ironic scratch on his arm, but anybody who could tell a stranger they had to pee, and do so without being vulgar or intentionally comedic, held a special place in his heart.

What position did she hold at the hotel? Sales? Front desk? Maybe she was a new museum gallery attendant. He imagined walking up to her and asking her out. He saw them having drinks up at the Starlight Room, sipping cocktails and staring out at the lights of the city below. He felt bad for mentally cheating on Georgia, but she was going to break up with him the first chance she got. And besides, he figured he would probably never speak a word to this person again.

Camden instead focused his attention on the upcoming meeting with the art thieves. If they were going to pay him to be a hostage, then fine, he'd take the cash. But that would be the limit of his involvement. If these people wanted him to fool with alarms or gather information or do anything active, he would turn around and leave. The money would be nice, but going to jail was not an option.

Just before exiting the hotel at seven o'clock, he heard the familiar chants and the clanging and banging from the picketers. By now he had lost interest, and he didn't even bother to turn his head at the spectacle. Better to gaze at the life-size cardboard cutouts of big-breasted women in the window of the sex shop. There was also a new diorama of porn star action figures engaged in poses he'd never even contemplated.

Making his way down Ellis to Fourth, Camden alternated his thoughts between Veronica, the cardboard cutouts, and the meeting with the art thieves. When he reached the corner of Fourth and Bluxome, he expected to have to wait. For whatever reason, he assumed crooks were not punctual.

"Please, step inside the vehicle, sir."

The voice, British or perhaps Australian, but clearly fake, came from within a black sedan with tinted windows parked a few feet away. The door opened and Camden stepped inside. A man, wearing a suit, black gloves, and ski mask, sat in the back seat. A darkened partition shielded the driver and anybody else who may have been up front.

"Please, allow me to blindfold you, sir," the man in the ski mask said.

Camden shrugged and allowed the man to place a piece of heavy black cloth over his eyes as the sedan began driving down the street. He tried to discern where they were going, noting the turns and stops. It was a valiant effort, but unfortunately after six months of living in the Bay Area, his knowledge of San Francisco was poor. He gave up when the car picked up speed and had most likely gotten on the freeway.

After about fifteen minutes of driving, the car pulled into a garage, and the man wearing the ski mask led Camden to a doorway. It was cool and damp, and the only sounds he could hear were the click-clack of the man's shoes on what he believed was concrete flooring.

"When you hear the door close and not a second before," the guy said, "you may remove your blindfold."

Following instructions, Camden could now see a wooden staircase illuminated by a single light bulb. He climbed the ten steps to the top and suddenly regretted saying yes to the Tall Woman. The metal door creaked opened before he could knock.

* * *

Veronica stood at the empty locker. Somebody from HR must have taken the backpack out of the locker, placed it inside a trash bag, and dumped it into a bin in the Scary Room. Although each bag was labeled and indicated which locker it came from, if Veronica was caught rifling through the bins there would be no plausible explanation for her actions.

Two women in their thirties, dressed in tight and ill-fitting jeans and T-shirts with the hotel logo, entered the locker room. They were discussing in detail their "total perv supervisor." Veronica wanted to hide until they left, but she had to make it to the Scary Room as soon as possible to find that backpack.

"Hey, that's the lady who gave us lockers," one of them said.

"You clearing out more?" another asked. "Mine is kind of smelly and Shirley's is hard to open."

"I'm sorry, but I'm not feeling well," Veronica answered. "I came in here to lie on the couch."

"Ain't no couch in here. They took that out last week. Treat us temps like dirt."

"Ahh, stop by HR later and I'll see what I can do," Veronica said as she moved toward the door.

Carmine would be back from lunch in less than fifteen minutes, and upon his return he would go straight to the Scary Room to begin preparing for the upcoming job fair. Pens, staplers, one-sheet behavioral interviews, and other assorted odds and ends needed to be brought up to the banquet space. Veronica hurried down the hall and entered the room.

It was called scary because of the clutter, and with the laundry bins of plastic bags there wasn't enough room for Veronica to move around. But she didn't care about comfort and began riffling through the bags to find number 333 in Ladies A. The bags were all jumbled and it could have been in any of the bins.

Grab, look at the tag, no. Grab, look at the tag, no.

Veronica's shirt dampened with sweat as time passed. She would search for another five minutes, and if the bag did not appear, she would show up at Lefty O'Doul's and let the Tall Woman know she had tried. But Veronica feared having such a conversation, and she bent over into the scratched plastic yellow laundry bin and kept at her task.

Eight minutes later she thought she found the bag. But when Veronica heard Carmine's voice in the hallway, she realized the tag read "338" instead of "333." Grab, look, no. Grab, look . . . yes! She held the plastic bag tight to her chest and began to toss all the unneeded ones back into the bins.

Upon the scratching of the metal key entering the lock of the Scary Room, Veronica panicked and jumped behind a filing cabinet. She could never explain why she was hiding in such a spot clutching a bag that did not belong to her. She was sure her last duty in human resources would be to add her name to the term list.

"Oh, shit," Carmine said from just outside the door. "Need a box."

Veronica scrambled to her feet, operating on pure adrenaline. First, she tore the bag off the canvas backpack, crumpled up that piece of incriminating plastic, and shoved it in the trash can by her desk. Next, she wiped off the sweat and dust from her forehead with a napkin, straightened her hair, and exited the Scary Room wearing the backpack. It appeared similar enough to the one she wore to work but felt as if there were big rocks in it. She wanted to put it in the locker as soon as possible.

A security guard from around the corner said, "And the guy actually had a bottle of beer in his pocket when he had the balls to say, 'No, sir, I didn't steal nothing.'"

"That's why we're having yet another job fair tomorrow," Carmine responded. "Gotta replace the replacements we keep firing for theft or incompetence."

Veronica scurried in the other direction to Ladies Locker Room A. It was empty, and she extracted the piece of paper containing the combination as she walked to number 333. Her hands were shaky, and it was difficult to get the tiny numbers to match up to the line on the lock. It took three tries, but it opened. She thrust the backpack in the place where the Tall Woman was expecting it to be, slowly closed the metal door, and snapped the lock shut.

Veronica then went into a bathroom stall and vomited.

* * *

Camden stared at the hardwood floor in the strange room and peeked up quickly to see redbrick walls and black plastic shades drawn down over all the windows. After taking one step inside, somebody grabbed his arm and shoved him against the wall. A cylindrical piece of metal jabbed at his abdomen, and a small chalkboard was shoved at his face. When his eyes were able to focus, he read the message:

Arms up. We must frisk you.

After being patted down, Camden was led into another room containing a crackling fireplace, an old, bulky television set, and another chalkboard. When the door closed behind him, he read the next note: *Press play on the DVD player. When it ends hit eject and throw the DVD in the fireplace.*

He followed the instructions and the TV screen lit up, revealing a man standing in front of a concrete wall wearing a suit and a ski mask. The camera had been placed just far enough away to muddle any distinguishing characteristics. It might have been the same man from the car, but there was nothing conclusive to confirm or deny it. When the person spoke, it was with the aid of a voice box.

"Good evening, Camden," the person on TV said. "Now you already know why you were chosen to carry out this job. As our colleague explained, we are professionals who pride ourselves in being prepared. Most mistakes are made from greed. Our organization does not hesitate to spend money to assure success. On the other end of the spectrum, we would not hesitate to kill you if you impede our goals in any way. All we ask of you is to be a docile hostage and never say you were paid to do it. I must stress the last detail. You were never here.

"Tomorrow, November first, just before the museum is to close, my associates and I will enter the hotel. One team will handle the regular hotel security and also disable museum security personnel. Team two will remove the sculptures. And the third team will take you hostage and ensure our escape. It is imperative that you are at your post at exactly eight minutes before the museum closes.

"While a hostage, you will not be treated gently. We will inflict harm on you to provoke fear and expedite our egress. This is how you earn your money. You won't experience anything that cannot be cured with ice and first aid; we need you to remain calm and just go along with your captors. That is all you need to know. We have left ten grand in an envelope behind the TV set. There is a blindfold on top of the envelope. At the end of this message, take the envelope and then blindfold yourself.

"Before you go, we must warn you: If you abuse our good faith, we will kill you. If you ever tell anybody you were here, we will kill you. If you tip anybody that there is to be a robbery tomorrow, we will kill you. That is all, Camden Swanson, who lives on Elm Street in San Carlos with his girlfriend, Georgia. Now, place the DVD and chalkboard into the fireplace."

Camden did as told, and just as the stench of melting plastic hit his nostrils, he grabbed the thick, unsealed envelope and the blindfold. He fanned the bills with his thumb, the currency crisp and the ink strong. After he donned the black cloth over his eyes, somebody gripped his arm and led him to the car. Twenty minutes later, the vehicle came to a stop and the door opened to a blast of cold air.

Camden was thrust out of the car, his palms bracing his fall against concrete. He didn't get the blindfold off quickly enough to see the license plate. He got to his feet and saw he was at the intersection of Mason and Bay Streets. He needed to find a bar.

After a few minutes of wandering, he emerged onto a brightly lit street where he had to push his way through crowds of people, many of whom dressed in Halloween costumes. They were entering and exiting shops that sold any item imaginable with "SF" or "Alcatraz" printed on it. Some of them held bread bowls filled with clam chowder, making Camden's stomach rumble. A tempting dinner, and so was the In-N-Out he'd just passed, but he wanted someplace where he could get a beer and contemplate what he had gotten himself into.

The bills in the envelope were of thousand-dollar denominations, and thus as useless now as Monopoly money. He stopped in front of a Hooters and searched his wallet, finding enough cash for a dozen wings and a pitcher of domestic beer. Sitting at the bar, with the women in short orange shorts and tight white shirts moving past him, Camden knew what he was doing was wrong. There were thieves who were going to rob a museum, and he had a civic duty to stop them. But there was another voice in his mind that said, *Fuck civic duty, you're feeling more alive than any other time since you were a reporter.* And most importantly, there was the matter of the clients' threats, and Camden's desire to remain above ground and breathing.

With each chicken wing and beer, his tenuous grasp on morality began to fade away. He was committed to being the thieves' hostage tomorrow and had taken the leap of faith in believing they would keep their word and not kill him. He peeked inside his envelope of thousand-dollar bills and tried to think of a place that would break one.

9

Hipple Gets Cold Feet

ON HALLOWEEN NIGHT, Larry saved his two most important duties until just before he left the museum. He first made the next day's shift chart for the opening manager, making certain Camden Swanson would end his rotation in the Matisse sculpture room. He then checked his email for the subject line "Radio invoices."

The clients, after hacking the purchasing manager's account, were to send him an email from the hotel employee with a PDF. To anyone, it would appear legit, but when downloaded, the file would allow the thieves to access every single camera in the hotel. Larry did as he was instructed and, with the malware in place, put on his rumpled suit jacket and fifteen-year-old London Fog overcoat and left his office.

He exited the hotel with a smile on his face, confident he could handle any cross examination. He would give the police nothing, and there wasn't enough evidence to make him a suspicious character. On the way home, Larry encountered a five-car accident on 101 South, but it did not in any way sink his buoyant spirits. When he arrived at his Burlingame condo, he was euphoric.

The feeling vaporized when saw Harry Hipple pacing in front of the garage.

"What the hell are you doing here?" Larry asked in an angry whisper after rolling down his window.

"I got a bad feeling, boss. I don't think—"

"Hipple," he said as if Harry had not spoken, "what the hell are you doing?"

"I got a bad—"

"Don't talk to me out here. When I get inside I'll buzz you in."

The night before, they'd agreed to never speak to each other outside of the museum. Larry mumbled obscenities directed at Hipple as he rode the elevator up to his apartment. He fixed himself a strong bourbon and water and downed half the glass by the time Hipple rang the doorbell. Larry dropped the rest of the booze on the floor when his employee entered and said:

"I think we should turn them in."

"Are you fucking nuts?" Larry asked.

"We're going to get caught," Hipple said. "I just know it. And I don't want to go to jail. I have a bad feeling."

"Fuck you and your feelings. You're going to keep that mouth of yours shut. And then you're going to go home and forget you ever came out to Burlingame."

"You're not nervous?" Hipple asked.

"Until you showed up, I was on cloud fucking nine. We did our jobs. Now let those people do theirs."

"I still have to finish my job, Mr. Aberlour. I have to take that backpack out of the locker, the women's locker room, and put it in the stairway outside the museum doors."

"And you're going to fucking do it," Larry said. "It's so simple. You know exactly which path you're going to take that's shielded from the security cameras. We went over it several times. And at that time of day, there won't be anybody in the women's locker room. Only room attendants use it. And they're on set break times. The locker room will be empty."

"I don't think I can do it."

"You fucking can, and you fucking will."

"I have a bad feeling," Hipple repeated.

"If you don't put that backpack in the stairwell, they're going to kill the both of us."

"I'm gonna throw up."

"Just relax," Larry said. "You're scheduled to take your last break one hour before closing. You will follow the path that has no security cameras and then you will put the fucking bag in the fucking stairwell. You do that, nothing to worry about. Only thing that can mess things up now is if you talk."

"What if they get caught?"

"They're professionals, Hipple. So they won't get caught. And even if they did, pros don't give cops information."

"But if we went to the police now, they couldn't arrest us. Right? We haven't really done anything yet," Hipple said.

"Do you have one piece of brain in that skull? They'll kill you, Hipple. And they'll kill me, too."

Hipple sat down on the couch and began to cry.

"I've never done anything illegal in my life. But they made it sound so easy. And all that money. I make minimum wage and all I got is a high school diploma."

"You now have a chance to do something with your life. It sounded easy because it is easy. Hipple, go home and forget you ever came here. For fuck's sake, forget everything you've done in the last week. Never utter a word to anybody, any-where, anytime. Just do your job."

"Okay," he said with no conviction.

"You will come to work tomorrow, be given the combination to a locker that the woman will give to me tonight. You will take the bag out of the locker and put it in the stairwell exactly where they instructed, and the clients will rob the museum tomorrow evening just as we're closing. You will not even look at a cop, much less speak to one. You have to promise you will not go to the cops."

Hipple hesitated but then said, "I promise."

10

Twist and Shout

EVERY WORD OF Larry and Hipple's conversation was being recorded via an electronic bug placed on the back mantle of an elongated gray, nickel-plated Ikea lamp. The Tall Woman listened to the exchange between the people entrusted to help her and her clients with the heist. After Hipple had left, the only sounds in the apartment came from the TV and ice cubes rattling around inside a glass. She waited fifteen minutes to see if Larry Aberlour would call somebody, but he didn't speak another word. She next switched to the various channels that covered the entire house where Veronica lived. The only noise came from her landlords' living room.

"Hobbits could beat the piss out of Gremlins. I mean, if they had to," Le Ned said.

"Think of the sheer numbers," Kutra shot back. "When those little dudes get wet they multiply. I'd root for the hobbits to prevail, but it wouldn't happen. Our boys are scrappy, but c'mon."

She had heard enough *Lord of the Rings* musings to make her cringe anytime Middle Earth was mentioned, but her clients paid her to listen. So she continued scanning the conversations of all the help she had hired. Usually it was silence, or else routine sounds or banal utterances. Until tonight.

The Tall Woman would listen in on Harry Hipple once he returned home, but it would take him more than an hour to get back to the city on public transit. So she pushed the button for Camden Swanson and heard only the hum of the refrigerator. Since listening in on Camden, so far she'd only learned that Camden's girlfriend was cheating on him. Georgia had entered their place the other night with a gentleman who had a slight French accent and called her "*mon ange.*" She had at least one orgasm.

When Camden was in his apartment, he never called anybody; he would only open the fridge, plop his behind on the couch, and pop the top off beer bottles. The other sounds were from movies or the various gasses his body expelled. But tonight Camden still wasn't home.

She had met Veronica at Lefty O'Doul's earlier in the evening. Amid a six o'clock crowd of people dressed in either Halloween costumes or business attire swilling beer and eating plates of meat and mashed potatoes, she received the locker combination and was assured the backpack was inside. She slid the envelope of cash to Veronica, who immediately shoved it in her bag as if it were radioactive.

"Don't you want to count it?"

"I just want to get out of here and forget this ever happened," she answered.

But that was hours ago, and Veronica had not returned home.

It had been easy to plant the electronic surveillance devices at all the accomplice's homes, but the place off Lake Street had been the definition of facile. A bearded and gangly man opened the door, grinning the whole time like he had just received a lobotomy, introduced himself as Le Ned, and then passed out on the couch ten seconds after the Tall Woman had entered. She was able to get excellent coverage, but it wasn't helping her tonight.

Where was Veronica? Where was Camden?

The Tall Woman switched over to Harry Hipple's apartment and waited. Eventually she heard the door open and then the sound of a grown man whimpering. Hipple did not speak one word. She was certain her clients would kill him and Larry Aberlour.

* * *

That night a dense fog came in from both the bay and ocean and engulfed the city in a spectral gloom. In addition to the increased calls to deal with Halloween celebrations, the police department responded to an excessive number of car accidents, muggings, and purse snatchings. But there was one crime that evening that would stand out from the rest.

A few minutes past three in the morning, a solitary man armed with a tranquilizer gun entered the Museum of the Twentieth Century on the top floor of the Matisse Hotel. Neither security guards nor surveillance cameras would get a clear view at him. He would leave with Henri Matisse's odalisque sculptures by jumping off the top of the building in a custom-made hang glider.

The hotel had been robbed—a full fifteen hours before the Tall Woman and her clients had planned their event to take place.

ACT TWO

11

Bo Knows Camden

AT 8:00 A.M. on November 1, after a night of drinking, it was too early for Camden to wake voluntarily, but the scent of perfume had jostled his slumber. The Tall Woman sat erect on the end of his bed, her long legs crossed over the side. She wore her usual knee-length pleated skirt and a tight black shirt. Camden blinked several times, thinking he was dreaming. As soon as he sat up, a gun appeared in his face.

"I don't think you're dumb enough to stash them here, but I'm going to search your bedroom now," she said.

The Tall Woman slid off the bed and began looking underneath it, in the closet, and inside the armoire. Camden, not convinced he wasn't dreaming, closed his eyes again. When he opened them, she was going through his dirty laundry.

"What makes you think you'll get away with it?" she asked.

"With what?"

"Mr. Swanson, my clients are willing to be civil. They are professionals."

"I have no idea what you're talking about."

"You can save your life."

"Did I oversleep? Did I miss the robbery?"

"I think you've played dumb long enough. It's one of the most brilliant acts I've seen," she said. "A flawless con job with the perfect cover. That said, I can't believe I fell for it."

"I'm sure you know what you're talking about, but I don't know what the shit you're talking about."

"Stop it right now. The best thing you can do is tell me where you've got the sculptures. And if you already had a buyer set up and moved them, I would advise you to buy them back as soon as possible."

"I'm a little hungover and I need about two more hours of sleep," Camden said. "My brain isn't connecting what you're jabbering about. You guys are stealing the Matisse sculptures tonight. I'm going to be your hostage."

"Your team beat us to it."

"My . . . my team? You're saying the sculptures were stolen last night?"

Camden grabbed the remote control and turned on the TV. There, on the bottom of the screen, was the title: "Breaking News: Hotel Heist." A reporter stood in front of the Matisse Hotel and spoke:

"What was once a battleground of labor relations and a fight for workers' rights has turned into an enormous crime scene. The Channel Six News Team was the first to arrive at the Matisse Hotel hours ago, getting firsthand accounts of what police are calling the biggest art heist ever perpetrated on the city of San Francisco. Earlier we spoke to Detective Clinkenbeard, who is leading the investigation."

The TV cut to a tall, ponytailed man wearing a pressed black suit of the discount rack variety. He cleared his throat, and then spoke in a resonant voice.

"At approximately 3:00 a.m. last night, an armed intruder stealthily entered the Museum of the Twentieth Century, located on the top of the Matisse Hotel. The perpetrator removed several objects of art, including the hotel's namesake Matisse statues, and then fled. The thief's mode of egress was a specially made hang glider designed to excel at low heights. Several eyewitnesses reported seeing a man in dark clothes flying through the air clutching sacks. The glider was later recovered in Golden Gate Park. If other perpetrators were involved in the crime, thus far we have no witnesses who saw them flee and have no knowledge of them. Presently nobody connected to the crime has yet to be found."

"Sound familiar?" the Tall Woman said.

Camden yawned, stood up, and scratched his crotch. The Tall Woman lifted her gun at him. He pretended not to notice.

"Sounds like Bo McClennan."

"Yes, your buddy robbed the Cordovan Museum in Boston exactly like that."

"Ain't never been my friend. And he's in jail."

"McClennan was released about six months ago. They reduced his sentence due to good behavior."

"My mouth is filled with cotton balls. Mind if I get a drink?"

Without waiting for her to answer, Camden walked into the kitchen. With the pitcher of ale at Hooters and the dozen or so cocktails he had in a North Beach strip club, his movements were creaky. The Tall Woman followed and watched him pour two glasses of apple juice. She declined the cold beverage, and he gulped both down.

"It's been eight years since the McClennan heist. That's so crazy. You know, I actually played against him in high school. Hockey. He checked me into the boards wicked good once, knocked me out cold."

"Nice to see you're connecting some of the dots," she said.

"C'mon, I didn't know the guy. We're the same age and went to nearby high schools, but I was never his friend. Hell, I haven't even thought of Bo McClennan in years."

"He was released six months ago. You got a job at the museum six months ago. A coincidence?"

Camden laughed and said, "You really believe I had something to do with last night? You think McClennan got me this job at the museum and together we robbed the joint?"

"My clients believe that, yes."

His head was starting to clear, and he finally realized how bad it must have looked to a bunch of pissed-off art thieves. If McClennan did rob the museum, Camden would certainly seem like a potential accomplice to both cops and robbers. To a rational person, it would actually strain credibility for him, linked with McClennan for a long time by circumstances beyond his control, to have no connection to the crime. But Camden had to do his best to convince the Tall Woman of the truth.

"Don't you remember that I'm a lazy drunk who's a complete loser? Masterminding an art heist, don't you think that's a little too ambitious for somebody like me?"

"McClennan was obviously the brains," the Tall Woman said. "You did as you were told. Maybe it was payback. If it wasn't for you, he wouldn't have gotten caught and spent years in prison. You owed him big time, and now you're even."

"I don't owe him shit. He admitted to the robbery," Camden said. "He said he was going to return the sculptures. That he did the whole thing for a bet."

"That bullshit was to reduce his sentence," she said. "You and McClennan must have had a big laugh when my clients decided to hire you for their heist on the same building."

"I haven't seen McClennan since I interviewed him in prison."

"Playing dumb isn't going to work anymore, Mr. Swanson."

"Frozen dinners, remember. Camden, please."

The Tall Woman grabbed him by his shirt and pushed him up against the fridge, dislodging a piece of paper that had been held by a magnet. "I am personally embarrassed for having fallen for your con and hired you on behalf of my clients, Mr. Swanson. It is the low point of my professional career."

"I really am a lazy bastard who works for minimum wage . . . Wait, what's this?"

Camden noticed that the piece of paper that had fallen to the floor had Georgia's handwriting. His back hurt when he bent over to pick it up, and he slumped down to the floor and began reading out loud:

"We've had so many problems since just about day one of our relationship, but it's tough. Even now, I see your potential. But I've come to realize I'm not the woman who can make you a better man. I wanted to have this conversation in person, and I'm sorry we haven't been able to do it. But it's over, and I think it will be easier on the both of us if you can move out in a few days. I will be staying at the cabin until you leave. Maybe someday we can be friends, but right now I just can't. Take care, and I really hope you can turn your life around. Sincerely, Georgia."

"I read the note. My condolences. But that's the least of your concerns. My clients wish to see you."

"I'm sure they want their money back, too," he said and walked into the bedroom. The Tall Woman followed him, and he grabbed the envelope the clients had given him out of his pants pocket.

"I think I spent around a grand," he said and handed the remaining cash to her.

* * *

Veronica's day began with push-ups, jumping jacks, and crunches. Not with the television. After showering and getting ready for work, she took the 1AX California Express bus to Montgomery Street and then walked ten minutes back toward Union Square. When she was a block from the Matisse Hotel, she noticed a distinct absence of noise. No clanging, banging, or chanting of any kind emanated from the surrounding area. But what was even more baffling were the cops, news crews, and police tape.

"Somebody stole the Matisse sculptures," a female bystander said. "Hella crazy shit."

Veronica immediately thought of the Tall Woman and the bag she put back into Locker 333. The notion came on hard in a sweep of guilt, panic, and nausea. She knew there had to be some connection to the robbery, and she could have been an unknowing accomplice. She began sweating and her heart raced. Would the unknowing part matter in the eyes of the police? She wanted to run, to leave San Francisco and never return to the hotel, but of course that would make her look extremely suspicious. No, she had to go into work as normal.

Veronica tried every entrance, but even her work ID, which was stamped "Temporary," could not gain access into the hotel. She learned that no temps were allowed in the building unless they were on the police's list. She wasn't sure if it was good or bad that her name was excluded.

While it was likely that the bag she put back into the locker was used in the robbery, it suddenly hit her that she had lucked into what could be the big break of her career. Veronica not only worked at the hotel, she potentially could have met one of the thieves. With her journalist genes in gear, she decided to conduct some interviews. None of the police officers would say anything other than "go away" and "stand back behind the yellow tape." But Veronica did chance upon a hotel security guard, a burly man in his fifties with a gray goatee, sitting against the wall of the sex shop. They had spoken once when the guy stopped by HR to change lockers. She crouched down next to him and began asking questions.

"Came up through an old laundry chute," the security guard answered. "The building's like a hundred years old, but it got refurbished. They dry-walled over the opening, but it led to the fucking control room. Should have filled it with, like, concrete."

"They busted through?"

"Bust?" the security guard said. "All that was there was dry wall and wallpaper. He could have used a box cutter or a switch blade. I saw the hole with my own eyes. He tranqued Charlie and Rich and that was the end of that."

"Tranqued?"

"Shot with a tranquilizer gun."

"Where were you?"

"Making my rounds," he said. "From the camera in the control room, the fucker knew exactly where we all were. Every last one of us was tranqued, except for me. Dumb fucking luck. He missed. Shit, I didn't even know I was shot at. I heard something hit the wall and I turned around. I thought I heard footsteps, but I just couldn't stop staring at the wall. Couldn't understand why there was a fucking dart sticking into it."

The man began to sob.

"When I got to the control room and saw the bodies, I thought they were dead."

"Did you get a look at the guy?" Veronica asked.

He shook his head and focused on his feet.

"Are you sure it was only one and not a team?"

"No, but I've heard it was just one guy. That it was the same guy who robbed that museum in Boston a long time ago," the security guard said.

"Wasn't there anybody inside the museum?"

"They only keep one part-timer inside," he said. "It's the snooze shift. Either students or fucking geezers."

"That's who's protecting all that art?"

"We're the protection," the guard said as he rose. "The hotel security. Us and the millions of dollars' worth of cameras and alarms and lasers. We do make our rounds inside the museum every hour, but we also have the entire hotel and our guests to protect and keep safe. There's no hotel security stationed inside the museum. But there shouldn't need to be with all the cameras and technology. I don't know how he disabled them."

The guard wiped the tears from his eyes, steadied himself against the wall, and plodded away toward the hotel. Veronica spotted Bonnie smoking a cigarette next to a door cop on the garage landing. She walked over, and after much cajoling by her manager, the cop allowed her into the building.

"What do you know so far?" Bonnie asked as they walked down into the basement.

Veronica told her, and her boss looked impressed.

"You'd make a good reporter."

"It's actually what I went to school for. But I just happened to see one of the security guards outside."

"The bums. My God, in this day and age, with all the technology. Shit, I get my picture taken for running a red light at three in the morning with no other cars for blocks, but they can't catch people leaving a major metropolitan hotel with priceless sculptures. Did you get a chance to see them?"

"Never got up there."

"Oh, Veronica, you should have. They were so beautiful, so remarkable. The imprints of Matisse's fingers and palms. Physical proof of a brilliant man's struggle for his art."

"You would have made a good critic."

"I majored in art as an undergrad," Bonnie said with a wink.

Back in the human resources office, the reception area teemed with people. Along with Ryan and Carmine, there were three men in suits and several uniformed policemen. All were engaged in conversation with grim expressions. At the sight of the blue uniforms, Veronica could only think the phrase *aiding and abetting.*

"We want to cooperate with you 100 percent," Ryan was saying as sweat poured down his face. "But we can't just let you rummage through all these confidential files without—"

"A warrant," one of the plainclothes detectives finished. "Trust me. It will arrive shortly."

The man speaking identified himself as John R. Clinkenbeard, a special detective with the San Francisco Police Force. There was one element to his appearance that didn't fit with his ensemble: his long ponytail. Although combed in a professional manner and tied back with a brown band, it made Clinkenbeard appear like a hippie forced to dress up for a wedding. But any bohemian expectations eroded when he spoke in his thunderous voice.

"Do you think Detective Slauson and I would attempt to take advantage of you?"

"Detective Clinkenbeard," Ryan answered, "I don't think you would do that. But one of the functions of an HR office is the storage and protection of private information."

"Understood. But as I said, the proper written documentation will arrive shortly. And Slauson and I have already interviewed everybody who works in your office." Clinkenbeard faced Veronica and said, "Unless this is the temp we've heard so much about."

12

Suspects à Gogo

GEORGIA HADN'T BOTHERED to call Miles after seeing the early news reports. When she learned of the Matisse robbery, she could only think of one person who had the balls, the motive, and the means to steal those sculptures. Georgia had a key to Miles's Victorian home on Nob Hill and she used it without knocking.

Upon entering, she expected to see Miles defecating on the sculptures while video cameras rolled. Or maybe he would be exploding them with firecrackers. Georgia was certain her former lover had committed the crime for his so-called artistic expression, as well as giving a big "fuck you" to the community who failed to recognize it. She figured Miles had paid piles of money for somebody to rob the Museum of the Twentieth Century.

The house was quiet, and Georgia moved over the marble floors through the foyer and then inspected the living room. Years before, when they were dating, original works from artists ranging from Renaissance to Pop Art hung on the walls. Now they were bare and painted solid black. The matching leather furniture were the only items in the room, and the sculptures were not behind or underneath the couches and chairs.

Next were all the closets on the first floor, which were empty save for stacks of vintage pornographic magazines. She paused at the wrought iron spiral staircase that led to the second floor and detected violins and cellos of a Bach symphony. She then took the stairs two at a time and threw open the door to the bedroom.

Miles sat in bed naked, holding an Uzi, while the London Symphony played a Bach concerto at full volume from his speakers. Georgia hit the floor as a round of bullets sprayed into the ceiling. Miles belonged to a gun club and fortunately was known for being the worst shot over the age of twelve.

"Holy fuck. Is that you, Georgia?"

She got off the floor, then walked over to Miles and slapped him in the face. He fumbled for a remote control and turned down the volume of the stereo.

"Fuck, sorry," he said. "Thought it was some right-wing group coming to get me again."

"You stole the sculptures," Georgia yelled at him. "I know you did."

"What sculptures?"

"The Matisse sculptures."

Miles giggled, grabbed a bong from his nightstand, and took a hit. He then flung his hands up and down as if he was conducting a symphony and repeated the bong ritual. He made no effort to cover his naked body with the blanket.

"Put some goddamned clothes on. How much did it cost you to rob a museum?"

Miles got out of bed and the Uzi fell to the three-inch-thick shag carpet with a thump. He then put on pajama bottoms that were covered with pictures of farm animals and began stretching.

"I can't fucking deal," Georgia said. "I just broke up with Camden, my show is coming up, and I'm sure my dad is going to want to have you killed."

When he began to practice Tai Chi, Georgia pushed him onto the bed.

"Is Camden involved somehow? Holy shit. I didn't even think of that until now."

Miles did not show any irritation at being shoved, and he swiveled his body to the side of the four-poster bed and took another hit from his bong.

"Don't you have anything to say?" she screamed. "I'll call the cops. I swear I will."

"Sweetie cakes, I don't know what you're mumbling about. I was doing acid all night with some chick, an art major at Stanford, from of all places Beaver Dam, Wisconsin. Lovely lady. What are you talking about? Sculptures and stealing and your dad killing me?"

Georgia grabbed the remote off the bed and turned on the fifty-inch plasma TV hanging on the wall. The local stations continued to report from the scene of the art heist. Miles watched the screen with glazed eyes and smiled placidly. He showed no shock or surprise over the robbery, but of course his head was swimming in marijuana, acid, and whatever brain-killing substances he had ingested.

Miles said, "I'm flattered you think I robbed the museum. But you're pissing up the wrong rope. Shit, I wish I had ripped off those sculptures. But the girl I was with last night was beaucoup demanding. College kids these days are ambitious. Probably a good thing she's gone. I'm exhausted."

Miles got back into bed and pulled up the silk covers to his chin.

"You swear you had nothing to do with the robbery?" Georgia asked.

"I swear I'm gonna find out who did and open my check-book to them. I could create a lot of art with those Matisse pieces of shit."

"I don't believe you," she said.

"Maybe you're close to cracking the case, Nancy Drew. And maybe it's someone in your own backyard. What about your dear old dad? Wasn't he brought in as a consultant before they opened the Museum of the Twentieth Century?"

"My dad isn't a thief."

"While never charged with a crime, the cops had a big hard-on for your dad but couldn't prove shit."

"Fuck you, Miles."

"You can dish the defamation of character out, but you can't take it? And, hey, didn't your dad pull some strings to get whiskey-dick Camden his job? Now who's looking guilty?"

"Defamation of character? You just said you want to buy the sculptures off whoever stole them."

"Whomever."

"Whoever is correct, you idiot. And if I find out you're responsible, either with Camden or my fucking dad, I'll kill you myself."

* * *

Veronica sat in front of Detective Clinkenbeard with her hands folded in her lap. She tried not to fidget, not to show the immense fear welling in the pit of her stomach. But her voice warbled when she spoke.

"Almost a month," she said. "I've been employed at the Matisse for almost a month."

"What did you do before that?" Clinkenbeard asked.

"Waitress."

"And before that?"

"Student. Berkeley."

"My alma mater. What did you study?"

"Journalism," Veronica said.

"Why aren't you working at a newspaper or magazine or on TV?" Clinkenbeard asked.

"They're laying off people from those jobs instead of hiring them."

"So your temp job is just a way to pay the bills," Clinkenbeard said. "You never had any ideas to write an article, freelance, about the strike?"

"It crossed my mind."

"So you're writing an article."

"No . . . I mean, yes. Well . . . I've been thinking of it."

"But now the strike is old news," Clinkenbeard said. "You have a story far more interesting to write about."

"I just heard about the robbery. I don't know anything," Veronica said a little too loudly. "I wouldn't know what to write about."

"You worked a lot with the strikebreakers," Clinkenbeard said.

"Temporary workers. They were temps, sir."

"My apologies. Temps. Your colleagues in the office said you helped hire them, give them lockers, maintain their files."

"Yes," Veronica said.

"Kind of ironic. A temp being in charge of the temps."

"I wasn't in charge," Veronica said. "And I was hired before the strike. The job that I do is nonunion. So I wasn't taking anybody else's job."

"Which piles on even more irony," Clinkenbeard said. "The strikers, by following their union and refusing to work, created a job that was nonunion. But I digress. The reason I ask you about the strikebreakers, the temps, or whatever they may be called, is that maybe one of them, or several, robbed the museum. Maybe one of the regular employees was involved also. Maybe no employee. But I have a hunch, Miss Zarcarsky, that one of the criminals used the unfortunate situation of the strike to their advantage. Everybody was concerned with the labor situation. Everybody was watching the workers who were on strike. I believe it was the ultimate diversion. What do you think?"

"Possibly. Makes sense."

"You seem a little nervous, Miss Zarcarsky. Now if you do have aspirations of being a journalist, you will have to deal with the other side of the law. The people who catch the scum of society that so fascinates your readers. I know several members of the San Francisco media and they all seem comfortable speaking to me. You do not."

"I apologize," Veronica said. "It's that this is all . . . unexpected. I was coming into work today and—"

"No apology necessary. I was only trying to help. Unfortunately many of the younger generation are distrustful and even contemptible about the police force. I can understand that because I was a member of SDS, and I marched at Berkeley and protested injustice. But honestly, Veronica, the cops are the good guys. We want to help. So if you could take a minute and think if any of the temps you hired seemed unusual."

Veronica was now confused. She had begun to think Clinkenbeard knew she was involved in some way. But now the guy wanted to sell her on the idea of law enforcement itself, thinking she was some sort of Berkeley radical.

"Off the top of my head, I can't remember anybody asking me about the museum or the sculptures," Veronica said. "I mean, we didn't hire anybody to work security or any of the gallery attendants. The security force is all another union, and they're not on strike. The gallery attendants are all nonunion. We haven't hired one of them since I've worked here."

Clinkenbeard said, "And any one of those individuals could be involved. But they are not my concern now. You dealt with the temps, the itinerant workforce that does not have ties to the hotel. Now if I wanted to rob the museum, and something like a strike occurred, I would have seen it as a golden opportunity to put a man or woman on the inside. Wouldn't you, Miss Zarcarsky?"

"I don't know anything about robbing museums," Veronica said. "And we also conducted background checks on everybody who was hired."

"But your peers said those background checks were spotty. You were sending so many to the third-party company that conducts them for you, they couldn't keep up. A temp could work for days, maybe even weeks, before their background check came in."

"You can't hardly blame the hotel for that. We needed to fill positions. We needed the hotel to keep on running."

"We aren't pointing the finger at any sort of ineptitude on the part of the Matisse Hotel," Clinkenbeard said. "The San Francisco Police Department only wants to catch the culprits of this crime. We also want to be able to return the Matisse sculptures to the museum for the benefit of society. I'm a lover of the arts, and I have no tolerance for such an outrageous act."

"I wish I could be of more help."

"We're working cold here. We got to shake a lot of branches before anything useful falls out. Time is my enemy, Veronica."

Detective Clinkenbeard's partner walked into the room with a file. The detective took the manila folder, inspected it, nodded a few times, and then glanced at it again. He handed it back to his partner and gazed at Veronica.

"Do you know anybody named Juan Wyman?" Clinkenbeard asked.

"No, sir."

"How about the names Bo McClennan or Camden Swanson?"

"I met a guy named Camden the other day in the hallway, bumped into him by accident. Gallery attendant in the museum. Only time I've ever seen or talked to him. Did the other guy work here as a temp?"

"We're asking the questions here, young lady. But thank you for giving me a few minutes of your time," Clinkenbeard said and handed Veronica a business card. "If you can think of anything that might help."

And at that moment the detective's cell phone rang, playing the first few bars of "Sugar Magnolia." He answered and got news of a murder down by Fisherman's Wharf. The evidence pointed toward the victim having a connection to the Matisse robbery.

* * *

The ride to see the Tall Woman's clients would have been completely silent if not for Camden whistling without skill in the back seat. The Tall Woman refused to put on the radio, so he decided to provide the entertainment. If he had been more adept, she would have recognized the song as "I've Got the World on a String."

She ignored Camden until he began snapping.

"Mr. Frozen Dinners, you could be dead soon."

"I haven't done anything that warrants getting killed. And I whistle when I'm nervous."

"If my clients want to kill you, I do not have a say."

"Sure, you do," Camden said. "I bet you're involved in every decision with your gang. If you wanted, we could take the nine grand I have left and put it all on black."

"The ten grand was given to you in good faith for your services. It is no longer yours. You abused that good faith by robbing the museum on your own."

"Do you really believe that?"

"My clients believe it," the Tall Woman said. "I'm about 85 percent certain."

"Maybe it's a *Fight Club* thing. And I have insomnia and do shit in the night I don't remember. I could be the head of a worldwide criminal organization."

She didn't speak again and the black sedan cruised at the speed limit down the James Lick Freeway, eventually exiting just before the home of the San Francisco 49ers. Soon they were on the cracked asphalt on Paul Avenue, where apartment complexes mingled with industrial buildings.

"Shit. Put this blindfold on," she said and tossed one in the back seat.

Camden stopped whistling and did as he was told.

"It's probably more like fifty-fifty I think you're involved," the Tall Woman said. "I had your apartment bugged, and I didn't hear anything that caught my attention. But that doesn't mean you didn't conduct your business elsewhere. And what about Georgia?"

"You read the note."

"You could have written it, for all I know."

"No, that was Georgia, all right. She's wanted to break up with me for a while now."

"Well, she's cheating on you. Only thing of interest I've heard in your apartment."

Camden didn't say anything. His stomach was swirling with imaginary Liquid-Plumr, his face drained of all color.

While he had suspicions, getting confirmation his girlfriend was unfaithful out loud hurt more than he expected. For all their problems, Camden believed they made a good couple.

"Sorry to be the one who had to break it to you," the Tall Woman said. "But it could be relevant. Was she using you?"

"Using me?" Camden asked. "You think Georgia, Bo McClennan, and I robbed the Matisse sculptures?"

"It is an odd threesome. No, I'm not sure Georgia was involved. But she did get you the job, along with her father. And she is an artist. It all somehow fits into the puzzle."

"Georgia is a respected artist, does well for herself. And her dad is filthy rich . . . she doesn't need money."

"Mr. Léveque, suspect extraordinaire in several art crimes, but never charged. It all seems too inbred, too many connecting dots."

Camden began to add some of these facts in his head. "This is exactly the sort of story that would have got me running in my investigative journalism days. When you piece it together like you're doing, I can possibly see how you think I'm involved. But why does Bo McClennan spend years in lockup just to get out and plan another heist? The guy was a gambler, sure, but when I interviewed him in prison he was genuinely remorseful. Sure, much like me, he's never going to be hired to do what he loves. I can't see any college or university on the planet bringing him on staff, but I think he's too smart to risk being sent back to jail. He even said to me, and I included it in my article: "You don't think about how wonderful freedom is until you're behind bars and getting strip-searched.""

Camden wanted to go back to drinking beers on his porch and watching squirrels, but there was a real possibility these were the last moments of his life. However, had he said no that afternoon to the offer to be their hostage, would the Tall Woman still have shown up on his doorstep because of his previous connection to Bo McClennan? Obviously she couldn't find the man, or they wouldn't need him. He had no clue as to McClennan's whereabouts, either, but he began trying to think up a lie if it could potentially save his life. His connection to the guy who robbed the Cordovan Museum could be his only value to them.

With the blindfold on, Camden had no idea where she was taking him, but he had not fastened it tightly. He pretended as if he was wiping his nose and used his knuckles to nudge the bandana slightly up. Through a crack, he studied the area as best he could. There were a lot of new condos mixed in with office space and the occasional taqueria, bar, and gas station. He caught a glimpse of the Third Street Metro.

"We're almost there, Mr. Swanson. I can't guarantee that you will walk out after the meeting. Do you have anything to admit before I bring you in to see my clients?"

"I admit that even though it doesn't seem like it, I'm really scared shitless right now."

13

The Game of Clues

ALREADY AT THE Matisse Hotel for eleven hours, Detective Clinkenbeard needed to eat lunch. Just how much sleuthing can a person do on an empty stomach? Mrs. Ellen Clinkenbeard had made him a grilled eggplant sandwich on homemade focaccia bread, complete with tomato aioli dressing. She had packed it in their tiny Grateful Dead cooler, a regular Coleman with the skull sticker, along with a vegan cookie and a bottle of pomegranate juice.

The ice in the cooler had melted but Clinkenbeard was pleased the lettuce hadn't wilted. And his wife's homemade focaccia would taste delicious even if it had rocks inside. But after questioning Veronica, he only got to eat three bites of the sandwich in his car on his way to a new crime scene.

Clinkenbeard learned at seven thirty in the morning, with less than ten feet of visibility due to the fog, that a homeless guy boarded a cable car at the Powell Street turnaround pushing a wheelchair. The disabled person in the chair was wearing matching sweatpants and sweatshirt with "SF" printed on them and sunglasses. The conductor and the brakeman, who had a combined forty years of service, did find this odd for a few reasons. One, with the thick fog there was no need for sunglasses. And two, the homeless guy had paid the man's fare. But when the vagrant hopped off, taking his stench with him but leaving the man in the wheelchair behind, the Muni employees just shrugged. They had a job to do.

The trouble began at the end of the line at the next turnaround near Fisherman's Wharf. The brakeman wondered why the guy in the wheelchair didn't answer when asked if somebody was meeting him. Thinking the person might also be mute, the brakeman helped the disabled gentleman onto the street. But the guy wouldn't push himself or even move. That's when the conductor wheeled him to the sidewalk and got a cop's attention.

"It was like that movie," the Muni employee would later say. "*Weekend at Bernie's*. How could I know he was dead?"

"You couldn't, sir," Clinkenbeard said.

"*Weekend at Bernie's*," he repeated with reverence. "But exactly. Hey, what do you think ever happened to that Andrew McCarthy? I really liked that dude."

Clinkenbeard had more pressing things to deduce. Why had the killer or killers expended so much effort and flair in their murder? The victim had been killed by one gunshot to the heart and wrapped tightly in plastic to keep from bleeding onto his clothes. The dead man had then been dressed in cheap clothes and sunglasses that could have been purchased at Walgreens or possibly in Chinatown. And why, after murdering him and making him appear alive, would they put his body in a wheelchair at one of the most conspicuous places in San Francisco?

But the most interesting fact of the case concerned the identity of the victim. The homicide detectives called Clinkenbeard because of what they found in the man's wallet, front shirt pocket, and pants pockets. Business cards identified him as the director of security at the Matisse Hotel.

"What can you tell me about the gentleman who wheeled the victim onto the cable car?" Clinkenbeard asked the brakeman.

"Pardon my French, but he was a fucking bum."

"How do you know for sure? Maybe it was a disguise."

"Not the way this dude smelled," the brakeman said. "Trust me, detective. I deal with bums all day. I have respect for all people, and I don't blame them for being the way they are. But when they try to catch a free ride or harass the tourists, I can't stand for that. Dude's clothes had stains on them, and his breath reeked of booze. And I've seen him at the turnaround before."

The police would soon track down Ken Synicker, the homeless man in question. He was sleeping and snoring on the corner of O'Farrell and Jones with five empty bottles of MD 20/20 next to him. Mr. Synicker said "some jerkface in a suit" gave him fifty dollars to wheel "some crippled fuck" onto a cable car. When pressed, the homeless man couldn't recall any details about who paid him the money. Not his height or age or even ethnicity.

"All's I remember is the fiddy. For some Mad Dog and a steak at Tad's."

The sketch artist worked with Mr. Synicker, but with repeated answers of "I don't know, man" there wasn't much to draw. The police kept coaxing, and finally Synicker began giving answers while he giggled. When the sketch was finished the person had a resemblance to George W. Bush. Synicker laughed so hard when he saw the picture he urinated in his pants.

Clinkenbeard drove his Toyota Prius back to the Matisse Hotel. While he always felt uneasy after leaving a murder scene, he was also pleased he had a lead. The director of security was somehow involved in the robbery of the sculptures. The why, how, and who else had participated remained mysteries.

* * *

Not wanting to risk the repercussions if anyone noticed his eyes weren't completely covered, Camden nudged his blindfold back as the car pulled into a driveway overgrown with weeds. The car now parked, he didn't move when he heard the Tall Woman exit the vehicle. His door opened and he was led by the arm inside a building that was cool and smelled of paint. After about ten steps they stopped, and he heard what he guessed to be a hydraulic cargo elevator. She nudged him forward and the elevator went down for what seemed like an excessively long time.

He was shoved out of it when they came to a stop, and as he stepped forward he was struck in the back of his head by a baseball bat and fell to the ground.

Camden felt dizzy but for some odd reason almost euphoric. There wasn't pain in the classic sense, but he knew something was wrong. He felt as if he had ingested five shots of tequila and had fallen down some stairs. He couldn't see anything with the blindfold on, and he curled up instinctively in the fetal position and covered his head with his hands.

"How much do you value your life, Mr. Swanson?" a man with a high-pitched voice yelled a few inches from his face. "You must have earned a nice payday for helping McClennan steal the sculptures."

Camden spat blood onto the floor.

"So I ask that question again," the man continued. "Do you value your life enough to cooperate with us? To do what is the right thing?"

Camden was able to get up on his knees, and he first felt the whoosh of air from the baseball bat in motion, and then the pain from the weapon striking his back. He fell and smacked his right ear on the concrete floor. The strange quasi-euphoria of the first baseball bat strike was gone. Now there was only sharp pain.

"You got the wrong guy," Camden said.

"You're fucking lying to us," a different man yelled at him in a booming, deep voice.

"I was drunk off my ass last night. I went to Hooters and then a strip club. I passed out when I got home."

"Your apartment has been bugged," the first man said. "You did not return there until four in the morning."

In his concussed brain, Camden began to recall some of the details of the previous night. Was it really 4:00 a.m. when he got in? After Hooters, he had a nice buzz and was horny. Who would break a thousand-dollar bill at midnight without questions?

A strip club.

North Beach had many, and he had stumbled into one that looked no different than any other. He couldn't recall the name of the place, but he did remember the mirrors, the creepy bathroom attendant, and the stunning half-Korean, half-Italian woman who enticed him into the VIP room. By the end of his time there, he retained one hundred and sixty dollars of the thousand bucks and an erect penis.

Next he remembered the massage parlor.

Camden's memory of standing outside the wrought iron gate somewhere in Chinatown was murky. A handwritten sign, barely legible over the graffiti, instructed him to ring the doorbell for service. After telling somebody in the building through the intercom he wasn't a cop, he was allowed inside where he paid a hundred dollars for the "extra-special massage." Camden had been disappointed they didn't call it a happy ending.

A thin Asian woman wearing a kimono led him into a dank room with one overhead low-wattage light bulb. The massage was a two-minute perfunctory shoulder rub, and then she asked him to remove his pants. The woman seemed disinterested, the massage table had the same type of sanitary paper that runs down a doctor's table, and Paula Abdul played from the speakers. Camden, despite being plastered, couldn't go through with it.

He said he would prefer to keep his pants on, and of course he didn't dare ask for a refund or discount. The woman felt bad and offered him a beer. Camden took it outside and walked down Grant Street drinking it in the cool night air. For some reason, he staggered all the way to the Caltrain station, even though the last train of the evening had left more than three hours before.

He got a taxi, but he couldn't remember anything about the ride. He did recall the driver waking him up, some money being exchanged, and then stumbling through the door of his apartment. Had he not been told, he wouldn't have believed it was after four in the morning.

"I went to a strip club and a massage parlor," Camden said to his captors. "I owe you a thousand dollars."

"When he gave me the money back, he was missing a thousand dollars."

"Easy cover," the guy with the deep voice said. "Hide a thousand somewhere and say you went to a strip club. Do you have anybody who can confirm your alibis?"

"I don't know the names of the places I went. It was a strip club in North Beach. A massage parlor in Chinatown."

"You could pay any stripper or any masseuse for an alibi," a high-pitched voice said. "There would be no credibility. You have better things to do, Mr. Swanson. Feel grateful we aren't going to splatter your brains out on the floor with a baseball bat. We're going to let you return the sculptures to us."

Camden tried to get to his feet, but he was shoved back down by someone's boot.

"I don't fucking have the sculptures," Camden shouted and then spit more blood out of his mouth. "I don't know who fucking has them. The only time I've ever fucking seen them is behind the fucking glass in the fucking museum. So fuck off, you fucking douchebags."

The bat struck Camden's kneecap. In a complete stupor from the hits to the head and back, the pain was throbbing but wasn't registering at full strength. It would later.

"Mr. Swanson, it shouldn't be so difficult," the Tall Woman said. "You find your friend, Mr. Bo McClennan, and you take back the Matisse sculptures. You bring them to us. How you accomplish these tasks is up to you."

"Or we kill you," the deep voice said calmly. "Maybe we should just kill you now."

Camden heard a gun cock, and in the five seconds or so of silence that followed, his mind went blank from fear. He heard a sound, which didn't seem to come from a pistol, and then felt a sharp pain in his thigh.

"There is no negotiation," the client said. "Today it's a tranquilizer dart. Next time it will be a bullet. You have three days to bring us the sculptures or you're dead."

* * *

After speaking with Detective Clinkenbeard, Veronica went to the Scary Room, sat down on the plastic folding chair, and turned on the laptop. She began inputting data into a spreadsheet, but her mind raced with the heist and how she could turn it into a great article. She grabbed a spiral notebook, logged on to the internet, and Googled the names Juan Wyman, Bo McClennan, and Camden Swanson.

Juan Wyman did not yield anything of interest.

With only a few clicks, Veronica learned that Camden Swanson was a reporter who had been fired for printing a fictional story in the *Los Angles Item*. His actions were credited with bankrupting that newspaper. Veronica recognized the face in the photos as the gallery attendant she had bumped into in the hallway the day before and accidentally scratched his arm. She scribbled, *Need to talk to Swanson*, in the notebook. She also made note to ask a manager at the museum for Camden's work schedule.

The Bo McClennan search yielded pages of information as well. The first item she clicked on was the story of the Cordovan Museum robbery in Boston eight years ago. Veronica read the article, which was written by then Boston reporter Camden Swanson. She then underlined her previous note about Swanson and added a few exclamation points.

The picture of Bo McClennan in the story was of a handsome man with dark red hair in his late twenties who wore a corduroy jacket and black T-shirt and sported a reddish-brown beard. He had grown up in the projects to parents who barely made an appearance in his life, but he'd excelled at school. He received a full academic scholarship to Harvard where he earned a 3.5 grade point average while being a four-year starting defenseman for the hockey team. How and why had he become a thief? In the next article, also written by Camden Swanson, more details emerged.

In addition to being an art professor, McClennan had become a high-stakes poker player. He was a frequent visitor to Foxwoods, Atlantic City, and Las Vegas during summer breaks, but he mainly sat in cash games among the reckless wealthy. McClennan was an exceptional player and won a high percentage more than he lost. The problem wasn't poker.

Bo McClennan had a passion for engaging in the most outrageous proposition bets. Somebody would say, "I bet you ten thousand dollars you can't eat more hard-boiled eggs than Paul Newman did in *Cool Hand Luke.*" He took such a wager and lost, vomiting after forty-one eggs. Another such stunt, or prop bet, as they were called, had him successfully swimming from Boston to Cambridge in the Charles River. Through the years there were many such prop bets, and McClennan was around even, money-wise.

That was until somebody wagered that he couldn't rob the Cordovan Museum of seven paintings without getting caught by the police.

McClennan would get five million if successful. If he failed or backed out after accepting the prop bet, he would owe two hundred and fifty thousand. In the article McClennan said:

"I was getting twenty-to-one odds on my money. Five million dollars! And it wasn't like I was going to keep the paintings. Nobody believes that, but it's true. I was going to store them in the proper conditions and leave instructions for where to find them. I have too much respect for the art treasures of the world."

The Commonwealth of Massachusetts might have gone lighter on the sentence if Mr. McClennan had provided any proof he had made such an outlandish wager. But he wouldn't supply the name of the person who had made the bet with him. He said the deal was that if he got caught, he could never reveal the other bettor's identity. Even after being pressured by confession-savvy cops and wise defense attorneys, he never did.

Veronica studied the picture some more. The face was familiar. Could Bo McClennan, under the alias of Juan Wyman, have worked at the hotel over the last couple of weeks? And why the hell was the reporter who wrote the articles, Camden Swanson, employed at the Matisse as a gallery attendant?

She rushed to the filing cabinet where they kept all the files of the temporary workers. It opened without any effort, as it was empty, the police having confiscated the contents. Every bit of information about the temp workers was contained in those files, except for their eligibility of employment papers. Veronica found the I-9 binder under a pile of picture frames and thumbed through the three-hole-punched pages until she came upon the name Juan Wyman. According to the document, he was thirty-five and a citizen of Mexico. Mr. Wyman had used a Permanent Resident Card to prove eligibility of employment, and Veronica's signature on the document verified it.

She had done hundreds of these and did not remember Mr. Wyman's face. Veronica moved to the term box, which was cardboard and wedged next to a similar one that spilled over with St. Patrick's Day and Fourth of July decorations that contained all the hotel IDs of the temps who were fired or quit. It took her several minutes of rummaging, but she eventually located the ID of Juan Wyman, who had worked in the property maintenance department.

Although the face on the Matisse Hotel ID had a bushy mustache, there was no mistaking that it belonged to Bo McClennan.

14

The McClennan Connection

CAMDEN AWOKE IN a Tenderloin alley, propped against a metal dumpster just off Turk Street. With consciousness came the urine, trash, and defecation odors. He gagged several times and then the chicken wings he had eaten the night before, in a more acidy liquid form, sailed onto the ground.

Using the dumpster to steady himself, he was able to get to his feet. The slime on the metal almost made him vomit a second time. His thigh, knee, back, and head all throbbed, but he managed to stumble out of the alley. He took a few deep breaths and tried to unscramble his brain. He began feeling a foreign emotion, white-hot anger. Camden hadn't seen any of the people who had beat him with the baseball bat, but he was thinking forward to a day when he could return the favor.

Before revenge would be possible, he had to find the sculptures. He was told he had three days to give them to the clients and the Tall Woman, or else he would be killed. Where to start? Bo McClennan likely pulled the job, but he could be halfway to Mexico or Canada by now. Camden was only a couple blocks from where he worked and the scene of the crime, and with no other viable option, he decided to start his investigation at the Matisse Hotel.

If McClennan had robbed the museum, it would make sense that he was employed as one of the temps filling in during the strike. Camden had overheard they had hired close to three hundred employees, and the guy could have used a phony ID to pass the background check. McClennan had definitely not worked for the museum security team, or else Camden would have known. And even if he didn't rob the place, there was a high likelihood it was in some manner an inside job. The best place to start looking for the sculptures was the place where they were stolen.

At Camden's usual entrance to the Matisse, the loading dock near the sex shop, a police officer stood with a hotel security manager he recognized. He was sure the cops weren't letting anybody into the Matisse, so he began devising a ruse. He then went to a fire exit on the other side of the building, which was open but manned by a lanky, twentysomething hotel security officer he had never seen before.

"Excuse me, sir," Camden said. "I'm a hotel guest. I have to get inside for my brain medicine."

"You're not a hotel guest," the guard shot back with excitement. "I remember Larry Aberlour yelling at you the other day. You're Swanson, and the police are looking for you!"

If the Tall Woman and her clients considered him a suspect in the robbery, it made sense the cops would as well. He thought of running, of sprinting to the BART stop, taking it somewhere in the East Bay, and then boarding a bus to a faraway state. Or maybe the police hadn't alerted the airports, and he could buy a one-way ticket to Honolulu.

The security officer coughed and expelled a hunk of phlegm. "They showed us your picture before our shift started and said you were a Bolo."

"Bolo?"

"Be on the lookout. Get your ass in there and report to human resources. This fire exit leads right to the basement. I'm gonna radio them to let them know you're here."

Camden descended the metal stairs, every step shooting pain into his leg. He wasn't yet sure if he would speak to the cops, so he continued down the hallway to the locker room where he hoped to find somebody who could give him information about the robbery. Any hint of a clue to possibly put him on the right path would do. But the place was empty.

Camden cleaned the dumpster slime off his hands and then rinsed out the bile from his mouth with warm water. After going to his locker and taking the two remaining aspirin from the bottle he kept there for hangovers, he heard a toilet flush. A few seconds later, Timmy, the gallery attendant who had argued with Hipple about unions, emerged from the stall.

"Wow, I'm surprised you showed up," Timmy said.

"What do you mean?"

"They all want to see you. The hotel, the cops, everybody."

"Larry Aberlour?"

"No, man," Timmy said. "Shit, didn't you hear?"

"About the robbery?"

"No, our boss, Larry. He's dead. Murdered. The cops think he had something to do with it," Timmy said. "Like a double-cross deal. They think you're involved, too."

"What have you heard?"

"Now, I'm just going on rumors, but supposedly there was a big art thief who worked here as a temp. Some guy named McClosky."

"McClennan," Camden said.

"Yeah, McClennan. And he's a friend of yours."

"Fuck. Was he really working here? Who told you?"

"The cops, man. He was working under the name Juan Wyman. That's funny, huh. Sounds like a porno name."

So the son of a bitch was responsible. After spending years in prison, he couldn't even wait six months before he went and robbed another museum. He must have been lying about stealing the paintings from the Cordovan on a bet and had to be a compulsive thief. But why this place, and why the Matisse sculptures?

"Timmy, I didn't know McClennan was working here, and he's not my friend."

"Go tell that to the cops," Timmy said. "They're in HR, I think. That's where I just was. Like I said, I'm surprised you showed up. They called all the gallery attendants and told them to come in for a mandatory meeting, but we figured you were in Paraguay or some random country by now."

Camden reached into the pocket of his grease-splotched jeans and pulled out his cell phone. He hadn't had a chance to look at it. The hotel number appeared on his missed calls log, along with Georgia's.

"Has everyone else shown up?" Camden asked.

"Everyone except Hipple and you. And of course, our boss, Mr. Aberlour, who's dead."

Could McClennan, under the alias Juan Wyman, have hired Hipple and Larry Aberlour to help him? And Larry had been killed. Camden didn't think McClennan was capable of murder, but he couldn't count anything out at this point.

"What did the cops ask you?"

"They were pretty cool. Asked if I knew anything about the robbery. Asked if I knew the names Bo McClennan or Juan Wyman. Asked what I knew about you and Hipple. They also wanted to know where I was last night. I mean, why would I be here if I had anything to do with it?"

"Precisely because of that," he said. "By not showing up you're arousing suspicion. You're throwing a spotlight on yourself."

"I guess that makes sense. Is that why you're here, Camden?"

"Do you think I robbed the museum?"

"I don't know, man. But it would be pretty cool if you did. Are you going to talk with the cops?"

The security officer who stopped him outside the hotel had radioed to the control room that he was coming inside the building, so the SFPD was expecting him. Every exit was likely being watched, so if he decided to flee, he would need to be creative. What to do? He felt that he was screwed if he talked to the cops or if he attempted escape. Camden really needed a drink.

"That's a damn good question, Timmy."

* * *

Harry Hipple woke to a dog urinating on his leg in Mountain Lake Park. A couple of hours earlier, he had made his way to the fringe of the Presidio and passed out behind thick shrubbery after hyperventilating. He could now hear the rush of cars heading up US 1 on their way to the Golden Gate Bridge.

The dog urine was not the worst thing that had happened to him that day.

Sometime before dawn, while Hipple slept in his twin bed, somebody slapped a piece of duct tape over his mouth. Opening his eyes in terror, he only got a few seconds to see the masked man before a bag was thrown over his head. Hipple was then rolled up in his mother's Persian rug, carried down his stairs, and tossed into the trunk of a car. It was hard to breathe, and even though the rug could only roll a few feet in either direction, the movement had made him nauseous.

When he was unspooled from the carpet and the bag was taken off his head, Hipple found himself in a corrugated metal warehouse full of boxes. His arms and feet had been tied with nylon rope, and he had been tossed on a plastic blue tarp against a concrete wall. Larry Aberlour, bound in the same manner, sat next to him on a separate tarp. He was sure his look of fear matched that of his boss.

A man dressed in black, with bulging muscles wearing a ski mask, walked into the prisoners' eyeline. He extracted a gun and lazily moved it back and forth between Harry and Larry. The duct tape muffled their screams.

"Which one of you is stupider?" the man with the gun asked. "Killing usually fucks things up. But we don't have the sculptures, and you've put all of us in jeopardy of getting arrested. We heard what you said to those hookers. We bugged your apartments specifically to determine if you could be trusted to keep your fucking mouths shut. And you could not."

The man in black began moving the gun back and forth in a steady aim. He chose his victim with a shrug, shooting Larry Aberlour once through the heart.

"I think you're stupider, Hipple, and I want you to have a few more minutes of your pathetic life so you can ponder just how much of a moron you are."

Two more men dressed in black, both slender with average height and sporting goatees, appeared and began to wrap Larry in plastic to stop the bleeding. They then used duct tape over the plastic, working efficiently, as if they had done it many times before. Hipple would have thought the whole scene of dressing his dead boss in matching sweat pants and shirt odd, but he was too busy defecating in his pants.

"What's that smell?" one of the slender men asked.

"It's gotta be the dead guy," the other answered.

"I don't think so."

The three clients turned to Hipple.

"We can't go to work on him if he smells like that."

"We gotta change him, then."

"Come fucking on. Let him clean himself up. He ain't going anywhere."

The one who did the shooting said, "I can't wait to do this to Swanson."

The muscle man approached Hipple with a ten-inch hunting knife. He raised it in the air, and then cut the rope binding his ankles and hands. He thrust Hipple up to his feet by grabbing his shirt and pushed him down a hallway. The man pointed the gun at Hipple's head.

"Go in there and clean yourself up. You have two and a half minutes."

Hipple shook violently and lurched into the bathroom. He removed his soiled underwear, tossing it into a garbage can, and used toilet paper to clean his behind and also to wipe the brown streaks from his legs. Then he threw up.

After wiping vomit from his mouth, Hipple looked up to pray. That's when he saw the grated heating vent. Being small and agile, he used the adrenaline coursing through his body to jump on the toilet and begin his first move toward safety. Angling his body through the opening would be easier than his routine activity of putting on pants without removing his shoes.

By the time the killer entered the bathroom and emptied his clip into the heating duct, Harry Hipple was almost out of the building. He could see light and smell the fresh air. But there was a metal grate blocking his escape. He pushed against it, but it didn't move. With the second frantic thrust of his hands, the obstruction inched forward. Gunshots thudded over Hipple's head. One last grunting shove broke the metal and it clanged onto the asphalt outside.

He shimmied out of the hole, crashed to the ground directly on his tailbone, and staggered down an alley to Third Street. He spotted the gray T line train with the red trim and ran hard to catch it. By the time he got to the stop, the train had already pulled away. A sweaty and exhausted Hipple then gestured his hands wildly at a cab making a corner. It stopped, and after receiving forty-six dollars up front, the entire contents of Hipple's wallet, the driver agreed to take the smelly, panting fare to Mountain Lake Park.

Harry ran up the sloping hill toward the small lake and collapsed behind the bushes next to the green metal storage bins that seemed like boxcars. He had been breathing so heavily he passed out from hyperventilation, an affliction he had suffered throughout his life. When Hipple awoke on the bluff overlooking the lake, he heard two women speaking Russian and saw the stream of yellow coming from a pug penis.

Mountain Lake had been the place where a young Hipple would go when he ran away from his Clement Street home. The park had always been a refuge, his safe place, and it was where his fear-addled brain took him that morning. The zooming cars on Presidio Boulevard on their way to Golden Gate Bridge blended together into a constant hum. The pug licked Hipple's face before bounding off toward a pigeon. He thought about his boss, Larry Aberlour, and began to cry.

* * *

Camden made the decision not to flee and now sat across from Detective Clinkenbeard in the HR office. The man's gaze was steady and unblinking, and his eyes, despite the ponytail and aging hippie vibe, were saying, *Don't fuck with me, boy*. He had come across many a police detective in his reporter days who tried to give off that sense, but few had reached the expert level of Clinkenbeard.

"You claim you haven't seen Bo McClennan since your reporter days in Boston. When you interviewed him in prison," he said. "What would you say if I told you there is a witness who saw you and McClennan drinking in a bar last month?"

"I would say that your witness is lying," he responded. "Or that you made that up to see how I would react."

"Very good, sir. There is no such witness."

"Because not only haven't I seen McClennan in years," Camden said, "I honestly had forgotten about him. I've had my own problems lately."

"Did you believe him when he said he stole those paintings in Boston on a bet? That he was going to return them?"

"I did back then. The guy was a pure gambler, an adrenaline junkie, somebody who craved physical and mental tests. The art heist combined both with the highest possible stakes."

"Do you feel guilty that you were the person to put him behind bars?"

"Guilty? No. I admire the size of his balls, but taking that sort of bet was stupid. He knew the risk, got off on the risk. He got caught. I think they were too harsh in their sentencing, but *c'est la vie*."

"Do you believe McClennan now, that he did it all on a bet? Actually, no need to answer that question. Do you think he robbed the Museum of the Twentieth Century?"

"The guy has a degree from Harvard and made millions playing poker. He could probably live off his investments and bring in a steady income at the tables. But the first thing he does after being released from years in prison is plan another heist. It doesn't make any sense."

"What if he spent all his money on legal fees?"

"A guy like McClennan doesn't go bust. I'm sure he's got plenty stashed in the Cayman Islands. But, hey, maybe not. What the hell do I know about the guy?"

"I've been studying your relaxed posture, the way you're holding your hands loosely on your legs. Your eyes are alert, but you're not looking down or away from me when you talk. Your answers and demeanor might be saying you're an innocent man, but my instincts aren't too sure. In contrast, I had a young lady in here not too long ago that I thought was ready to confess. But my instincts tell me she was just a nervous, wholesome kid and not a calculating grifter."

"And you think I'm of the latter variety."

"Well, you sure ain't wholesome, and I don't think you've been a kid for quite some time. Camden, when you came in here to speak with me, you had to figure there was a good chance that we would detain you."

Such a fate had crossed his mind, but talking to the detective was the right move. While he couldn't find the sculptures from behind bars, at this point there was no evidence linking him to the crime other than his association with McClennan; the likelihood of walking out of the hotel in handcuffs was slim. Second, if Clinkenbeard did detain him, Camden could be completely truthful and hope for police protection while the criminals were hunted down and caught.

"When I arrived at the hotel, I knew nothing of McClennan being out of prison, knew nothing of him working here under the alias of Juan Wyman, and knew nothing of the robbery except what I saw on TV," he said. "I met a coworker in the restroom who told me the cops wanted to see me. I have nothing to hide. So here I am."

"So here you are."

Camden watched Clinkenbeard scribble in his notebook. The detective then stared at his eyes, held the gaze, and then wrote more on the pad. Camden looked right at his inquisitor and held his placid poker face.

"What do you know about Jean Francois Léveque?" Clinkenbeard asked.

"He's the father of my ex-girlfriend."

"Ex?"

"Broke up with me today. A damn fine written note, I must say," Camden said.

"Sorry to hear that. Have you met Jean Francois?"

"I consider him a friend."

"Your tangential involvement in the art community is interesting," he said. "There's the heist you covered in Boston, you are or were dating a prominent young artist, you're friends with her father, and you now work in a museum that was robbed. It's all incongruous, yet with the right kind of eyes, it could make sense."

"If one were prone to crazy conspiracy theories, detective," he said.

Camden limped over to the water cooler and poured two paper cups. He gave the detective one and then leaned against a filing cabinet. He smiled and took a sip.

"Having fun, Mr. Swanson?"

"In some perverse way, I am. You're already aware I used to be an investigative reporter. I used to spend hours of my day with cops and crooks and all kinds of shit that would make a normal person's hair stand straight up. I was good at it and I loved the work. It's been a long time."

Clinkenbeard stood up, moved within a foot of Camden.

"You're limping and you also got some cuts to your face. Can you tell me what happened?"

"Not sure. Had a few too many last night. If I wasn't so drunk, I could probably provide you with an alibi."

Clinkenbeard kept a foot away from Camden and said, "I think you're involved in the heist. I don't know how, but conspiracy theories aside, there're too many connections for you not to be."

"Detective, I generally don't care about much of anything these days, except watching movies, getting drunk, and writing a few poems every now and then. Why the hell would I get involved in an art heist?"

"Money. And you were on the inside."

"My coworker told me about Larry Aberlour getting murdered. So you're thinking the director of museum security recruited some people to help. Harry Hipple also. The only other gallery attendant not to speak with you today."

"His locker was right next to yours," Clinkenbeard said. "There are several people who said you were friends with him."

"Friends? No, I had the unfortunate luck of having to dress next to the guy every day and be subjected to ignorant diatribes. If you do some further police work, there are many people who will attest that I was in no way wild about Harry."

"Doesn't mean you couldn't have worked with him," he said.

"The only work we did together was standing next to pieces of art."

"What about Aberlour? How would you describe your relationship with him?"

"The guy was a complete ass," Camden said. "Never once had an actual conversation with him, unless you count being yelled at. He barked orders and I mostly did my job the way he wanted, mainly so I didn't have to have to spend any time with the douche."

"Did he order you to help him rob the museum?"

"No. As I said earlier, I had absolutely nothing to do with the robbery."

"Okay, Mr. Swanson, I think we both have a pretty good idea where we stand with each other. Game time is over. I'm not going to detain you, even though I have a gut feeling you're somewhat involved. Gut feelings are important in police work. But hard evidence is what pays the bills."

"So you let me go," Camden continued for Clinkenbeard. "You watch me and hope I lead you to some hard evidence."

"And if you run, I'll catch you," the detective said.

15

Smells Like Team Spirit

WHEN VERONICA LEARNED that Camden Swanson was talking with Detective Clinkenbeard, she stayed in the HR office and pretended to straighten up. When Camden left the office, she announced to nobody in particular that she was going on break and followed the gallery attendant up the stairs of the employee exit. With his limp, she had to slow her pace so she wouldn't pass him. She wondered what had happened to the guy, who was clearly injured, as she trailed behind him all the way to the barstools of the Gold Dust Lounge.

She paused at the swinging doors of the bar, took a deep breath, and then entered the dim room. She sat down next to Camden, and the only thing she could think to say was, "Can I buy you a drink?"

Camden appeared perplexed, and she didn't know what to utter next. Should she tell him everything she knew? Should she take a more insidious approach? Finally he spoke.

"You work at the Matisse."

"We bumped into each other a few days ago," she said. "I work in human resources."

"You had to pee . . . what are you doing here?"

"I need to talk with you."

"For fuck's sake. Is this how they're firing people these days? Over cheap margaritas?"

"I'm not here to fire you. That's not what I do. I'm a temp, and I'm not here to talk about your job performance or official HR business. It's, I, ummm—"

"You seem like a very nice person, but I kind of have a lot of shit I'm dealing with here. I need to stay focused."

She watched Camden rub his temples and tried to figure out what she was going to say to him. She couldn't reveal her involvement with the tall lady, and it didn't make much sense why the temporary HR assistant would want to question him on the robbery. But if she told him the truth, that she wanted to write a story, maybe he would feel simpatico to her.

"I can help you," Veronica said. "I know who you are—I read about you online, and I know that you're a suspect in the robbery. I'll get you another margarita."

With a diet soda for her and margarita number two for Camden, they took their drinks to the long red velvet couch on the opposite side of the bar.

"All right," Veronica began. "I probably should be coy, and even a little deceptive. But I don't think that's going to work with you. You're the reporter who broke the Cordovan robbery in Boston. Are you working here because you're undercover for a story?"

"I'm not a reporter anymore."

Veronica was hoping that Camden had followed Bo McClennan here because he had been tipped he was going to rob the museum, and the only reason he had been working as a gallery attendant was for an investigative piece. But that did seem a long shot, especially since he had not stopped the sculptures from being stolen. When the Cordovan was robbed, he had been successful in doing that. But maybe he tried and failed.

"I didn't have time to get all the details, but I did read that you got fired for making up stories in the paper you worked at in LA. But you could be working freelance."

"The only thing I've been working on is my drinking game," Camden said. "But when I met a certain tall woman, all that went to shit."

"Tall woman?" Veronica asked in a shaky voice.

"You've met her?"

"No."

"Bullshit. What did she ask you to do? How much did she pay you?"

Veronica tried to speak but no words would come from her mouth.

"Are you working for her?" Camden asked. "Are you wearing a wire? Is she listening?"

"No, none of that. I want to be a reporter. I'm working at the hotel because nobody will hire me to do that yet. I'd been planning on writing an investigative piece about the strike. With the robbery, I got a much better story. I don't want to abandon the strike, but it can wait. I'm hoping this will be my big break, like the Cordovan was for you."

"So how do you know the Tall Woman?"

"I didn't say I know her," Veronica said.

"Your reaction did."

She sipped her soda and glanced up at the chandeliers and then at the back of the brass sculpture of the miner panning for gold at the entrance.

"If you know who she is," Camden said, "then I do need your help. I'm in a lot of trouble. Hell, if you know her, you could be in a shit ton of trouble, too."

"I need your help for the story," she said.

"Then let's be honest with each other."

Veronica shifted in the velvet seat, took a deep breath. She looked around the bar, but the ten or so patrons inside weren't paying them any attention. She said, "There was a bag inside a locker. I gave her the combination so they could get the bag."

"What was in the bag?" Camden asked.

"I didn't look. But when I put it on my back, it was very heavy."

"And she paid you?"

"I'm broke with tons of loans. But I feel terrible about it. It was so much money, and I didn't know they were going to rob the museum. She kept talking about her clients. How her clients needed the bag."

"Okay, relax. So that's all you did for her? Did you meet the clients?"

"No. That's it. I returned the bag to the locker because it had been confiscated by human resources, and I gave her the new combination. Nothing else. I didn't know anything about the robbery. I wouldn't have done it."

"It's okay," he said. "I believe you."

"What did you do for her?"

Camden didn't answer. He gulped the rest of his cocktail and signaled the waitress for another.

"You can trust me, Camden. We're both reporters. Well, I want to be one, and you used to be. We could work on the story together. My byline first, but we could team up."

"I want to stay out of jail and the morgue. You should be thinking the same."

"I gave out that locker combination without knowing anything about the robbery," Veronica said. "Technically, I didn't do anything illegal. Did you?"

"I never got the chance."

"What does that mean?"

Veronica watched Camden pay the cocktail waitress for his margarita, take a long sip from it, and then put his hand to his chest and wince as if he had heartburn. "Under different circumstances," he said, "I would love to help you. And you're right, it would be a mutha f'er of a story. But right now I have much bigger problems than writing articles."

"I can help you."

"Do you realize how stupid this is?" he said. "There's a police detective and a team of violent art thieves who are gonna want to know why we're talking to each other."

Camden's cell phone vibrated in his pocket and shook his head when he saw the number on the screen.

"You gotta be shitting me," he said to Veronica and answered the phone.

* * *

"You're a tough person to reach," Georgia said.

"I got your letter," Camden replied. "What else is there to say?"

He slipped off the couch and walked outside, noticing that Veronica seemed bewildered at his abrupt departure. The air was cold and the fog that had receded in the morning had started to drift back in from the bay. Scores of people passed him going up and down Powell Street and he stayed close to the building so as not to be trampled. Georgia was silent.

"I didn't want to write a letter and was planning on doing it in person," Georgia said.

"The letter was fine. Honestly. It captured the essence in just the right tone."

"We still need to see each other," Georgia said. "With what happened, I doubt you're at work. Where are you?"

There was no longer a reason to lie, so he said, "The Gold Dust."

"When aren't you at a goddamned bar?" she mumbled and then said in a normal tone, "I'm actually in the city. Have you had lunch yet?"

With all that had happened during the day, food had been absent from Camden's thoughts. But with the mention of lunch, his brain sent signals to his now rumbling stomach that he hadn't consumed anything solid all day.

"I need to eat at some point."

"I'm at a collector's place in Sea Cliff. There's a brewery not too far from where I am. You'd like it."

"Georgia, you know I don't have a car. I wouldn't even know what bus or combination of busses to take to get out there."

"Take a cab. I'll pay for it."

"You have a car. Why don't you drive down here?"

"Camden, let's not end this with petty arguments."

"Fine," he said. "You can break up with me in person down by the ocean. It's more poetic that way."

"It's called the Beach Chalet. I'll meet you out front."

Camden put his phone back into the pocket of his jeans. He watched clanging cable cars rumbling by in each direction on Powell. When both had passed, he saw the Tall Woman behind the plate-glass window at the luxury soap store across the street. He thought about waving to her but instead walked back inside the swinging doors of the bar.

"Our tall friend is across the street," he said to Veronica.

"Really?"

"Do you want to help me?"

"Definitely," Veronica answered. "We can help each other. But I do have to get back to work. It won't do either of us much good if I get fired."

"No, that's perfect. Go back and get Harry Hipple's phone number and home address. I'm sure you have access to his file."

"I can do that."

"I also need your help with another very important thing," Camden said. "It might be harder. I need you to see if that bag is in that locker."

"Why would it be?" she said, lowering her voice so it was just audible. "They must have used it for the, ah, you know what."

"Maybe not. I'll explain later why I really need to know. But it's extremely important we find out whether that bag is still in the locker."

"I still can't believe I did it, that I could have some responsibility with what happened. I've never done anything illegal in my life. I'd be so happy if the bag was still there."

"Either way, what's done is done. I need to find out who stole those sculptures."

"I'll help you if you help me with the story."

Camden ignored her and said, "Give me a call when you're leaving work."

* * *

The Beach Chalet was located at the western edge of Golden Gate Park. A Dutch-style windmill loomed behind it and the Pacific Ocean shimmered across the Great Highway. As the cab pulled into the parking lot, Camden watched Georgia stride toward the vehicle. With a fedora hat over sandy-brown hair that swirled in the breeze, she was wearing a double-breasted black peacoat and blue jeans that fit tightly. He handed the driver a debit card before Georgia could reach the taxi.

"I just sold one of my paintings," she said. "I'm paying for lunch. So don't even try to take out that wallet of yours."

The surf was barely discernible over the buzz of the traffic and the gusts of wind. They both remained silent, and neither made eye contact. Camden watched the breeze billow Georgia's coat. He caught her inspecting his jeans and became self-conscious of the grime and how, since they were too long in the leg, the bottoms were in tatters.

They walked past the columns of the entrance, which supported an overhanging glass-enclosed balcony, and into the visitor's center for Golden Gate Park. Camden looked at the 1930s WPA murals covering the walls, which were beach-scene frescoes with a Cubist flavor. He also noticed the squat glass-enclosed display cases throughout the room, but there would be no time to inspect any of the artifacts as they quickly exited the visitor's center. They went down the stairs into the Park Chalet section of the restaurant and sat at one of the high-top tables next to the bar.

The waitress appeared and took their drink orders—Golden Gate porter for Camden and a pinot noir for Georgia. The glass-enclosed atrium was bright despite it being a cloudy day, and salt air drifted through the one open door. He eyed the bronze statue of a dog next to the fireplace. The creature was looking up, as if scouting for ducks or other game.

"We should have bought a dog," he said. "It might have saved us. A beagle or a maybe a French bulldog."

"What the fuck are you talking about? I don't want a dog."

"I've lived here six months, and I'm pretty sure this is the first time I've ever been west of Van Ness."

"That's not true. We went to Golden Gate Park once. Remember, the Japanese Tea Garden? You kept saying that the Huntington in LA was much better."

"Huntington Gardens is in Pasadena," he said.

"It's actually in San Marino," she corrected with a sigh. "I was hoping we could have a civil conversation."

Just then the waitress dropped off their drinks and took their food orders, a salad for Georgia and a burger for him. He accidentally hit his knee against the high-top table, causing his beer to spill. She closed her eyes for a few seconds and appeared annoyed but did not comment. He raised his pint glass and Georgia, with a frown, clinked her wine goblet to his.

"To the bitter end," he said.

"Feels strange to toast us breaking up."

"Honestly, I don't know how you put up with me for so long."

"Don't do that."

"I'm genuinely sorry that we met at the wrong point of my life."

"We had a lot of fun when we first started seeing each other."

"I was probably beyond saving even before we started dating," he said. "I was already on the way down. So don't blame yourself. Wasn't your fault."

"Please don't bring out the violin, Camden. Anyway, I have to be truly honest now. I have to come clean."

"You cheated on me."

"You knew?" Georgia asked.

Camden didn't answer. He sipped his beer and looked at the dog statue.

"I am really, really sorry. I'm embarrassed."

"Was it one guy or lots?"

Georgia was silent and gazed out toward the park.

"I guess it doesn't really matter."

"I don't want to talk about it," Georgia said. "Please."

He took a sip of his beer and said, "Don't want to, either. But, hell, I can't help myself. I don't even blame you for cheating on me. I never did any of the things you asked me to do when we moved to San Francisco."

"I loved you, and the beginning of our relationship was great. But I'm going to be honest, I stayed with you because you were easy. You didn't ask anything of me. There came a point when I knew it wasn't working and would never work, but breaking up is hard. Doing nothing is easy. You're attractive, you can be charming when you try, you always held the door for me, and it's really nice waking up with somebody every day."

Camden had trained himself to not show his emotions. It first started growing up in New England, where it was part of his family's DNA to be stoic. It continued when he became a reporter, where he took seriously the need to be unbiased. Then over the last several years, he had read a lot on Zen Buddhism, and he loved the philosophy and idea that you should acknowledge emotions but not hold on to them.

He knew he had the ability to be in control of his emotions, but all rational thought was slipping away. Everything bad that had happened to him over the last year and his poor choices were all pulsating in his brain. He was struck powerless to stop the pity party he was throwing.

"If you weren't with me when I got fired from the paper, I'm not sure what I would have done. I wish I could have been a better boyfriend over the last several months instead of walking around with my head up my ass."

"It's been more than several months."

"Touché. I've been a three-ring shit show. Even though the end's been coming for a long time, it's sad. I'm going to miss you. But as you said, we stayed together because it was easy."

"Now it's messy. You have to find an apartment. Will you stay here or go back to LA?"

"My problems right now are a little more complex than cities or apartment hunting."

"We need to talk about that." Georgia leaned in closer and said in a hushed voice, "Please tell me you're not involved in the robbery?"

"I was going to ask you the same thing."

"Why?"

"Because of your dad," Camden said. "He does have a reputation. I consider Mr. L a friend, but it doesn't mean I think he's singing with the Tabernacle Choir."

"Camden, you're the one who was involved in that museum robbery in Boston."

"As a reporter. I covered the goddamned story."

"I don't think you had anything to do with what happened at the Matisse," Georgia said. "But do the cops? Have they talked to you?"

"Yes," he said. "And I'm sitting here across from you and not in jail."

"It's been all over the news how the Matisse was robbed in exactly the same way as the Cordovan in Boston. The press hasn't mentioned your name, but that guy Bo McClennan is a suspect and you do have a history with him."

"I'm a suspect, too. But not a newsworthy one yet. That's why I have to find out who stole the sculptures. Your dad is a helluva great guy, but I need to make sure he didn't have anything to do with the robbery."

"I remember when those Matisse sculptures went up for auction. He could have bought them. But out of courtesy to David, he stopped bidding."

"David?"

"Bouchon. The owner of the Matisse. Why would he want to steal from his friend?"

"Maybe they're not friends anymore."

"They were never friends in the sense they palled around together, but there is a great professional respect that is mutual. I just came from David's house and we talked about that."

"You're hanging out at the house of the dude who owns the Matisse Hotel?"

Georgia sipped her wine and spoke softly with the glass next to her lips. "The Board of Trustees voted to buy one of my pieces. When they reopen the Museum of the Twentieth Century, they're going to display it."

"Congrats," Camden said. "I can tell the museum patrons that I used to date the artist."

Georgia flipped him the bird.

"All right, your dad probably has nothing to do with the robbery. But I have to see him. I don't have many leads here. He's a person who knows things."

"It's a free country, Camden. You can call my dad whenever you like. Are you going to talk to Miles?"

"I didn't even think of that ass-clown," Camden said. "I saw him this morning."

"In bed?"

Camden knew saying that was out of line, but he needed to take a verbal jab at her because he hated himself right now. Pity, jealousy, self-loathing, and boorish behavior. He had to snap out of it, and instead focus on the robbery and finding those sculptures.

"C'mon, Camden. I can't believe I ever dated that guy. He's my friend in a fucked-up way, and I'm worried about him. I think he's losing his mind. No, I went over there because I thought he robbed the museum."

"To videotape himself destroying the sculptures. That makes sense, but is he that stupid? He'd get arrested."

"I thought of that," Georgia said. "He could say they were replicas. How could the police prove they were real? They would be destroyed. There would be no evidence."

"You're right. He probably has some connection to this. Can you give me his address and phone number?"

"I'll text it you," she said and then did so using her phone.

The waitress set their food down on the table, and before taking a big bite from the sesame bun, Camden ordered another porter. His hunger did nothing for his already poor manners, and he was shoving fries in his mouth before he had completely chewed the meat. The smoky and juicy burger improved his sprits until Georgia spoke.

"I wouldn't feel right if you learned about it in some other way. I have to tell you about the guy I'm now seeing."

"I don't need to know his name, for Christ's sake," Camden said.

"At first it was just an affair, but it's getting serious now."

"Fuck me. All right, who is he?"

"David Bouchon."

16

Hot Pocket

COPYING HIPPLE'S PHONE number and address in her notebook only took a few seconds, but Veronica's mind buzzed from doing a task that could lead to a story. Soon afterward, she hurried toward the ladies locker room to see if the Tall Woman's bag was there, but ran into a gauntlet of housekeepers. They were in the midst of a shift change, and scores of ladies in Matisse Hotel T-shirts and black pants entered and exited the room.

Veronica detoured to the Scary Room to do some research. She flipped open the laptop and scoured the internet for any new developments on the heist, but no website had facts she didn't already know. She then clicked through pages to find out more about Camden Swanson. One of the articles she read was titled "Reporter Fired for Posing Science Fiction as News."

Los Angeles—Harkening back to the days when Orson Welles terrified radio listeners by convincing them Martians were attacking the earth, a local columnist published a page-one article yesterday declaring the city was being invaded by half-monkey, half-snakelike creatures. The story was written in the first person and told of a government experiment with gene splicing gone awry. Completely fabricated, it contained dozens of harrowing eyewitness accounts and quotes from "top scientists."

But while Welles was clearly pulling a prank, Camden Swanson, an award-winning journalist, claims he believed what he had published. When reached for comment on the morning of publication, Swanson said by phone, "They're out there, and they're winning. The monkey-snakes have mobilized into a powerful player in our city. Opposable thumbs AND sleek maneuverability. We're doomed."

The spurious article appeared in the Los Angeles Item, *and officials at the newspaper have issued the following statement: "We regret the unfortunate and egregious fabrications of Mr. Camden Swanson. If his words caused any anxiety or fear to our readers, we sincerely apologize. Our thorough investigation has proven this inopportune incident was perpetrated solely by Mr. Swanson, who surreptitiously placed the article in our publication and with no knowledge of anyone else. In fact, his means of deception in doing it were borderline criminal. He is no longer employed with our paper, and the* Los Angeles Item *will once again move forward with high-quality journalism."*

Swanson wrote a popular column and appeared on many local TV and radio programs. None of the other media outlets where he contributed would comment on the incident.

"Yes, I do expect to be fired from everywhere I work. I will most likely never get hired as a journalist again," Swanson said via phone interview. "There's not much room in today's media for people who speak the truth. But none of that matters. The only hope is that the monkey-snakes will not leave LA County. Because you can't stop them. You can only hope to contain them."

With her face scrunched up in the longest wince of her life, Veronica read more articles about how the Swanson debacle escalated. Not only had the columnist made up a ludicrous story, but he also laced the article with profane language. Advertisers pulled out of their contracts, readers canceled subscriptions, and lawsuits were settled out of court. The *Los Angeles Item*, established in 1982, went bankrupt less than a year later.

Weeks after, in an interview with the *LA Times*, Camden said he had been "tripping his balls off" on LSD. He claimed it was all an accident. Swanson alleged he swallowed a piece of paper containing the acid after it had landed on his half-eaten Hot Pocket.

"I was in the park eating my lunch when I saw two teenagers running toward me. They were screaming but I had no idea they were yelling at me. I took a bite of my Hot Pocket and one of them yelled, 'He ate my hit of acid.' The guy said a breeze had blown blotter acid off his finger and onto my Hot Pocket. I didn't believe them. I went to work, and the next thing I knew, the whole monkey-snake thing happened. If I didn't lock everyone that could have stopped me that night in a closet, I would probably just have slept it off."

Veronica began to wonder if she had been too trusting with Swanson. But she was also somebody who never judged without all the facts, and she would get his side of the events later. But first the locker room.

The dim fluorescent lighting cast eerie shadows on the floor. She took short, deliberate steps to locker number 333 and did not need to check the combination. Those three numbers were seared in her mind forever.

Right, left, right.

The locker opened.

The blue nylon backpack was there. She slowly unzipped it and found a heavy plastic black garbage bag. She inspected it without touching anything and found several handguns, knives, and smoke bombs. Veronica snapped a few photos with her phone and zipped the backpack, shoved it back inside the locker, and unintentionally slammed the door shut. The metal on metal echoed and resounded in her ears long after leaving the locker room.

* * *

After Georgia said she was dating David Bouchon, Camden's head percolated with information. It ran through the Matisse robbery, Veronica, being dumped, the Tall Woman, getting hit in the head with a baseball bat, needing to find a new place to live, and having his life threatened. Georgia's last piece of bad news wouldn't compute. He asked her to repeat the name.

"He's older than your dad," he finally said.

"David's actually three years younger".

"What is Mr. L going to say?" Camden asked. "Fathers don't usually condone their buddies banging their daughters."

"Don't be crude. He respects my choices. I've known David for a long time. There's always been an attraction there, and we've denied it because of my father."

"I think I've heard plenty," Camden said. "*Au revoir, merci beaucoup* for lunch. I need to find those sculptures. Peace out."

He stood up with shaky legs, which caused the high-top table to rumble, and strode back up the stairs and through the lobby with the murals. He walked into the cool ocean wind with a keen sense of being in the moment. It was a sensation he hadn't felt in a long time.

In front of the painted wooden Beach Chalet sign, Camden took a few deep breaths. It was then he spied the Tall Woman across the highway standing at the concrete wall separating the beach from the sidewalk. She was turned away from him, wearing a peacoat much like Georgia's, smoking a cigarette while talking on her cell phone.

There was traffic zooming in both directions of the Great Highway, but Camden did not wait for a light to cross. Finding a break in the speeding cars he sprinted across the street. Upon seeing Camden moving toward her, the Tall Woman's composure sagged, and she took a step back when he reached her.

"You know, instead of tailing me around the city you could put yourself to use and try to find those fucking sculptures," Camden said. "I didn't steal them."

"My clients have paid me to watch you."

"Your clients. The same clients who want to murder me. If they really want to get their hands on those Matisse sculptures, they should get off their asses and start looking."

"Mr. Swanson, they have people searching for the art. My job is to watch you."

"Did you ever think your clients are trying to pull a fast one on you?"

"Come again?"

"Sure. You're a key part, the person who has put the whole thing together and who probably found the buyer."

The Tall Woman puffed her cigarette and turned her head in the opposite direction of the wind to exhale the smoke.

"Thieves need buyers in art heists," Camden continued. "Because even if you can steal the stuff, who's gonna pay you for it? Not many people on this earth could display the shit in their homes without fearing arrest."

"So what if I did set up the buyer?"

"What if your clients found somebody else who was offering more money? Maybe they wanted to screw you out of your cut."

The Tall Woman threw her cigarette on the ground and then instantly lit another with her Zippo, which took a few tries in the wind. She flashed a Mona Lisa smile when she took her first drag. She held up her pack of cigarettes to Camden as an offer, but he shook his head no.

"I completely underestimated you," she said. "You could be innocent, could not. But I truly misjudged your character. You're not the complete loser I thought you were."

"Can I get that on a greeting card? And can you answer my question?"

"This isn't the first job I've worked with them on. My clients are professionals. Devising an intricate con to cheat me out of my percentage goes against who they are. It's far too risky for them. Can you even comprehend just how complicated it would be to make two completely different sets of plans for such a robbery?"

Camden said, "One of the best pieces of advice I got when I was first starting off as a reporter was, 'Never underestimate the power of greed.' Greed is what drives people to do all kinds of things that don't make much sense."

"The clock is ticking on you, Mr. Swanson. Arguing with me isn't getting you any closer to returning the sculptures to my clients."

"They're paying you to watch me. I'm making it easy."

"I am being compensated for my time," the Tall Woman said. "But naturally, the real money comes when we get those Matisses back."

"I don't have them. But follow me," Camden said. "You'll have good company. The police think I was involved in the robbery, too. Associating with me, like the friendly conversation we're having, could lead to you becoming a suspect."

The Tall Woman leaned toward him, put her left arm around his back, and kissed him. Her mouth tasted of cigarettes, and he thought back to a night when he was thirteen. Alice Fowler, who had the typical "bad girl" reputation because she smoked and wasn't the best student, asked him to dance at a party. While "Total Eclipse of the Heart" played on the stereo, she kissed Camden and tasted of cigarettes and grape lip gloss. He zapped back to the present when the Tall Woman took her lips off his, hugged him tight, and ran her fingers through his hair.

"If the police ask," she whispered, "I am your lover. That is all. If you drag me into any police questioning, I will put a bullet in your face."

She had delivered all her words with a smile. Camden shuddered when she blew him a kiss and strode away as if vamping for a runway.

* * *

Detective Clinkenbeard sat in his unmarked vehicle in the Beach Chalet parking lot. He was looking through his binoculars, attempting to figure out what to make of Camden's encounter with the mysterious woman. *The guy had just eaten lunch with his girlfriend, a prominent and very attractive artist, and now he was sprinting across the street to speak with a lady who resembled a model. What am I doing wrong with my life?*

At first Clinkenbeard thought he had another suspect, but could that explain the kiss at the end? He was adept at reading lips, but the angle wasn't right for it. From that distance, it seemed like the woman was Swanson's mistress.

He considered following the woman but didn't have the luxury to waste time on guesses. As for Camden, he had watched the guy limp into Golden Gate Park. Clinkenbeard knew he'd be easy to find, and radioed for the closest cruiser to pick up the tail.

Rich people, on the other hand, could be much more challenging to find than their poor counterparts. Clinkenbeard exited his vehicle and with the wind blowing his ponytail, he walked to Georgia's Mercedes. When she emerged from the restaurant a few minutes later, he flashed his badge and introduced himself.

"Just need a few minutes of your time, Ms. Léveque," Clinkenbeard said. "As I'm sure you know, the Matisse sculptures were stolen last night."

"I am aware."

"You have a relationship with Mr. Swanson, who is a gallery attendant at the museum. He is a person of interest in this case. Now, your personal life is just that and of no business to SFPD. But I ask because it might be relevant. Did you break up with him because he's cheating on you?"

"Cheating on me?"

"I assume that means no."

"Did you see him with another woman?"

"A few minutes ago I saw him exit this restaurant and kiss a woman who is thin, about six feet five, and strikingly attractive," he said. "Know anybody who fits that description?"

"I do not."

"I had to ask, because if you had any information regarding the woman I witnessed him with, it might be helpful to our case."

"Camden and this chick were kissing? I need to know. We broke up, and if he was cheating on me it might make me feel a little better."

"I would think it would make you feel worse."

"That son of a bitch," Georgia said.

"Ms. Léveque, I'm here to speak with you about the Matisse sculptures. Since you don't know her, let's move past the lady I mentioned. We think Camden might be involved. Do you think that's possible?"

"Before what you just said, I wouldn't have thought he had the drive to do anything except finish a case of beer."

"I'm seeking your honest opinion, Ms. Lévheque, which I don't want clouded by what I told you. Have you noticed anything strange with Camden lately? Did you overhear any conversations he had that might have been a little off?"

"We haven't seen much of each other lately. I've been so busy with my upcoming show, and honestly, I haven't really wanted to see him."

"Do you know who Bo McClennan is? Have you ever seen Camden with him?"

"I've never seen Bo McClennan in my life, with or without Camden," Georgia answered. "I only know who he is because as an artist, everybody has heard of him. And then of all the stuff they've said on the news recently. Camden has never mentioned him at all."

"Do you think Mr. Swanson would rob the museum?"

"The notion that Camden, as the person he's become over the last year, could be involved in an art heist, is about as believable as him kissing a runway model at Ocean Beach."

"Let's move on, then," Clinkenbeard said. "How about your associate Miles Krakow?"

"It's too windy out here. Can we talk in my car?"

"I apologize. Of course."

Georgia pushed a button on her keys and both front doors automatically opened. Detective Clinkenbeard and Georgia sat on the leather upholstery, which was the most comfortable car seat he had ever felt. Clinkenbeard sniffed his runny nose brought on by the wind and detected a hint of cinnamon from an unseen air freshener.

"First off, Miles is my friend. Sometimes I hate him and I'm now starting to believe he's losing his mind, but he's still my friend. I went to see him this morning and he completely denied any involvement."

"What did he say?" Clinkenbeard asked.

Georgia recounted her meeting with Miles and how he was acting bizarre, even for him. How he claimed he spent the night with an art student, but the girl was not there. She left out the part about the Uzi.

Detective Clinkenbeard scribbled in his notebook, and when Georgia had finished speaking, he asked, "Can I ask you where you were last night?"

"Am I a suspect?"

"No, but you have ties to certain individuals we are interested in knowing more about. Camden, Miles, and, of course, your father."

"My father?" Georgia asked. "Again with that shit."

"After the previous accusations, which date back over thirty years, you cannot be surprised that your father's name would come up."

"Surprised? No. Disgusted and pissed off that my family has to be yet again dragged into shit that has nothing to do with us. My dad is not an art thief."

"Ms. Léveque, there is no reason to get upset. I must find those sculptures. My job is to ask a lot of people a lot of questions. Most of the answers will lead nowhere. I am not accusing you or your father of anything. But I must ask you again, where were you last night?"

"I spent the night at a friend's."

"And who was that friend?" Clinkenbeard asked.

Georgia stared down at her steering wheel and did not answer.

"Who were you with last night, Ms. Léveque?"

"David Bouchon."

17

Hipple in Harm

CAMDEN WANDERED INTO Golden Gate Park to the windmill, its towering reddish-brown features making him think of Don Quixote. He opened his phone and saw he had received a text message from Veronica providing Hipple's number and address. Camden wanted to sit down for a few minutes and formulate some sort of plan, and the tulip garden underneath the windmill seemed like a good place. But all the benches were full, so he passed by the colorful flowers billowing in the breeze and continued down JFK Drive. Just as he was about to put his phone back in his pocket, it rang.

"Were you able to reach Hipple?" Veronica asked after he answered.

"Haven't tried yet. But I had an interesting encounter with the Tall Woman."

"What did she want?"

"We'll talk about it later. Where should we meet? I'm way the hell out by the ocean, by that windmill."

"You're not too far from where I live," Veronica said. "We can meet at my apartment. It's around a forty or so minute walk from where you are. I'll text you directions."

"Was the bag in the locker?" Camden asked.

"Yes."

"That's probably a clue, but I'm not sure where it fits yet."

"I opened it," Veronica asked. "Guns and knives and smoke bombs. Why wouldn't they have used that stuff to steal the sculptures?"

"It doesn't look like the clients stole the sculptures. Not sure about the Tall Woman. We have a lot to talk about. First, I'm going to call Hipple. Let's see what that son of a bitch has to say. I'll see you in an hour."

Camden continued down JKF Drive and noticed a narrow road curving to the left leading to city streets. Ahead of him were lush green trees and the enormity of Golden Gate Park, which he remembered reading somewhere was bigger than Central Park in New York City. He thought wandering around and exploring might help him think, but it was getting dark and he didn't want to get lost. So he turned on the road leading out of the park and dialed Harry Hipple's number.

"Who the fuck is this?" the man asked in a panicked voice.

"Camden, from work."

"Camden, holy shit," Hipple said. "You gotta help me. I'm in big trouble. They're gonna kill me."

"Who's gonna kill you?"

"I don't know why I ever said I was gonna help them. But it was so much money and it seemed so easy. And that woman was so gorgeous. Camden, you gotta help me."

"Where are you?" Camden asked.

"Oh, fuck. How do I know you're not with them? They could have a gun to your head."

"Hipple, I'm by myself. I want to help you, but I can't if I don't know where you are."

"Oh, shit," he said. And then his voice became more strained and out of breath. "That's gotta be them. They found me. I have to get out of here."

"Where are you?"

The signal went dead. Camden hit the redial button several times, but it went straight to voicemail. He left his number on the message, repeated that he sincerely wanted to help, and urged Hipple to call as soon as he could.

So Hipple had been involved in the heist, and he was hiding and feared for his life. Their boss, who was murdered, had also played a part in the robbery. But how? And why was he killed if the clients didn't steal the sculptures? Camden's head, lethargic from months of apathy and booze, blooped and bleeped with data he could not compute. So he read Veronica's text message to get her address and took a right on Fulton.

He exited the park at 47th Avenue, and to his left, houses lined the street and sloped down the hills leading off Fulton. Veronica lived on 20th, so there remained a long way to walk. What was it about those Matisse sculptures, he wondered, that made them so valuable? Sure, Matisse was a famous artist, but there were masterworks hanging everywhere in the world. Why did the thieves want those particular pieces?

Did the "why" matter anymore? The Tall Woman's clients were going to fire bullets into his brain unless he found those sculptures. It could just as well be bowling balls he was trying to recover.

He passed the intersection at Fulton and 25th Avenue, where the wide, divided road cut through the park with cars speeding in either direction. After crossing the street, he took a left on 24th Avenue and decided to call Sal, who he believed was the brightest member in the Unsuccessful Men's Club.

Sal was an obscure trivia junkie, who on several occasions had referred to himself as a "czar of esoteric facts." In addition to co-owning the baseball card shop with the other two members of the group, he ran a website devoted to San Francisco-based conspiracy theories.

Sal answered and asked, "Are you calling to complain about the film, Camden?"

"Huh? What film? No."

"Didn't you get the email I sent?" Sal asked. "Since nobody could find a copy of that Korean film, I thought it would be nice to change gears. I know *Twin Peaks* was popular, but I think it's worth revisiting. David Lynch is brilliant, and that Agent Cooper is such a great character. Pies and Douglas firs."

"Sal, I need your help," Camden said as he walked down the steep decline of 24th Avenue. "What can you tell me about the Matisse sculptures?"

"They were stolen."

"Yeah, genius, I know that. But what can you tell me about their history?"

"You're the one who works there," he said. "Don't the people who go to the museum ask you questions?"

"Yeah, and I send them to somebody who knows more than me. C'mon, Sal. I need some help here."

"Are you trying to find them?" he asked. "Gonna become a reporter again?"

"Something like that. I can search information about the sculptures online, but I'm looking for details that might not be public knowledge. You always brag that you know things that few others—"

"I don't brag."

"Well, do you know any obscure facts about the sculptures? Anything you can think of that might help."

"Hmmm . . . I know David Bouchon is the co-owner and chairman of À Venir Fantastique, the hotel group that built the Matisse. I know he got into a fierce bidding war to acquire the sculptures. But everybody knows that. However, there was some intrigue about the mystery person bidding against Bouchon. There was a proxy sent to the auction . . . proxy, I think that's what they call them.

"Anyway, on my site we did have a few discussion threads after they announced they were putting them in the Matisse Hotel in San Francisco. The mystery person was bidding strong and then suddenly dropped out. I guess it went too high."

"How much was it?" Camden asked.

"One hundred million, I think. And there are three sculptures in the collection. That much for things hardly bigger than a bread box. It's a crazy world we live in, Camden."

"You never found out who the mystery bidder was?"

"Wasn't a big issue on the site," Sal answered. "One member said it was Zuckerberg. Apparently, he has a soft spot for Matisse. But I don't buy that for a second. A hundred mil to that guy is like a fucking Happy Meal to me. I always figured it was the government of France. You know how they have such a strong national identity. Matisse is one of their own and they probably wanted to be certain the sculptures would remain in France."

"That's it?" Camden asked. "No conspiracies?"

"We don't do conspiracies. I've told you that a thousand times. We uncover interesting facts the public should know. Anyway, with the Matisse thing, nobody decided to pursue it. I have a lot of active members, and we focus more on local politics and government. If a discussion thread dies, it dies. I'm sure something more important happened a day or two later."

"Is a hundred million a lot for three sculptures? Especially small ones?"

"Dunno. David Geffen paid one hundred forty mil for a bunch of scribbly paint dripping by Jackson Pollock, and around the same for a de Kooning that was done in 1953. A five-thousand-year-old Mesopotamian statue found near Baghdad went for something like sixty recently. A Picasso sculpture recently sold for around thirty mil, and it was a bronze cast. These Matisses are the original wax jobs and there's three of them. But maybe it went so high because they were lost for so long. Some dude found them in a crate under a floor in the South of France. Maybe it was in the walls. And I believe they were done when Matisse was younger, so that always plays a factor in art. I'm not an expert, Camden. Again, you're the one who works in a museum."

"Thanks, Sal. If you have any time, it would mean a lot to me if you could ask around about the sculptures. Anything you could dig up. I'll call you later."

"Remember, Camden. *Twin Peaks*. The pilot. And if the discussion goes well, maybe we'll continue with the whole first season. Laura Palmer, that was a mystery."

* * *

With two of her fingertips on the side of a plastic seat for balance, Veronica got jostled by the people surrounding her on the 38 Limited bus as they hunted for a bit of extra space. She only wanted fresh air, and her nose and lungs searched for any bit that snuck through the small windows. She was once told that the 38 Limited traversed Geary Street as well as the goodwill of all commuters who rode that bus line. Even though it was the quickest route home, she normally walked the longer distance from work and took the less crowded number 1 or 2 busses.

But Veronica braved the Geary Limited at rush hour because she was eager to return to the heist story and to ask Camden about those monkey-snakes. By the time the bus reached her stop in the Middle Richmond District, the dense bodies thinned and she stepped off without having to use elbows. She walked up 20th toward Lake and saw Camden sitting on the front steps with her roommate, Kutra.

"One day I smoked a whole bowl and started digging all the palm trees," Kutra was saying to Camden. "There's one on 11th Ave. and Cali that is hella cool. But I couldn't understand what the hell they're doing in San Francisco. Can't figure it out. When I think palm trees, I think Miami or LA."

"They're not native there, either," Camden said.

"At least they make sense. It's warm in those places, like Saudi Arabia or some shit like that. San Francisco is cold and foggy. Not today, but out here in the Mid it's like fucking London. Man, wouldn't it be cool if we were in London?"

"What's the Mid?" Camden asked.

"Middle Richmond. People always say Outer or Inner Richmond. We're at 20th . . . the Mid, man."

For the first time, Kutra noticed Veronica.

"Hey, V-Ron. Well, I gotta bail. I'm meeting Le Ned in the InSun," she said and took a crumpled piece of paper out of her jeans. "Not sure why, but I did write it down. Inner Sunset, Lincoln and 9th at 6:30 p.m. Later, kids."

Veronica motioned Camden to follow her, and they entered the house through the side door and walked through the darkness into her basement apartment. It was a small in-law studio, and when she unlocked the door, the stale air gave the place an almost muggy feel. Sabrina, her French bulldog, cocked her head at them when they entered and then zoomed up to Camden and began licking his shoe. He got down on the floor to her eye level, and the dog assaulted him with puppy kisses.

After Sabrina tired of playing, she left the apartment through her doggie door. Camden sat down on a love seat while Veronica took the chair at her desk. The walls were painted a yellowish color and had hardly anything hung on them. There were only a few photos of Veronica and her friends wearing graduation gowns, and a framed poster of *All the President's Men*.

"Any luck with Hipple?" Veronica asked.

"I talked to him briefly and he sounded scared out of his mind. Said he was in trouble but wouldn't tell me where he was. Before he hung up, he said, 'They've found me.' I've called back a bunch of times but he won't pick up."

"Should we call 9-1-1?" Veronica asked.

"I thought of that, but we don't know where he is. And the cops are already looking everywhere for him. He's also got a phone and could do that himself."

"We have his address," Veronica said. "Do you think we should go there?"

"That would be a stupid place for him to go, figuring whoever wants him dead likely knows where he lives. Then again, Hipple probably struggles with spelling his own name."

"I remember we pulled his file a few days ago because he had just been nominated for Employee of the Month. Everybody in HR was curious why."

"The kid might seem like he's had multiple lobotomies," Camden said, "but I don't want to see him hurt. We gotta find him before the clients do."

"Do we know it's the clients who are after him?" Veronica asked.

"No, but he thought so. He mentioned them specifically, as well as the Tall Woman."

"Do you think it's all a lie with her?" Veronica asked.

"What do you mean?"

"She always talks about her clients, but do you think she's the one who's in charge?"

"She could be. But that bag was in the locker."

Veronica said, "They paid me all that money to put it there. Why wouldn't they use it? I mean, I know about McClennan, but could he be one of the clients?"

"I could be wrong, but I don't think McClennan had anything to do with them. I never told you what my role was. What the Tall Woman recruited me to do. I was supposed to be the client's hostage."

"I don't understand."

"The clients had the whole robbery planned out down to every minute detail. They were supposed to come into the museum just before it was closing, take me hostage, rough me up, and storm out of the place. Because I was being paid, they knew I wouldn't try to be a hero or else keel over in fright. Most of the gallery attendants are retired people or students. They didn't want to take any chances."

Veronica said, "But the museum was robbed overnight with no hostages. It was robbed exactly like Bo McClennan did to the Cordovan Museum in Boston."

"And the clients don't have the sculptures. Somebody else does, probably McClennan. But none of that matters. The clients and the Tall Woman think I teamed up with him."

"Are you guys friends?"

"'Cause of me, he spent years in jail. I haven't exactly got any Christmas cards from him."

Veronica stood up. "We need to keep working through the facts, but I'm starving. I have some chicken and veggies I can stir-fry for us if you're interested."

"Had a burger not too long ago, so I'm good. If you don't mind, I could actually use a catnap. Ten, fifteen minutes would help. This has been the most shit I've done in one day since I don't know when. I'll leave my cell phone turned up in case Hipple calls."

Veronica pointed to her queen bed, made smooth and taut with burgundy sheets and matching duvet and plush pillows. It took up nearly half the studio. Camden flipped off his shoes, slid them under the bed, and hoped his new friend would be kind enough not to comment on the odor. He turned the ringer of his cell phone to full volume and then tossed it on the white particleboard nightstand. Sabrina climbed into bed with him, and Camden was asleep by the time Veronica had heated her wok.

* * *

She ate her dinner at her desk out of a plastic bowl with chopsticks while her new partner and her puppy snored loudly. After finishing and washing the dishes, she called Hipple from Camden's phone, but it went straight to voicemail. She flipped open her laptop and with a new Word document began typing all the facts she had learned about the heist, including her recent conversation with the slumbering man in her room.

At ten fifteen she nudged his shoulder several times, and he finally woke with a snort. He gazed up at her as if she were a stranger, blinked a few times, and then went back to sleep. Veronica shook him awake again, noticing her guest had drooled on her pillow. Sabrina was now up and began licking his face.

Camden enjoyed the dog kisses, but turned away from Sabrina to ask, "Hipple call?"

"Nope. I tried him, but it went straight to voicemail. I guess we wait, and then if he doesn't call, you can crash here on my floor."

"I really appreciate that," Camden said as he sat up. He grabbed his cell phone, inspected it, and put it in his pocket. "And thanks for letting me sleep."

"Let's get some fresh air."

From a door in the basement, Veronica and Camden walked into a small backyard. A floodlight shone down from the side of the house, illuminating a cracked broom wrapped in duct tape, a stack of broken chairs, and dead plants in pots that poked up from the overgrown grass and weeds. On a patch of concrete there were painted wooden beach chairs, and they each took a seat. They could barely make out the sound of the surf crashing down onto Baker Beach.

"Did you know McClennan was working at the hotel under an alias?" Veronica asked.

"Found out today. And of course that makes it seem even worse for me. I talked with a police detective and he's pretty sure I'm involved."

"Detective Clinkenbeard? He questioned me, too. Terrifying."

"Clinkenbeard throwing me in jail is much better than what the clients are offering. I've got three days to return the sculptures or they kill me."

"Oh my God, Camden."

"The Tall Woman forced me by gunpoint to see the clients this morning. They whacked me in the head with a baseball bat and shot me with a tranquilizer gun."

"I talked to one of the security guards who was there during the robbery. He said everyone had been shot with a tranquilizer dart during the robbery except for him. And these guys used the same thing on you. Coincidence?"

"Has to be. Unless the clients robbed the museum the day before to screw the Tall Woman out of her cut. Maybe they got in business with McClennan. It's possible. But what I'm getting at here is that the more time you spend with me," Camden said, "the more danger you're gonna be in. I know you want a story, but it's best if you walk away."

"I can't."

"It's easy," Camden said. "Get out of the city and forget all about it. Take that money they gave you and go on a long vacation."

"How did I get that money? I did something for the people who want to kill Hipple and you. Who have already killed Larry, the director of security."

"But you didn't know what you were doing."

"Doesn't make me feel any better," Veronica said. "I'm not going anywhere. We're going to find those sculptures and we're going to write an article about it."

* * *

The nap had helped Camden, and he was feeling another strange sensation that had been absent in his life for over a year. A sense of purpose. He thought that even though his life had really gone to shit in the last twenty-four hours (a cheating girlfriend who left him, becoming a prime suspect in a major crime, and being beaten with a baseball bat and having his life threatened), the self-hatred was gone. He didn't have to define himself by what happened in Los Angeles. What was occurring now, whether he found the sculptures, got thrown in jail, or killed, would be all that mattered going forward. He had the opportunity to change his life.

Camden felt his cell vibrate in his pocket before it rang, and he stood up to answer. It was Hipple and he spoke in a desperate whisper. "They found me. Fucking help me. Please fucking help me, Camden."

"Where are you?"

"They finally found me. I'm fucked."

"Where are you?" Camden repeated.

"Golden Gate Park. Got a friend who works the overnight for the de Young Museum. Said he'd hide me. Somehow they found me. Fuck, I'm going to die like Mr. Aberlour did."

"Do you want me to call 9-1-1?"

"Fuck no. I don't want to go to jail. You gotta help me."

"Okay. We're coming to get you."

"We? God, is the Tall Woman with you?"

"No, I'm with a friend. She wants to help, too. The park is huge, Hipple. Where specifically?"

"On the hill overlooking the lake."

The line went dead.

"Do you know where the hill is by the lake in Golden Gate Park?" he asked Veronica.

"Has to be Stowe Lake. Strawberry Hill. It's not too far from here, probably twenty-five minutes to walk."

"Hipple could be dead by the time we get there."

"We'll take bikes. My roommates own about three bikes apiece. They're stacked in the basement and we'll be there before a cab could even show up."

18

The Showdown at Golden Gate Park

THE TALL WOMAN had been listening to Camden and Veronica via her leather-padded headphones. She had almost not bothered to put an electronic bug in Veronica's yard due to its shabbiness but was now glad she had made the effort of slipping the device in a cracked planter. Veronica's meeting with Camden in the Gold Dust Lounge was not a fluke, and their peculiar partnership had yielded the location of Harry Hipple. She called the man she referred to as Client A on her cell phone.

"Hipple is in the park," she informed him.

"Yeah, we know. We followed him there."

"Do you want to know specifically where he is?"

"No, we'd like to keep guessing."

"You learn a lot about people when things go wrong. If I wanted to have a conversation with a dickhead, I could have called my ex-husband."

"Sorry, but we've been out here combing the fucking park for hours now," Client A said. "We should have had him at the de Young."

"Yes, you should have. After I told you where he went."

"He got away, the little fucker."

"Like he got away from you before."

Client A did not respond.

"From what I heard," she said, "Hipple is most likely on Strawberry Hill."

"Where the fuck is Strawberry Hill?"

"Over Stowe Lake. Use the map I gave you."

"We'll be in contact when we have him."

"Mr. Swanson is on his way to try and help him. He's traveling with a young woman. Kill her if you must, but we need him to lead us to McClennan."

"Our PI thinks he found McClennan."

"Don't kill Swanson," the Tall Woman yelled. "Even if your detective has found McClennan, we should have a backup. Make sure you reiterate this to your team."

"Hey now, missy. Who the fuck works for who?"

"I'm the one moving the items, remember? If we don't deliver, and I mean we, the whole lot of us is fucked."

* * *

Camden and Veronica rode the bicycles up 22nd Avenue toward Golden Gate Park, the road turning hilly once they passed Balboa Street. She gave him a Navy Cal pullover that an ex-boyfriend had left when she was a senior, and she had changed into jeans, a black T-shirt, and a zip-up dark raspberry nylon jacket. Camden hadn't been on a bike since he was in college, and five minutes of pedaling yielded heartburn and a stitch on his right side. Veronica stopped so he could catch up, and his breathing was the only thing he could hear.

They crested the hill and reached Fulton, and after crossing the street they made a sharp left onto a paved path next to a bus stop. The trail crossed a divided street, and soon they were inside Golden Gate Park. It was dark, but the moon provided enough light in the mostly cloudless sky as they rode under a bridge.

A few seconds later they turned right and rode up a paved path, Camden once again struggled with the incline as Veronica pedaled with ease. They were now facing a wooden cabin-like building that had "Boating and Refreshments" painted in large letters on it. Just beyond the structure, a group of paddle boats were tied to each other on Stowe Lake.

The paved trail continued around the placid body of water, which resembled a moat that surrounded the forested Strawberry Hill. Camden followed Veronica up the path, turned right over the arched stone bridge and onto the island, and skidded to a stop on the dirt. Camden dug his phone out of his jeans and called Hipple.

"We're here, just by the bridge," he said in a whisper.

"I'm on top of the hill," Hipple answered in hushed fear.

"C'mon down. We'll get you out of here."

"I can't, Camden. I'm so fucking scared I can't move."

"Did they follow you?"

"I don't think so. Think I lost them again."

"If they're not here, Hipple, you can do it. Come down."

"Please come up, Camden."

Camden angled his bike to the ground and climbed off it.

"This is ridiculous," he said.

"I'll go up," Veronica said.

"No, I'll get him."

"It's probably more dangerous down here. You keep watch. I'll get him."

This girl had balls, Camden thought. Beauty, intelligence, and an inner fortitude that most people he met these days, be they men or women, did not possess. Under different, less life-threatening circumstances, he would have recognized his emotions for a full-blown crush.

Camden nodded and spoke back into the phone, "All right, Hipple. Veronica is coming up. She's my friend so don't be scared. It isn't the Tall Woman."

* * *

Veronica stepped onto the overgrown path that led up to the four-hundred-foot-high Strawberry Hill. She moved quickly up the railroad ties and dirt, and after a switchback she heard water trickling down rocks. The trees blocked most of the moonlight, but her eyes adjusted to the darkness and after crossing a short wooden footbridge she was almost at the top. She passed a pile of woodchips and now stood at a small, fenced reservoir that fed the manmade waterfall. She turned back and could make out the tip of the Transamerica building over the ridge of trees. She called out to Hipple in a hushed voice.

She did not get a response, so she continued on the right side of the dirt path that curved around the reservoir. She arrived at a clearing at the top of the hill, which in the moonlight revealed a shallow pit surrounded by jagged rocks. Veronica now felt sand under her feet.

Hipple emerged from the darkness and crouched low next to a green trash barrel. "Veronica?" he called out in a childlike voice.

"Yes," she answered. "Let's get the hell out of here."

Hipple sprinted to Veronica and grabbed her hand like a child would with his mother. Moving quickly, they soon reached the waterfall, which had been turned off and could only be heard as a trickle. In the darkness, she missed the trail she had used going up, and instead descended the main steps that hugged the waterfall. She could smell the moss that clung to the rocks. They were both breathing heavily when they reached another short wooden footbridge, and Veronica swung her head around the area to get her bearings.

She heard a crack of a branch.

Suddenly a stocky man wearing a dark track suit and a ski mask darted out from behind a tree. She screamed. The guy grabbed Hipple and they stumbled to the wooden parapet on the bridge. The man outweighed both Hipple and Veronica by at least one hundred pounds and had six inches of height on them. Veronica rushed to the wrestling bodies and swung her fist as fast as she could at the attacker's ear.

The man used one beefy arm to toss her to the ground, and then he elbowed Hipple in the nose. He extracted a gun and moved it toward Hipple's head.

From out of the darkness she saw Camden rush the guy in the ski mask and deliver a hard hockey-style check. The guy stumbled back against the wooden railing. Camden lowered his shoulder and rammed Hipple's attacker with another check, which splintered off a chunk of wood and the guy crashed through the bridge.

There was a three-foot section of rock before it dropped off thirty or so feet below. It all happened in a matter of seconds. When the stocky man tried to stand up, his feet went out from under him before he was halfway up, and he staggered backward. He tumbled off the precipice and out of her vision.

An ugly-sounding thud echoed against the rocks.

Veronica grabbed Hipple's hand and the three of them raced down the trail. When they reached flat ground, they all looked at the bottom of the waterfall, the large man in the track suit was facedown and not moving. They rushed over the stone slates and back toward the bicycles.

"Get on behind me," Camden said to Hipple.

"No," Veronica said. "I'm the better rider. You could barely make it up those hills."

"Are you sure?" Camden asked.

"Get on," Veronica yelled.

Hipple did as he was told and the three of them sped down the trail toward the main road. When they passed underneath the bridge, Veronica felt a bullet whiz by her ear. Headlights blasted out from across the street and a car zoomed toward them.

She was moving at a fast pace even with Hipple on the back and cut over to the right and went off the main road. She turned around and saw that Camden followed her, and she wished he could go faster. She led them past another lake, through a narrow dirt path in the trees, and emerged into an open meadow. The sound of screeching tires and a whirring engine weren't far off from them.

* * *

Tall branches and leaves shielded the moon as Camden followed Veronica up a barely visible dirt path and left onto another. He kept pumping his legs and prayed he wouldn't run head on into a rock or tree. For a moment he lost control and skidded up to a post, his face now next to a sign that told him to watch for flying discs.

He got the bike back in motion and tried his best to keep up with Veronica, but she was no longer in his sights. It got brighter as he approached a clearing from the narrow path. He didn't see Veronica and Hipple, but he continued pedaling until a bullet hit his front tire.

Camden tumbled over the handlebars and skidded across to the side of the paved road. With his scraped and bleeding face planted on the ground, he watched the dirt next to him jump upward from more bullets. He clawed his way to his feet and started running. After the crossing at 30th Street, the dirt path continued to a bluff and he stumbled down it as fast as he could.

Fulton Street, which he had walked down earlier in the evening, was bathed in streetlights and beckoned safety. But he didn't even consider leaving the park without Hipple and Veronica. He continued down the now sandy trail making his progress even more sluggish.

He eventually came to another body of water, the flat and diamond-shaped Spreckles Lake. He paused to suck in as much of the cool air as his lungs would allow, but the body of water exposed him to the people with the guns. He only heard his own breathing, and after scanning the area in all directions, he could not see a car or any person moving.

He took off in a sprint down the paved path.

Bullets thudded against trees inches from his head, and Camden dove off the asphalt. Scurrying back to his feet and running as fast as he could, he cut over to a narrow path and was scraped by stray branches.

At 36th Street the lake ended, and he followed another side trail that ran parallel to the main road. He skidded down the dirt and rocks with numb and bloodied hands, crossed a paved ranger road and came upon an eight-foot-high chain link fence that stretched out in the distance.

He heard footsteps but didn't know from which direction they were coming. The crunching on the ground could have belonged to Veronica and Hipple or the men who wanted to murder him. He tried to control his breathing, which was heavy and gasping.

He grabbed the fence and shimmied himself over it.

He had to hop a second fence about three feet high and made of wood and rope. Camden then dashed behind a tree and watched two silhouetted men come toward the fence. They were holding guns with silencers on the ends.

"It sounded like he climbed over," one of them said.

Beyond the trees a meadow as big as a football field offered nowhere to hide. In a low crouch, Camden moved toward the next grouping of trees. He heard the clanging of the men going over the chain link fence. If he ran for the other side, they'd have an easy shot at him.

He jumped up to a hanging branch, dug his fingers into the bark, and climbed up the tree.

Camden watched the men, who both seemed to be of slight build, walk with their guns pointed straight ahead. They wore ski masks and track suits like the person he had pushed off the bridge. The men stopped just beneath him, close enough for Camden to notice the white skulls on top of the ski masks.

In his mind he kept repeating, *Walk away, walk away*, over and over. He did his best not to audibly sigh when the guys turned and began heading into the grassy meadow. But after pausing and sweeping their heads to the left and right, the gunmen turned back around toward the trees. Camden could see the whites of their eyes through the ski masks as their heads craned upward.

"Mr. Harry Hipple?" one of them asked. "I see you."

"No, it's your mom," Camden answered without thinking.

The Tall Woman said they were giving him three days to return the sculptures, and he was hoping they were good to their word. But antagonizing people with guns was not a smart move. He was pissed off about getting caught, and his mind was churning with ideas on how to talk himself out of not being killed.

"Ahh, Mr. Swanson. You're supposed to be returning the sculptures to us and not hiding in trees."

"I'm trying to find them."

"Then why are you chasing after Hipple? He doesn't have them."

"I could ask you the same thing," Camden responded.

"Hipple is going to die because he couldn't keep his mouth shut."

"But you didn't get to rob the museum."

"But we are going to get those sculptures. And when we do, we can't have any loose ends blabbering about town. We were always going to pin the crime on him and Aberlour."

The other man said, "Now why don't you come down so you can bring us to Mr. Hipple?"

Camden had an intense hatred for the two people below him but needed to play it smart.

"Why don't you go eat a dick?"

Shit, he thought, *my adrenaline is overpowering my brain.*

"Mr. Swanson, we have orders not to kill you until your three-day window ends. There are members of our team who think you can lead us to McClennan. I disagree. I think your usefulness has already expired."

The man aimed his gun toward Camden.

"We'll say we thought it was Hipple. That it was an accident."

He fired the gun.

The bullet thwacked into the branch next to Camden's head.

"You've always been a shitty shot," the other man said and then fired his pistol.

The bullet again hit the branch.

Camden heard what sounded like galloping horses. He was watching the men to see which way they would angle their guns and hoped the branches would provide protection. The rumbling noise got louder, and he peered down at large humps and sets of horns.

That's when a herd of buffalo charged into the two clients.

The creatures were enormous, and their force crumpled and slammed the men's bodies into the trees. The buffalo snorted and circled their victims. Camden was stunned but thanked the bison as they lumbered away.

He had read somewhere that there were buffalo inside Golden Gate Park. Bison had roamed the park for more than one hundred years and were a popular tourist draw. He had learned about it from an article he had read online a few weeks ago, about how four new buffalo were introduced into the aging, thinning herd.

Camden shimmied down the tree and hurried over to the bloodied men whose bodies rested at odd angles. Neither held their gun, and he began searching the dewy ground to retrieve the weapons. He could only find one and now rushed back to the men to see if they were alive. One was certainly dead, his head crushed against a large boulder next to the tree. Blood oozed from an ear and he didn't make a noise. The other did not have any visible wounds, but he wasn't conscious and he labored to breathe.

Camden searched them both, but neither had wallets or any identification. The only item he found was a cell phone that belonged to the man who was still alive. He pocketed it and went toward the fence, all the while being mindful of the buffalo. Hearing the galloping of hooves, Camden ran toward the low wooden fence and jumped over it.

The four aggressive buffalo slowed as they reached the fence. They smelled like cows, but the stench was more powerful. One snorted, the spray landing on Camden's scraped face, and then the herd clopped away.

Lying on his stomach, Camden called Veronica. They spoke in whispers.

"We're looking for you," she began.

"You're not going to believe what just happened."

"Where are you?"

"With the buffalo. Are you guys all right?" Camden asked.

"We're okay," she answered. "We're hiding, but we're okay."

"They followed me. One's dead, the other isn't doing so well. I don't know if there's more. Probably, so we have to be careful."

"You killed one?" Veronica asked.

"The buffalo did. I don't have the bike anymore."

"Just get out of the park. We're fine. We'll get out and find a place to meet."

"I'm not going to leave you guys in here. And I have a gun now."

"Okay. If you keep going past the Buffalo Paddock you'll eventually come to a road, I think it's 42nd. There's a lake there. We'll meet you."

"Be careful."

Camden climbed back over the chain link fence and moved as fast as he could down the dirt trail. He came to a bluff overlooking the paved road and hid behind a tree, noticing how the moonlight reflected in the lake below. He hadn't held a gun in years, and it was heavier than expected. He heard the whoosh of air through tire spokes and saw Veronica and Hipple cruising on the bike.

They were racing down the walking path next to the lake, which seemed more like a lagoon surrounded by trees and shrubbery. Camden then heard tires screeching and a car engine accelerating. Headlights beamed down the main road below him.

Shots erupted from the speeding black Cadillac, and Veronica and Hipple went flying off their bicycle.

Camden raised the gun and squeezed the trigger as fast as he could. Several bullets hit the car, shattering the side and back windows. The vehicle continued down the road, careened left, and sped toward the ocean.

Camden skidded down the hill and found Veronica sitting up in a patch of bushes, her face scraped and cut. Dirt caked to her sweaty forehead. He helped her to her feet, noticing there was blood on her hair and face.

"Are you shot?" Camden asked.

"No. I'm okay," she answered, trembling. "Where's Hipple?"

They found Hipple facedown in shrubbery next to the water. In the moonlight it was easy to see he had been shot and was no longer breathing.

19

A Drink Around the Fire

CAMDEN STOOD CLOSE to Veronica under a tree on the corner of Cabrillo and 43rd, just one block down from the park. He had tried to talk to her, but she just shook her head. He had seen murder victims when he had the police beat in Boston, but he figured it was a first for Veronica. However, he had never known any of the dead people he reported on, and he was sure that his face, one of disgust and fear, matched hers. And no matter how many times he had covered a homicide, it was always unnerving.

It was best not to think about what just happened and instead focus on their survival. They both listened intently for cars or footsteps as the cold wind blew against their backs and ruffled the leaves above them. Just minutes earlier, Camden had called Sal, and the Unsuccessful Men's Club member said he would leave immediately to pick them up.

Sal's 1993 Honda Civic Hatchback pulled up to the curb, and they both rushed inside and sat in the back seat together.

"What am I, a cabbie?" he asked. He was dressed in ripped cargo shorts and wore a sweater with a unicorn on it.

"I'll explain what happened later, if I even can," Camden said. "Right now we're both pretty goddamned freaked out. Thanks so much for coming to get us, Sal."

"Roger that," Sal said. "I have some Japanese whiskey that I bought the other day. Should help. So should Lou Reed."

Sal popped an old cassette tape into the player, and Reed's "Street Hassle" began to play. The three of them drove without speaking to the apartment in the Upper Haight neighborhood shared by the other members. As he climbed out of the car, Camden noticed that some of Harry Hipple's blood had leaked from Veronica's hair to form tiny droplets on the tan faux-leather upholstery.

An hour later, Camden sat on a faded leather couch next to Dickie and Rubbish, who were both dressed in plaid pajamas. Sal was on his laptop at his desk, searching for any information that might help Camden's cause. They were all drinking beers as the fireplace in the old Victorian house crackled. Veronica had been in the shower for more than thirty minutes. Camden knew he needed the Unsuccessful Men's Club's help and decided to recount every detail of the evening.

"Fucking buffalo!" Dickie said for probably the fifth time.

"I saw some in Yellowstone once charge at a car and dent the fucker. Big sons of bitches," Sal said.

"What a way to go," Rubbish offered.

"They would have killed me," Camden said.

"You're a lucky bastard," Dickie said. "That poor dude Hipple sure isn't."

Camden finished his beer and grabbed the bottle of Japanese whiskey off an old scratched and worn travel trunk that served as the coffee table. It was called Fuji-Sanroku, and there was a drawing of the eponymous mountain on the label. He drank straight from the bottle, not once wincing, and noticed the antique piece of luggage. It seemed to be made of honey-colored pine, had double locks, and in between the tattered canvas bands were the "D C" initials of the long ago previous owner.

"Pretty damn good whiskey, huh?" Sal said.

"Veronica has been in that shower an awfully long time," Rubbish said.

"She's gotta be completely freaked out," Dickie responded.

"What about you, Camden?" Sal asked.

"It's a combination of sickness, excitement, anger, elation, and bone-chilling fear. I never liked the guy, but I feel awful that he got killed. We should have saved him. We almost got Hipple out of the park alive. We were so fucking close."

"But you guys got out. You're safe."

"Yeah, Rubbish, but he's got two more days to get those sculptures," Dickie said, "or he's gonna end up like that Hipple guy."

"Maybe he doesn't even have two days now," Sal said. "Sorry, Camden, but don't you think you've pissed them off? Two of their guys are dead, and maybe two more. You pushed one over a waterfall."

"He slipped. But you're probably right," Camden said.

"Oh, great," Dickie said. "Could they track you down here? Are they going to be shooting at us?"

"I don't think so," Camden answered. "These guys are pros. They said they had to kill Hipple because they thought he would go to the police. He was a liability. If they really wanted to kill Veronica they probably would have."

"You should go check on her," Sal said.

Camden used the side of the travel trunk to steady himself off the couch and lumbered to the bathroom. He knocked lightly on the door and then opened it a crack, the steam wetting his face. He'd known Veronica for less than a day, but he was starting to fall for her. Smart, brave, and beautiful, she was the kind of woman who made you feel better by just being near her. But he had to be as respectful as possible, and they of course had more pressing things to deal with than romance.

"Just checking to see if you're okay," Camden said.

"Do these guys have any wine?" Veronica asked from inside the shower. "I could really go for a glass of wine."

"Just beer and whiskey."

"Thanks for checking in on me. I'll be out shortly."

Camden hobbled back into the living room and over to the computer. Sal held the gunman's flip phone and was scribbling all the incoming and outgoing numbers onto the back of a ripped envelope. He smiled at Camden with his pockmarked face, showing chipped teeth and a lot of gums.

"I found the private detective you were wondering about," Sal said. "The one they mentioned to you. It's the only thing of interest from the phone numbers on that dude's phone."

"What private detective?" Dickie yelled from the other side of the room.

"Everybody is looking for this Bo McClennan guy, right?" Sal said. "One of the bad guys told Camden he hired a private detective who found McClennan. When I Googled a number I found on the phone, it came up as 'Cronjager & Bryan Detective Agency.' They have an office near Broadway and Kearny. It has to be the detective he was talking about."

"Thanks, Sal. Can you write down their address and phone number for me?"

"Already done."

* * *

Veronica, wearing a baggy sweatshirt with a chicken on it and checkered pajama pants, stepped into the living room on bare feet. She sat on the black, thickly cushioned reclining chair next to the fireplace and was grateful Camden brought her a shot of whiskey and a glass of beer. She drank a good amount of beer and then downed half the shot while holding her nose. She finished the rest of the beer in three long gulps, her sweatshirt the recipient of several ounces of the brown liquid.

"Thanks for letting me borrow some clothes," Veronica said. "And for picking us up and for letting us stay here. I'm very grateful."

"Of course," Sal replied. "Any friend of Camden's is a friend of ours. Let me get you another beer."

"Do you think the cops are in the park now?" Veronica asked as she took a fresh bottle from Sal.

"When we first got there, I thought that Clinkenbeard might have tailed us," Camden said. "But there definitely weren't any cops."

"Gotta be there by now," Dickie said.

"Maybe," Camden answered. "But they were shooting with silencers. A bike crash isn't going to draw much attention, neither does screeching tires. Depends if there were witnesses."

"Sooner or later, somebody is going to find the bodies," Sal said.

"Camden, could you be charged with murder?" Dickie asked.

"How?" Sal answered for him. "Self-defense."

"I wanted to board him," Camden said. "Like in my hockey days, when you check somebody into the boards to make them go down."

"But he went over the railing," Veronica said. "That sound on the rocks was sickening."

She hoped some day she would forget that sound. She wanted to erase everything that had just happened from her brain, scrub it clean like that Jim Carrey and Kate Winslet movie. Veronica felt like throwing up but managed to hold back the bile.

"I've never been shot at before," Camden said. "Those bullets didn't miss by much."

"Do you still have the gun?" Rubbish asked. "Can we see it?"

"When we came in and I took off my shoes, I put it in one of them. I'd recommend leaving it there."

Sal stood up and after yawning ostentatiously said, "I'm going to find out as much as I can about those Matisse sculptures tomorrow. But I can barely keep my eyes open. We were all up late last night watching the whole first season of *Twin Peaks*."

"There's some extra pillows and blankets in the closet," Dickie offered.

After the three members of the Unsuccessful Men's Club said their good-nights, Camden took two more beers from the fridge. Veronica sat cross-legged by the fireplace and he kneeled next to her after he set the bottles on the oval, multi-braided rug. She watched him grab the Japanese whiskey, put it up to his lips, and close his eyes with a look a relief.

She wanted that same reprieve from what was replaying in her brain and snatched the bottle from his hands. It burned a bit going down, but she liked the numb feeling that was spreading throughout her body. On the next sip of whiskey, she savored the earthy, smoky taste and tried her best to keep Hipple's image out of her head.

"Are you okay?" Camden asked. "If I were on that bike, I don't know if I would be."

"The blood was pretty awful, everything was pretty god-awful. I don't want to talk about it," she said and grabbed a beer from the rug and took a sip.

She wiped away the tears that ran down her cheek and leaned closer to Camden to put her head on his shoulder. The burning logs crackled and hissed, and she watched the murky blue flames dance in the fireplace. Veronica guzzled half the beer, the coldness of the ale stark against the warmth from the hearth.

"Hipple was so terrified," she said. "We were hiding and I kept shushing him. But he just kept talking, kept saying he saw his boss get shot. He kept repeating how they moved the gun back and forth and he could have been the one who was killed. He just wanted to live. Shit, why am I talking about this?"

"I'm sorry, Veronica."

"You warned me. You told me our lives were in danger. The sound was so awful when he got shot. So much worse than the guy hitting the rocks."

"I'm sorry."

"Stop saying that."

"Tomorrow you leave. Like I said before, you take the money the Tall Woman gave you and go to Europe or," he picked up the bottle of whiskey and continued, "Japan. I've always wanted to see Mount Fuji. Shit, maybe both of us should go."

"I'm not going to do that. And you can't leave, either, Camden. We can't go on the run for the rest of our lives."

"Veronica, this is a blip in your twenty-four years. You will become a great investigative journalist and you can do it somewhere else. There will be more adventures for you. I admire you and you're brave as shit, but staying here is just plain stupid."

"I'm not going anywhere. We're going to find McClennan and the sculptures and help get the clients and the Tall Woman arrested and held responsible for Hipple's and Larry's murders."

While part of her wished she would play it safe and go into hiding, she was hit with a rush of relief that Camden was going to be her partner. After what happened, she could trust him. Finding the sculptures would be a near impossible task, but she believed together as a team they could do it. Camden said the guy who got killed by the buffalo claimed their private detective had found McClennan. They now knew the agency's name, and the two of them would need to formulate a plan.

"Could the clients find us here?"

"Oh, fuck," Camden said and walked over to Sal's desk. The gunman's cell phone was next to the laptop. He turned it off.

"You think there's a tracking device in there?"

"I don't know if that's just movie stuff. I think they probably can."

"Shutting it off won't do any good. It's too late."

She watched Camden crouch next to the window and peep down onto Parnassus. "See anybody?" she asked.

Camden shook his head no.

"I'm not a thrill seeker," Veronica said after he turned from the window and faced her. "I have no interest in skydiving or bungee jumping or, hell, even getting a tattoo. But you know it wouldn't be right for either of us to leave. Jesus, I hope I'm right."

Camden took a long drink from the whiskey bottle then said, "I agree. But that means we have to figure it out. Gotta think it through. What do we know so far?"

They both returned to the floor in front of the fireplace. Veronica grabbed the metal fire poker and used it to rearrange some logs to keep the flame burning. She then tapped it absently on the bricks and looked pensive. She took a few sips of beer before she spoke.

"The Matisse sculptures were stolen, but we don't know for sure who did it. The cops, the clients, and the Tall Woman all figure Bo McClennan for it. And he worked under an alias at the museum."

"It had to be McClennan. But I don't understand why," Camden said. "The guy was released from prison and immediately flew across the country to get involved in another art heist? Hard to believe."

"Could someone he met in jail be forcing him? Maybe the mob?"

"I knew the guy," Camden said. "I just don't see him associating with mobsters. Of course, he could have got mixed up with them in prison, but he stole those paintings in Boston on a bet. Or so he says."

"Somebody in jail made another bet with him?" she suggested.

"That's what I'm thinking as well. But Frankie in cell block C who's in for boosting cars isn't going to have the kind of dough to dangle in front of McClennan for such a bet."

"Does it have to be a bet? And does it have to be somebody in jail? Another person wanted those Matisse sculptures and figured McClennan was the guy to get them?"

"Possibly. Could have been offered enough money to allow him to hide away forever."

"From whom, then, if that's what happened?"

"Miles Krakow," Camden suggested.

"I've read about him," Veronica said. "What kind of a sick person destroys art treasures and then videotapes it?"

"That nutjob is one of my ex-girlfriend's pals," Camden said. "He's filthy rich and nobody will sell him any more pieces of art."

"So tomorrow we find the private detective who hopefully gets us to McClennan. But we also talk with Miles."

"What about the Tall Woman? What if she hired McClennan to steal the sculptures and double-cross her clients?"

"When we were hiding in the bushes, Hipple kept talking about bringing a bag into the hotel and putting it in a locker, and then he was supposed to get it out right before the robbery so the clients could use it. I gave the Tall Woman the combo to the locker."

"Why was the bag still there?"

"Like you said, she could have paid McClennan to steal the sculptures and everything else was just smoke and mirrors."

"Or maybe the clients did and it's all a cover? A double-cross-type deal on their side."

"Does that make sense?" Veronica asked.

"The Tall Woman had the buyers lined up. It's very possible the clients could have found somebody else and were going to screw her out of her cut. I said as much to her, but she didn't think it was possible."

"Why?"

"'Cause she worked with them before. Honor among thieves. That they were pros, and pros wouldn't go through all that trouble to screw over a trusted partner. Maybe she was saying that because she's guilty of doing it."

"We can speculate the shit out of everything, but I guess we gotta focus on McClennan," Veronica said. "The one thing we do know is that the clients are desperate to find him, even going so far as to hire a private detective."

"And tomorrow that's where we begin. Cronjager & Bryan Detective Agency. Since I don't think they're just going to lead us to McClennan by asking nicely, let's each come up with some plans and compare in the morning."

Camden gazed into Veronica's hazel eyes that were blood-shot from the exhaustion and alcohol. She smiled and angled her head onto his left shoulder. It was the happiest Camden had been since he left Boston.

Within seconds she was breathing deeply, her eyes closed and her body limp. Camden gently scooped her up, carried her to the couch, and covered her with the thick, handmade quilt

Dickie had left on the floor. Camden popped open another beer and went back to the window, the streetlights revealing only asphalt, parked cars, a fluffy cat, and the vaporous, drifting fog.

20

Camden's Got a Gun

THE NEXT MORNING, Detective Clinkenbeard craned his head upward from the base of the waterfall on Strawberry Hill. When he was a teenager, he had spent a whole afternoon there lying against a tree with his girlfriend, smoking marijuana, studying the clouds, and talking about changing the world. The smell of the water on the rocks transported him to that time and place.

Now, decades later, Clinkenbeard turned his attention down to a dead man wearing a dark track suit, whose face had been smooshed by the slate rock at the bottom of Strawberry Hill. He was the second corpse found in the park that morning. The other was Harry Hipple, a museum gallery attendant at the Matisse Hotel who lost part of his brain about nine feet from where his body lay. Clinkenbeard didn't know the identity of the man at the waterfall yet because nothing was found in his pockets and he was waiting for the prints to come back.

Hipple had been murdered, a fact easy to discern from the giant bullet hole in his head. But the guy here could have been out for a late-night jog and somehow slipped. That theory was doubtful, but Clinkenbeard would only rule it out until proven otherwise.

There was also the matter of the gun found on the wooden footbridge above. Would a jogger arm himself for a midnight run? Possible, but again, all rational thought would conclude otherwise. With a nonjudgmental mind, he studied the broken and splintered wood on the railing of the bridge.

The footprints in the dirt revealed little. Strawberry Hill was a popular destination for joggers, bikers, Segway enthusiasts, and families out for a stroll. However, Clinkenbeard had ordered pictures taken of the dirt paths and stairs surrounding the crime scene, because at some point random facts congeal into evidence.

Earlier that morning he had visited the other murder scene in Golden Gate Park. Harry Hipple had been shot to death on the banks of North Lake, and that crime scene had yielded some clues. There were fresh bicycle wheel tracks next to the body. Was Hipple riding a bike when he was shot or had some random person wiped out while pedaling earlier? The former was more likely, as the position of the body indicated it had been thrown to the ground, but the bike was nowhere to be found.

"Detective," a uniformed officer said. "We just finished interviewing a resident on Fulton. Saw a brand-new black Cadillac screeching out of the park last night. Was out walking her dog. Then she saw a man and a woman run down 43rd Street toward Cabrillo. Was too dark for her to make out faces, but she seemed to think they were in their twenties or thirties."

* * *

Veronica heard male voices and then that of a woman speaking clearly and authoritatively. She had just woken from a dream where she was being chased by a herd of buffalo, each of them ridden by their own Harry Hipple. In unison, each of the Hipples were screaming, "You could have saved me."

She opened her eyes and realized she was in the worn-down Victorian House in the Haight, and the first thing she saw was Rubbish staring at the TV with his hand down his pants. She was still sleepy and closed her eyes.

"Darya is so hot," she heard Rubbish say. "She seems so cool and just super smart. If I could have brunch with any celebrity, I would choose her. No fooling."

"When Darya wears those tight shirts . . . my goodness," Dickie said. "Cougar with a capital C. And I say that with complete respect; she's foremost a top-notch reporter."

"Agreed. She sure knows her stuff," Sal said. "I'll take our peeps on channel four over any of the affiliates."

"C'mon," Dickie said. "As much as I'd like to, we can't keep watching the news report about the robbery. Plus, we know more than they do about what happened in the park last night. Boyos, we gotta get the shop open."

Veronica wanted the guys to shut up because her head was throbbing. She again opened her eyes and realized she was lying next to Camden on the couch, covered by a thick brown afghan. Sal walked toward them with heavy steps, and she was now fully awake. She opened her eyes and shot up from the couch.

"What time is it?" she asked.

"A few minutes past eight," Sal answered.

"I have to call in sick," she said and got to her feet and grabbed her cell phone. Camden grunted but did not wake up.

When Veronica spoke with Carmine, she apologized that she would miss the job fair. She said, in a grave tone, there was an emergency she had to attend to. She thought it was cryptic enough to imply seriousness but bereft of any details as to discourage follow-up questions.

"That detective called and wanted to speak with you," Carmine said. "I'm not sure if you've seen the news, but Harry Hipple was killed in Golden Gate Park. They're pretty sure both him and Larry Aberlour were in on the robbery. The detective said to inform him of every person in the hotel who called in sick or otherwise did not show up for work. I know there's no way you're involved, Veronica, but I have to tell him you're not coming in."

"It's okay, Carmine. It's a family emergency. My grandfather is sick."

While she was on the phone Veronica rubbed her temples and watched Rubbish take pieces of food out of a box and throw them at Camden. They were Cap'n Crunch's Crunch Berries. He did not stir until one of the tiny colored balls hit him in the eye. When she walked back into the room and sat down on the edge of the couch next to Camden, Rubbish stopped his cereal assault.

"What if you get to the private dick, who then gets you to McClennan, and he ain't got the statues?" Rubbish asked.

"Sculptures, you moron," Dickie corrected.

"I don't think he wants to think about that scenario," Sal said.

Veronica could tell Camden still needed more time to wake up, and she laughed when Rubbish gave Dickie the finger, after pantomiming sticking the same middle digit in his butt. Dickie returned the gesture. She jostled Camden after she saw him close his eyes.

"I was thinking about how we go about approaching those private detectives. Show up at their office and follow them? Or I can call and say we want to hire them for a case?"

"Both good ideas," Camden said in a gravelly voice. "But we have the gunman's cell phone and we know he had called the private detective's number."

"You could impersonate the client, get the detective to tell you the info."

"Genius. I say we go with that."

"We'd like to help but we got a business to run," Dickie said. "Make sure you lock the door."

"So you know," Sal said. "None of the news reports said anything about the buffalo. They only had two deaths in Golden Gate Park—Hipple and the guy who fell off the rocks."

"The clients must have grabbed the guys in the Buffalo Paddock after they shot Hipple," Camden said. "One was dead for sure, the other was in bad shape."

Rubbish flashed the peace sign and three members of the Unsuccessful Men's Club exited the room, the heavy wooden door slamming shut.

* * *

Camden got slowly off the couch and lumbered over to Sal's desk. He picked up the gunman's cell phone, turned it on, and it vibrated in his hands. When he flipped it open, a red light blinked in the corner, and he began pressing buttons on the phone like it was his own.

"Doing my best to get the voicemail," he said. "This is just like the first cell I ever owned. Shit, it's asking for a password."

"Let's just call the detective agency," Veronica said. "Sal said he wrote the number down, should be on the desk."

He found it, dialed, and held his phone out so she could hear the conversation.

"Hello?" a man answered in a bad-tempered voice.

"It's me," Camden said in a nonchalant voice.

"Me, who?"

"I'm sure you're looking at your fucking caller ID now and you can tell who it is. And don't even try to say it's coming up as blocked or unavailable, because if you don't have a device to counteract that, then I've been wasting my fucking time."

"What do you want now?" the man asked wearily. "I already spoke to your boss. The meeting is all set. And I don't understand why you can't come into the office. The Ferry Building at high noon? So goddamned dramatic, don't you think?"

"There might be people following us and we need to keep the information secret. It's for your protection as well as ours."

"Sure, whatever. So what do you want?"

"Well, I was thinking the Ferry Building might not be the best place. But forget it, my boss is probably right. Don't tell him we spoke."

"Yeah, when we're having tea and biscuits afterward, I'll keep it a secret. All I care about right now is getting paid. I'll see you near the ticket booth in a few hours. Finding that guy wasn't easy."

Before Camden could put the phone down, it rang again and he answered.

"Are you coming outside soon?" the Tall Woman asked. "I watched your friends leave the apartment. I've been parked in front of a fire hydrant all morning and a cop is bound to ask me to move."

"Fuck. Tracking device on the phone."

"You're lucky you and your friends are alive," the Tall Woman said. "It took a lot of convincing on my part."

"Are you with your clients outside?" Camden asked.

"No, I'm alone. I'll see you downstairs in a few minutes. It's the gray Prius one block down behind the tree. If you needed the reminder, I have my gun with me."

"I have a gun as well," Camden responded. "See you soon."
He pocketed the phone and said to Veronica, "Our long legged
friend is outside waiting for us. Just her, no clients."

"We have more than three hours to get to the Ferry
Building," she said. "But we have to ditch the Tall Woman. We
have to be careful with her."

"That's what the gun is for."

"She is the enemy."

"Agreed."

A few minutes later, Camden and Veronica exited the
Victorian house and walked one block down Webster Street
wearing the same clothes they had on the night before. The
Tall Woman, donned in jeans and a hooded gray fleece, stood
next to a Prius. She wore designer sunglasses even though fog
engulfed the area. After lifting up the fleece a few inches to
show a pistol handle against a flat stomach, the Tall Woman
pointed at Veronica and waved her to the driver's-side window.

Veronica squinted at her and said, "I'm not a dog you can
beckon." She paused a few seconds for a reaction and, after
getting none, entered the vehicle and got behind the wheel.
Camden took the back seat and the Tall Woman slid into the
passenger side with the gun in her hand.

"Drive," she said to Veronica.

"Where?"

"I don't fucking care. Just drive."

"Go to hell," she replied.

"Now, ladies," Camden said, "let's play nice."

The Tall Woman pointed the gun at Veronica's head. "The
time for being nice is over. If I tell you to do something, you
do it."

"After what happened last night," she said, "you can't scare
me. You kill us, you've got nothing to show for it."

Camden began slowly moving his hand toward the gun that was tucked into his pants. His heart sped up. He tried to remain calm and was thinking whether he could pull the trigger if the Tall Woman did.

"You might be an excellent shot," he said. "You might be able to kill us both before I pull this gun out. But it doesn't make sense. If you wanted to kill us, you wouldn't have called and said you were here."

"I'd lay odds," the Tall Woman responded, "you'd blow your balls off trying to get that thing out of your pants. But you're right, it doesn't make sense. Please drive, Miss Zarcarsky."

Veronica sighed when the Tall Woman lowered her weapon. She started the Prius and drove noiselessly down the hill on Webster, passing multimillion-dollar Victorians and several people walking their dogs.

"I'm impressed. Nice job recruiting her on McClennan's team," she said.

"We don't know anything about McClennan," Veronica snapped. "There is no team."

The Tall Woman ignored her and faced Camden. "You both could be dead now. You killed two of my clients; the other is lucky he walked away from the buffalo with just a bruised face and a concussion."

"The guy at the waterfall was self-defense," Camden said. "And technically he slipped and fell over the waterfall on his own. The others were hit by the buffalo. While it would be nice, I don't possess Doctor Doolittle powers, and the bison were acting on their own accord."

"They followed you into the Buffalo Paddock. You are responsible."

"That wasn't on the news. No mention of the buffalo, no bodies found there. I'm guessing you guys got them."

"We did, and cleaned up the scene as best we could to keep our affairs quiet. Unfortunately, we did not know Client B had died falling on the rocks. We tried to get Hipple, but only succeeded in taking the bike. Was the first thing they saw, so they grabbed it. While looking for his body the sirens got too close."

They had almost come to the end of the street, and Veronica turned right onto Hermann toward Duboce Park.

"If it weren't for that buffalo, I'd be like Hipple," Camden said.

"They had orders not to kill you."

"Your clients don't listen for shit. They said they didn't need me anymore because the private detective found McClennan."

Driving up Duboce with the green expanse of the park on their right, a Muni train passed them in the other direction. A space opened on the hill and Veronica pulled over and parked. The Tall Woman glared at her.

"We're leaving," Veronica said.

"Excuse me?"

"Camden, it sounds like they're close to getting McClennan. Once they do, why do they need us?" She turned to the Tall Woman and said, "Maybe your job today is to keep us occupied until they have McClennan, and then you'll turn us over so the clients can murder us like Hipple. Why should we stay with you? You have a gun, Camden has a gun. There are hundreds of people around us now. Your affairs would not be too quiet if you went guns ablazing on us."

Camden smiled when he saw the Tall Woman's face turn red but recoiled when he saw the gun thrust against Veronica's neck. He immediately raised his weapon. The Tall Woman noticed this, but she did not speak.

"We're going to find those sculptures," Veronica continued. "Isn't that what you and your clients want? We can't do that in your car."

Camden watched Veronica slowly exit the vehicle but kept one eye on the Tall Woman's hands the whole time. He studied the gun for any movement, and then caught a glimpse of her bemused grin. Camden kept his weapon pointed at the Tall Woman. The driver's-side window was open, and Veronica spoke into it from three feet away.

"What happens next?" she asked.

The grin left the Tall Woman's face and she went rigid, exposing a hint of crow's feet around her eyes and a few more forehead wrinkles than he had noticed before. She did not say a word. Veronica could no longer see her gun.

"What happens is the gun goes back down my pants and we're leaving," Camden said.

"Go ahead," she said to them. "I'll find you again, or else one of my clients will. Or we'll find somebody you care about and give you a choice on whether you value their life."

Camden exited the vehicle without shutting the door and walked with Veronica quickly down Duboce toward the Muni stop. Neither of them turned around. There was a group of people waiting to board the train and she was sure they blended in with them.

"Everything about her disgusts me," she said. "And you're attracted to her. I can tell. You practically drool at her like a puppy."

"I don't exactly drool," Camden said.

"For some reason that really pisses me off."

21

Watching the Detectives

JEAN FRANCOIS LÉVEQUE arrived at David Bouchon's Sea Cliff estate at nine in the morning. The white neoclassical-style home with views of the Golden Gate Bridge sparkled when the glint of the sun hit its eastern side, but today there was only fog. He didn't pay attention to the weather or the architecture and only had deep suspicions of Georgia's breakfast invitation. When his daughter greeted him at the ten-foot-high double doors, he soon lost his appetite.

Georgia and Bouchon were dating.

He could not get the notion to settle inside his brain, and the news swirled around there like dirt in a glass filled with water. Bouchon had held Georgia when she was a baby. There was a creepiness factor to that which could not be put into either English or French.

"It was a long time coming," Georgia said. "We've been seeing each other socially for years. He makes me happy."

"It's not a simple affair," Bouchon said. "We are in love."

Mr. Léveque stood there catatonic.

"Daddy, say something."

"*Nom de Dieu*," he finally uttered.

"Jean Francois, you should be happy your daughter is with an equal. Somebody who values her as an artist and a woman."

"I should be happy? *Vous êtes fou?* We have known each other for a long time. Over the years you've made several business deals that put you in direct competition to me. Those were fine. I can accept that. You did what was necessary to help your business. But this I consider a personal attack."

"You're being unreasonable," Georgia said. "It's not an attack."

"Jean Francois, we have not seen eye to eye through the years, but I have always held you with the utmost respect. And we are fellow countrymen who have much in common. Our business rivalry has settled down as we've gotten older. And I thought when you stopped bidding for the Matisse sculptures it was a sign of goodwill toward me. A sign that we could put our differences in the past."

"I need a cognac," Léveque said.

Bouchon had one of his servants bring in a bottle of Frapin Cuvee 1888 and three snifters. He loved the design of the bottle, which he believed resembled an amber pawn chess piece, almost as much as the taste. Only two glasses were poured because Georgia did not want any of the seven-thousand-dollar booze. At a few minutes past nine in the morning, she said she was happy with a cup of coffee.

"A nice salve to the situation," he said after taking a sip. "But I apologize for my reaction, Georgia. I may not like it, but you're an adult and should do as you wish."

"But that's not how I want it to be," Georgia said. "I want you to be okay."

"I don't know if I can be okay. I need it to settle in my stomach. Maybe some food will help me digest it."

The three of them went to the dining room and were served breakfast by a uniformed staff of five. As they ate their omelets and drank their cafés au lait, Léveque did his best to listen to Georgia and Bouchon explain their relationship. He respected his daughter and wanted her to be happy. But he eventually changed the subject to politics in France, to art that was coming up for auction, or to places he had taken Georgia on vacations when she was young. When they both again started to justify why they were together, he finally found a topic to end the romantic discussion.

"Any news on the robbery?"

Bouchon slammed his fist on the table, knocking over a silver serving tray of caviar. Three of the servants rushed over to tend to the mess as Georgia put her hand on his shoulder.

"I think it was that scum of the earth, Miles Krakow," Léveque said.

"You think so as well, honey," Bouchon said.

Léveque winced on the word *honey*.

"I don't know," Georgia answered. "Right after I saw it on the news, I went to his house. Miles denied it, but he was out of his mind on drugs. It didn't seem like he was trying to hide anything, but how could you put it past him?"

"Must have paid somebody to do it, then," Léveque said. "Such a *branleur* could outwit an entire museum security system."

"Acquiring those sculptures and building a hotel and museum for them were my legacy. Now they are gone. Just like that," he said and snapped his fingers.

"Hopefully they'll be recovered, David," Georgia said.

"With each day they are gone, the odds keep plummeting," he said.

"I believe that McClennan character helped Krakow," Bouchon said. "I have people scouring the Bay Area for him. I will get the sculptures back."

"Possibly it was McClennan," Léveque said. "But I heard he was just released from prison. You'd think he'd be scared of going back."

"You cannot assess logic to a thief," Bouchon said. "And I have to wonder if Mr. Swanson helped him."

"I talked with Camden yesterday," Georgia said, "and he said he hadn't seen McClennan since his Boston days. I would have known, and I don't think he's that good a liar."

"Are you sure?" Bouchon asked.

"With Camden you never know. *Sure* might be too strong a word."

"I've gotten to know Camden," Léveque said, "and squirrel watching is much more his speed."

* * *

Detective Clinkenbeard sat in his brightly lit office, sipped his wife's homemade kombucha tea, and flipped through the printouts of Harry Hipple's phone records. He had already investigated the incoming and outgoing calls of Larry Aberlour, the director of security for the Matisse Hotel, but nothing peculiar materialized. By the time he had finished two cups of kombucha and had a slight buzz from the caffeine and fermented alcohol, Hipple's phone gave him some clues.

The major point of interest was the connection with Camden Swanson. From late afternoon yesterday up to within an hour or so of the coroner's estimated time of death, several calls were made back and forth between him and Hipple. But after Mr. Swanson left the Beach Chalet yesterday, his whereabouts were unknown.

Clinkenbeard stared absently at his framed red and yellow Jefferson Airplane Fillmore Concert poster and shook his head in disappointment for that mistake. The cruiser never was able to pick up his tail. He had been sure Camden would go back to his apartment and gather his belongings, but neither he nor Georgia had gone in or out of their residence in San Carlos all night.

There was no doubt of Mr. Swanson's involvement in the robbery now, but Clinkenbeard was unsure of the particulars. Regardless of whether his role was major or minor, there was enough suspicion to detain him for questioning. Except it was better to find him and watch from a close distance. The Matisse robbery trail had turned cold, and Camden Swanson was the smoldering ember that might set off the fire of arrests.

But where was he? Swanson's picture, obtained through the personnel files at the Matisse hotel, was included in the APB given to every member of the San Francisco Police Department. The orders were to find the suspect and to contact Detective Clinkenbeard immediately before taking any action.

* * *

Camden and Veronica arrived at the Ferry Building almost two hours before the clients were to meet the private detective. They ate breakfast at Boulettes Larder, sitting at an outside table even though the fog shrouded most of the bay. Camden sipped his coffee, inhaled the salt air, and hoped he wouldn't have to use the gun he possessed.

"Do you think the Tall Woman is going to be with the clients?"

"Doubtful. I kept an eye out on the Muni but I didn't see her get on."

"Agreed. But I'm sure she knows that the clients are meeting the detective here."

Camden felt his phone vibrating in his pocket.

"Bonjour, Camden," Mr. Léveque said after he answered. "I just had breakfast with Georgia and David Bouchon."

"She upgraded well for herself," Camden said. "Like going from an '84 Buick to a brand-new Bentley. Or rather a 1940s Bentley."

"I know your humor is a mask. I need a bit of it now myself. Of all people, David Bouchon. Life always finds a new way of twisting the knife into your gut."

"I'd really like to talk to you, Mr. L, but I'm a little busy right now."

"One café au lait. I need to vent to somebody who can vent right with me."

"How about later on today?" Camden asked.

"It would mean a lot if you could spend a few minutes with me now. I'm in a car, outside of Union Square. Where are you?"

"Can't do it, Jean Francois. I have an important meeting I have to attend."

"Bullshit. Fifteen minutes."

"Well . . . I'm close to Embarcadero Plaza. Do you know where the cinemas are? I think there's a coffee shop right below there."

"Camden, my construction company helped build the place."

"My meeting is at eleven thirty, so I won't have long."

"I'll see you there in fifteen minutes," Mr. Léveque said.

Veronica's eyes narrowed and she opened her mouth, but then took a sip of her coffee and looked out into the foggy bay.

"My ex-girlfriend's father," Camden said to her.

"And you're going to talk to him now?"

"There's plenty of time before the clients show up. It'll be quick."

"I don't understand why you have to meet with your ex-girlfriend's father."

"He knows the owner of the Matisse Hotel and he might be able to help us. He might even have info on the robbery."

"Just hurry up and get back."

* * *

Camden walked over to the coffee shop, ordered two cafés au lait from the counter girl who radiated boredom, and took a seat by the window. As much as he admired Mr. Léveque and enjoyed his company, he did not want to talk about Georgia. While the cheating and the breakup were lower on his list of concerns than gun-toting clients and finding the sculptures, it hurt to think about her. Mostly it pissed him off to realize that his lethargy, drinking, and depression were the reasons he was now single.

Léveque arrived a few minutes later and after perfunctory greetings, neither spoke. Camden took a sip of his drink and then swirled around the foam with his finger.

"Thought I needed to vent," Mr. Léveque finally said. "But the fog of discouragement has filleted my mind."

"Dylan Thomas?"

"One of your poems, you asshole."

Camden laughed and said, "For me, I just want to put Georgia out of my mind. I knew she was going to leave me, but doesn't make it sting any less. And I guess it doesn't matter who she replaced me with. Hurts all the same. *C'est la vie.*"

"Is that true? I remember when I was twenty-three and saving money to start my first business venture. At the time I was working as a bartender in New York. I fell madly in love with a waitress, one of the deepest loves I've ever felt."

Léveque took a sip of his drink and continued, "We were together for three months until one day Lauren left me for a cook. He was a gaunt simpleton whom I considered not worthy to mop the floors she walked. It hurt so much and it left me bewildered how she could have chosen the cook over me. I hated myself for that."

"You would have hated yourself regardless. That's what happens when you break up with somebody you love. Whoever she leaves you for, it sucks all the same."

"We can respectfully disagree. But of course with my daughter it is different. I want her to be in love, but to my rival? A man of my own age?"

"Didn't you stop bidding on the Matisse sculptures because he's your friend?"

"We keep up the appearance of being friends. I stopped bidding on the sculptures for other reasons."

"What reasons?" Camden asked.

"Ancient history. The sculptures are gone." Léveque got up and went to the front of the coffee shop. He returned with two bottles of Evian and said, "Since when do you have important meetings?"

"A potential job offer."

"Doing what?"

"Advertising," Camden said.

Mr. Léveque drank from his water, stared at Camden, and then laughed.

"Realized that was a terrible lie the second it left my lips," Camden said.

"Is it an AA meeting?"

"It is. A church close by."

"Bullshit."

"And I'm usually a pretty good liar," Camden said. "But there are always people you just can't lie to."

"Are you meeting Bo McClennan?"

"That's a curious question to ask."

"Why? It has been on the news that the Matisse was robbed in exactly the same manner as the Cordovan in Boston. The perpetrator of that crime was Bo McClennan, and you were the one to break that story. He was released from prison not too long ago."

"So you've jumped on that bandwagon, too."

Mr. Léveque smiled. "Of course not, Camden. I am asking if you might know where Bo McClennan might be."

"I haven't seen or heard from the guy in nearly a decade. Why do you care so much?"

"For the protection of fine art."

"Then maybe you should check up on Miles Krakow."

"That imbecile. He could be involved as well. But I sincerely hope you are not entwined in this *merde*."

"I could say the same for you."

"I didn't think you believed any of those rumors," Léveque said.

"No, but I'm pointing out the possible connection. You told me you're rivals with Bouchon. You were also in a fierce bidding war with him for the Matisse sculptures until you stopped. Did you stop because you were inevitably going to be outspent by Bouchon?"

"Camden, David could never outbid me. It was his À Venir Fantastique that had the deeper pockets."

"The hotel group?"

"And he had just been appointed CEO. I knew of their plans for the hotel and museum and I realized they would drive the price up too high."

"But you wanted them."

"Henri Matisse is a passion, and these are unique pieces. Truth be told, if the odalisque sculptures hadn't been lost for so long, I doubt they would have been in such demand."

"The prices people pay for art I'll never get. I'm sure Matisse did a ton of sculptures. Why would somebody go to such great lengths to steal a few out of a museum?"

"Do you really have to leave soon? Your phantom meeting?"

"Yes."

"Then we don't have time for an art history lesson."

"And anyway, we came here to talk about Georgia being with a guy your age."

"I don't have the stomach for it anymore," Mr. Léveque said. "Doubt you do, either."

"How long are you in town for?" Camden asked.

"No plans to leave any time soon. I'll be in my suite at the St. Francis. You are welcome to stop by at any time."

Mr. Léveque took a hotel key card holder out of his pocket and slid it over to Camden.

"And I know you do not have a place to live now. My suite is *enormé*."

"Mr. L, I'll be okay. We'll talk soon."

"Yes, we will. And you will take the key. The room number is written on the key holder."

Camden grabbed it and stuffed it into his pocket.

* * *

From a dusty window near the top of the Ferry Building, the Tall Woman trained her binoculars on the ticket booth. She bit into an organic Fuji apple bought at the marketplace below when her cell phone rang. She finished chewing and then answered Client A's call.

"Do you have Swanson and the girl in a safe place?" he asked.

"Regrettably, no."

"Good fucking lord."

"There were unforeseen complications due to your mistake," she said.

"My mistake?"

"They have a gun now. One of your partner's, I presume. Procured when it took you hours to take care of business that should have taken minutes."

"We got the job done," the client said. "One less problem to worry about."

"You made a giant mess in the process. A mess that is known to the whole city of San Francisco. Now we have problems on top of problems on top of problems."

"After we find McClennan it shouldn't matter," Client A said.

"No guarantees we will. Which makes me wonder if Swanson was telling the truth."

"What truth?"

"That you tried to take him out."

"If we wanted to, it would be a done deal."

"Just act like the professional you are," the Tall Woman said.

"I shall ask the same of you."

"Don't worry. I'll find Swanson and the girl. They couldn't have wandered far. Now, is your meeting at the Ferry Building on as planned?"

"We are there now waiting for him. Are you sure they will not intrude?"

"How could they? They are far too concerned with their well-being. I'm tracking them as we speak, and I'll let you know when I find them. You do the same after your meeting."

"Yes, ma'am."

The Tall Woman put her cell phone away, took another bite of her apple, and once again used her binoculars to study the area below. Many people were buying tickets to Sausalito and Tiburon, but no client or private detective had made themselves visible. The clock above her, the one that towered over the Ferry Building that she could not see, would read five minutes to twelve to those outside. Nearly an hour ago, while she was buying her apple, she spotted Camden Swanson shoving a biscuit into his mouth. And now he and his new partner, Veronica, lingered by Sinbad's Restaurant, doing a poor job of looking inconspicuous.

The Tall Woman had stopped trusting the clients after the fiasco in Golden Gate Park. But being lied to about their meeting with the private detective was something she had not suspected. Maybe Swanson was onto something; maybe the clients had stolen the sculptures to make it look like McClennan had. Hell, they could have partnered with the guy. She felt as if she were back in Hollywood.

22

Desperately Seeking McClennan

VERONICA WIPED SWEAT from her brow and tried to ignore the apprehension that had permeated her body. It didn't help that the usual blasé Camden looked tense. She ripped a piece of bread from the sourdough loaf and flung it into the water, where seagulls and pigeons furiously fought over it.

"We're a couple of tourists feeding the birds. And our cover only cost seven dollars," she said.

"Hope the gulls appreciate the locally farmed, organic whole grains."

"So what's the plan?" Veronica asked.

"We follow the clients once they get the information on where McClennan is hiding."

"How do we know who they are?"

"I guess we won't be completely sure, but the private detective is probably going to show up by himself. He'll hand something to the clients, who will be in a group. That's who we follow. We should be able to figure out who they are."

"There's so many people walking around here," Veronica said. "Lots of them buying tickets and standing around talking."

"That's why we need to pay attention," he said.

The white clock tower, which Veronica had told him was designed after a twelfth-century one in Spain, kept advancing its hands while nobody unusual approached the ticket booth. They went from tossing bread into the water to eating it. They both were shifting their gaze from the booth to the clock, which now read twelve forty-five.

"I think we've been had," Camden said.

"Maybe they're running late," Veronica said without enthusiasm.

"I think that son-of-a-bitch detective lied to me. The Tall Woman could have told him that we had the cell phone."

"Should we go?"

"Let's give it a little bit more time," he said. "I doubt it, but they still could show.

Veronica felt doubt sneaking back into her mind, that maybe she had made a poor choice in aligning herself with Camden in an effort to find the sculptures and break the story. She had been shot at and nearly killed the night before, witnessed a murder, and had a gun pointed at her head before breakfast. And then there was her new partner's embarrassing past.

She tossed the remaining pieces of bread into the bay. "I was going to ask yesterday but didn't get a chance. What happened to you? I'm sorry, and you don't have to answer. But I did a little research."

"Monkey-snakes."

"I read about that. But what happened? You were a successful reporter and columnist and then suddenly a hit of acid lands on your Hot Pocket inadvertently?"

"That explanation is what is referred to as a dirty rotten lie."

"What's the truth? I get it if you don't want to talk about it, but at this point, I would really like to know."

"Let me first ask you a question. Why do you want to become a reporter?"

"Because I want to make a difference. Because the country needs an independent press to watch the system for flaws."

"That's a good classroom answer," Camden said. "And I'm sure you believe it. I once did. But what, from a personal level, made you want to become a reporter?"

"What drove me to majoring in journalism at college? You'll probably laugh."

"No, I won't."

"It was a play. I was a little girl visiting my cousins in Boston and I went to a play about Nellie Bly. Do you know who she is?"

"Can't say as I do."

"She was a famous reporter from the nineteenth century. More than a hundred years ago—can you believe that? Hell, women didn't even have a legal right to vote until 1920."

"Seems like I should have heard about this."

"Look it up, Camden. It's all true. After I saw the play, I went to the library and researched. Nellie Bly went undercover in a mental hospital to show how horrible those places were. She even went around the world faster than Jules Verne. This was the 1800s! A huge influence on my life, along with my aunt."

"I bet when you tell that story people ask why you're not a reporter now," he said. "They probably want to know why you're working in a hotel. I won't ask that. It's hard to get a job. Isn't it crazy? For a profession that pays so little there're so many people flocking to it."

"I don't want to get started on that subject."

Veronica watched a man in a puffy black coat, leading four French bulldogs on a leash, buy a ferry ticket. They were each grunting and snarling and it made her smile and think of Sabrina. She was glad that even though certainly stoned, Kutra would make sure her puppy was fed. She would call her landlord soon and make that request.

"I answered your question," she said. "Now you answer mine."

"I might have started out on the Nellie Bly path, but by the time I got to LA, I was writing all fluff."

"You had an audience. You had readers."

"But it didn't mean anything. I wasn't doing real reporting. It was just silly stuff, the equivalent of posting cat videos on YouTube. I could have had my own investigative team if I stayed in Boston, but I sold out."

"You realize I would have killed to have what you had."

"I get that. A lot of people would have, but it was completely wrong for me. And I admit, there was part of me that enjoyed the easy fluff pieces. Which made me feel even guiltier."

"So you decided to drop acid and piss everything away?"

"Already had nose-dived my life long before I saw the monkey-snakes. As my old friend Bradleigh used to say, that was just the natural progression of events. N-P-O-E."

"Did you really see half-monkey, half-snakelike creatures plotting to take over LA?"

"Unfortunately I did."

"Why would you take acid while working?"

"You majored in journalism because of Nellie Bly. I pursued the field because of Hunter S. Thompson."

"Now you're making a little bit of sense."

"What do you know about him?"

"*Fear and Loathing In Las Vegas*, that's it."

"A terrific book. But read *The Great Shark Hunt* or his collected letters. That guy was on the front lines of everything important happening in our country in the sixties and seventies. You'll learn more about America than any history book can teach you."

"So you took acid because your hero did."

"I met this intern named Regina. Red curly hair, tall, and lips that drove me crazy. Extremely well read and very deep. We would talk for hours. Her parents knew Hunter Thompson, or so she claimed. Regina also said if I ever wanted to be like my idol, I had to experiment with drugs like him. And she also wanted to screw me after we dropped acid."

"You blame an intern."

"I blame only myself."

"Regina was your girlfriend?" she asked.

"We had a three-day romance that ended after I dropped acid with her. I had a bad trip with those monkey-snakes. She wouldn't return any of my calls after I got fired."

"I'm sorry that happened to you, but like you said, you can only blame yourself."

"Yup, I take 100 percent blame. And we've 100 percent been had," Camden said. "They ain't showing up."

"But we can make a visit to Cronjager & Bryan Detective Agency."

* * *

Lars Cronjager slapped a manila file folder into the hands of the person he only knew as Abel, which naturally was not the man's real name. Abel's associate was called Cain, which was clearly spurious also. Cronjager, a former police officer with puffy red cheeks and thinning gray hair, thought the two looked like they belonged in some nerdy rock band. Each were of average height, thin, had goatees, and dressed in black suits that accentuated their gauntness. But Cronjager wasn't interested in what the men did or their proper identities. He only cared about the shiny metal briefcase full of cash on the musty bed.

The meeting was never supposed to take place at the Ferry Building. The spot all along had been a wino hotel on Eddy Street. Rates had been available by the hour, but for discretionary purposes they had paid for the whole night.

Abel inspected the folder and said, "You're sure Bo McClennan is hiding here."

"Look at the pictures," Cronjager answered, lifting his Hawaiian shirt up a few inches to scratch an itch on his belly. "You see him going in and out of the building in West Portal multiple times. It's where he's living."

Abel studied each photograph and wondered aloud, "He's always alone."

"We never saw anybody else go into the building."

"And he never carries a bag or anything else that could hide objects of art?"

As Cronjager counted the money in the briefcase he spied a cockroach moving across the bed. He let it make the journey across the tattered linen before answering. "Nope. Always alone, and only carrying the clothes on his back."

"You tailed him, right?"

"To restaurants, bars, and to a house I personally know to be a high-stakes poker club. Oh yeah, he once went to a movie. A romantic comedy, I believe."

"How do you know about the poker club?" Cain asked.

"Case we did about six months ago," Cronjager answered. "Wife thought her husband was cheating. Guy disappears for hours on end and was bleeding their bank account. She thought he had a girlfriend and was buying her expensive presents.

Bastard was blowing his paycheck at a poker club. And a rather large paycheck it was. Bigwig at Google."

"Pictures of people he met at the bars and restaurants?" Cain asked.

"None. Like I told you. I never once saw McClennan meet or talk with anybody other than waiters and bartenders. Never even used his cell phone out in public. Had a long-range mic to pick up anything he said. Fucker was quieter than a mime. He would read the paper, smoke cigarettes, have some drinks, some food, and go play poker for hours."

"You're sure it is a poker club."

"I'd bet my life on it."

"Why didn't you follow him inside? You must have gone in there for that case you did."

"Actually, I didn't. They won't let you sit at the table for less than ten grand. Won't even let you in the door. I got all my information from reliable witnesses."

"Maybe he was conducting secret business in there."

"Perhaps."

Cain handed a photograph of Camden Swanson to him and asked, "Have you ever seen this man?"

"Nope. Is he the one I spoke to on the phone this morning?"

"Yes, he stole my associate's cell phone. We want you to find him and follow him."

"Consider him tailed. What should I know about Swanson? Dangerous?"

"Not in any way, shape, or form. He's been going around with a young woman, Veronica. Her address and his are on the photograph. Also his cell phone number."

"What else about Swanson?"

"Mr. Cronjager, we have been doing business with you for a few years now. Have I ever put you in any danger when I've contracted your services?"

"No, and I'd like to keep it that way."

"You have my promise that Camden Swanson poses no threat to your safety. He does have a gun, but I'm sure he's too scared to ever use it."

"Fuck, I had to pull that out of you. Are you sure?"

"The guy is harmless. We need to know where he might be at any given moment. But there is something else. There is a woman watching him from afar. She is also in our employ."

"Then why do you need me?"

"Because her trust has recently come into question. That is why she also believed our meeting was to take place at the Ferry Building."

"Won't she be pissed off now? Is she dangerous?"

"She is a professional, like us. I will tell her we had to change the meeting place because Camden had gotten wise."

Cronjager, satisfied with the answer and with his payment, shut the briefcase and said, "How often you want updates on Swanson?"

"Just keep him in sight. If he leaves the city, let us know. We'll be in contact with you. Once again, we greatly appreciate your complete discretion."

"Briefcases full of money will always assure that. I won't let the man out of my sight."

* * *

The slope of the street was so steep it gave Camden the sense he could topple backward at any time. He was breathing heavy once they reached the door of the Victorian house off Broadway, and he was surprised to see Veronica was as well. There was a small wooden sign above a doorbell that said in faded letters, "Cronjager & Bryan Detective Agency." He pressed the button next to the chipped doorframe, but nobody answered even after several more attempts.

"Should we wait?" she asked.

"And ask the detective nicely if he'll tell us where Bo McClennan is?"

"We could pay him."

"Got about fourteen dollars on me."

"I have around sixty."

"Seventy-four bucks won't make the nut. I'm going to break in."

"Camden, it's broad daylight."

"Usually a cliché to say, but my life truly does depend on it."

"How do we get in?"

"Good question."

He looked up and down the steep street and scanned the windows of the Victorians. The only living creature he saw was a fluffy cat sitting on top of a rusted VW Bug.

A small patch of overgrown green-brown grass to the right side of the house made a path to the back. Camden motioned for Veronica to stay in front while he rushed behind the house. He returned a few seconds later and smiled.

"There's a tiny balcony on the second floor. I think I can jump up to it from a tree and get to the window."

"You look winded from running ten feet and back. Let's say you get up to the tree. Then what? Hope that it's open?"

"They don't call it breaking and entering for nothing. Keep your eyes peeled for anybody coming. Whistle if somebody shows."

"I can't whistle."

"Then yell. If I hear your voice, then I'll know to get out."

"Maybe somebody else might yell. We should have a code word."

"Okay . . . how about Rice-A-Roni?"

The old advertisements for the San Francisco treat flashed in Camden's mind for a second, and then he looked up the slender, ten-foot-high ficus tree he needed to climb. He had gotten up the tree the night before in Golden Gate Park, but it had been sturdier. He tried to think thin.

With a grunt he jumped to the first branch he could reach, and as his feet dangled in the air, all he could hear was crackling sounds. After struggling, he was able to pull the rest of his body up onto the ficus but could tell it was about to give way. There was a thicker limb two feet above, and Camden got his butt on it just as the lower branch snapped and tumbled to the ground.

He steadied himself with his scraped hands and studied the side of the house. The windowsill was at least five inches wide and he quickly calculated he had about a 40 percent chance of landing on it without the wood and his body crashing to the ground. It was a two-foot leap and almost a fifteen-foot drop.

Camden jumped.

He got his feet onto the windowsill, but he teetered while attempting to balance himself. His fingers gripped the top of the window frame to keep from falling and cracking his skull open. He carefully reached forward with one hand and tried to open the window.

It was locked.

At this point it didn't matter if anybody was watching. In a deliberate motion, he lifted his foot up and carefully removed his shoe. A car alarm went off down the street and it startled him. When he turned his eyes to the asphalt, his vison became blurry, and he swayed after losing his footing. He hoped that if he fell he wouldn't damage his spine or brain.

But the swaying stopped, and Camden tightened his grip on the ledge and regained his balance. He tapped the shoe in his hand against the top part of the window until it splintered and broke. He then reached for the latch and was able to lift the window up and shimmy into the room, which smelled of marijuana.

He wasn't alone.

A man, who he figured to be Billy Bryan, the partner of Lars Cronjager, sat at his desk wearing a San Francisco Giants game jersey smoking a joint. The pear-shaped guy wore headphones and was bobbing his head up and down. Luckily, he faced the opposite direction from the window, and smoke rose and eddied around him.

Camden took the gun out of his pocket and inched toward him, hoping the narcotics would slow down the man's reactions. He thought the safety was on, but he wasn't entirely sure. He pressed the gun against the back of the man's head and with his other hand knocked off the headphones.

There was a shriek to make a thirteen-year-old girl jealous, and he watched the man swat at his ears as if a giant bug hovered over him. Carefully holding the gun, he used his other hand to push the man back into the chair and to keep him from swiveling around.

"You changed the meeting," Camden said in an awful British accent.

"What meeting, man?"

"Bo McClennan."

"McClennan? Whaddaya mean we changed it? The meeting was always at that flophouse hotel. That whole Ferry Building thing was subterfuge, man. Talk to your partner."

"That means I've been lied to," he continued in his fake British voice.

"C'mon, man. I don't know anything about that. You guys are Cronjager people. I don't deal with you. I'm Bryan. I do divorces and runaways."

"Where is McClennan?"

244   MICHAEL OSTROWSKI

"The meeting was at that hotel. If you're with those guys, you shoulda been there."

Camden wanted to cock the gun but was too nervous it would go off and blow a hole in the man's head. Instead he pressed the weapon hard against Bryan's back, his finger not on the trigger.

"Where is he?" Camden yelled.

"Oh, man. Are you guys trying to screw Cronjager? He said you were paying us a lot of money. I spent a couple days myself at McClennan's apartment. We deserve the money."

"I won't ask again," Camden said in his most menacing tone.

"McClennan's in West Portal," Bryan said in a quivering voice. "Lives on Dorchester Way, near the Muni. There's a copy of his file on that desk over there."

"Turn around and I'll shoot," Camden said as he moved toward the desk. Inside the file were pictures of Bo McClennan and a map printed from a website.

Camden's adrenaline surged as he felt a strange sensation that had been absent in his emotions for over a year. Pride. Wherein just a few days ago it had been a chore to get off the couch, he was now climbing trees and jumping through windows to solve a mystery. Yes, there were people who wanted to execute him and there was no certainty McClennan had the sculptures, but he was thoroughly enjoying the endorphin rush.

"Lars is gonna kill me," Bryan said.

Camden bolted out of the room and sped down the creaking stairs to the heavy oak door. Clutching the file, he nearly tripped over his own feet when he tasted fresh air. He regained his balance, and when he saw Veronica he pointed down the hill. She quickly took the lead with her loose-limbed strides, but he surprised himself when he nearly caught her by the time they reached the bottom.

23

Poker Face

BO MCCLENNAN, DRESSED in a black blazer and jeans, sat at a green felt table with more than one hundred thousand dollars' worth of colorful clay chips stacked neatly in front of him. He peeked at his hole cards and nonchalantly tossed five pink chips into the pot. The remaining players of the no-limit Texas Hold'em game, each old enough to be his father, all folded and made varying faces of disgust at the victor.

McClennan shrugged and exposed his hole cards, a three of clubs and a nine of diamonds. He raked in the pot and began stacking the chips into his orderly and bulbous pile. At that moment a new player sat down in the one empty seat at the table. McClennan looked at the gentleman, who was now the youngest person in the room, and kept a blank face even though he knew his identity.

"Woo! I'm harder than I've been in years," the new player said as he extracted the chips from the three racks he had bought. "I'm fucking panting at the opportunity to push all these bad larrys into a pot."

"Partner, I'll be happy to take them off your hands," a skinny man wearing a suit and cowboy hat said with a laugh.

The next hand was dealt, and everyone folded in front of the new player, who McClennan recognized to be Miles Krakow. The big blind was five hundred dollars, and the standard raise was three times that amount. He watched Miles peek at his two cards, lick his lips, and push his entire thirty-thousand-dollar stack into the middle of the table.

McClennan was the big blind, the last to act in this round of betting, and the remaining players folded to him. He held an ace and a queen of the same suit and called. "Licking your lips was a little too ostentatious."

"That's a big word for a poker player," Miles said.

"And that's a big bet for an artist who hasn't sold anything in years," he responded.

A queen came on the flop, giving him a pair, and the remaining cards did not improve Miles's tens that he flipped over with a shrug.

"Consider that a down payment," the guy whose work he once taught in art class said.

"I'll consider that a hand of poker I won."

"Mister, ahh, Smith, can we talk somewhere in private?"

"Everybody in the room, including you, knows my name is Bo McClennan."

"The discreetness of gentlemen," Miles said. "Warms the heart to be around my fellow filthy rich brethren. But all the same, I'd like some privacy."

"We were close to taking a break, Bo," the dealer said.

"Fifteen minutes it is, then," McClennan said and got up from the table.

McClennan, with Miles behind him, walked down a hallway filled with original oil paintings featuring scenes from the Old West, and ended up in a room that exactly replicated an

1800s saloon. He went behind the polished-mahogany-paneled bar and poured himself a Johnnie Walker Blue Label. He did not offer Miles a drink.

"I don't have the sculptures," McClennan said after taking a sip.

Miles grinned and grabbed an open bottle of Bordeaux he could reach from behind the bar. He poured himself a glass, swirled three times, and sniffed the wine. He downed it in one gulp and said, "Bullshit."

"I came to San Francisco for the fog. It's good for the complexion."

"So is money," Miles said. "Even though I haven't sold a painting in years, I have fuckloads of cash. I will double whatever you were paid."

McClennan shook a cigarette from his pack and lit it with a Zippo. After taking a long drag he blew out rings of smoke, which he alternated with small and large circles. Miles coughed, spit into a tall brass spittoon, and clapped his hands.

"You learn how to do things like that after nearly eight years in prison," he said.

"Can I ask you why, after just leaving the big house, you would pull another art heist before your release papers could even dry? In the same exact fucking manner. And then stay in the same city afterward. You're either brilliant or immensely daft."

"I'm a law-abiding citizen now. I'm in San Francisco to play poker."

"And the fog."

"Out of curiosity, how did you find me?"

"I've lived in this town my whole life. I got connections on top of connections."

"Who was it?"

"One of my doctors plays here."

"A doctor who broke the code of the house. Never discuss another player's name outside these walls. To my knowledge, it's never been done before. Your doctor is banned for life."

"Oh, shit," Miles said absently as he popped a pill. "He told me not to say anything. Fuck him. The important thing here is that we conduct some business."

"Let's say I had the sculptures. How would you destroy them?"

"It involves Pop Rocks, carbonated urine, three speed metal bands, and a kangaroo. Afterward, my retirement from art. I'm going to open a whorehouse/theme park in Kazakhstan called Miles World. There will be all kinds of rides, lots of sex, and dick and boob characters walking around, greeting people and taking pictures with them. And churros, naturally. Whores, both men and women, included in your price of admission."

"Too bad I don't have the sculptures. But I would like to buy whatever it is you're on."

Miles emptied his pockets and scattered onto the bar a handful of various colored pills.

McClennan gulped the rest of his scotch and said, "I was joking."

"I'm not. I want those Matisses."

"You've come to the wrong place."

"Did Léveque hire you? That fucking Frenchman. He's your buyer."

McClennan exhaled more smoke rings and said, "I have no idea who he is."

"If you weren't such a good poker player, I just might believe you."

"Speaking of poker, did you bring more money, Mr. Krakow? You obviously have plenty of it that you don't mind losing."

"I could be back in an hour with millions. You hand me the sculptures and it's all yours."

McClennan snuffed out his cigarette and drank off the rest of his scotch. "It was nice meeting the world's worst living artist. See you in the funny pages," he said as he stood up from his wooden chair.

"Did you pull the job with Camden Swanson?" Miles asked.

"Who's he? Your mother?"

"All right, all right, Bo. You can play hard to get now as long as you come to your senses later." Miles handed him a business card. "I will top any offer you have."

* * *

Camden and Veronica had taken a cab from North Beach and twenty minutes later were deposited into the West Portal neighborhood in San Francisco. Since the Tall Woman had a knack for following them, they had the driver let them out under the blue and white awning of the Muni station at the base of the Twin Peaks tunnel. Wires hung over the street and spread out along the tracks leading away from the square to power the electric trains.

"Never been here before," Veronica said. "The streets seem like they turn and twist all over the place. It should be left, up the hill."

"Figures a guy from Boston would get a place on Dorchester Way," Camden said.

They turned left on Ulloa Street and began the walk up Claremont in the direction of the red-and-white-pronged Twin Peaks Tower that loomed over the hill. The sign for Dorchester Way was visible on the right, and Camden grabbed Veronica's arm. He led her back around the corner to the gas station.

"Either the clients or the Tall Woman are waiting outside McClennan's apartment. We need to be someplace where we can see the street but be hidden. I'll stay here and patrol the block. If any car or person turns down Dorchester, I'll move in closer to check it out."

"Won't you look suspicious hanging around on the corner? It's super residential here."

"I'll pretend to be talking on my phone and seem as if I'm out for a walk. You should go back down toward all the shops. There's a café right across from the Muni, Squat & Gobble, I think it's called. Take a sidewalk table and keep your eyes out for him. If McClennan's taking public transportation or out in the neighborhood, you should see him. If he's driving or coming from the other direction, I'll pick him up. Whoever sees him first will call the other."

Veronica nodded, and Camden continued up the hill on Claremont Street to a streetlight and leaned against the pole. Looking down Dorchester Way, he held his cell phone up to his ear as if he were speaking to somebody. Camden viewed a black Cadillac with tinted windows across the street from the white Spanish-style house where McClennan was staying. He could only make out the back of the vehicle, which he hoped meant whoever was inside could not see him.

Whenever a person approached, Camden started talking to himself, inventing a lucrative business deal involving robot butlers. Nobody walked down Dorchester Way, but a few cars drove past McClennan's house and did not stop. The sky began taking on a charcoal tint and the cars cast long shadows by the time Veronica finally called.

"I see McClennan," she said. "He's going into a bar."

Camden hurried down Claremont and saw Veronica getting off her chair at the sidewalk café. She pointed across the street to the old neon sign that identified the bar as the Philosopher's Club. Camden and Veronica met at the medieval-style door and paused before going inside.

"What are we going to say to him?" Veronica asked.

"I don't think I'll ever make his BFF list because of the whole ruining his art heist and him going to jail thing, but we're a better alternative than the Tall Woman and the clients."

"Do you think he has a gun? Is he dangerous? I know we're in a public place, but when people are trapped, they do stupid things."

"Good points to consider. I'd say he very likely has a gun, but so do we. I don't think McClennan will feel trapped because I guarantee he thinks he can outsmart us. And he very well is capable of that. Let's both be on our A game."

The tavern was narrow and dark, a wooden bar stretching down the right with a row of high-top tables paralleling it. Flat-screen televisions flanked either side of a large mirror. On the right side was a Giants jersey, while the left featured, curiously, Camden thought, a Red Sox one. The place looked clean but worn and cozy.

Bo McClennan, wearing jeans and a faded black T-shirt, sat at the far end of the bar. The blazer he had on earlier at the poker house was draped over the wooden chair. He took a San Jose Sharks hat from his back pocket, smoothed out the crinkles in it, and put it on his head. After taking a sip of his scotch, he glanced in the direction of the door.

"Not my day," McClennan said when Camden made eye contact with him.

"How are you doing, Mr. Juan Wyman?" he asked.

"Camden Fucking Swanson," McClennan said and slapped him on the back. "Do you see a doctor, most likely a proctologist, who plays in high-stakes poker games?"

"Been a long time, Bo."

He downed the rest of his drink, looked at Veronica, and said, "You were the one that hired me."

"It was a convincing mustache," she said.

After Camden ordered a beer for himself and a glass of red wine for Veronica, McClennan said to the bartender, "Another Johnnie Walker Black. On my friend here. It's too bad they don't have the Blue. Then again, if they did, I probably wouldn't like the place as much. It would mean rich people drink here. If you want to know what God thinks of money, look at the people he gave it to."

"W. C. Fields?" Camden asked.

"Dorothy Parker," McClennan answered as his eyes swept the bar. "A cute girl with tattoos quoted that to me here last week. I've come to consider the Philosopher's Club my second home. Much nicer than prison."

"If prison isn't such a lovely place, maybe you shouldn't steal stuff. But the least I can do for you after all these years is buy you a drink."

After the beverages arrived, McClennan clinked Camden's and Veronica's glasses with his, took a sip of his scotch, and smiled. He then tipped his cap, grabbed his blazer off the chair, and walked into a small back room. They followed him to the pool table.

"Thought I picked a good spot in the city to hide," McClennan said.

"We're not the only ones who found you," Camden said. "There are a bunch of pissed-off art thieves in front of your house now."

"And you brought them here. Thanks again, buddy."

"We had nothing to do with it. They found you through a private detective. We got the information from the detective's partner."

"I've really come to love this neighborhood," McClennan said. "Did you get a chance to walk down West Portal Ave.? Man, you got the streetcars going up and down and the store-fronts are amazing. The fucking neon signs. Vacuum and shoe repair. Carpet and linoleum. The front door of this bar. It's how I imagine a 1950s or early '60s Main Street."

Bo finished his drink, put on his blazer, and left the back room. Camden expected a dash out the door, but instead the art thief caught the bartender's attention and ordered another round. He returned with three shot glasses filled with crimson liquid, a beer, a glass of red wine, and what looked to be another scotch for himself.

"Redheaded Sluts," he said, handing the shot glasses to Camden and Veronica. "Same girl who told me the Dorothy Parker quote turned me on to these. She had red hair and liked the irony. Anyway, where was I? Honestly, I could see settling down here. Marrying a terrific woman, raising a family, and playing Hold'em for a living. There's a house down the street where you can play high-stakes poker night or day."

McClennan raised the little glass and downed the booze. Camden did the same but winced a bit when he tasted the Jägermeister. Veronica smelled the shot and then set it on the side of the pool table, where it only sat for a few seconds before McClennan finished it.

"Sounds like you have a nice future planned out. Too bad there are people in front of your place who want to kill you. And kill me, too," Camden said.

"Why do they want to kill you?" McClennan asked.

"They think I helped you steal the sculptures."

"Why?"

"Because you robbed the Matisse in exactly the same way as the heist in Boston. Because I was the one who caught you. Because I now work for the museum as a security guard and you were working there, too, under an assumed name."

"Why do these people who supposedly want to kill us care about the sculptures?"

"Because they wanted to steal them."

"Interesting, but let's back up. How did the great Camden Swanson become a museum security guard?" He took a sip of scotch. "Just fucking with you. I know how it happened. Hell, I don't have any bad feelings. I did give you that interview after the trial when I was in prison."

"Unexpected, but appreciated."

"It's taken me many years to come to grips with the unfair randomness of it. You happened to be watching the sky when I was in my hang glider."

"Dumb luck."

"Exactly," McClennan said and then inserted quarters into the pool table. He pulled back the silver lever, and after the balls clacked down he began racking them. "Gambling successfully, especially poker, requires a tremendous amount of skill. It also requires guts, determination, and about a hundred other intangible character traits that few can cultivate. But no matter how good you are, you can lose. You can get screwed by dumb luck or one poor choice."

McClennan lined up the cue ball and broke, scattering the rest of the balls in every direction. None fell into a hole, and he nodded to a stick leaning against the wall. Veronica picked it up, and then rolled it on the table to see if it was straight.

"Four ball, corner pocket," she said and then sank it with ease. "Still don't understand why you robbed that museum in Boston."

"The *coup de grace* of my prop bet career."

"You were a college professor. How could you risk stealing art treasures on a bet?" Veronica asked as she sank another ball.

"I'd run through a tiger's cage or swim in a shark tank if somebody bet I couldn't do it."

"So childish," Veronica said.

"It is. But at what time in your life did you feel truly alive? It's when we were kids. Being curious, wondering what was on the other side of a door or down a street. Children experience life as it should be, in the moment. When you get older the moment becomes a thing to forget about. We drink, we watch TV, we numb our heads in any way possible to forget we're living our lives exactly the way we said we wouldn't when we were younger."

Veronica lined up a shot but did not strike a ball as McClennan continued to talk.

"When you're a child you take a lot of risks," he continued. "You climb trees. You jump off roofs. You hop in strangers' pools on hot days. You do it for the rush, the experience."

"I never did any of those things," Veronica said and sunk the eight ball.

"But you probably took a lot of people's money shooting pool," Camden responded.

"Poker," McClennan continued, "became a surrogate for those types of adrenaline rushes. When you have a couple hundred thousand of your own money in a pot, you're in tune with The Moment better than a fucking Buddhist monk."

"Then why do stupid bets?" Veronica asked.

"As much as I love poker, I need more flavor in my life. I know enough rich people spread out across the country willing to propose all kinds of crazy bets for all kinds of crazy money."

"Who bet you to steal those paintings in Boston?" Camden asked.

"If I didn't answer after eight years in prison, it would be goddamned silly to do it now in West Portal, San Francisco. But you reporters are paid to ask silly questions."

"Here's another one," Veronica said. "Did you steal the Matisse sculptures?"

"Perhaps," McClennan answered.

"Well," Camden said. "If you did, you've pissed off a group of people who had planned to rob the museum in a different way."

"The ones waiting for me outside my place?"

"Were you working with them?" Veronica asked. "But then decided to go on your own?"

"I only work alone," McClennan said.

"Do you know the Tall Woman?" Camden asked.

"The Tall Woman?" McClennan repeated with a laugh. "Does she work with Jack the Bean Stalk? Or maybe she's friends with the Mad Hatter?"

"I'm thinking she could have hired you to steal the sculptures to double-cross the clients."

"You've been hanging around Monkey-Snake Boy a bit too long, kid," he said and then finished off his scotch.

Camden held McClennan back when he tried to take a step toward the bar. He wasn't necessarily surprised to see the Tall Woman walk through the door, but he was hoping he had more time alone with Bo. The reason the clients hadn't killed him yet is because he could potentially lead them to McClennan. And now he had. There was nowhere to run.

She strode though the room wearing a black blouse and a pleated skirt that showed off her perfect legs. There was a crowd of middle-aged softball players who had congregated at the bar a few minutes prior to her arrival, and they all parted so she could pass. The place got quiet and the dominant sounds in the room were her shoes clicking on the floor and the grunts, groans, and sighs of the men staring at her as she walked to the back room.

"At last I find Camden Swanson and Bo McClennan together," she said when reaching the pool table.

"It's not what it seems," Camden said. "Shit, it really isn't."

"We tracked him here, just like you," Veronica said.

"You weren't kidding about her, Camden. If we're playing a basketball game, I'm picking you first. I didn't catch your name, though."

"Nice try, Mr. McClennan."

"We just call her the Tall Woman," Veronica offered. "She won't give her name."

"Whether you are or aren't in on it together," she said, "you're all going to take a ride with me to see my clients."

"I'll politely decline that invitation with a big fuck you," McClennan said.

"You are in no position for protest."

"Of course I am. I can't remember if I have those Matisse sculptures. But if it turns out I do, if you want to see them, you can't if I'm dead."

"Do you have them?" she asked.

"Maybe. Maybe not."

"Well, maybe or maybe not you'll be shot in the head when you step outside. Maybe my clients have already gone through your house and found them."

"I'm going to call you the Feisty Woman," McClennan said. "But think for a second. If I did steal the Matisse sculptures, I wouldn't be so dumb as to hide them where I'm living."

"Perhaps they'll kidnap you and torture you until you tell them where they are," she offered.

"Why are we engaging in this kind of barbaric talk?" McClennan asked. "If I did steal the sculptures, negotiating their sale would be beneficial to everybody. Let's go to my place and discuss such an option. It's close by and I have snacks."

24

A West Portal Soirée

DETECTIVE CLINKENBEARD GAVE instructions to be informed of any police call in San Francisco concerning a black Cadillac. That such a vehicle was seen screeching out of Golden Gate Park the night of Hipple's murder was one of the few clues he had. Seven people owning cars fitting that description, who had recently been involved in either parking tickets or moving violations, had been questioned. The search thus far had been a waste of time.

That was until Mrs. Lucy Browning had reported a suspicious dark Caddy on Dorchester Way in West Portal.

The eighty-year-old former postal worker had been sitting at her white-sheer-curtained window waiting for her granddaughter to come home. She told the police the young lady was fifteen and seldom returned at agreed-upon times. Ms. Browning kept vigil behind the curtains every evening, and that's when she noticed a black Cadillac pull to the curb across the street.

"Nobody got out of the Caddy," she said. "Those tinted windows are spooky. They could be raping me with their eyes right now."

Mrs. Browning had made the call to the police station several hours ago, but Detective Clinkenbeard was not notified because of the source. The officers said the grandmother routinely phoned the station complaining of "shifty" characters in the area. Such people always turned out to be neighborhood kids or food delivery employees.

Thankfully, after the woman's third call, a desk sergeant finally contacted him. He had been taking a shower and listening to the Dead's "Cosmic Charlie" when he got the message relayed by his wife. He slipped rushing out of the tub and bruised his knee, but he managed to dress and drive to West Portal in less than thirty minutes.

While taking the turn onto Dorchester Way, Clinkenbeard saw seven people walking into a house. In the darkness, they were unidentifiable, so he double-parked and took out his gun as he slipped out of the car. He took cautious steps as he approached the black Cadillac across the street. The windows were tinted, but pressing against the glass with the help of the streetlights he could see the vehicle was empty. He called for backup.

* * *

Camden watched McClennan unlock the door, and he, Veronica, the three clients, and the Tall Woman followed him inside the house. They entered the living room, which contained worn couches and chairs once in style in the 1970s. The host went to a stereo that had to be at least thirty years old and put an album on the turntable. There was a crackle on the speakers and a bossa nova song began playing.

The Tall Woman had her gun pointed at McClennan and looked annoyed. Two of the clients, who each had trim goatees and wore plaid sweaters, black slacks, and thick-rimmed eye-glasses, kept their weapons at their side but were jittery. The fact they appeared more like accountants seemed spooky to Camden. The third client, a guy who could start left tackle in the NFL or be chief bouncer at a trucker bar, was even more menacing. He did not show his gun, which could nonetheless be discerned under his tight black shirt in a holster.

Motioning everybody to take seats in the living room, McClennan continued toward the kitchen. He stopped at a swinging door and asked, "Camden, can you give me a hand?"

He did as asked, and the Tall Woman followed them into kitchen with her weapon raised. True to his word and without the slightest acknowledgment of the gun, McClennan poured chips, mini pretzels, and popcorn into three earthenware bowls.

"I know Camden will take a beer and his friend a glass of wine. What would you and your pals like?"

"Those three men in there will do anything necessary to get back the sculptures. I will also have no problem shooting you."

"That's marvelous," McClennan said. "But would you all prefer scotch, beer, or wine? Those are my three choices."

"I wouldn't have a clue," she said in an exasperated way. "But I'll take wine if you have anything decent."

"Got a nice little red from the Rhône I think you'll enjoy," he answered and poured two glasses. He then popped the bottle cap off a Stella Artois.

"Camden, if you can take your beer and Veronica's glass of red, and Stretch, if you can get your wine, I can handle the rest."

McClennan grabbed a bottle of Johnnie Walker Blue, along with four tumblers and the bowls of snacks, and placed them on an antique silver tray. He grooved to the bossa nova song as they walked back into the living room. He deftly set the tray down on the coffee table and poured the glasses of scotch for the clients and himself.

Camden noticed one of the "accountants" had bruises and scratches on his face and figured him as the client lucky enough to survive the bull. Even though they both looked like they could file a damn good tax return, there was sufficient menace in their eyes to make him nervous. The third client was capable of eating all of them. Camden of course still had a gun stuck down his pants, but he was clearly outnumbered.

"I'm going to search for the sculptures now," the enormous client said. He walked over to the coffee table, downed one of the scotches, and then left the room.

"Search away, amigo," McClennan said. "Is he related to Andre the Giant?"

"I'm glad you seem to be enjoying yourself," the bruised-face client said. "But this is hardly a fondue party."

"Manners and decorum are the pillars of society," McClennan responded. He put the tumblers of scotch in front of the two accountant-looking clients. Neither touched them.

The Tall Woman once again pointed her gun at McClennan. "While we appreciate the snacks and the drinks, our little soirée is going to turn dark quickly if you do not cooperate with us. Do you have the goddamned sculptures?"

"The Feisty Woman continues to live up to her name. I guess it's the proverbial time to lay my cards down on the table," McClennan said. "Yes, I stole them."

"Either return them to us," bruised-face client said, "or else we kill Mr. Swanson and Miss Zarcarsky right now."

McClennan flipped open his Zippo, lit a cigarette, and, after inhaling, deeply blew three smoke rings. "I don't want to see them killed, but neither are my friends or my partners. I spent eight years in prison. If you think I'm going to hand those things over to you without a big payout, guess I'm dealing with rank amateurs."

"How much do you want?" the client who was free of blemishes asked.

McClennan sipped his scotch and said, "You were going to rob the museum. How much was your buyer going to pay?"

Neither the Tall Woman nor the clients answered.

"I'm going to be honest with you. Because that's the kind of guy I am. Fifty million. That's my payday for the sculptures."

Camden watched the Tall Woman sip her wine, stare at McClennan, and then grab the pack of cigarettes from the table. She shook one out, lit it, smelled it as if she were enjoying the nose of a glass of wine, but then snubbed it out on the blown-glass coffee table.

"That's about right from our side," the Tall Woman said.

"For fuck's sake, I have ashtrays. But let's forget about that and be professionals here," McClennan said. "I have the sculptures. Only I know where they are, and you'd never see them again. Without me, you got a big bag of dicks."

"If you think you're getting fifty million from us, I might just shoot you right now," the injured client said.

"You all seem like such nice people. I'll forgo ten and put those sculptures in your hands for forty million."

"Fuck you. I would rather shoot the three of you than settle for a lousy ten million. And you forget, we have the option of torturing you to find out where you hid the sculptures."

Camden stood up, took a long sip of his beer, then said, "C'mon, people. How much do you all need? Why don't you split it evenly? C'mon, Bo, twenty-five mil is fair."

"Hey," McClennan said. "Who stole the sculptures?" He thrust his thumbs toward his face. "This guy, that's who. I took the risk, I made it happen. Why should I give you guys half?"

"'Cause we would have robbed the museum if not for you. We'd have the fucking sculptures," the bruised client said.

"And if my grandmother had a dick, she'd be my grandfather . . . I know how it is when you have meticulous plans and something out of your control fucks it up," McClennan said while staring at Camden. "It cost me nearly a decade of my life. So I'll repeat it again. I have what you desire. I'm the one who robbed the museum. Not you. If you want them, you'll have to pay me off in a big way."

"Torture would fuck this up even more," the Tall Woman said. "But we cannot settle for twenty-five million as our eventual payout. Not acceptable after everything that has happened. I'd be okay to walk away with thirty-five, which means we would have to pay Mr. McClennan fifteen mil to give us the sculptures."

The Andre the Giant client returned to the room and said, "They're not here."

The doorbell rang, causing everybody to become catatonic. The only sounds were the hum of the refrigerator and Astrud Gilberto on the stereo singing about the girl from Ipanema. The doorbell rang again.

"Nobody, other than you all, knows I live here," McClennan whispered.

All three of the clients and the Tall Woman had their guns out and ready to use.

"There's no way out the back," McClennan whispered. "The yard is surrounded by fences. But if we go on top, we can jump to the garage next door and then to the next one behind that yard. Trust me, I've plotted my escape route very carefully."

McClennan led the way up to the top floor, unhooked the latch on a five-foot-wide skylight, and climbed through it to the roof. The entire group followed, with the clients and the

Tall Woman leading the pack. Veronica and Camden hesitated and listened to the scuffling of feet on the roof.

"I can say I forced you to come here," Camden said.

"Get your ass through that skylight," Veronica replied.

The two of them shimmied up through the skylight in time to see McClennan point to the red-tiled roof of the garage of his next-door neighbor. The three clients and the Tall Woman, who was now holding her designer shoes, moved toward that direction without waiting. One by one each leapt over the three-foot chasm to the roof in the next yard. Camden was about to follow their tracks, but McClennan grabbed his arm, shook his head, and then jumped through the skylight. He hit the floor with a thud but kept on his feet and headed quickly down the stairs. Camden and Veronica could now see blue and red flashing lights, and a siren blared. Holding hands, they went down through the skylight together, barely squeezing through the opening, and followed McClennan to a door at the back of the house.

"They'll probably get away in that direction, but we can't go with them," he whispered. "And there's an easier route that will take us to my car."

McClennan sprinted out of the house into the darkness of the backyard toward a white picket fence, and Camden and Veronica followed. The grass was wet from the sprinkler that had just watered the lawn, and he lost his footing and crashed into a horseshoe pit, landing inches from the spike used to keep score. Veronica and McClennan had made it over the picket fence, and when they landed on the grass of the neighbor's backyard, a voice yelled out in the darkness.

"Freeze. San Francisco Police. Move and I'll shoot."

Camden wiped the sand from his lips, stayed on his belly. A shadowy figure held a gun about eight feet from Veronica and

McClennan on the same side of the fence. The two of them thrust their arms in the air. Gunfire crackled close by.

"Do not fucking move," the law enforcement officer screamed.

With hands in the air, they stood inert, save for their heavy breathing.

With his gray ponytail dangling over the back of his pressed suit, Camden could tell it was Detective Clinkenbeard when he got closer. He stared up at the detective, and felt around the sandy pit with his hands until he found a horseshoe. Was he really going to do this?

Camden scrambled to his feet, cocked his arm, and flung the iron object as hard as he could at the detective. The horse-shoe whistled in the air and hit Clinkenbeard in the jaw, causing the second ugliest thud he had ever heard, and the man crumpled to the ground. Camden hopped over the fence, did not turn back, and trailed McClennan and Veronica after they jumped a chain link fence. The three of them were now out of another neighbor's yard and were sprinting down Allston Way toward a blue Volkswagen sedan.

Gunfire, screeching tires, and sirens echoed on the other side of the block as the three of them rushed into the car. Before Camden could even shut his door, McClennan had put the vehicle in gear. They drove the speed limit in the opposite direction of the noise toward Twin Peaks. He stared out the window for signs of the police, the Tall Woman, or the clients, only finding houses illuminated by streetlights and the fog curling around the Twin Peaks Tower as they drove upward toward it.

"A lot of commotion," McClennan said, "for a bunch of sculptures that are fakes."

ACT THREE

25

Bo Knows Sculptures

MCCLENNAN KEPT HIS eyes straight on 19th Avenue and would not elaborate on his claim. He did not speak at all. Despite a barrage of questions from Camden and Veronica, the only sounds that came from him were his singing of a bossa nova song in perfect Portuguese.

After passing a donut shop with a flickering neon sign, McClennan took a left on Ortega, drove for several blocks before taking a right on one of the avenues, and then parked at an open spot in front of an old hatchback. Like many of the houses in that part of the city, they were sleek stucco fronted and were connected like bricks in a wall.

"And here is where you two get out of the car and my life," McClennan said.

"Don't think so, pal," Camden answered.

"Vamoose, Swanson, I got things to do."

"Bo, you are the only thing that's keeping us alive right now," Camden said. "We're not letting you out of our sight."

"We have a gun," Veronica said.

"So fucking what? I have one on me, too, plus a few in the trunk and even a pretty sharp knife. Get the fuck out of my car."

While McClennan was speaking, Camden slowly reached into his jacket pocket. His hand gripped the cold metal of the gun and it rested on his lap with the barrel pointed at the driver. Camden coughed, stared McClennan in the eyes until the gaze was returned, and then nodded at the gun. McClennan laughed.

"Fucking A, I thought she was bluffing."

"We need those sculptures or they're going to kill us."

"Your personal safety is pretty far down on my priority list, Swanson. But, hey, I guess you're the boss now 'cause you got the gun. Where do you want to go?"

"The cops probably have roadblocks on both bridges," Camden said. "And all up and down the 101. The clients, the Tall Woman, and the police would figure us to head out of town. A friend of mine has a suite at the St. Francis. The car is off the road and we have a place to stay for the night."

"What if he isn't there?" Veronica asked.

"I have the key. He told me to stop by anytime."

"Fuck it, maybe you're right," McClennan said. "But here's an even better idea. Let's ditch the car and cab it over there."

The three of them got out of the Volkswagen, zipped, buttoned, or pulled tight their jackets or sweat shirts to counteract the cold wind, and McClennan called a cab. The taxi picked them up on the corner near a dry-cleaning shop and soon they were heading back up 19th Avenue and cutting through the park. Then a straight shot down Geary Boulevard to O'Farrell toward Union Square. Nobody spoke a word the whole ride. At the entrance of the St. Francis, the picket-wielding employees shouted at them as they left the cab and made their way to the revolving doors of the hotel. With all that had been going on, Camden had forgotten about the strike. While McClennan had used the workers as a diversion, their labor action against management was still going strong.

It was after 10:00 p.m., and their shoes click-clacked against the marble by the front desk. Camden took the key holder out of his wallet and looked at the room number. It was on the twelfth floor of the old building, and the three of them entered the vintage elevators with the gold trim.

"Who is your friend, Swanson?" McClennan asked.

"He's an art guy, so you probably know him. My ex-girlfriend's father, Jean François Léveque."

McClennan extracted a tooth pick from his breast pocket, put it in his mouth, and with the little wooden instrument lodged in a tooth he answered, "I've heard of him."

Once on the twelfth floor, the group followed the signs to the suite and walked across the mini promenade made of hardwood flooring. Camden knocked several times, but nobody responded. He shrugged and used the plastic key; the lock lit up green and made a beep.

He gazed down a long entryway, and all the doors leading to the rooms were closed. They could hear music and voices coming from down the hall. Veronica grabbed Camden by the arm.

"Are you sure we should be here?" she asked.

"Safest place on earth right now," Camden said. "Between the cops and the clients, they're probably searching every roadside motel."

"We could have got our own room here," McClennan said.

"We'd have to use a credit card, and that's too risky," Camden answered. "Mr. Léveque is one of the few people I trust. He might help us get out of the city quietly or he might tell us to go to hell. But he would never screw us over."

Camden felt his cell phone vibrating and took it out of his pocket. It was Sal, and he let it go to voicemail.

Veronica sniffed. "Something smells real good."

The door opened to a long banquet table with glassware and china set for three people. Seated at the table were Mr. Léveque, his daughter Georgia, and her new boyfriend and owner of the Matisse Hotel, David Bouchon. When Camden, Veronica, and the famous art thief walked inside, all heads turned to them. Every person in the room experienced some sort of recognition shock.

"What the fuck," Camden said, probably summing up all sentiment.

Mr. Léveque rose. "Camden, you must have a little bit of French in your ancestry. You have such perfect timing."

"I apologize for the intrusion," he said, his eyes drifting toward Georgia and Bouchon. "We'll be leaving now."

"Don't be foolish. C'mon in and introduce your friends. We have plenty of food and wine to go around."

Bouchon stood and pointed at McClennan. "I think we all know this gentleman. Many law enforcement officials believe you stole my sculptures."

"What do you think?" McClennan asked.

"I don't know. Did you?"

"I'd be more inclined to speak freely if I could have some food. I don't know about Veronica or Camden, but I am damn hungry."

"Of course. Please sit," Mr. Léveque said.

Georgia seemed distressed but remained silent. Camden couldn't help but look at Bouchon, and he fought back the anxiety welling inside. Veronica was wide-eyed and alert, while McClennan and Léveque appeared relaxed. The servers, dressed as if it were the 1920s, put place settings down for the new guests.

As the wine was being poured, Léveque first went to Veronica and introduced himself. She explained she was a friend of Camden's through work.

"You are employed at my hotel also, young lady?" Bouchon asked.

"Gallery attendant?" Georgia asked.

"Human resources," she corrected.

"I know how hard you all have it," Mr. Bouchon said. "The strike has been so difficult for not only our union members, but for the management team that has to keep the hotel running. Thank you for your efforts."

"You're welcome. But I'm a temp, mostly filing and administrative tasks."

"You're very much appreciated. Hopefully our unfortunate labor situation will end soon," Bouchon said. "It's bad for everyone."

"And David is contending with other issues now," Mr. Léveque said.

"I would do anything to get my sculptures back. And perhaps tonight Mr. McClennan will be able to help me."

Léveque moved toward McClennan and shook his hand. "We met many years ago at an art conference in Florence. Or maybe it was Siena."

McClennan bit into a dinner biscuit and said, "Don't remember." He then glared at Bouchon, making him shift in his chair and stare at his half-eaten shrimp cocktail. "You talk a good game, but I consider reading people one of my greatest skills. And you don't seem overly concerned."

"Who are you to speak to me in such a way? A common thief. I've been sick over what happened to the Matisse sculptures."

"The museum reopened today for the first time since the robbery and set an attendance record," Léveque offered.

"I never even thought of that," Georgia said. "People eat that shit up. They'll come because it was the site of a 'daring art heist.'"

"And for the important pieces in the museum, honey," Bouchon said.

"For fuck's sake," Camden said and then downed half his glass of wine.

"Don't I know you?" Bouchon asked Camden.

"We play polo at the same club."

Bouchon laughed. "No, I think I read some of your poetry the other day. You work in the galleries. It went something like, 'charbroiled soul on penny loafer bread.'"

"Wing-tip bun," Camden corrected.

"Since when do you write poetry?" Georgia asked.

"*Bon sang*," Bouchon exclaimed. "This is your Camden!"

"The one and only, honey," Camden answered for Georgia.

"Now let's all be civil," Mr. Léveque said. "Manners and decorum are the pillars of a decent society."

Camden turned to McClennan, but he wasn't sure why.

As the food was being served, Mr. Léveque stood and with an expansive smile said, "Bon appétit."

Camden ate as if they would be ejected at any minute, and Veronica and McClennan both clearly shared his hunger by the way they went at their plates. The other three in the party picked at their petite filets and assorted vegetables and starches. There were several bottles of red wine on the table, and Camden commandeered one for himself. He was determined to replace the nauseous feeling in his stomach with a buzz in his head.

"They really make the suite up special for you, Mr. L?" he asked after pouring himself more Bordeaux. "It must be nice to be filthy rich."

"You have the brains and the wit to be filthy rich, too. Just not the ambition."

Camden raised his glass in a toasting fashion and downed the rest of his wine. Georgia gazed at him, shook her head, and put her hand on Bouchon's arm. He smiled at her with purple teeth and refilled his glass, spilling some wine onto the table in the process.

The table went silent.

"Let's start a new thread of conversation," Veronica said. "The view of Union Square is amazing."

"It's nice here, but normally I stay in the Arbuckle suite on this floor," Léveque said. "They don't officially call it that, in fact they don't advertise it at all. But it is the famous suite where a young woman was found killed during a party in 1921. Arbuckle was accused, and even though he wasn't convicted, it was quite a scandal. Highest paid actor at the time. In 1950, Al Jolson, who starred in the first talking film, *The Jazz Singer*, died of a heart attack during a poker game in the same suite. It's a bit ghoulish, but there's so much history in those walls."

"Speaking of history and interesting stories," McClennan said in a theatrical voice, "I think the opportunity is perfect to tell one."

He grabbed the bottle of wine closest to Camden, but it was empty. The next one yielded a glass and he drank off half of it and stood from the table. Everybody in the room stared at McClennan.

"Mr. Bouchon, your precious Matisse sculptures are imitations, spurious as a toupee on a bald man's head," he said.

Georgia said, "Get the fuck out of here."

"The gentleman who made the sculptures is not named Matisse, and he is actually still alive."

"Bo is clearly joking," Léveque said.

Camden looked at him and said, "Is that why you bid heavily on the sculptures and then stopped?"

"I have no idea what you're talking about," he answered while looking at the table.

"I'm certain the real reason is that you received a letter," McClennan said. "A letter sent from Paris. Penned by a man named Victor Roux-Fuzie."

Camden had still been eyeing Léveque and noticed his friend's face drop.

"How could you . . . I never showed that to anybody."

"While I was in prison, Monsieur Roux-Fuzie became an accidental pen pal. He wrote me saying how impressed he was that I robbed the Cordovan Museum. When you're in prison, you appreciate correspondence from anybody. Luckily, I'm fluent in French and could answer him."

"I figured Victor Roux-Fuzie to be a crank," Mr. Léveque said.

"Victor told me he had contacted you before the bidding. He was friends with your grandfather. You must have read the letter around the time the sculptures went to auction."

Léveque sighed and took a sip of wine. "I got the letter that day. I didn't believe him, but when the bidding got into the upper stages, I couldn't stop thinking about Roux-Fuzie."

"Why didn't you tell me, Jean Francois?" Bouchon asked.

"Hell, David. You were determined to get those pieces. And I had no evidence! Just a letter from some ninety-year-old man."

"He's seems as vibrant as a thirty-year-old," McClennan said.

"What proof did he give you?" Veronica asked.

"None," Léveque said. "And without hard evidence I could not announce to an auction that I thought the pieces may be fake. They had already been scrutinized by experts and found to be authentic. There were a few who wouldn't authenticate, which is normal these days, but the majority were convinced they were done by Matisse. I would have appeared like an imbecile."

"Roux-Fuzie created one of the greatest forgeries in the history of art. It was perfect. There was no way to prove it was not a Matisse." McClennan drank more wine and then said, "I only know they are fakes because he gave me proof."

All eyes locked on him.

"The Matisse sculptures are actually Victor Roux-Fuzie sculptures."

26

F Is for Fake

"WHO THE FUCK is Victor Roux-Fuzie?" Georgia asked.

McClennan lit a cigarette then said, "He was a student of Matisse who wanted to follow in the steps of his master. Unfortunately, the art world would not recognize his genius. So he turned to grifting, to bending society's rules in his favor."

"He was a con man?" Georgia asked.

"Victor wouldn't have referred to himself as such, but sure, in today's world that is what he'd be labeled. I like to think of him as a sort of spiritual brother of Elmyr de Hory."

"Elmyr de Hory?" Camden asked.

"One of the best-known art forgers of the twentieth century," Georgia answered for McClennan. "Picasso, Modigliani, even Matisse . . . he fooled a lot of people."

"I don't know if Roux-Fuzie or de Hory was better," McClennan said, "but my boy did a helluva job with the odalisque sculptures that used to be up in Bouchon's hotel. Made them when he was just in his early twenties."

"I find this terribly hard to believe," Bouchon said. "There were Matisse scholars who verified the authenticity of my sculptures. And, hell, they were found under the floorboards of his studio."

"Which is why they were believed to be the work of Matisse. The sculptures were not signed. If there is no documentation on a piece, as you know, authenticity is ambiguous. Scholars can debate it, and we've seen it throughout history from works ranging from Botticelli to Basquiat. As long as you get the right people to say it's real, there will be buyers. There are always buyers. These were found inside the master's studio and bore every mark of the artist's style. The argument against authenticity was weak. That is why Roux-Fuzie is such a genius."

"What proof do you have?" Georgia asked.

"In time, Georgia. First let me continue with the tale. Roux-Fuzie quit art for more lucrative endeavors, but he kept close ties with Matisse. Not only that, his girlfriend and love of his life, Ms. Claudette Leblanc, owned a house not far from Matisse's studio in Nice. They were frequent visitors and friends of the artist. And Victor, being a professional grifter, soon found a way to exploit his friendship with his famous friend.

"Victor, above all, was an artist. He learned by copying Matisse, and he practiced so frequently, he could produce work almost identical to his master. It's how Victor found his angle. When Matisse was away from Nice, he would invite wealthy people to visit his girlfriend's chateau there. They would wine and dine them, and then casually mention they were authorized by Matisse to sell his work.

"Victor would replicate a Matisse, usually a painting but sometimes a sculpture, and hide it in the studio. He pried open a loose floorboard and dug underneath the ground to make a hiding hole. When he took a mark to Matisse's studio, which he had stolen the key to and made a duplicate, he would quickly remove the spurious piece, and then sell it for huge sums. But

Victor was smart. He never sold to anybody who would question them. And you must remember, back then word traveled like a slug. He sold to Russians and South Africans and even to rich Americans, people not involved in the art community. Always private collectors who wouldn't think of donating to a museum. Through the years he made millions."

"You're claiming there're a lot of fake Matisses out there now," Bouchon said.

"Hanging in private residences. The ones brought back into the market were most likely outed as counterfeit. The reason the sculptures in question were not is because Victor never got a chance to sell them. And those pieces were to be his retirement. Faking those three sculptures took him a long time, almost all of 1939.

"He hid them in the usual spot under the floorboards, awaiting his buyer. Unfortunately, he never got to make the sale. The police had tracked him and Claudette down for other crimes and busted them in Nice. Claudette was killed trying to escape, and Victor Roux-Fuzie spent the next twenty years in jail.

"By the time he got out, there was no way of getting inside Matisse's studio. The master had died and he had no access. They changed all the locks. He thought of breaking in but couldn't bear the thought of spending more time in jail. He then lived quietly . . . until that auction about two years ago."

Mr. Léveque said, "That is exactly what Roux-Fuzie said to me in the letter."

"What's the proof?" Veronica asked.

"As I said, Victor had worked a long time on the sculptures. Claudette documented his progress by taking pictures."

"You have the pictures," Bouchon said glumly.

"Indeed, I have the photos and the negatives."

"Okay, McClennan," Veronica said, "why would you get out of prison and steal these sculptures if you knew they weren't real?"

"Because Mr. Roux-Fuzie paid me shitloads of money to. He knows death is near and he believes those sculptures to be the best things he created in his life. Even though he was imitating Matisse, Victor said they were his creations. He wants them back, to be buried with him. After Victor got out of jail, he used all the money he'd made grifting and invested it wisely. The guy is as filthy rich as either of you two."

"So you stole my sculptures," Bouchon said.

"I sure did, sir."

"Then why shouldn't I call the police right now?" Bouchon asked.

"Because I'll expose that they're fake. You can have me arrested, but I'll get the pictures to people who will get them in the newspaper."

Camden finished another glass of wine and stood.

"Fake or not, there are people right now who want to kill me and Veronica if they do not get the sculptures. And they'll surely kill you, too, McClennan."

"They'll never find me," he said with confidence.

"Who do you speak of, Camden?" Mr. Léveque asked.

Camden took a deep breath, gulped some wine, and said, "There is a group of people who'd planned to rob the museum, but McClennan beat them to it."

"I don't believe that," Mr. Léveque said.

"It's true. I think there's an excellent chance Miles Krakow paid them to do it."

"Miles," Georgia said. "I knew it."

"I can't prove that yet, but it makes sense," Camden said. "There's also a tall woman that somehow fits into the puzzle. I don't know if she's the one pulling all the strings or just one of the puppets."

"Tall woman?" Georgia asked. "The one you were kissing?"

"You saw that?"

"No, but that police detective, Clinken-something, he told me."

"After seeing you with a guy old enough to be your dad, I'd love to make you jealous. But that kiss was an act. She did it so the detective would think she was my lover. It was a calculated move."

"Who is this tall woman?" Mr. Léveque asked.

"She works for the guys who wanted to steal the sculptures. Maybe she's the boss."

"You said your life is in danger," he said. "I don't understand how or why."

"They gave me three days to get them the sculptures or they would kill me," Camden answered.

"Why you?" Georgia asked.

"Because I was going to help them rob the museum."

"Oh, Camden," Léveque said.

"They were going to pay me seventy-seven grand to be their hostage," he said. "I didn't have to do anything except let them push me around and not try to stop them. Paying a hostage was insurance against one of the old gallery attendants dying of a heart attack or a younger one trying to be a hero."

"Another stellar choice by Camden Swanson," Georgia said.

Camden drank his wine and said, "One of hundreds."

"So the group of thieves thought you worked with McClennan to steal the sculptures before them?" Mr. Léveque asked. "Because of what happened in Boston all those years ago?"

"Bo got a job working at the hotel under an alias . . . I'm a gallery attendant at the museum in hotel. It doesn't look good."

"We have to figure out what to do now," Léveque said.

The room got quiet.

Camden walked to the corner window and peered down at Union Square hundreds of feet below. He admired the lights illuminating the palm trees in the sloping park made mostly of concrete. Veronica went to him and put her arm on his shoulder.

"Are you okay?" she asked.

"I've felt better."

"It has to be tough seeing your ex with somebody."

"Somebody richer, thinner, and, even though much older, better looking than me," Camden said. "Kinda sucks."

"You have to get your head somewhere else," Veronica said. "We have to figure out what to do. Let's state the facts. McClennan has the sculptures. He wants to get paid for stealing them. Bouchon of course wants them back, even if they are fakes. And he doesn't want the public to learn they're bullshit. The clients still want them, and Detective Clinkenbeard wants to arrest somebody for the crime."

"And I want to be on a beach somewhere with a bottle of rum and an iPod full of Jimmy Buffett songs."

"Shut up and think."

Camden looked at Veronica and asked, "Do you really believe in me?"

"What?"

"You don't assume I'm going to fuck up."

"You were a great reporter," Veronica said. "You're a smart guy, regardless of any of your past mistakes. I've watched you the last few days handle a lot of shit."

"You, too," he said. "I mean it. We make a pretty good team."

"Then why are you acting like my Cousin Karl?"

"Cousin Karl?"

"Every family get-together he drinks too much and rambles on and on about how he messed his life up. I could never understand why he didn't do anything about it. Who cares about the stupid monkey-snakes? Right here, right now, Camden. We need to stay alive and we need to get the sculptures and break the story."

Camden put his head against the window, his breath steaming the glass, and watched the red and white lights of the vehicles navigating Powell Street. After a couple of minutes, he turned around and smiled at Veronica. He held up his hand for a high five and she slapped it.

"No more Cousin Karl, I promise."

Camden strode back to the table, a little wobbly but his eyes were sharp. There was a discussion going on but he did not wait for a break in the conversation. He held both arms up in the air like a third base coach frantically signaling a runner to stop from going home.

Everybody stared at him.

"Here's what we're going to do," Camden said. "Veronica spelled out the situation perfectly. It's all about satisfying needs. McClennan has the sculptures and needs a big payday. Bouchon needs the sculptures back and doesn't want, for the sake of the museum, the public to learn they're forgeries. Veronica and I need to stay alive. And there's a detective eager for an arrest. So here's what we do. We set up an exchange with the Tall Woman and her clients. We then alert Detective Clinkenbeard and have him arrest them. Bouchon gets the sculptures back and we don't have to worry about getting killed."

"What about me?" McClennan asked. "Why do I just hand over the sculptures to set up those people? I don't want to see you killed, but I need to get what's due to me. I spent eight years in jail and I need to make up for lost time. I have my future to think about."

"That's where Bouchon comes in," Camden said. "He's going to pay you to give us the sculptures. In return you take his big check, give him the pictures and the negatives, and do not say anything about them being fraudulent."

"*Pourquoi?*" Bouchon asked with incredulity.

"Your hotel, which is called the fucking Matisse, depends on it. Veronica and I keep our mouths shut, too. McClennan does it for the money, we do it for the gratitude of staying alive. Mr. Léveque and Georgia, we'll have to ask for your word to keep quiet. I mean, it does neither of you any good to be involved. Endeavoring to explain to people how and why the Matisse sculptures are fake . . . can't see either of you interested in embarking on such a quixotic journey. With no hard proof, you'd both wind up seeming like a bunch of nutters."

"How much is Bouchon going to pay me?" McClennan asked. "I have a guaranteed fifty million from Victor Roux-Fuzie."

"Fifty million, then."

"You are crazy," Bouchon said.

"If it gets exposed, it would be a huge embarrassment," Veronica said. "Maybe you'd get through it, but your hotel and museum would be synonymous with fraud."

"She's right," Georgia said. "It wouldn't be the cool place of a daring robbery. It would be the museum that fobbed off to the public a bunch of imitation Matisse sculptures."

Mr. Léveque said, "A fifty-million-dollar loss would hurt, but you and I both know there are plenty of ways of covering up such a thing. I'm sure À Venir Fantastique has accounts all over the world that wouldn't even be dented by such a figure. But if you want to be stubborn and cheap, I would be more than happy to help with some of the cost. People's lives are at stake."

"Keep your checkbook in your pants, Mr. L," Camden said. "With Bouchon's combined income with Georgia, I don't think he'll be sweating it. Her upcoming show should be a huge success."

"It will be," Georgia said. "And fuck you, Camden."

"What do you say to this, David?"

"You are all insane," he answered.

"The Museum of the Twentieth Century," Camden said, "forever known as the embarrassment of the art world."

"Fine," Bouchon barked. "I will pay. But I don't understand why you insist on getting that, what do you call her, tall woman arrested. It seems too dangerous. I will pay you more if you do not involve the police."

Veronica answered, "Because they want to kill us, and unless they're in jail, they'll probably be able to do it."

"Won't the police arrest you?" Bouchon asked Camden. "How can you explain your involvement in it?"

"Shit," Veronica said. "He's right. We're both in danger of that. And losing our story."

"Veronica, you'll be fine," Camden said. "I'll leave your name out completely. Hell, the bag you put in the locker was never even used. I'll set it up with Clinkenbeard, lie about my involvement with the Tall Woman. I'll say they threatened to kill me if I didn't help."

"What if the police don't believe you?" Veronica asked. "You'll end up in jail."

"Possibly, but if the sculptures get returned and I give them people to arrest, I should be okay. And it won't be you, McClennan. I've never even seen you."

"I'm game," McClennan said. "Roux-Fuzie will be disappointed about not getting his sculptures back, but I guess it's how it has to be."

"Fine," Bouchon said.

"I don't care about setting up that woman and her partners," McClennan said. "I want to get paid first. I'll bring the sculptures once I get the money. I'll let you know where to wire it."

"It's not like I can hand it over now," Bouchon said. "I will have to make certain arrangements to get it."

"We'll wait here," McClennan said. "I'm sure you can get it in the morning."

Bouchon stood up quickly, knocking over his water glass in the process, and put out his hand for Georgia. She accepted, smoothed the wrinkles in her black cotton dress, and rose without making eye contact with anybody. Camden watched them stride toward the door.

"We will be back tomorrow by noon," Bouchon said before exiting. "I want those photographs of that despicable Victor-person faking the sculptures. Along with the negatives, or else I do not pay."

"I can do that," McClennan said.

Camden followed Georgia and Bouchon out in the hallway and could smell his ex-girlfriend's perfume as he exited the door. The urge to be like Cousin Karl was strong. He wanted to say something but instead turned around and headed back toward the suite.

* * *

The hotel staff were in the process of eliminating all traces of the night. As the plates, silverware, and glasses clinked and clanked from being bussed, Camden snatched a full bottle of Burgundy. He poured himself a glass and slumped into one of the oversized plush chairs. Veronica sat next to him, her body warm against his, and her hair smelled like lavender.

"It's going to be more challenging, but we can write that article," she said.

Camden drank his wine and did not look at her.

"We'll have to leave out the part of the sculptures being fakes, which really sucks because that would be the scoop of a lifetime. But we'll have more than enough material for a great story. Any newspaper or magazine would buy it."

"Veronica, I'll help you with remembering quotes and details, and I give full consent to use me in the article. But I'm not a reporter anymore."

Camden tried to take a sip of his wine, but Veronica stopped him. "I'm not letting you off that easy," she said. "You promised no more Cousin Karl. The story is going to start my career and give yours back to you."

"It will be a church-sanctioned miracle if I don't end up dead or in jail."

"Don't even joke about that."

"How can Georgia be with that guy?"

"Who knows why people fall for each other. Who cares?"

"You're right. If I mention her again, please punch me in the face."

"Deal."

"You're pretty amazing, you know that. It's your character, your fortitude. I'm drunk and I'm babbling, but I'm speaking the truth now."

Camden turned to Veronica and thought of all the beginnings of every relationship he ever had. The beginnings were the best. There was hope, promise, admiration. He had felt not only a physical attraction toward Veronica, but he respected her determination and was impressed with her toughness. He angled his head toward her for a kiss on the lips. She turned away and instead put her head on his shoulder.

"I like you, Camden. We've been through a lot these last couple of days. You're the kind of strange, flawed, funny guy I've been looking for. But I can't be your rebound girl. Not now. Not with all this craziness going on. Let's try to keep focused on what we have to do."

"You're right. Sorry, I'm a goddamned hot mess right now. But please know I did mean what I just said to you. Hot mess and all."

"No need to be sorry. There could be a chance someday."

"Like a 47 percent chance?"

"Let's call it 41.3."

27

Abracadabra

CAMDEN OPENED HIS eyes to Veronica's curly auburn hair inches from his face. He did not remember falling asleep or even getting into the room. He brushed some of the lavender-scented strands of hair away from her eyes and he smiled.

After wandering through each room of the suite searching for a bathroom, it took Camden, in his highly groggy state, a few minutes to realize something was amiss. Both Bo McClennan and Jean Francois Léveque were missing. But his mind, numbed by last night's alcohol consumption and focused on finding a place to urinate, could not grasp what that fact meant.

Veronica continued to sleep, the fluffy, white duvet pulled up to insulate herself from the air conditioner, and Camden wanted to enjoy the moment for as long as he could. He slid back into the bed and felt content to simply be next to her. After only a few minutes in ignorant bliss, he began to worry about the disappearance of McClennan and Léveque. He wanted to believe they were at breakfast or had stepped outside for a cigarette, but Georgia's father was not the type to leave guests unattended.

Camden slipped out of bed gingerly as to not wake Veronica and checked his cell phone. The only missed call was from Sal, who also left a message, but the Unsuccessful Men's Club was not a priority. He eschewed his voicemail and instead he called Mr. L, who did not answer.

He poured two glasses of water from the kitchen and returned to the room. Veronica's smooth, rosy cheeks on her serene face made him think of a Botticelli painting. He would have liked to let her sleep, but he gently shook her shoulder until she opened her hazel eyes. It took her a few seconds to realize where she was, and when she sat up she grunted and put her hand up to her head.

"How much wine did we drink?" she asked with a scratchy voice.

"Several gallons, I believe."

"I'm not a big drinker."

"Neither am I," Camden said.

"How can you say that with a straight face?"

He handed her the glass of water and she gulped it down, spilling some on her undershirt. He gave her the other one and she took a long sip and put it on the nightstand with a groan of somebody not used to a hangover.

"McClennan and Mr. Léveque are gone," Camden said.

"Where?"

"Don't know. Mr. L would have taken great pleasure providing us with a lavish breakfast, but he's not here and did not answer his cell phone."

"I'm sure they'll be back soon. Try Mr. Léveque again."

Camden called Georgia's father several more times, only getting the man's silky French voice on the outgoing message. After speaking with somebody at the front desk, he learned that

Léveque and a friend left at five in the morning and requested a limousine. The desk did not know where they were going, nor would they share that sort of information even with a guest of the man paying for the suite.

"I didn't think they knew each other before last night," Veronica said after Camden gave her the information.

"What the shit? I really thought we could trust him."

"Camden, maybe that means Mr. Léveque paid McClennan to steal the sculptures."

Camden began pacing and said, "It's possible. But it doesn't make sense. The Matisse sculptures aren't genuine."

"Maybe McClennan was lying," she said. "Isn't he a champion poker player, probably really great at bluffing? We can't trust anybody."

"But why would Léveque risk such a scandal, especially after all those rumors from way back that he was behind the Rembrandt robberies in the seventies, and being a suspect in both the Gardner and Cordovan heists?" Camden asked. "He hates that he has that reputation. It can't be money; he's worth a lot more than those sculptures."

"Where is he, then?"

"Could McClennan have kidnapped him?" he suggested.

"Why?"

"I don't know. Sure, he's my ex-girlfriend's dad, but we're close. He wouldn't fuck me over. McClennan could have forced him at gunpoint. Shit, there's got to be some logic here."

"Let's search the suite. Could be a clue as to where they went," Veronica said.

"I'll call downstairs to get the name of the service they used."

"I'd like a limo," Camden said after he dialed the desk and spoke to the same person he talked with earlier. "The same service that Mr. Léveque uses."

"Unfortunately, that is not possible, sir," the hotel employee said. "Mr. Léveque hired the limousine for the day and Corningstone only has but one limo. They're more of a private security service, but they do rent out their limousine occasionally."

"Could you give me the number for Corningstone?"

"Absolutely, sir."

Camden scribbled down the number on hotel stationary and thanked the agent for his time. The kidnapping theory could now be discarded since McClennan and Léveque had left together in a limo run by a private security company. And what to make of that?

Getting Corningstone to release where they took a client would be impossible. He instead joined Veronica in searching the suite. Maybe they would find an old-fashioned clue.

Léveque's personal belongings did not yield any receipts for train tickets or letters hinting of where they were going or any piece of information that could tie him with McClennan. They only found expensive clothes, a few books, and toiletry items. They could not even be sure if Mr. L was coming back since he could request the hotel staff pack up and ship his belongings to wherever he wished.

They decided to give them one hour to return and to order room service. When Veronica expressed disappointment in having to put on her dirty clothes, Camden asked what she would like to wear. She said she'd feel a lot better wearing a business suit, but she did not agree on his idea of having one sent up to the room courtesy of Léveque.

"Breaking the plan and putting our lives in danger entitles you to at least a thousand or so dollars' worth of clothes. I'd order some for myself, but Mr. L and I are about the same size."

Veronica finally acquiesced and provided her size and preference of designers, and Camden called the concierge. Not long after showering and putting on a terrycloth robe, he answered the door and a uniformed man in his sixties carried in a tray with two stainless-steel-covered plates, a pot of coffee, and two ceramic cups. Veronica soon joined him in a matching robe and a towel wrapped around her head, and they both enjoyed their breakfast. Just as they were finishing, the clothes arrived, and Camden gave the employee a generous tip on Mr. L's tab.

While Veronica put on her new outfit, Camden donned one of Léveque's suits that had a French name sewn on the inside pocket that he didn't dare pronounce. He was sure he couldn't have guessed how much it cost if he had ten chances. The jacket was a little tight in the shoulders, but it was far superior than the blazer and clip-on tie Camden wore as a gallery attendant. But it did feel strange to be out of his jeans and T-shirt.

Veronica entered the living room wearing her new Chanel suit, and Camden couldn't help but mouth the word "wow."

"Do you have anything to say, Mr. Swanson? Sorry, didn't mean to use your last name."

"After what we've been through, you can call me whatever you want."

"Cool it. We have a lot of work to do today. Just give me ten more minutes and I'll be ready to go. And you clean up well yourself."

"Thanks. I like that the gun fits well inside the jacket pocket."

Camden figured Georgia would hang up on him after hearing his voice, but she might know where her father went. She picked up on the third ring and barked, "What do you want?" as if he were a telemarketer.

"I'm sorry, I'm sorry, I'm sorry," he said. "I promise I'm not stalking you."

"David is off getting the money for your thieving asshole of a friend. He's been gone since early morning."

"C'mon, Georgia. McClennan isn't a friend."

"After the shit I heard last night, I don't know what to believe. Two different groups of thieves, the Matisse sculptures being fakes, and you saying you were going to be paid to be a hostage, which of course you never told me about."

"Hell, Georgia. You'd been avoiding me."

"Camden, I can't deal with you now. David will be over at the St. Francis as soon as he can. What do you want?"

"Your father."

"What about my father?"

"He's disappeared. McClennan and your dad left at five in the morning in a limo."

"That's insane. We made that plan. David will give the money to McClennan. Dad wouldn't jeopardize that, especially if what you said was true."

"What I said is true. If I don't give the sculptures to the Tall Woman today, they are going to kill me, and likely Veronica as well."

"My father wouldn't do that to you."

"Agreed. That's why I'm worried. Maybe McClennan tricked him to leave. Maybe he's got a much bigger deal lined up. I don't even know if I believe anything he told us last night."

"My dad's really missing?"

"Missing isn't the right word. I'm sure he knows very well where he is, but we don't. Will you call me if you hear from him?"

"Of course."

"And Georgia, I honestly want you to be happy. It stings to see you with somebody else, but if you're happy then I'll have to deal with it."

"When I'm with David it feels so nice to be the one who doesn't have to be responsible all the time. I don't have to take care of him."

"I get it," Camden said. "And Bouchon is a cool guy. Shit, he complimented me on my poems. I'm happy for the two of you. Truly."

"Find a girl who's more laid back. That's what you want. We're not right for each other, and you know it. Maybe we can be friends. Maybe not. But right now, that's not my biggest concern. I want to know where my father is."

"I'm going to do my best to find him. And please call me the minute you hear from him."

28

The Clinkenbeard Conundrum

WHILE CAMDEN STRODE down the hotel hallway with Veronica to the elevator, he listened to Sal's voicemail from the night before. "Dude, you're not going to believe it, but McClennan and Léveque have known each other for a long-ass time. Léveque, through one of his organizations, gives scholarships to gifted high school kids so they can attend college. McClennan got one when he graduated high school. Somebody brought that up on one of the discussion threads on the site. Sorry I don't have any more info, but figured you should know. Seems to be an intriguing coincidence."

As they rode the elevator down to the lobby, Camden gave Sal's information to Veronica and then said, "Would have been nice to have known that last night."

On the third floor, the elevator stopped and the doors opened, but nobody stood on the plush carpet on the landing. When the doors shut, Camden pulled the stop button and said, "Not sure if we can trust the cops, but I'd feel a lot better knowing somebody had our back. Do you think Clinkenbeard could ID you? It was pretty dark."

"No, he couldn't have seen either my face or McClennan's last night, but I don't think that matters. He could arrest us anyway."

"For what? You put a bag in a locker that's still there, and I said I'd be a hostage and never was. We weren't accessories because they never robbed the museum. It could help having the cops on our side."

"You threw a horseshoe at Clinkenbeard's face," Veronica said.

"He doesn't know that."

"I don't like it," Veronica said. "I certainly don't want to die, but I also don't want to go to jail."

"I won't call if you think it's a bad idea."

"You really think it's a good one?"

"All I know is that we're fucked right now. McClennan is gone, we don't have the sculptures, and we've both seen what the clients can and will do to people who piss them off. And I'm sure the Tall Woman is probably outside the hotel waiting for us."

"Okay," Veronica said. "Make the call."

"I'll be careful of what I say. I won't tell him we know about McClennan. Of course, Clinkenbeard's not stupid and probably figures McClennan did steal the sculptures. But we can't throw the guy under the bus, because he could help us. In the most evasive way possible, I'll tell him about the Tall Woman and the clients. We were going to have to do this anyway, we're just moving up our timeline."

Camden released the stop button on the elevator and they rode the rest of the way in silence. The lobby teemed with people as they walked over the marble and rugs and into the revolving doors at the main entrance. It was gray outside and many people bounded up and down Powell Street carrying umbrellas to keep dry in the mist.

But there were no chants or pickets or people banging trash cans. The striking employees were gone. And that's when Veronica said she had to make one more trip to the human resources department at the Matisse Hotel.

"I've never no-called, no-showed to a job before," Veronica said. "We have far more important problems to deal with, but it's only a few minutes' walk from here."

"Do what you have to do. I'll call Clinkenbeard. We'll meet in fifteen minutes at the ticket booth right there in Union Square."

* * *

When Veronica walked into the human resources department, Carmine and Bonnie stopped what they were doing and stared at her. It was after 10:00 a.m. and the team had been trying to reach her all morning. During the entire time of her temp assignment, Veronica had never called in sick, been late, or failed to do one thing that was expected of her.

"We thought something had happened to you," Bonnie said.

"Are you okay?" Carmine asked. Before allowing her to answer, he continued. "'Cause we're going to need you now big-time. Probably for the next month or so at least. I'm sure you've heard. The employees are coming back."

"They signed a contract?" Veronica asked.

"Nope," Carmine answered. "Basically, it's a draw. The hotel wouldn't crack and neither would the union. But both sides know the labor dispute is stupid, so they called a truce."

"For how long?"

"For however long it takes for a contract," Bonnie answered. "Last time it took two years for both the sides to agree."

"So the strike was for nothing?" Veronica asked.

"I wouldn't go that far," she said. "But you basically had two very powerful opponents scheming to outmaneuver one another. Both sides, me and you included, were pawns for the Wizards of Oz behind the curtains."

Veronica approached Bonnie and asked in a whisper if they could speak alone in private. They went to her manager's office, which was small and crammed with binders and papers. She was surprised at how difficult it was to say good-bye to her temp job.

"I appreciate how everybody here treated me, especially you," she said. "It's been an amazing experience where I've learned so much. But I have another job opportunity."

"Doing what?"

"Journalism. It's what I went to school for. What I've always wanted to do."

"I'm happy for you, Veronica. I guess that's why you didn't seem so thrilled at taking a full-time position here."

"It's a great hotel and I'd be proud to take any job here. But all I've ever wanted to do since I was a kid is be a reporter. I'd like to stay on and help train the new temp, but I have to start the new job right now. I wish I could tell you more, and some-day I promise I will. But I'll call the agency when I leave and they'll send somebody immediately to take my place."

"Whoever it is they won't be as good as you," Bonnie said. "And while I'm sad we won't be working together anymore, I'm happy to see you get on the career path you want. Makes me want to dust off my art books and make a go of it one more time. I'll be looking forward to reading your byline in the future."

"Hopefully very soon," Veronica said.

* * *

While Veronica took care of her business at the Matisse Hotel, Camden strolled into the concrete center of Union Square. Among a throng of tourists and under the shadow of the nearly hundred-foot column with the woman holding a trident on top, he dialed the number for the San Francisco Police Department. After giving his name and being put on hold for a few minutes, he was connected to Detective Clinkenbeard.

"I have enough evidence to get a warrant out for your arrest, Mr. Swanson," the man said as a greeting.

"I'm not the one you want, detective. Trust me. But I can help you get that person."

"How?"

"Let's talk in person," Camden said. "I'm in Union Square. Can you meet me here?"

"Do you know where Grace Cathedral is?" Clinkenbeard asked.

"The one on the hill?"

"Yeah, about a ten-minute walk up. California and Taylor. It's next to the park."

"Are you feeling spiritual now?" he asked.

"Some asshole this morning threatened three people out here with an Uzi. Could be connected to the Matisse robbery. I'll meet you on the front steps."

Camden didn't think the clients or the Tall Woman would randomly threaten people with an Uzi, and it was doubtful McClennan had, either. However, anything was possible and he had to be careful. He possessed the loaded gun that was not registered to him, which wouldn't bode well for him if Clinkenbeard discovered that.

Shunning the steep walk up Powell, Camden boarded a cable car at Post Street after he heard the bell clanging behind him. He hoped he could jump off before the conductor could collect the tourist-priced fare, but no such luck. He paid with one of the few bills he had left and called Veronica to arrange to meet in the park across from Grace Cathedral. At California Street, he hopped off and landed hard on his sore knee and limped the two blocks up the hill to meet with Clinkenbeard.

With its stained glass, gothic design, and overall medieval appearance, Grace Cathedral loomed majestically over Huntington Park on Nob Hill. The fog had rolled up there and, along with the mist, made it impossible to see the bridges and the bay. Camden spotted Clinkenbeard, who had a large bandage on his purplish face, leaning over the railing on the top of the steps facing down California Street.

"I almost didn't recognize you in that suit," he said. "Did you change tailors?"

"And I almost didn't recognize you with the whole look you got going on. Go a few rounds with Mayweather or Pacquiao?"

"I'm assuming you were in West Portal last night," Clinkenbeard said. "But I have no evidence to prove you were. We believe that it was McClennan's hideout and we have a neighbor who identified him in a photo. But given the source, we're trying to find a second witness who can positively ID him."

"Where's West Portal?" Camden asked.

Clinkenbeard stared at him with the gaze of a drill instructor and asked, "Have you seen Miles Krakow lately?"

"He's Georgia's friend, not mine."

"Krakow matches the description of the guy with an Uzi earlier this morning."

"Dude's a nutjob. Seems like his MO."

"From all accounts he's lost it," he said. "The man, whom we believe was Mr. Krakow, was videotaping the cathedral all morning. When a couple of tourists asked him if he was a movie director, he showed them an Uzi in his bag and started raving that they should never bother an artist while he's working. He then flashed them for good measure. Scared the hell out of a couple from Bugtussle, Kentucky. By the time we got here, Krakow was gone."

"I thought Miles might have been involved in the robbery, but now I'm not so sure," Camden said. "And whipping his dick out at a couple from—"

"Bugtussle, Kentucky."

"Doesn't exactly point to him being a master thief."

"I'm thinking Krakow paid you and McClennan to help him steal the sculptures."

"I wouldn't help that piece of shit across the street for any amount of money."

"Krakow or McClennan?" Clinkenbeard asked.

"Either. I had absolutely nothing to do with stealing the sculptures. I've never seen them except behind the glass in the museum," Camden answered.

"But you said on the phone you could help me get the person who did steal the sculptures. How can you do that if you were not involved in the theft? Are you a detective, Mr. Swanson? Are you working undercover for the SFPD?"

"You know I was a reporter before. I've decided to use the heist as my comeback tour."

"I believe you as much as I believe Jerry Garcia is going to rise from the grave and give a concert in Golden Gate Park," Clinkenbeard said.

"There are a group of thieves involved in the robbery," he said, "who have nothing to do with McClennan."

"How do you know?"

"They contacted me a little while back. Wanted me to help them, but I said no."

"If you had knowledge that a crime was going to be committed, why didn't you contact the police?"

"They threatened to kill me if I did," Camden said. "The morning after the sculptures were stolen, one of them, possibly the leader of the crew, showed up at my apartment and accused me of robbing the museum with McClennan. I think that's all a ruse. Maybe McClennan did want to steal the Matisse sculptures, but this other group beat him to it with their end game to cheat the person I've come to call the Tall Woman, who I think is the leader, out of her cut. I don't know the Tall Woman's real name. Makes sense, right?"

"Nothing you have said so far makes sense."

"The group of thieves want to keep all the money they get from selling the sculptures for themselves. So they come to me because they know I have a connection to McClennan. They then rob the museum on a different day than their original plan and accuse me and McClennan to shift the suspicion. Which brings me to the second and most important reason I need to find the sculptures. They gave me three days to get them or else they kill me."

"Who are these alleged group of thieves? Who is this tall woman?" Clinkenbeard asked.

"I could identify three of them in police lineup, but the others were wearing masks. Two look like accountants or even your average tech guys. The third probably used to compete in body building competitions and consumes whole chickens for breakfast. The Tall Woman is the person who asked me to help them rob the museum. She looks like a model and could play shooting guard in the NBA."

"Six feet five with dark hair and a trim-to-athletic build?"

"That's the one. You saw us kiss outside of the Beach Chalet," Camden said.

"Why would a master thief, the leader of the crew, as you say, kiss you if she believes you stole the sculptures?"

"As deception. She figured the cops would be watching."

"I don't believe anything you're saying, Mr. Swanson. I've yet to figure out how you fit into all of it, but my instincts tell me that you're not innocent. The case has run cold and right now you're all I have. Tell me why I shouldn't arrest you?"

"If I were guilty, why would I call you? My life is in danger and I wanted to tell the police what I know about it in case bad shit happens to me."

"Bad shit? You could be in major fucking shit. But what have you told me?" Clinkenbeard asked. "You've given me a tall woman and a bunch of guys wearing ski masks. C'mon, Swanson. We figured McClennan for the robbery with you, Hipple, and the Matisse's director of security. Two of those people were murdered, and you think you're next. You're scared because you're the last loose thread."

"Detective, what evidence do you have that I was involved?"

"We don't have any proof yet."

"And you'll never find any. It sounds crazy, but you have to believe me."

"That's where you're wrong. I don't have to believe you. I don't have any evidence you're involved in the robbery, but I can't let you leave. I need to bring you downtown to be properly questioned. I want detailed descriptions of everyone and everything you know. A couple of hours under a hot light might get the truth out of you."

As Clinkenbeard took out his handcuffs, a girl screamed from inside the church as if she had seen a vision of fire and brimstone. The detective rushed inside with the piercing sound echoing off pews and stained glass, and it would take him about one minute to realize it was a hoax. By this time Camden was gone.

He learned a teenage girl from the Marina on a class outing was paid a hundred bucks to scream as loud as she could. She described the person who gave her the money as being "like way volleyball player tall" and "super swankalishious hot."

29

Scofflaws

WHEN CLINKENBEARD RUSHED past the copies of Ghiberti's golden Gates of Paradise into the cathedral to investigate the scream, Camden turned to see the Tall Woman bounding up the steps. She yanked him by the arm, and her grip was strong. Seconds away from being arrested and a gun now stuck in his ribs, he had little choice but to follow her down to Taylor Street.

"We have Veronica in our car," she said, giving him another reason to not resist.

The Tall Woman shoved him inside a black sedan with tinted windows double-parked on Taylor. Veronica sat a foot away from him with her hands bound with duct tape next to the muscular client holding a gun on her. The vehicle shot out into traffic just ahead of a cable car and began heading down the steep slope of California Street.

"We'd like our gun back," said the client who resembled Andre the Giant. "Put your goddamned arms up."

Camden did as requested and said, "It's in my suit jacket pocket."

The guy reached inside his jacket and took the gun.

"All we want is McClennan," the Tall Woman said. "If you tell us where he is, and we're able to get the sculptures, then you both can live. Simple."

"What if we don't know where he is?" Camden said.

"Then I would say that you're lying."

"It's the truth," Veronica pleaded.

"Then you're both fucked," the Tall Woman responded.

"We don't know exactly where McClennan is now," Veronica said with a shaky voice. "But we're meeting him later."

"When?"

"He's gonna call us."

"I hope for your sake that's true," she said. "And you'll both wait with us until he does."

The driver, who Camden recognized as the client who survived the bison attack, slowed down to the speed limit, and just before the road began sloping upward, he took a left on Van Ness. After ten minutes, they reached a redbrick warehouse that had been recently tagged with graffiti. The car then maneuvered down a driveway of cracked asphalt toward a gated garage.

"I don't think I like the fact we weren't blindfolded," Camden said.

"It doesn't matter now," the Tall Woman responded. "You've seen everyone already. Either they kill you both or else we won't be staying long enough for either of you to hurt us."

"It's starting to come together now," Camden said.

"Excuse me?" she asked as the gate to the underground parking structure began to open.

"You must have followed us out of the hotel. How did you know we would be at the St. Francis this morning?"

"We followed you from the hotel up to Grace Cathedral. I have my connections."

"Perhaps," Camden said. "But I think it's because Bouchon told you we were there."

"Why would the owner of the hotel, whose sculptures we wanted to steal, tell us anything?"

"Because he paid you to steal them," Camden responded as the car drove into the underground lot. "He knows they're forgeries and wants them gone. Simply removing them from the museum would cause far too much suspicion and he's out millions of dollars. You rob the place, he at least recoups some of the money through the insurance. That's exactly it. He paid you to steal the Matisse sculptures, but McClennan beat you to it."

"Could that be true?" Veronica asked.

"I think it is. But whether or not she knew she was dealing with Bouchon is another story. He could have used a third party, a go-between. Maybe they don't even know the sculptures aren't real. But that hardly matters. The clients want them back, so they can give them to Bouchon. He's going to pay for that service no matter what. But no sculptures, no money."

"Makes sense," Veronica said. "Remember last night, Bouchon said he didn't want to get the police involved."

"Whatever crackpot theories you have, please keep them to yourself," the Tall Woman said. "The only thing that should matter to you both is whether or not you can deliver McClennan. Get out of the fucking car."

The vehicle had parked close to a wooden staircase, and she led them upstairs to a dimly lit apartment that Camden recognized as the one he had entered days ago. The client who looked like Andre the Giant followed behind them, and he jabbed his weapon into the small of Camden's back either to make him go quicker or just for fun. He shook off the pain and tried to piece together all the events since he'd accepted payment for being a hostage.

The four of them rounded a corner and Camden felt a tap on his shoulder.

He instinctively turned around and a fist slammed into his nose. With teary eyes he crumpled to the floor.

Veronica screamed.

The driver of the car kicked Camden as he lay on the ground. "That's for your buddy McClennan stealing the sculptures."

He then lifted Camden up, threw him against the wall, and punched him in the cheek.

"I wanted to do that last night. That's for what the buffalo did to our partner in the park," he said with a grin.

Camden wobbled up on his feet, hunched over in pain and bleeding in several places. The man grabbed him by the hair and threw him to the ground. Camden covered his face with his hands, and the kick that followed likely broke one of his fingers.

"That's for our partner who fell over the waterfall," the man attacking him said.

A thought flashed in Camden's head while he got in the fetal position to protect himself. He remembered his first byline at his college newspaper, how he had truly felt proud of what he'd completed. It was a story on one of the football players, how he had risen from the projects and now had a 3.5 grade point average. Why hadn't he stuck to the sports page?

"Stop it," Veronica screamed.

The large client grabbed Veronica and threw her against the concrete wall. Camden, with all the strength he could muster, kicked him in the groin. The guy fell to the floor and screamed like a toddler. He would only enjoy the satisfaction for a moment, as the other client beat him until he passed out cold.

* * *

Camden, with a piercing headache and his shirt covered in blood, felt plastic against his hands. Slowly regaining consciousness, he was able to focus his eyes on a blue tarp underneath his supine body. His arms and legs weren't bound, which he considered a good thing, but glancing up he saw Andre the Giant pointing a gun at his face.

"Your friend informed us that you have a meeting with McClennan and Mr. Léveque later on today. True?"

"Yeah," he croaked.

"You better hope for her sake that it is."

With sweaty and stinging palms, Camden pushed himself up to the seated position. He saw Veronica duct taped to a chair, her mouth covered and looking frightened. In addition to the pain he felt in his head, face, and ribs, Camden's stomach rippled with nerves.

"We will hold her here and expect you to deliver us the sculptures by midnight tonight," he said. "If you do not, she will die and so will you. We will accompany you to your meeting. If all goes as planned, you will both live."

"Like you let Hipple live," Camden said.

There was no response.

"McClennan doesn't give a shit about us. He wants to get his money. We had nothing to do with him robbing the museum. It's not our fault."

"You are our best chance at getting the sculptures, and that is all that matters."

"What if I can't make McClennan turn them over?"

"You shouldn't have that attitude, Mr. Swanson. You should be thinking of ways to make him give you the sculptures."

"McClennan has no alliance to me."

"It's simple. You either get us the goods by midnight or you and your friend are dead. We will shoot you, wrap you up in plastic tarps, and dump your bodies in the bay. We will continue to search for McClennan. But that is the messy and inefficient way of doing things."

"I doubt he'll answer, but I'll try calling him," Camden said.

"You have his cell number?"

"I do," he lied. "I'm sure it's one of dozens of prepaid ones that he has, but I can try." He dialed his own number, waited ten seconds, and said, "No luck."

"I'm calling bullshit," the large client said.

Camden got to his feet, wobbled on weak knees, and heard the whoosh of an arm moving a gun at him. He spit blood out of his mouth.

"Did your tall friend tell you?" Camden asked with a bloody smile. "That the sculptures were not done by Matisse?"

"Complete bullshit, but even if it's true it doesn't matter. Our buyer believes they're real and is going to pay us for them."

"I'll get you the fucking things," he said. "But I'm not handing them over until Veronica is safe. Take the tape off her mouth. She looks like she can hardly breathe."

The room went silent.

"C'mon," Camden yelled. "Even if she screamed, who the hell is going to hear her? Show a little fucking class."

"Fine. But if she gets loud, the tape is going right back on."

Camden tripped when he took a step, regained his balance, and then walked toward Veronica. As delicately as he could, but not able to stop the ripping sound, he removed the tape from her mouth. She gasped and took several deep breaths.

"Are you okay?"

"I'm fine," she said.

He hugged Veronica but was pulled away by Andre after only a few seconds.

"Enough of that shit. The clock is on, Mr. Swanson. And don't fuck it up."

Seconds later, the Tall Woman strode into the room and ushered Camden at gunpoint to the black sedan they had arrived in earlier. Once inside, he wiped the blood that trickled from his nose as his captor started the engine. The car moved toward the garage exit, and as the automatic door began to rise, Camden pondered his options. She carried a gun, but he could try to wrestle it away and make her his hostage. He could demand Veronica's release or even go in there Rambo style and kill all the bad guys.

Unlikely.

His reflexes were far from catlike and he didn't want to shoot anybody. But, if not violent carnage, what was the next course of action? McClennan and Léveque could be sipping champagne on the Champs-Élysées for all he knew. Camden couldn't let the clients harm Veronica in any way.

"Do you have a tissue?" he asked. "My lip is bleeding."

The garage door droned upward but stopped before it reached the top, almost enough for the car to sneak under. The Tall Woman kept pressing the red button on the opener and did not answer Camden's question.

"Or if you'd rather stop for an ice pack, that would be nice," he said.

"Mr. Swanson, I'm going to get out of the car and press the manual button by the garage door. You are going to exit the vehicle as well with your hands in the air. You are lucky you are just bleeding. I was sure the clients would kill you."

"You're ridiculous, you know that?" Camden said.

"Excuse me?"

"You keep talking about 'the clients' in some sort of abstract manner. They're not some business partner in a stock deal. They've killed people, and they've beaten the piss out of me twice. It might be about money, but you're a fucking accessory to violent crimes, whether or not you think you are. Shit, you might even be the head honcho here, the Grand Poobah."

"They are my clients, and I am brokering our deal," she said before she got out of the car.

"Pull this leg and it plays 'I Left My Heart in San Francisco,'" Camden said after he stepped out of the vehicle. "You are involved in every detail one way or the other. What I don't understand is why or how. My God, you're extremely smart, educated, well-spoken, and attractive; the world is fucking yours for the taking. Why be a common thief?"

"Nothing I do is common. Arms up."

Camden was sore in almost every nook and cranny of his body but was able to do as requested. Maintaining his arms in the air was difficult. He wanted to keep the Tall Woman talking and maybe he could get the gun away from her.

"You seem like you should be the CEO of a company, not involved with criminal menace in a parking lot."

She showed a slight frown. But the emotion disappeared quickly and was replaced by a grimace as she went back to pressing the garage door clicker while pointing it at the sensor. Camden persisted with his questioning. The gate would not open, and maybe he had a chance.

"What did you want to do when you were a kid? I'm sure it wasn't stealing Matisse sculptures."

"I'm exactly where I want to be in my life," she said.

"Bullshit. Hardly anybody is, and I can tell you're not one of the elite few. What did you do before?"

"I'm not divulging personal information to you."

"Does it matter? Either I'm going to get killed or else you and your clients are leaving far, far away from here."

"Why do you care about my past?" she asked after moving toward the wall and pushing a large red button. She did not lower her gun.

"Curiosity, I guess," Camden said. "Because I am one of them, I'm interested in stories about people who ruin their lives in some fashion by making poor choices. I have to imagine every scofflaw such as yourself started off with parents who loved them and noble dreams. Always wanted to use the word scofflaw in conversation, felt like the right choice."

With a loud clang, the garage door inched open. With her gun, the Tall Woman motioned for him to return to the sedan, which he did. She followed without putting down her weapon.

"Am I living the life I wanted for myself? Is that what you're asking?"

"More or less," he said.

"The answer is no, Mr. Swanson. I'm not going to tell you what I did, but I had a good job and I loved it. But then somebody I worked with raped me. He spread lies to the whole office, ruined my reputation, and then fired me. Is that what you wanted to know? Is the story of how I ruined my life enough for you?"

Camden was not expecting to hear such raw honesty. Of course, there was a chance she was lying, but he put it very low. Here was a person who was part of a group who would murder him if he could not return the sculptures, and who dragged him into this shit show. He wanted to hate her but suddenly felt genuine compassion.

"Not a failure story. If he hasn't already, I hope that scumbag gets what he deserves."

"During our lives we're all kicked in the face at one time or another," she responded. "Shouldn't be that way, but it's the choices we make that ultimately define us. I decided to go into this profession and am now a millionaire. You chose to become a drunken loser."

Camden was still trying to process what the Tall Woman had said when she leaned over, put her hand on his shoulder, and kissed him. It was the second time she had put her lips on his, and he was sure it was done with a purpose, but he couldn't figure out what. Nobody was watching like outside of the Beach Chalet.

"Why'd you do that?" he asked. "The first time I could understand, deceiving the cops. But now you're fucking with me."

"I'm proving a point. I might be a scofflaw, as you say, and despicable by your judgment. But if I said let's go to a hotel room and have sex, you'd do it. And you would have the time of your life. Your so-called morals would crumble in an instant. So I'd make my choice over yours a thousand times over."

30

Miles Does Not Go Gently into the Good Night

THE TALL WOMAN turned the car onto Bluxome Street as the garage door thudded against the cement behind them. Camden, thinking about how he could rescue Veronica, heard tires screech and a car accelerate somewhere nearby. He saw a glimmer of chrome as another vehicle slammed into the driver's-side door.

With the explosion of glass, the Tall Woman was thrown at Camden.

Metal crunched into metal as the seat belt then jerked the Tall Woman right to left and her head slammed into the airbag protruding from the steering wheel. The car was filled with melting rubber and a burning chemical scent. Camden's skull smacked against the side window and then grazed the side of the airbag. His ears were ringing.

A hand reached into the smashed driver's-side window. The Tall Woman pawed under the seat for her gun but stopped when an Uzi rested up against her bloody nose. Miles Krakow stood over her, grinning with a cigarette in his mouth.

"I love it when a plan comes together," he said as the lit cigarette bobbed up and down. "Hands up, bitches."

"You're making a big mistake," she croaked out.

"I don't make mistakes. I'm rich and I'm clever and I'm high as the fucking moon over my hammy. I'm taking Camden as my hostage."

"You fucking idiot, Miles," he screamed. "Don't do this. I have to stay with her. They're going to kill Veronica."

"You speak gibberish. Always have and always will. I made my decision: I'm getting those sculptures no matter what. It's my Vision Quest. I've been on a big eighties kick lately. While I'll never get to 168 and wrestle Shute, I was meant to get those Matisse pieces then destroy them for the world to see! Now get the fuck out of the car."

"I have nothing to do with Miles," Camden said to the Tall Woman. "Don't hurt her. I'll get the sculptures."

"The fuck you will," Miles said. "Now out!"

Miles pointed the Uzi at Camden as he stumbled out of the wrecked car. The sound of sirens grew louder. He steadied himself against the black sedan and limped toward the crumpled passenger side of Miles's vehicle.

"No," Miles barked. "Follow me and run. C'mon! Down the street and go right."

After being beaten up and absorbing the shock of a car wreck, Camden could not run. He loped down the street and felt pain everywhere. For the first time that day he wanted a drink. Instead he brushed some crunchy glass out of his hair.

Gunfire popped three times and Miles screamed.

"You fucking cunt," he yelled.

Camden stumbled behind a gray SUV and peered over the hood. He watched Miles fire a burst of bullets and then hobble toward him dragging his left leg like a broken stick. Blood poured down his thigh as he stumbled behind the SUV next to Camden. The windshield shattered and the Tall Woman's bullets ripped through the car.

Miles positioned himself where he could aim his Uzi, and his rapid counter fire provided enough time for them to escape around the corner to a gray minivan. Miles yelled at Camden that he was to drive and threw the keys at him, and they bounced off his chest to the cement. Reaching down to grab them and then getting up so quickly made him woozy, but Camden was able to get into the vehicle and start the engine.

"Drive normal," Miles said. "Luckily, I'm tripping my balls off and I can't feel a thing. But we gotta get some bandages to stop the bleeding. Find a fucking pharmacy."

"Then what, you goddamned lunatic?"

"Then we go to see Mr. Bo McClennan and Mr. Jean Francois Léveque."

"You know where they are?"

"I hired private detectives to follow all of you motherfuckers wherever you go, and I've been in constant communication with them. Calls, text messages, even been Skyping, bitch. How do you think I found you in that warehouse?"

"The sculptures are fake, Miles."

"Bullshit."

"It's true."

"It's a filthy rotten lie and I don't believe it. Hey, there's a Walgreens. Pull over. We need to clean up our lives a little, and get me some pants while you're in there. Here's a couple hundred dollars." Miles reached into his jeans and pulled out two crumpled bills and tossed them at Camden.

He parked in front of a fire hydrant and wiped the blood and sweat off his face before entering the store, but he still looked like a guy any sane person would consciously avoid. Using one of the wadded-up hundred-dollar bills Miles gave him, he purchased bandages, towels, rubbing alcohol, and aspirin so he would be able to take care of his wounds as well. There were nervous stares from the other customers, but the guy with the neck tattoos rang him up without hesitation. Camden, as requested, also bought a pair of sweat pants that had "SF" printed in large letters on them.

Back in the car, Miles had already removed his jeans, and he grabbed the bag from his hands when he opened the door. He ripped it open and began to go to work on his leg. Camden shimmied into the back where he had more room to clean the gashes on his body.

"Cheap sweat pants! I love them," Miles said. "But you gotta go in and get me the matching sweat shirt with the big 'SF' on it, too."

"Fuck you, Miles. They have Veronica hostage and they're going to kill her unless I bring them the sculptures."

"Well, that's not going to happen. I got the Uzi. The sculptures will be mine."

The rubbing alcohol stung Camden's face as he swabbed the affected areas. He winced and responded, "If you know where McClennan is, why do you need me?"

"Because I need to trick Frenchy and him into showing me where the sculptures are. Uzi or no Uzi, they're not going to just hand them over. But you, Camden, you will make my dreams come true."

"How? Mr. L and McClennan ditched me. I thought we had an arrangement made, but they took off this morning without telling me where."

"I know where."

"That's great, but as you said, what makes you think they're going to show us where the sculptures are hidden. What do I have to offer that you do not?"

"Fuck," Miles said. "I should have kidnapped Georgia. That was the smart thing to do. Pepé Le Pew would have caved without a fight. But Georgia's my friend. My only friend in our shithole of a world. You, you are a cheap loser who didn't deserve to mop her floors, much less have sex with her. I was sort of hoping you could lead me to the pieces and then I could kill you. No offense, but I think you suck."

"If you ever stop popping pills, you'll see you've turned yourself into a joke. And when I get the chance, I'm going to split your nose open."

"I kind of like your whole macho thing you got going on now. But remember, I'm the one with the gun. You're going to figure out how to get those sculptures. For me. To keep."

With their cuts and wounds dressed, Camden put the car in gear and drove in silence. He knew there could be an opportunity to take the Uzi away from Miles, but the guy was so gone on drugs there was an even greater chance he could get shot. The minivan had GPS and he followed the directions from the electronic voice. As they headed west down Geary Street, a country song played, one with flawless musicians but strange and irreverent lyrics.

"Who is this?" Camden asked.

"Ween."

"God, I hate that I like anything you like."

"Every song is perfect on this album, but 'Piss Up a Rope' is a masterpiece."

"So, genius, what do I do when we get there?"

"I don't know," Miles responded. "What do you think?"

"You can do what the song suggests."

"We can't go in cowboy style and start shooting. I wouldn't have needed you for that. No, it has to be subtle."

"Why not just pay McClennan?"

"You don't think I tried that?"

"How much did you offer?" Camden asked.

"Whatever he wanted for them. He knows I have the money. So why wouldn't he even listen? Everything wouldn't be all higgledy-piggledy now, with the crashing into a car and the Uzi and kidnapping you and getting shot. I mean, it's been damn fun, but too much work."

"Strange he wouldn't listen to you. McClennan is clearly all about his payday."

"I would have doubled any offer," Miles said. "It has to be his buyer. And that buyer has to be Georgia's dad. Fuck me, you really think the sculptures are fucking knock-offs?"

"I don't know," he said. "But I don't think Georgia's dad is the buyer."

Although Camden couldn't be sure it would compute in Miles's drug-soaked brain, he told the story McClennan had related the night before. As they cruised down the divided and heavily trafficked Geary Street, he spoke of Victor Roux-Fuzie and the long journey of the counterfeit Matisse sculptures. Miles laughed and then spit at what he thought was an open window.

"It's all bullshit," he responded as he wiped the greenish phlegm off the glass with his hands. "McClennan probably wrote the letters and had somebody send them from France."

"It's possible."

Camden turned right on 25th Avenue and then left onto Lake Street. They had gone from honking horns, busses, and billboards in several languages to the sound of the ocean, empty streets, and million-dollar homes. He recognized that they were close to Veronica's apartment. Camden had to go left again on 28th and then a quick right to stay on Lake as the road split off and became one way on each side. The path on the left rose above the one they traveled down, and the surrounding homes were of varying architectural motifs but all fit into the dominating theme of money. They were in the Sea Cliff district of the city and the GPS directed him to a street off El Camino Del Mar where he parked.

"It's actually a couple blocks away," Miles said. "I didn't want us to drive by in case they're watching out the window."

"I ask again. Now what?"

"Time for some more medicine. I'm actually starting to feel some pain in my legs."

Miles took his hand off the Uzi on his lap and reached toward the glove compartment. Camden used all his strength and whipped his fist toward his captor's face. The side of his hand landed square on the bridge of Miles's nose.

With a scream, Miles instinctively put his hands up to his face, and Camden snatched the Uzi from him. He then brought his fist down hard in the spot where he guessed the bullet wound to be and felt warm and sticky blood. Miles let out another piercing shriek.

"What's the address?" Camden yelled at him.

He hit him in the leg again after getting no answer. Through grunts and heavy breathing, Miles told him the address of the house. With one hand on the gun, Camden grabbed a dirty towel from the back seat and gave it to him to help stop the bleeding.

"C'mon, we're going in cowboy style. Get out of the car."

31

Nouveau Plan

AS MILES STUMBLED out of the minivan in a daze, Camden shoved the Uzi under the seat and locked the doors. He rushed over and pushed Miles toward the house where they hoped to find McClennan and Léveque. A middle-aged woman in tight-fitting spandex jogged toward them, and he expected a screech of horror at their bloody intrusion to Sea Cliff. Luckily the jogger wore headphones and concentrated on the ground as she passed. Nobody else was on the street.

Miles was struggling through the pain, and Camden helped him up the stone stairs to the ten-foot-high French doors. With creaky knees, he bent down and yelled through the mail slot, "It's Camden. Open up before there's a big scene out here."

Heavy footsteps moved across hardwood floors and the doors opened. Léveque's face was a fusion of puzzlement and anger, and all Camden could do was shrug. He steered them both into the house with a stream of French obscenities.

Miles stumbled onto the sofa and smashed a lamp and vase in the process. When he began screaming in English, French, and Polish, McClennan entered the room and aimed a gun at him. The shot fired before Camden could protest, but luckily for Miles it was only a tranquilizer dart that hit him in the leg. After a few seconds of spitting and wheezing, he collapsed to the floor.

"Always dreamed of shooting that imbecile and punching him in the nose," Léveque said.

"He'll be up in an hour or so. We'll have to tie and gag him before we leave," McClennan said. "Tranquilizer guns are the best. Perfect for robbing museums and putting down hipster artists."

"Camden, you do my suit justice. A little short in the leg, but you are a different person."

"Thanks, but why did you leave this morning, Mr. L? Can understand McClennan because he doesn't give a shit about us, but the bad guys have kidnapped Veronica. I thought we had a really great plan."

"I was going to call and let you know of the new one," Mr. Léveque said.

"Veronica is tied up in some warehouse and they beat the shit out of me again. Great fucking plan you switched to."

"Sorry that happened, but all will be well," Léveque said.

"I love you as if you were my dad, but fuck you."

"We will give you the sculptures in the morning."

"The clients want them by midnight or they're going to kill me and Veronica," Camden said.

Léveque put a hand on his shoulder. "Please, have a seat. You're best to be off your feet for what we're about to tell you. And you'll surely need a drink."

"They're going to kill her, Mr. L. I can't believe you would do this."

"Camden, I promise I was going to call. I wasn't going to let anything happen to you or Veronica. I honestly thought you would stay in the suite. Why didn't you? You were safe there."

"You could have left a note. You could have called me."

"Too risky. You see, we are at the finish line. To the *coup de maître* of my career. I cannot take chances now."

"I have no idea what you're talking about," he said.

McClennan had left the room and now returned with a bottle of Cristal and three glasses. He popped the cork, letting it fly against the wall, and poured the drinks with a wide grin. While McClennan and Léveque toasted, Camden put his glass down without taking a sip.

"Did you hear what I told you? I'm certainly not toasting champagne while Veronica's life's in danger."

"Tomorrow we give you the Matisse sculptures. You will save her and we'll all be rich. That is what we are toasting. Our friend Bo here was only telling part of the truth last night. He left out many key details about Roux-Fuzie and made other things up."

"Are the sculptures fake or not?" Camden asked.

Léveque walked back toward him, grabbed the glass of champagne off the table, and shoved it in his hands. "Drink," he said. "They're fake. Victor Roux-Fuzie, a Matisse protégé, made them."

"Then what's the big deal?"

"What's inside of the sculptures."

McClennan finished off his glass of Cristal and poured himself another.

"Easy there, Bo," Mr. Léveque said. "We have some digging to do tonight."

"Champagne is like water to me. I'll be fine. Now, Camden, what I told you last night about Victor Roux-Fuzie is mostly true. He was a Matisse protégé who got frustrated that he could not find success with his art. He also did have a girlfriend named Claudette Leblanc, the love of his life, who had a house nearby to Matisse's in Nice. But Victor did not support himself by making fake works of his master and then selling them. I made that up on the spot last night. In truth, he only produced three fake Matisse pieces, the ones that ended up in the Museum of the Twentieth Century, and he never intended anybody else in the world to possess those infamous sculptures."

"Then why bury them in the floorboards of Matisse's studio and let them stay there for decades?" Camden asked.

"He buried the sculptures to hide them because of what's inside the pieces," McClennan said. "He was never able to get them back because he was in jail. And that's where Victor died a few years ago. I played with the facts last night when I was telling my story. Much of what I said was true, but a lot was creative bullshit."

"If he wasn't in jail for being a con man by forging fake Matisses, why was he?"

"For stealing diamonds," Léveque said.

McClennan moved toward Camden and put his hands on his shoulders. He stared him straight in the eyes and said, "There is half a billion dollars' worth of beautiful diamonds inside those sculptures."

* * *

After the shootout with Miles, the Tall Woman abandoned her smashed sedan on the street and ran two blocks to where she had a motorcycle parked. Climbing on the black Suzuki, she called the clients and informed them they had to evacuate the hideout as soon as possible. They had a secondary location for such an emergency and would rendezvous there.

"Don't leave the surveillance equipment," she yelled.

"We gotta throw it in the warehouse furnace. That was the plan all along. It's gonna slow us down," responded the person she referred to as Client A.

"It's our only hope of seeing the sculptures ever again. Do as I fucking say or I'll kill you."

"Okay, okay. We're packing them up now."

The Tall Woman heard sirens and shoved her phone into her bra. She pulled back on the throttle and maneuvered the motorcycle at normal speed down Townsend Street and then onto Kansas. She hadn't prayed since she was twelve, but as the cold wind hit her face, she asked the universe to help her clients escape with the surveillance equipment. If they did, she knew they would get hold of the sculptures.

And David Bouchon, after all of the trouble they'd endured, would have to double his price to get them back.

* * *

The three remaining clients all looked at Veronica.

"Should we just kill her?" the hulking mass of a man said. "I also think it's a fuck-all idea to lug around all this shit. Both are going to slow us down."

Veronica closed her eyes and thought of the play about the life of Nellie Bly she had seen when she was as kid. Before that show, she had just wanted to get married and live in a big house. But she was certain afterward that she had to be like Ms. Nellie, as she called her back then, part superhero, part reporter, and someone who would make a difference in the world. She hoped she would get the chance to do it.

"You heard what our Big Bird of a friend said," the client with the bruised face said. "I don't trust her anymore, but she's gotta have someone bugged. We gotta take the shit with us."

"What about the girl?"

"It's fucking risky to be lugging around a prisoner, but we need her for insurance. Let's get a move on."

While her hands were bound tightly together, Veronica was happy to be hustled through the warehouse and down to the garage. She was thrown in the trunk and her head whacked against a piece of metal, which she believed was a tire iron. She ignored the pain and tried to use the object to get her hands free, but to no avail. Fifteen minutes later, the car slowed and she could hear a garage door open, and soon they were parked and taking her out of the trunk.

Veronica was taken to a folding aluminum chair in the corner of a redbrick room, and her feet were bound by duct tape by the two clients who looked like accountants. After finishing with her, they prepared two computer stations as quickly as your average IT person, donned headphones, and stared at their monitor screens.

The ginormous client wearing all black stood in the doorway, holding a pistol at his side. Every so often he pointed it at Veronica and pretended to shoot her with a smile.

She did her best to ignore the bulky black mass in the doorway and instead tried to free her hands of the duct tape. Veronica had paid close attention to the layout she had seen and felt she could make it out of the building and onto the street, given the chance. First she had to get her hands and feet free, and then there was the matter of the giant with the gun and murderous grin.

Camden would do whatever necessary to help her, but what if he couldn't find Léveque and McClennan? There would be no article, no more trips to North Beach to read poetry at City Lights, no more walks on the beach, no seeing Camden again, no more anything. The duct tape was not tight, they had rushed the job in favor of setting up their computers, and Veronica believed she could wrestle free if the client holding the gun left the room. The two other men were engrossed with their headphones and computer screens and might not be able to react quickly enough to stop her.

Veronica got her chance thirty minutes later when the steroid-inflated gunman said, "I gotta take a shit, keep an eye on her."

Neither of the other clients paid any attention to the announcement, so the man with the gun took two steps their way, towered over them, and smacked them both in the back of the head. The smaller clients appeared annoyed but lifted the headphones off an ear when he said, "I gotta drop a deuce; watch her."

Both nodded, but as the big man left the room they snapped the earbuds back on and continued to stare at the computer screens.

Veronica felt sweat dripping down her ear as she tried to shake her hands free of the duct tape while making as little noise as possible. Her wrists burned, but within a minute she wiggled them out. While keeping her body and face as motionless as she could, she reached down and peeled the silver adhesive from her feet.

She studied the two clients as she mustered the courage to run. Neither was paying any attention to her, but both wore side holsters that contained automatic weapons. She didn't know where the bathroom was located in building, or whether the roided-out lunatic actually went there.

Veronica rose to escape.

One of the clients turned around and locked eyes on her.

She started to run but her heel hit the bottom of the aluminum folding chair, sending it and her to the ground. She scrambled to her feet and out of the corner of her eye saw the client reach for his gun. Veronica heard the bullet splinter wood as she ran down the stairs toward the exit.

She was pumping her legs as best she could and she didn't look behind. The door was ten feet away, the light from the street spilled onto the concrete floor in front of it. She was now steps from escape.

The door opened to the Tall Woman, and Veronica ran right into her.

They both fell to the ground at the doorway, Veronica feeling quite woozy. She tried to get to her feet, but something held her back. Her eyes now focused on a swath of black clothing, and the silver barrel of a gun pointed at her face.

32

Will the Real Victor Please Stand Up?

"I CAN'T BELIEVE you gentlemen showed up at my suite last night," Léveque said to McClennan with a laugh.

"Didn't know you were the friend Camden was talking about," he responded. "And I thought you said you were at the St. Regis. Anyway, at the moment it was a lot safer than being on the road. On the way there, I thought up the story of Roux-Fuzie sending me the letters."

"Brilliant," Léveque said.

"If there were no letters," Camden said, "then how do you know the sculptures weren't made by Matisse and that there are diamonds in them?"

"There were letters," Léveque answered. "But they were sent to me. Bo was never Roux-Fuzie's prison pen pal. A clever bit of storytelling."

Camden grabbed the Cristal and drank it straight from the bottle. "You were the one who bet McClennan that he couldn't steal the paintings. You hired him to steal the Matisse sculptures. You're the puppet master pulling the goddamned strings."

"You make it sound so sinister," Léveque said. "It is not so. Yes, I was the one who bet Bo way back when. But I didn't force him. It was his idea and I tried to talk him out of it."

"It's true," McClennan said. "I was so sure I could do it. Didn't turn out that way, but I take full responsibility. And that's why I kept my word and never revealed Jean Francois's name."

"You received a scholarship from Mr. L," Camden said.

"Good investigative work," Léveque said. "Yes, my foundation paid for his entire schooling, but I actually never met Bo until he became an art professor. Whenever I was in Boston, I would sit in his poker game. All those years he spent in jail were tragic. So when this little business opportunity arose, I offered him a fifty-fifty partnership."

"Doesn't make up for the lost time," McClennan added. "But two-hundred and fifty million dollars will help me forget about it."

"So Roux-Fuzie wrote you letters," Camden said to Léveque. "Then why did you drop out of the auction when the sculptures went up for sale?"

"Because the crazy bastard didn't tell me about the diamonds until it was too late. The first letter said they were fakes, that he had made them. What I said last night was true; I didn't know if he was lying or not. But it was enough for me to drop out of the bidding."

"And after what you told me about the two of you being rivals, I'm sure the last person you wanted to get those sculptures was Bouchon."

"Never hated the man until now. Seeing my daughter with him makes me ill. I was so glad you crashed the dinner party last night. I had only arranged it to mollify Georgia."

McClennan went to the silk-draped bay window and smiled at the pink and gray sky. "Maybe another hour or so before we should take off."

"So how in the hell did half a billion dollars' worth of diamonds end up in those sculptures?" Camden asked.

"As I said before, McClennan's story was mostly true. Yes, Victor was a Matisse disciple and his friend. But he and Claudette hardly ever went to visit Matisse. The only reason they were in Nice was to hide after they pulled the biggest robbery in the history of Paris. They actually had the balls to hit Chaumet."

"I guarantee Swanson doesn't know what that is."

"One of the most iconic jewelers in the world," Léveque continued. "They robbed the place where it all began in Place Vendôme. Late 1930s, a brilliant heist. Did it overnight and used knockout gas. Claudette conned the guards to let her inside, and they basically had the run of the house."

"Bouchon couldn't have known there were diamonds concealed in the sculptures," Camden said. "Or else he would have cut them open a long time ago. But I think he knew they were fakes."

"I begged Roux-Fuzie not to, but the crazy old fool sent Bouchon a letter telling him he made the sculptures and even included a photo of him in the act."

"So Bouchon hired the Tall Woman and her clients to steal the sculptures," Camden said. "Like we discussed last night, if word got out that they were not done by Matisse, it would have been an embarrassment to him, and his investment would have been worthless. But have them stolen, he's insured for who knows how much and plus his museum gets more attention and attendance goes up."

"I have a lot of connections in the art world," Léveque said. "Both legitimate and not so much. I got word of his plans right at the time Bo was getting out of jail. I had to act fast. I couldn't let all those diamonds disappear like that."

"You could have told Bouchon about them," Camden said.

Both McClennan and Léveque laughed.

"So what else about the story was true? Did Claudette, the girlfriend, get killed in Nice?"

"Yes," Léveque said. "After the robbery, that's where they fled. Victor hadn't seen Matisse in years, and the master was happy to have coffee with his old protégé. Claudette had a place there in Nice, it was her uncle's summer house, and it was the perfect spot to lay low.

"Victor had been a thief for many years. Small jobs, a few banks, some trains, but nothing of a diamond-heist magnitude. He suddenly was in possession of a fortune and was scared. He decided to make sculptures exactly like Matisse's just so he could hide the diamonds and feel safe. But Victor was also terrified of having the stones in his possession, whether they were in sculptures or not. The guy was an artist at heart, and the thought of going to prison chilled him to his bones.

"Claudette broke into Matisse's house after he left for a lecture in Paris and hid her boyfriend's sculptures containing the diamonds under the floorboards of the studio. In the letter Victor wrote, he said it was intuition. He knew the police were closing in on them. Sure enough, the next day they showed up at Claudette's house. There was a shootout. Claudette killed two policemen before being shot down herself."

"Real Bonnie and Clyde shit," McClennan said.

"So they arrested Roux-Fuzie," Léveque continued. "They arrested him for the Chaumet heist, but he was never convicted for that because the diamonds were never found. But he was charged with two counts of murdering officers of the law."

"But you said Claudette shot the cops."

"Victor was shooting at them as well. She was dead and they had to give the public somebody to lock up," he said. "Every year Roux-Fuzie tried to escape from prison. Every year he got caught and more time was added to his sentence. He didn't have anyone he could trust to get the diamonds for him, had no living family members or close friends to give them to anyway. And they were useless as he rotted away in jail. By the time he had reached his seventies, Victor had given up hope of ever getting the diamonds. Just before the sculptures were put on auction, he found out he was dying of cancer. So the old man decided to tell his story. He needed to find somebody who had the means to get the sculptures back. Victor kept up with the doings in the art community, knew I was such a guy."

"How were the sculptures discovered underneath the floorboards?" Camden asked.

"The house was sinking," Léveque said. "Contractors found them during the restoration."

McClennan moved toward the oak liquor cabinet and extracted a bottle of Johnnie Walker Blue. He poured himself a tumbler of scotch and drank half.

"Steadying nerves is one thing, Bo, but we need you focused."

"I am focused, and when have I ever been nervous?" McClennan said and drank the rest of the scotch. "I buried the bag. I know where it is."

"It'll be dark there," Léveque cautioned.

"And we'll have flashlights," he said and took another swig from the expensive scotch.

"Victor wrote me that first letter, telling me he had crafted the sculptures to look like the master's work," Léveque said to Camden. "He didn't mention the diamonds because he wanted to see how I would respond. My stupid fault for waiting so long to get back to him. I answered Victor after Bouchon bought the sculptures, and then I went to the prison to see him."

"Why did you believe him?" Camden asked.

"He showed me the photos. Victor had them in a safety deposit box and paid a private detective to get them and bring them to the prison. They were explicit. The photographs showed him making the sculptures. Clearly it wasn't Matisse. Victor said he had everything documented because of insurance. He figured if they ever lost the sculptures they would be able to get them back easily if he could prove he made them. Victor was a meticulous thief."

"Not thorough enough. He got caught."

"The curse of dumb luck," McClennan said with a sigh.

"I feel for Roux-Fuzie, but he's gone and we're going to keep what he could not," he said. "The sculptures are hidden not far from here on Lands End Trail. We're going to dig them up and bring them back here. We got a guy flying in tonight who will cut them open with lasers and extract the diamonds. Bo, being the foremost Matisse expert, will then mold the artworks back together exactly as they were before."

"Which was the plan all along," McClennan said. "I was always going to return the sculptures back to Bouchon and the museum, otherwise I'd be hounded the rest of my life."

"And," Léveque said, "nobody will be the wiser. In the morning, you can use them to rescue Veronica. Everybody is happy."

"We'll cut you and Veronica in for a piece for your efforts," McClennan said. "Jean Francois insisted on it. A very tiny piece."

"Camden, I was never going to leave you and Veronica to die. So can you call that woman and tell her you'll give her the sculptures in the morning? Tell her it is impossible to get them until 8:00 a.m."

"I don't like it," Camden said. "And you can keep the money for the diamonds. I don't want anything to do with it."

Camden called the Tall Woman and said, "First, I want to let you know that I had nothing to do with that asshole, Miles," he said.

"I know that," she said calmly.

"The only reason I'm talking to you now is because I got the Uzi from him. I split his nose open and then punched him on the bullet wound. He's had better days."

"So now what? Are you with McClennan?"

"I am. And he's agreed to turn over the sculptures for the price we discussed last night," Camden said. "What do you say?"

"Let's arrange a drop," she said. "My clients and I are professionals. Paying for convenience and safety is worth it. It's too dangerous to drag on any longer."

"Then we're on. But McClennan said he can't get the sculptures until the morning. He won't tell anyone where they are but swears there's no way to get at them until 8:00 a.m."

"Keep in contact. We'll arrange a meeting sometime after nine."

"Can I speak with Veronica?"

"This isn't a chat line, Mr. Swanson. I assure you she's fine and will be if you follow through and get us those sculptures in the morning."

"Let me talk to her," Camden insisted.

There was a pause and then Veronica's voice came over the line. "I'm okay, Camden. We moved locations but I'm okay. I hope—"

The connection went dead.

Camden closed his eyes and said, "Veronica is okay for now, and they're going for it."

"No problemo, as expected," McClennan said.

"I don't know," Camden responded. "I'm not used to her being so accommodating."

* * *

Earlier the Tall Woman had taken the headphones from the bruised-face client and put them on her ears. Courtesy of a tiny electronic bug planted under Camden's collar, she was able to hear the whole story of Victor Roux-Fuzie and the stolen diamonds. She had put the bug there when she had kissed him earlier in the car, just before Miles Krakow had smashed into them.

Client A was listening as well, and he said, "You may be a pain in the ass, but you are a genius."

"I'd say it's more that Camden Swanson is an idiot," she responded.

The Tall Woman looked at Veronica tied to a chair. She had tried to escape, which is why her wrists and ankles were likely swollen from the tightness of the duct tape. Her three remaining clients began loading weapons, ammunition, and night goggles into duffle bags. Veronica had closed her eyes and looked, with her controlled breathing and index finger on each hand touching her thumb, like she was trying to meditate.

"Where do we ambush them on Lands End?" the body-builder client asked. "I say three of us take a high position and make some noise so they hear us, while a fourth sneaks around and takes them by surprise."

Veronica opened her eyes.

33

Lands End

WHEN THE INDIGO sky turned black and the fog nestled into the Sea Cliff district, Bo McClennan led the way up El Camino Del Mar holding a shovel. Camden and Mr. Léveque followed him up the rising hill that curved slightly away from the ocean. Soon they had reached the big, brown square sign that read, "Lands End, Golden Gate Recreation Area." Just beyond that on the beginning of the trail another warned, "Cliff and surf area, extremely dangerous, people have been swept from the rocks and drowned."

"Great," Camden said. "We can hardly see anything."

"Tourists walk up and down these paths every day," Mr. Léveque said. "Besides, the moon is out and we have flashlights."

"Your eyes will adjust," McClennan grumbled.

The only sounds were the surf crashing against the rocks, the trees rustling in the wind, a few sea gulls cawing, and the intermittent blowing of a guttural horn. The moonlight mixed with the fog and created a diaphanous haze. They passed a wooden observation deck and fragments of the Golden Gate Bridge could be discerned.

Camden looked away from the scenery and instead focused on his own feet, concerned about taking a wrong step into the abyss. He lost Léveque and McClennan for a few minutes but caught up with them on the narrow and sandy trail. Cyprus trees and Monterey pines loomed over them on their left, while to their right various shrubs and bushes clung to the side of the cliff. At some points it appeared as if the drop to the ocean went straight down over a hundred feet.

It doesn't feel right being here without Veronica, Camden thought. He never would have made it this far without her help, and she deserved to be walking next to him instead of being tied up in some warehouse. He had thought of Mr. L as a true friend, but after he abandoned him and Veronica at the hotel, Camden could no longer trust him. For all he knew, Léveque and McClennan's new plan could involve shooting him and burying him in the hole after they dug up the sculptures.

If he and Veronica somehow got through the ordeal, would they write a story? It had been over a year since he'd written anything longer than a haiku. If Mr. L did stay good to his word and help them escape and they were able to write an article, would they be able to keep him out of it? These questions were premature. Camden knew he was a long way from getting to that point, and he needed to stay focused.

Up ahead was a clearing that during the daylight hours and in good visibility would have offered outstanding views of the Pacific. Tonight, in the foggy darkness, there was nothing but a black and gray void. The wind was stronger here and the path rose sharply up the hill. Camden wasn't sure if the wooden planks made the walking easier or more problematic. Regardless, he was out of breath about halfway up.

"You're going to take some money whether you like it or not," Léveque said to him. "If only for a gym membership."

Camden couldn't spare any breath for a clever comeback. Instead he plodded onward and soon crested the hill. The wood and sand steps now went down steeply, and he used the rope fence on the right to keep himself steady. At the bottom, McClennan hopped over the barrier and began walking down a path.

Camden read a sign indicating they were at a place called Painted Rock, and it warned visitors to keep out because "People Have Fallen To Their Death From This Point." There were two yellow diamonds on the sign with the word "Warning" printed on them. Léveque climbed over the low fence and grinned. The foghorn sounded just as he said:

"The adrenaline is what keeps my arteries clear. Diamonds not seen in nearly seventy years await us, Camden."

"All I care about is getting Veronica back safe, and for all of us to continue breathing."

"Shut up," McClennan said. "Do you hear that?" He pulled out a gun and pointed it at Camden. "Did you let somebody follow you here?"

"What the fuck are you doing?"

"Are you wearing a wire?"

"You're being paranoid now, Bo," Mr. Léveque said.

"We're close to digging up half a billion dollars. So I'm feeling fucking cautious right now. Not paranoid, cautious. They could have forced you to wear one."

McClennan patted him down in frantic fashion. Finding nothing, he then began staring up at the cliffs and tried to detect any movement in the fog. He then pushed Camden in the chest.

"There's somebody coming. They're getting closer," he said.

"Oh, shit," Camden said.

"What 'oh, shit'?" Mr. Léveque said.

"The Tall Woman could have bugged me. She said she bugged all of our houses . . . shit, she could have put one on me."

Camden then thought of her kiss a few hours before when they were in the garage. She wanted to make a point of why she thought she was a winner and him a loser, but it would have been a perfect distraction. It was the only time she had gotten close enough to do it.

Camden began running his fingers through his hair and then over his shirt as if a cockroach was crawling up him. He found the tiny electronic device on the inside of his collar. Now in his hand, the three of them stared at it in complete shock.

Camden put it on the ground and stepped on it. He then scooped it up and tossed it into the black and gray void. Léveque's and McClennan's faces in the moonlight were drained of all color.

"I swear I didn't know," Camden said.

"Son of a bitch. You fucked me again, Swanson. Jesus Christ. C'mon, we gotta dig fast now."

McClennan ran down the narrow path and then up to the right behind a pine tree. He got on his hands and knees and then shined the flashlight on a large rock. He left the light pointing there and got back to his feet. He tossed the shovel at Camden and pulled out a handgun.

"You dig."

McClennan then took out another gun and handed it to Mr. Léveque. "C'mon, Jean Francois. We'll shoot anything that comes down the hill."

"There's not enough time," Léveque said. "We should leave immediately."

"McClennan, you're nuts. Let's get out of here," Camden said. "Let's keep moving and get safe. They don't know where they are. We can always come back."

"Fuck the both of you. Dig. I'm not going to let those ass-holes get the diamonds. I didn't spend all that time in jail to give up now. Just dig!"

Camden jammed the shovel into the soft earth. All around him were roots and rocks, but the soil was fresh from when McClennan dug it up after the robbery. After only a few min-utes, the shovel hit a large object in the hole, and Camden got to his knees and began to claw at the dirt with his hands. He felt burlap, and then pulled a large sack out of the ground.

McClennan pushed him out of the way and grabbed the sack. He reached inside and pulled out the objects that had been packed in bubble wrap. Camden saw the whites of McClennan's eyes and teeth as he paused for just a second to smile at the Matisse odalisque sculptures that were filled with diamonds. He then put them back in the bag.

A gun appeared in McClennan's face.

The bruised-faced client held it, and he extracted a sec-ond one, pointed it at Camden, and whispered, "Don't fucking move."

Camden remained on his knees, and he became catatonic as requested.

"Hand the bag over slowly," the client said.

"If you're going to shoot us," McClennan said, "please do Camden first. I really want to see him die."

"Just give me the bag and you both can live," he responded.

As the client reached for the bag, the hand pointing the weapon at McClennan drooped just a little bit. Bo lunged at the man. The first bullet fired came within a few inches of blowing Camden's head off his shoulders, rendering him momentarily deaf. He dropped to the ground, covering his ears and eyes.

The client fired the other gun at McClennan, sending him to the ground. Camden leapt up and swung at the shooter, connecting on his jaw. He then hockey-checked him to the ground and wrestled the weapon free from his hands. They struggled and both of them rolled to the edge of the cliff.

The foghorn blew.

Gunshots crackled all around them.

Camden didn't hear anything except the rustling of clothes scraping on the dirt in between the ringing in his ears. His attacker elbowed him in the nose and his eyes filled with water. Camden kept pumping his fist against the client, and he felt bone where he was connecting. It could have been the man's face or his arm or leg.

Both Camden and his attacker were now half off the side of the cliff, their legs dangling just below their kneecaps.

Camden saw the glint of metal move toward his face.

Using one hand to keep him steady, he brought his free fist down onto the weapon. The attacker lost his grip on the cliffside. So did Camden, but he was able to grab on to a thorny shrub that spiked into his palm.

The client grasped at air and plummeted down to the rocks.

The ringing in Camden's ears lessened and he could hear bullets thwacking into trees inches away from him. Keeping low, he scrambled to his feet and grabbed the bag with the sculptures. He was soon out of the light and off the path behind the trees. McClennan lay a few feet away on his stomach with his gun pointed toward the cliff stairs. Camden flopped down next to him.

"You all right?"

"No," McClennan uttered with great strain and fired his gun.

"I have the bag. I have the diamonds."

"Fucking Swanson," McClennan said. "All I can think of right now is that Winslow Homer painting. The one of the old man in the little boat with the big fish, too far out to sea."

"Where's Mr. L?"

"Over in those trees, I think. Shots are coming from there."

Camden fumbled for his cell phone, cupped it so it would not emit a burst of light, and pushed the button for the police department from his call history. Clinkenbeard was put on the line within seconds.

"I hope you're with a lawyer, Mr. Swanson," he said.

"I'm on Lands End. The Painted Rock area. Get down here now. McClennan is shot and they're going to kill us."

"Why don't I believe you? Smells like some kind of diversion."

"Listen to the fucking gunfire. Lands End! Send a helicopter!"

Camden hung up and heard somebody from the top of the hill yell. He couldn't understand what the person was saying through the wind and the foghorn. The figure moving down the hill was using another person as a shield. When they were halfway down the stairs, Camden saw the six-foot-five shadow and understood what the person was saying.

"I have Veronica," the Tall Woman yelled. "If you want her, give me the sculptures."

Camden looked down at McClennan, but he wasn't moving. A puddle of blood had saturated the dirt underneath him. Camden got closer and listened for a breath, but there was only silence. *Why didn't you just give him the bag?* Camden wanted to scream. *Why did you have to rob another museum right after getting out of jail? You could have just moved to Vegas and been a professional card player instead of dying here on Lands End and probably getting me killed as well. Why didn't you let us leave when we knew they were coming for us?*

The ocean slammed into the rocks and the foghorn blew. Camden spat out sand from his mouth and his adrenaline got his mind to survival mode. He pried the gun from McClennan's hands and moved slowly through the trees.

The Tall Woman had reached the bottom of the wooden stairs and held the gun to Veronica's temple. They were both silhouettes in the darkness and fog. Camden's hand was shaking and he couldn't keep the gun straight.

"Come out with your hands up, all three of you," the Tall Woman yelled.

"McClennan's dead," Camden yelled. "I don't know where Léveque is."

"Then you start. Drop the gun and put your hands in the air."

"So you can kill us both?"

"Just give me the sculptures and I won't kill anybody."

"Where are your clients? I don't think they'll have a problem killing us."

"I think they're all dead."

"I don't believe you."

"We're not playing truth or dare. Get out from the trees or I'm going to kill her."

"Then I'll kill you."

"Is that what you want?"

Camden came out from the trees with his hands over his head but kept a finger looped around his gun. He left the bag on the ground and kicked the half a billion worth of diamonds a few feet behind him. The Tall Woman pointed her gun at Camden and with her other arm held Veronica as a shield.

"Where are the fucking sculptures? I listened to every word you all said. I know there are all those diamonds inside them, and they're mine now."

"Let her go."

"Give me the goddamned sculptures!"

"Not until you let her go."

The Tall Woman pushed Veronica to the ground. She lay there, hands covering her head, as the fog drifted past them. The Tall Woman kept her gun steady on Camden.

"Throw your gun to the ground," she said.

Camden dropped the gun to the dirt and it landed with a thud. A helicopter approached.

"Run, Veronica," he said.

"Go ahead," the Tall Woman said. "But you better give me those sculptures or else I shoot both of you."

"They're in a bag just behind me."

Veronica scrambled to her feet and turned away from the Tall Woman as if to run. But instead she pivoted on the balls of her heels, swung back around, and tackled her captor. The Tall Woman flailed and fired her gun before hitting the ground.

As the Tall Woman struggled to raise her gun up, Camden rushed over to them and stomped as hard as he could on her hand. She yelped, and Veronica punched her in the face and rolled to the side. Camden scooped up the gun and watched the Tall Woman get to her feet and run off into the woods like a track star. Veronica followed after her.

The whoop of the helicopter grew louder, but he was able to hear rustling over by the bag containing the sculptures.

"Mr. L?" Camden yelled just as he got shot in the arm.

The impact sent him to the ground and his gun flew out of his hand. The man who shot him, the client who could pass for a professional wrestler, was attempting to speak. But the whirring of helicopter blades drowned out his speech.

The large man in black grasped the burlap sack containing the diamond-filled sculptures and looked up at the helicopter. A giant beam of light blasted down onto him, and he instinctively shielded his eyes with his arm and fired up at it. Camden took off in a sprint and jumped at him. He felt his shoulder crack against swollen pectoral muscles, but the force carried them both off the side of the cliff.

Camden skidded onto a bush that sprung up the cliffside. He could hardly breathe, and his arm throbbed from the bullet; he was sure his shoulder was separated. His eyes focused on the burlap sack just below him on an overhanging rock.

The helicopter engulfed all sound as it hovered above him. A ladder dropped and hung within a foot of his head.

Camden reached up toward the swinging rope ladder with his good arm and lost his footing. He slid down and landed on the rock next to the bag of sculptures. He dug his fingertips into the rocks, and although his left arm was sticky and throbbing, he was able to use the hand. It grabbed the burlap with as tight of a grip as he could muster.

The ladder hurtled toward him once again. Camden propped his butt onto the rock and snatched the rope, but the bag began to slip from his left hand. His eyes watered and sweat ran down his face and neck as he tried to steady the sack.

One sculpture slid out, and then another, and finally the last of the objects holding the diamonds plunged hundreds of feet down the rocky cliffs.

Camden's fingertips were numb, and while he could see them clenched around the rope ladder, he couldn't feel them. He had to get his bloody hand onto the rung or he would never keep his grip. He felt as if he had been burned with a branding iron, and he swiped at the rope and missed.

The foghorn blew.

The last remaining client had not fallen off the cliff, and he now grabbed Camden's foot. He was lodged against a skinny cyprus tree but had a solid grip on Camden's shoe. His eyes were bloodshot, and he swung his other hand toward Camden's foot, which would have ripped him down into the rocky cliffs but missed by an inch.

Camden's fingers began to quiver and come off the rope, and now only the index and thumb separated him from death. He flailed his wounded arm once again toward the ladder to steady himself, and he was able to grab it just as the other hand lost its grip. With the last bit of energy, he wiggled his foot out of his shoe and kicked the client in the nose.

Camden heard just one second of a scream and the man disappeared into the fog.

34

Feeling Good Again

HIS WOUNDS SWABBED and dressed, Camden lay inside an ambulance in the Legion of Honor parking lot above the Lands End Trail. Through the open door, he watched the flashing red and blue lights disappearing in the drifting fog. His head swam in painkillers and it was hard to focus for more than a few seconds. He didn't have much strength to talk, but he was grateful when he saw Clinkenbeard's horseshoe-bruised face approach because he wanted information.

"While you're in the hospital, you will be in police custody," Clinkenbeard said.

"Am I being arrested?"

"There are four dead bodies tonight."

"Two fell off the cliff because they attacked me. I was trying to save my own life."

"Two others were shot, including McClennan. The two women and you are the only ones alive. Ms. Zarcarsky is fine, but we're not too sure about the unidentified one."

"The Tall Woman?" Camden asked.

"We have an APB out on her. We'll find her."

Why hadn't Clinkenbeard mentioned Léveque's name? He feared for his friend's life, but then he added up the numbers. Four dead meant Léveque must have gotten away when he heard the helicopter approaching.

"What about the sculptures? They're fakes with diamonds inside. They're probably scattered all over the rocks and cliffs. Well, depending on how well the bubble wrap worked."

"That is what Ms. Zarcarsky has said as well. While she was being held, she heard her captors talk of it. We're sending teams down there to try and recover them."

"Bouchon paid those guys to steal the sculptures. He knew they were fakes and he didn't want the museum tied to a scandal. I'm sure the dead guys had cell phones on them. Get the records and I guarantee Bouchon's number will show up. We know where their hideout is."

"Ms. Zarcarsky gave us two different locations. We have people going there now."

"Those guys also killed Harry Hipple and Larry Aberlour. Hipple told us he saw them shoot Aberlour. We saw them shoot Hipple."

"Ms. Zarcarsky also informed us of the incident in Golden Gate Park. She's been cooperative. And if what she has told us checks out, then you most likely won't be charged with anything. Most likely. But we got a lot of questions for you."

"Shit," Camden said. "I almost forgot about Miles Krakow. He's tied up in McClennan's house off El Camino Del Mar."

"You've had an interesting night, Swanson. I'll find out why he was tied up later. Give me the address and we'll pick him up. Mr. Krakow needs to answer for what he did yesterday at Grace Cathedral. Menacing, possession of an illegal weapon . . . enough to keep him to get his story."

Camden began piecing together a lead for the story that he now knew he would write with Veronica. *I was literally clinging for my life to an inch-thick rope when the Matisse sculptures, which were filled with diamonds from a Parisian heist decades ago, began to drop one by one into the ocean.* He knew they each would need to have first-person narration in the article because they were participants in it, but "clinging for my life" was too much of a cliché. *I'm out of practice,* he thought.

"Going to be a helluva article, detective."

"You're lucky to be alive," Clinkenbeard said.

"Like the great Robert Earl Keen song, feels so good feeling good again."

* * *

Camden wasn't allowed any visitors while in police custody in the hospital, and under the influence of morphine he spent several hours with Clinkenbeard and other cops answering questions. At ten the next morning, a male nurse with his arms covered in tattoos approached him. Camden could be discharged if he could walk up and down the hallway three times.

"Are they going to arrest me?" he asked.

The tattooed nurse shrugged and helped him to his feet, and he felt wobbly. In his bed gown with the air nipping at his bare buttocks, he was able to sufficiently shamble fifteen paces up and down the hallway three times. His shot arm was numb, and while he wanted to touch the bullet hole, he knew that would be asking for trouble even with the painkillers.

When Camden got back to his room, the nurse pointed at a crisp designer shopping bag in the corner. There was no note in the bag, but the slacks, shirt, sweater, and shoes were of similar style to those he'd seen Léveque wear before. After the painful ordeal of dressing, with shaky and scraped hands, Camden signed the necessary documents to be released from hospital care. Out of the corner of his eyes, he saw the glare of handcuffs on a uniformed police officer's belt as he approached.

"You're free to go," the officer said.

Camden hobbled into the lobby and the smile on his face grew bigger when he saw Veronica's curly hair peeking above the magazine she was reading. She leapt up and rushed to him with a big hug, almost knocking him over.

"Are you okay?" he asked.

"You're the one who got shot," Veronica said. "I'm fine. They didn't touch me while I was tied up. How do you feel?"

"Physically like shit, but mentally as good as ever. I can't wait to start our article. We should get a hotel room as soon as possible and write without any distractions."

"Mr. Léveque already got us one at the St. Francis."

"Is he okay?"

"He is," Veronica answered. "And he's in the parking lot waiting for us."

"Clinkenbeard never asked me any questions about Mr. L so I didn't bring up his name."

"We've talked a lot and he's grateful for that. I didn't even know Mr. Léveque was at Lands End last night until he told me."

"I'm not sure why I didn't tell the police about him," Camden said.

"Because he's your friend."

"Because of him, McClennan's dead."

"C'mon, Camden. McClennan isn't some innocent guy. He willingly stole the sculptures. As he said to us in the bar, he loved taking risks. It's what made him feel alive. Léveque didn't force him to do anything."

"The Tall Women is still out there somewhere."

"I ran after her but she was too quick."

Outside the hospital, a white limousine idled close to the entrance. Léveque, wearing one of his custom-made gray, pin-striped suits, stood outside the vehicle smoking a cigarette. He tried to give Camden a hug, but he took a step back.

"I'm sorry I wasn't more help last night," Léveque said. "When McClennan started firing, I got behind a rock for cover and lost my footing. I slid down into a bush and was stuck. When the gunfire stopped and I heard the helicopter, I took off to the other side of Lands End."

"Would have been pretty hard to explain to the cops why such a respectable businessman was partners with Bo McClennan," Camden said.

"Quite true, but I have spoken to the police at length and told them everything about the night in my suite. That I was merely doing my best to help you and Veronica. The DA's office has all the evidence that McClennan stole the sculptures and they know about the Tall Woman and the clients. And of course, the pièce de résistance, David Bouchon."

"The police are building their case against Bouchon," Veronica said and then took a manila folder from her bag. "Mr. L was able to get us copies of some phone records that link Bouchon to the clients. He's got connections inside the SFPD. We'll have just enough time to write our article before his involvement becomes public."

"How is Georgia taking it?" Camden asked.

"She's fine. What do you call it, a rebound? I think David was simply a rebound for Georgia. I spoke with her last night and she was happy we are both okay."

"Both."

"She still cares about you, Camden. Even though I was going to do it anyway, she insisted I use my connections to ensure nobody digs more into your involvement."

"And I appreciate that. Why don't I feel better about what happened?"

"I feel terrible that Bo is dead," Léveque said.

"But worse, you never got the diamonds."

"I cared deeply about Bo, he was a good friend. And I feel the same about you and Veronica. I understand that we've been through a lot, but—"

"You listen, Jean Francois. Veronica and I have been through a lot. With all due respect, you haven't been through shit. I was shot and almost died last night. Veronica was kidnapped and a few days ago was pedaling a bike when one of my coworkers was murdered inches behind her. McClennan is dead. You've ridden around the city in limos and stayed in your fancy suite and you hid in a fucking bush."

"I would have helped if—"

"Mr. L, through strange circumstances we became friends. And I'll always consider you one. That's why I didn't tell the cops you were at Lands End last night. But your world is one I'll never understand. One I don't even want to."

Léveque looked at the ground and said, "I have a suite for you and Veronica so you can write undisturbed. And of course, there's going to be some money to help the two of you get your freelance careers off on the right foot. I am terribly sorry that you and Veronica had to endure so much, and I played a part in it. That is why I want to help."

"I appreciate the offer," Camden said. "But I don't want the suite and I don't want the money. All we'll take is what you've already given to Veronica. The phone records linking Bouchon to the clients, and of course any other info you can provide."

"Camden—"

"Mr. L, I value friendship above just about everything in this world," he said. "Ours is pretty fucking damaged right now. I need some time. But when this is all over, I hope we can share a bottle of Burgundy from one of the finest plots in France."

"One that tastes like menacing clowns?" Léveque asked.

Camden smiled and the sliding hospital doors opened. Clinkenbeard stepped outside and walked right past the limo, his ponytail swaying in the breeze, and with a stony glare in the other direction, pretended not to see them. Camden took Veronica's hand and the two of them walked toward the bus stop.

"C'mon, you can at least let me give you both a ride," Léveque said.

"Nothing wrong with taking the bus," Veronica answered.

"I haven't written anything longer than seventeen syllables in a long time," Camden said as they waited by the curb.

"The last article I wrote was about how to cope with your dog's excessive flatulence."

"We can do it, right? I think we make a pretty damn good team."

"You bet your ass, Swanson. But as I said when we first met at the Gold Dust, I get my byline first."

"I'm good with that. But the next story is by C. Swanson and V. Zarcarsky."

EPILOGUE

TWO MORNINGS LATER in the misty darkness of dawn, Camden and Veronica practically skipped to the newspaper kiosk around the corner from her apartment. They both wore heavy wool coats over their pajamas, and Veronica brought Sabrina along on her leash. Camden thrust the quarters into the machine and he grabbed four inky newspapers from the rack. When the green door whipped closed, Veronica narrowed her eyes at him ostentatiously, and then inserted the proper number of coins to pay for the papers Camden took.

They stood on the corner and each read the front page of the city's leading newspaper as pages ruffled in the wind. The article they wrote, which appeared over the fold, had a large-font headline declaring that David Bouchon had been arrested for conspiracy to attempt capital fraud. The police had also recovered the diamonds, and pictures of them appeared in the spread inside the paper devoted to the robbery. Photos of McClennan, Bouchon, the sculptures, and the bag that Veronica had put into the locker, were also included. The tale of Victor Roux-Fuzie was a sidebar, and they used quotes from the deceased French thief courtesy of the letters Léveque had provided.

Miles Krakow was another sidebar to the story, and it included a detailed description of his actions that pertained to the sculptures. The picture printed was his mugshot that showed a smiling face with a broken nose and wild hair. What would never be reported is that Miles would soon get all charges dropped because of secret help from Léveque. It was done in exchange for forgetting he'd seen him at the house in Sea Cliff. The story also said Miles had checked into rehab.

The Tall Woman was never found.

Back in Veronica's apartment, where Camden and Veronica had spent the last two days writing, they now relaxed on her bed and watched TV. They each sipped coffee and flipped through various stations reporting what they had uncovered. Sabrina was nestled between them, her bat ears sticking straight up as she enjoyed being petted.

As the day went on, they would be besieged with requests for interviews, but they declined them all. The only calls they took were from national magazines wanting an in-depth article on the robbery. Veronica negotiated a deal, which included advances for three more stories of their choosing. Camden said he would use his share of the money to get an apartment.

"You can stay here until you find a place," Veronica offered.

"We can look for a two bedroom," Camden said.

Veronica sat up in bed and replied, "Let's take it slow. We're going to be spending a lot of time together writing these articles. I'm probably going to get on your nerves."

"After what we went through, I can't see that ever happening. Thank you."

Camden wasn't sure if their relationship would last a few weeks, months, years, or if they would someday in the future get married or just become good friends. But he decided in that moment, he was going to enjoy every minute of their time together. Furiously composing the article with Veronica to make deadline was the most satisfying thing he'd done since he left the paper in Boston. She was a talented writer, more eloquent than he had ever been. Her prose complemented his perfectly. Camden only wanted to savor the now.

Gratitude had been a foreign concept in his life, but the amount he felt right then made him realize it was exponentially better than any high alcohol could bring. He knew it couldn't last forever, but he was okay with that. Because there was one thing he was sure of now. No matter what happened in the future, he would never give up on himself again.

Camden raised his coffee mug and toasted Veronica.

* * *

The next day, Camden called Georgia.

"I can't talk now," she said. "I'm late for a meeting at the gallery."

"Are you finished?"

"My show premieres next week."

"Congrats. Do I get an invite?"

"Do you want one?"

"Of course, Georgia."

"I'll be glad to have you and Veronica there."

"Will you be around the apartment later?" Camden asked. "I need to pack my stuff up."

"Been waiting for you to do that," she said. "But I understand you've been busy."

"What did you think of the article?" he asked.

"If David was involved like you and the police say, he deserves what he gets. I'm happy my dad is safe, and he had almost nothing to do with it."

"Almost is too generous a description."

"Thank you for keeping his name out. I'd be answering questions until the day I die if you hadn't. I owe you big. I'll start the payoff by buying you dinner."

"You don't owe me anything, Georgia. Dinner would be nice, but my treat."

"As I said before, I don't know if we can be friends, Camden, but I'm willing to try."

"Same here."

* * *

Camden had rented a small van and drove it down the 101 Freeway to San Carlos, catching glimpses of the Caltrain as it rumbled along the tracks toward San Francisco. Even though his belongings didn't add up to much, he sweated through an entire afternoon boxing the items and loading them into the vehicle. The painkillers helped, but his body throbbed throughout the process and he was out of breath as he sat on the carpet and surveyed the apartment. Minus his stuff, the place was much less cluttered and seemed peculiar. It was strange to think he had spent over six months of his life there, and these would be his last looks at it.

Camden got off the carpet and went to the fridge for a cold drink. A few of his beers rested in the vegetable crisper, the dogs on the labels inviting him for a taste, but he chose a bottle of water instead. He took it to the porch and sat in his frayed camping chair to spend some time with the squirrels.

THE END

GRAND PATRONS

Jamie Amerault
Craig Boon
Shaun and Jeanie Borges
Dan Cassely
YooBee Ciminieri
David & Sarah Ditchfield
Yohei Egashira
Rachel and Ed Gunderson
Tania Higgins
The Horlyk & Markham Families
Tina & Jeff Krasovec
James Lancaster
Oscar Lara
Tim McGrew
Alana Miranda
Barbara & Stewart Moncrieff
Jodi Munson

Jane Myung
Patsy and Deems Narimatsu
Kathleen Naughton
Mark O'Connell
Brian Ostrowski
Mary Jane & Michael E. Ostrowski
John and Beth Perullo
Ann Pierce
Pam & Dave Pittenger
Michael Ranahan
Rob & Erin Robinson
Christina Tang
J'Nell Thomas
Valerie and Peter Williams
Todd Wonkka
Joseph Yamaoka
Ada Yan

INKSHARES

INKSHARES is a reader-driven publisher and producer based in Oakland, California. Our books are selected not by a group of editors, but by readers worldwide.

While we've published books by established writers like *Big Fish* author Daniel Wallace and *Star Wars: Rogue One* scribe Gary Whitta, our aim remains surfacing and developing the new author voices of tomorrow.

Previously unknown Inkshares authors have received starred reviews and been featured in the *New York Times*. Their books are on the front tables of Barnes & Noble and hundreds of independents nationwide, and many have been licensed by publishers in other major markets. They are also being adapted by Oscar-winning screenwriters at the biggest studios and networks.

Interested in making your own story a reality? Visit Inkshares.com to start your own project or find other great books.

CPSIA information can be obtained
at www.ICGtesting.com
Printed in the USA
JSHW051019101120
9474JS00001B/34